# In the St. Nick of Time

# In the St. Nick of Time

## William Pepper

Carnival of Glee Creations

*In The St. Nick of Time*

© 2008 by William Pepper.

This book is published in the United States by Carnival of Glee Creations. This novel is a work of fiction. The characters, events, dialogue and plot are products of the author's imagination. Any similarities to actual persons or events, living or dead, is purely coincidental.

Cover Design by Patricia Rasch.

ISBN #978-0-9818647-0-9

Library of Congress 2008907881

First Edition, November 1, 2008

# DEDICATION

This book is dedicated to Mr. Dale Harmon, my high school writing coach, who I suspect never quite forgave me for missing that weekend writer's retreat my senior year. (I had a prior commitment.) I hope this makes up for it.

# ACKNOWLEDGEMENTS

I'd like to thank the many people who helped make this book a reality, including: Jill and Sophie; the folks who live and work in the real Santa Claus, Indiana; the Santa Claus Chamber of Commerce; the entire Howie family; the entire Pepper family; Patricia Rasch; Jean and Wally Kelding; and many, many others.

A special thanks also to my parents, Merrill and Judy, who never discouraged my believing in St. Nick. I still do.

# DECEMBER 1

A multi-colored mongrel peed on the back of Santa Claus's head as the jolly old elf lay in the gutter where he had been many times before. A small stream of melting slush, stained with road grit and canine urine, flowed along the curb, making its way out of town.

Humans get coal in their stockings when they've been bad. What do dogs get? Maybe grapes, the cursed defier of canine mouths. If so, it was sure to be an unhappy Christmas for one local pooch.

An old man, grunting an old man grunt, bent and picked up the corrupted Kringle with one green-mittened hand. He righted the cardboard cutout with an affectionate pat. "There you go, old friend," he said to the decoration, then paused to admire it. "Not a bad likeness." He stood next to the cutout comparing abdomens for a moment. Then he turned to set up his kettle, nearly colliding with the nervous little schnauzer of a woman—though presumably not the one who had peed on Santa—who scurried from the adjacent store front.

"What are you doing?" the suspicious shop owner asked.

"Madam, this ornament was sullied. I was putting it right."

The woman wordlessly snatched away the cutout Kringle and went back inside, never taking her eyes from the man.

"Well, I didn't do it," the old man said, a little petulantly. He looked at the gawkers passing by. "I really didn't. I'm not from around here, but I'm sure you have many fine water closets."

The old man straightened the Santa hat on his head and prepared to spread yuletide cheer. In the Noel game, negativity is a lead fruitcake that can flatten the toe of the holiday spirit.

"Merry Christmas to all," the sidewalk Santa said in a clear, confident voice. No one passing by responded, but that was okay. He believed they heard it, even if they pretended not to.

The weather was unseasonably warm in Santa Claus, Indiana, that December first, relieving the old man from having to worry about spilling his collection kettle when he slipped on icy walks. This was not cause for rejoicing, however, as all that warm temperatures this time of year in the Midwest really accomplished was to melt the snow and ice for a while, only to have it refreeze when temperatures dropped at night. This rendered roads and sidewalks even more treacherous, reducing the citizenry to mitten-wearing penguins mincing along the walkways toward their pickup trucks. And in a town that bore the name of Christmas's second most famous icon, not having a lot of snow just seemed wrong.

Nearby, on this mild day, Cameron Jones, who in his relatively short life had gone from budding writer to bestselling author to budding schizophrenic sat in a sparsely furnished conference room at the Spencer County Courthouse in Rockport—a community about thirty minutes south of Santa Claus, feeling not particularly mild at all. Cameron's attorney, Everett Franken, was pleading with his client, but Cameron was having none of it.

"Please, Cameron. We're talking about one day per month," Everett Franken said.

"It's one day less with my daughter," Cameron replied. Cameron cut an almost-fine figure in his suit. The suit was black, sharp, and well-tailored. Somehow, though, it looked more like a reminder of the man he was long ago, than it was an expression of who he was sitting in the courthouse that day. The suit was complemented by a tie as flamboyant as Cameron was subdued. It all looked out of place, though, topped by a head of dark hair that seemed conflicted itself, with a minimum of four cowlicks pushing the mane in all directions.

"If you don't agree to this temporary change in the visitation schedule," Everett Franken said, "We'll have to have a hearing. That means testifying."

"Let's do it."

"But, Cameron, if you testify in court, people will hear it."

"So?"

"Let me be more specific. The *press* will hear it. You are a well-known author. This case has already drawn media attention in a town that, well, doesn't usually draw media attention other than at Christmas time."

Cameron snorted. The *media attention* directed at him these days consisted of a mention of the case a couple times on the MSNBC "crawl" and a mini-blurb in *USA Today*. Once your latest book falls down a few notches on the best-seller list, you don't rate the verbal mention of your name on cable news. The local paper tried only once to get an interview. Cameron didn't follow up and neither did they.

Cameron considered Everette Franken's words. No, not really. He paused and tried to look as if he *was* considering, but really his mind was full of white noise. Well, white noise and, oddly, the plots of the first eight episodes of "Gilligan's Island." There had been a marathon on cable the night before.

"Fine," he said, finally. "As long as they know I'm only doing this temporarily, only to avoid dragging this thing through court."

"Good," Everett Franken said. "Just remember it's not over until trial on December 26."

The "they" Cameron had referred to were Wally Bass, attorney at law, and his client Susan Wentworth-Jones, Cameron's ex-wife and mother to their daughter Holly, now age five.

Susan was the first person ever to ask Cameron to sign a copy of his first book, *Quality, Not Quantity*. What choice did he have, but to fall in love with her? The day novel number two, *The Dead Man's New Hat*, cracked the top ten on the bestseller lists, they were married.

Holly was born two years later, about the time an expanded version of novel number three, *Sandstorm*—with more self-indulgent character backstory added in—was going into paperback.

A year after that, Susan left Cameron and announced she wanted a divorce. On Christmas Day. Ho, ho, ho. Reading the final divorce decree nearly gave Cameron a body length paper-cut. Seeing "Susan Jones shall have primary physical custody of the minor child Holly Jones, age 2" typed out so baldly in Times New Roman was devastating.

The final decree terminating the marriage was signed December 24, Christmas Eve.

And now another December was here, the third since the divorce was final, the fourth since Susan left; not that Cameron was obsessively keeping track or anything. They were in court today because Susan was moving overseas and taking precious Holly with her. And Cameron, for all his authorial status and wealth, could do nothing about it. Except, maybe, listen to his lawyer, who Cameron now realized was talking to him.

"If you're ready, I'll bring them in," Everett Franken was saying; the words drifting lightly into the small outer chamber of Cameron's mind that was not consumed by these thoughts, like so many autumn leaves floating to the ground. Cameron nodded vacantly.

Everett Franken stepped out of the conference room and quickly returned, followed by Susan's attorney, Wally Bass. Everett Franken had warned Cameron that Bass was a formidable litigator, but Cameron couldn't help being amused by the sight of him. Wally Bass was short, pudgy and balding. He wore a sport coat and pants that complemented each other only in the sense that one item served the function of a sport coat and the other served the function of pants. Otherwise, the two had nothing in common. The stout man looked especially comical next to the lanky, white-haired Everett Franken.

"Mr. Jones, sir. A pleasure to see you," Wally Bass enthused, thrusting out a gaudily-ringed hand.

"It'd be nice if I could say the same," Cameron responded.

Everett Franken shot him a look. Wally Bass, however, seemed not to have taken offense. He took a seat at the end of the conference table opposite Cameron.

"Coffee?" Everett Franken asked no one in particular. Wally Bass waved a "no" as he looked for something in his briefcase. Cameron likewise shook his head.

Susan Wentworth Jones entered the conference room. Her entrance so disrupted the atmosphere that Cameron's heart compressed into his chest cavity.

"Sorry I'm late," Susan said. She brushed her dark hair back from her face self-consciously.

"Even with all the alimony, you still can't afford a working wrist watch?" Cameron asked, his breath having returned to him in a rush. He truly had intended it to be funny, but it came out flat and mean-spirited.

"Hello, Cameron," Susan said, smiling and ignoring the remark with minimal visible discomfort, a well-worn mechanism she had developed to block out the non-sequiturs and hostile rantings that had increasingly defined the last years of their marriage.

Cameron also said "hello," but did not smile.

"We're just getting started, Ms. Jones," Everett Franken said. "Would you like some coffee?"

"No thanks," she said. Susan caught Cameron's eye again for just a moment before turning her head and her chair ever so slightly toward some document Wally Bass had just put in front of her, just enough to break the sight line with Cameron.

Everett Franken closed the conference room door and sat next to Cameron. He also slid a piece of paper in front of his client.

"Cameron, Ms. Jones, as you know, Mr. Bass and I have been discussing Cameron's request for additional visitation with Holly pending the modification hearing on the twenty-sixth. You each have in front of you a copy of the letter I sent to Mr. Bass with our proposal.

"Currently, by the terms of your decree, Cameron has Holly every other weekend and several weeks in the summer. We would propose adding a weekly Wednesday night visit and also adding a portion of Christmas Day in addition to the Christmas Eve visit provided for in the dissolution of marriage decree."

Susan shook her head. "Then he gets her the whole holiday?"

"You're taking her halfway around the world next month," Cameron said, an edge to his voice. "I don't think I'm asking too much." Rather than looking at Susan, he said all this to the wood grain on the table as if mapping the route of his escape in the pattern.

Both Susan and Wally Bass started to protest, but Everett Franken tried to intervene. "This is all pointless anyway," Susan managed to get out. "I am moving to London, Cameron. With Holly. I won't be able to do any extra visits once this is over."

"That worked out pretty well, didn't it?" Cameron said.

Before Susan could fire back, both lawyers stifled them.

"I think for now we should focus on the current visits," Wally Bass suggested.

Everett Franken agreed. "We are still negotiating a modified, but expanded, visitation schedule that will work with your move, as you know, Ms. Jones. For now, let's just deal with Christmas. Any permanent changes would go into effect next year. I think we can save that debate for trial. For now, pending the outcome of our petition for expanded visitation, an additional visit this month is not unreasonable."

"Are you sure that's...best for the child?" Wally Bass said with a glance at Cameron. "Given Mr. Jones's problems, we're not so sure increased visitation is in the best interests of the child at this point."

"You mean because I'm crazy?" Cameron spat.

"Cameron, let's not do this now," Everett Franken said, somehow making his voice stern, while still retaining its pleasantness.

Cameron fumed and said nothing.

"Wally, I think everyone would be better served by saving the issue of Mr. Jones' psychological fitness for trial," Everett Franken said.

"He can't be trusted," Wally Bass said. "What if he flips out on a visit again?"

"The incident you are referring to was a year ago. Mr. Jones has had a number of visits with Holly since then that have gone quite well."

"Holly thinks her dad is weird," Susan said quietly, rejoining the conversation, but appearing to speak to the same point on the table top that Cameron had addressed.

Cameron's impulse was to mount a vigorous defense; to reject Susan's words. Holly loved her father. Certainly she did. And he loved her. The reality was, though, that Holly probably did think he was weird. Cameron wasn't all that sure himself that he wasn't weird.

"The psychological records do indicate mental instabilities," Wally Bass said. "We'd be foolish to ignore that."

"Wally, you know those records might not be admissible in trial," Everett Franken said evenly. "Besides, there are conflicting reports."

"Bipolar was a good one," Cameron said. "But I thought manic depressive was a little over the top." He chuckled at his own joke.

"This isn't funny, Cameron," Susan said.

Cameron shrugged. "Right. Well, maybe a little. Maybe I'm just pissed off at the world and don't care who knows it." He laughed again. "So my choice was either to write country music or go over the edge. Tough call."

He had tried once a couple years ago to get serious about psychiatric treatment, got overconfident and went off his meds. He felt great when he did that though. He hadn't been so in control of his emotions and his psyche in years. Even his writing went better. He was actually able to focus on his new untitled novel. Things were great again. Until that last Christmas Eve.

What happened that holiday, far from being a conquest of Christmas-dom, resulted in weeks during which Holly wouldn't talk to her father, much less visit him again.

"Cameron, please be serious," Susan snapped before her lawyer motioned for her to relax.

"Serious?" Cameron asked, incredulous. "These days, *everything* I do is serious. Christmas, the happiest fucking time on Earth, is a goddamn torture session."

"That's enough, Cameron," Everett Franken admonished.

Of all the visitations with his daughter throughout the years, Cameron agonized over the Christmas Eve visit the most. The possibility of a Norman Rockwell Christmas was as cold and dead as Mr. Rockwell himself. The echoes of Holly sobbing as Susan retrieved her from Cameron's home last Christmas still echoed in his mind.

No. Cameron would not, could not, think about that today. That was then. Things were different now. *He* was different now. He needed more time with his daughter, needed to show her he wasn't crazy. His daughter would not grow up without him. Bet your big, shiny, jingle bells on that.

He looked at Everett Franken who was deftly outlining a litany of case law supporting an increase in visitation pending a custody trial. He looked at Wally Bass shaking his head and rejecting Everett Franken's argument. He looked at Susan Wentworth Jones, still intently gazing into the wood grain tabletop, seemingly entranced. It was time for a bold move. He needed to stage a strategic retreat and regroup.

"All right," Cameron said. When no one reacted, he repeated it a little louder. "All right. Just forget the extra visit. But I still want my Christmas Eve visit."

Everett Franken looked at his client and gauged that he was serious. Then he looked expectantly at Wally Bass.

Wally Bass was caught a little off guard, but rallied quickly. "Well, then. I guess we're done here."

Susan looked at Cameron, making eye contact for only the second time that afternoon, but said nothing.

Wally Bass thrust out his hand to Everett Franken. "Thanks, Everett," he said. "Good to see you again."

"Yes. Thank you," Everett Franken responded, without returning the pleasantry.

Wally Bass motioned to Susan and headed out of the room. Susan left also, still not looking at Cameron.

After they had gone, Cameron laid his chin in his hands and sighed. "Merry Christmas to me," he said.

"Tell me about it. Now, I have to spend my Christmas holiday preparing for trial." Everett Franken grinned.

"Sorry, buddy," Cameron said.

"Ah, well. No big deal. I'm Jewish anyway."

They shared a laugh; brief and light, but still a laugh.

Out on the street, a less tumultuous, more traditional, form of Christmas was in full force. Cameron stood by his jeep in the parking lot and cursed as he dropped his keychain in the slushy road grit. As he bent to pick it up, a pair of snakeskin boots stepped into his field of vision.

"Mr. Jones?" the boots asked.

"Yes," Cameron responded, then stood.

The man before him was tall with a paunch visible even through a heavy parka. He had a huckster's grin that went well with the boots.

"I'm Ben Steene," the man said, politely enough, though his outstretched hand was spurned.

"Lawyer or reporter?" Cameron asked wearily.

"Reporter," Steene replied. "If you're gonna punch me, wait 'till the photographer gets here."

Cameron winced. One of the joys of living in a small town like Santa Claus was that it was far from the media jet stream. His troubles had gone largely unreported. "Who are you with?" he asked.

"*Perils of Prose-Masters.com*," Ben Steene answered, offering a business card. It also went untouched. Cameron feared what he would catch if he made contact with the man. "Sometimes I write for the print version too."

"Good for you. But I'm not doing any interviews right now, thanks," Cameron said diplomatically.

"Oh, c'mon. Just a few questions." Ben Steene grinned ingratiatingly, revealing a prominent chipped tooth.

"No thanks," Cameron said still calmly, but with a bit more tone. "This isn't the best time." He depressed the button on his keychain to unlock his doors, but Ben Steene had maneuvered himself between Cameron and the driver's side door.

"Yeah, I understand," Ben Steene said. "How's Holly doing?"

Cameron's teeth clenched. "Don't," he said simply. "Please."

"Been a rough time, hasn't it?" Ben Steene asked. Cameron wondered if he had a tape recorder hidden somewhere. "Get to see her much? You know...anymore?"

Cameron resisted an urge to add a few more chipped teeth to this guy's collection. "I said no interviews, thanks."

Ben Steene glanced down and made a face. "Oh, would you look at that? Got salt on my new boots. Guess that's what you get for wearing snake skin to the Midwest in the winter. Well, we all got problems, right?"

"Goodbye, Mr. Steene."

"Till we meet again, Mr. Jones." He handed Cameron the business card again. Cameron snatched it away, glaring at the reporter.

Ben Steene stepped aside with a bow and Cameron climbed into the jeep and pulled away.

Ben Steene glanced around and smacked his lips as if savoring the last of the Figgie pudding.

Cameron drove mechanically back to Santa Claus, cruised without interruption through the two stoplights, parked, and walked. Just walked. The sidewalks of Santa Claus, Indiana were bright and crunchy with brilliant white snow crystals underfoot, evidence of a recent, cursory effort at snowfall.

Santa Claus, Indiana, is a town of a couple thousand people, two main residential developments, two state highways, two caution lights, and one shopping plaza. There are also numerous references to favorite son Abraham Lincoln who spent a lot of time in Spencer County, a bunch of fake elves and reindeer, and this one quasi-celebrity who wrote books.

The people of Santa Claus, Indiana are a hardy, Midwestern bunch who are pretty blasé about the whole Christmas thing, probably a consequence of being steeped in yuletide spirit the whole damn year. Still, they put on a good show. Light posts, storefronts and other businesses were lined with garlands of silver, gold, green and red; as well as the occasional Santa Claus and more than a few Rudolph the Red-Nosed Reindeers. It seemed like when you entered the city limits to Santa Claus, Indiana, you were struck with some odd form of color blindness that prevented you from appreciating any colors other than red or green.

It was a perfect winter wonderland, so long as your eyes didn't wander too far from the patch of snow on the middle of the grassy areas to the patches of brown grass around them and the muddy streets. Cameron hated all of it. Well, he kind of appreciated the dead spots in the grass, but not the rest of it.

It wasn't all Susan's fault either. He had to give her that. When Cameron was six, his parents, Helen and Stan, got him a puppy. It was a beautiful...well, it was a beautiful mutt. But it was playful and smart. He named it "Baxter." Cameron and that dog were inseparable. For two weeks. Then Baxter died. Some sort of quirky, intestinal thing. He never owned another pet.

When Cameron was eleven, four days before Christmas, the family home burned down, taking the Christmas tree, the presents, and everything else they owned.

When Cameron was nineteen, his father Stan passed away. He was a life-long smoker and cheese Danish devotee. It was something of a miracle that his heart limped along as long as it did. But the loss still sucked.

And now, this holiday season, Cameron was losing his daughter.

In between all those dreadful holidays was a series of peaceful, joyous yuletide events that went normally, yet somehow were unsatisfying in some intangible way. The presents were nice, the holiday ham/turkey/steaks/oriental stir fry (that last was the culmination of an odd year) were always good; the family and friends were great company. Somehow, though, the holidays never quite lived up to whatever it is they're supposed to live up to. Instead of being full of good will, he was usually left full of starchy foods and little else. Yet, every time he turned on the television, there was that smiling, singing, jolly old elf, babbling about peace on Earth and goodwill and all that crap, oblivious to Cameron's holiday dissatisfaction.

Santa Claus—what a motherfucker.

And still Cameron pressed on; quirky oddities of the mind or not. He had come to think of his bi-polar disorder, or whatever it was, as just a big joke his mind played on him. So much of the time, he was fine. But then at the strangest, most awkward times, he would flip out. Getting ready to go on a talk show to promote a new book? Launch a crying jag. Trying to focus on writing the end of a manuscript that is grossly overdue to the editor? Instead, find yourself distracted by a phantom voice telling you, "You suck. Give it up." Finally out on your first date since the divorce? Stare intently at the ghostly image of a little girl in pigtails carrying a meat cleaver racing back and forth through the restaurant instead of gazing intently into your date's gorgeous hazel eyes.

"And a big steamin' hunk of Noel to you," Cameron muttered to no one.

"Is that any way to talk during the merriest time of year?" a voice said.

Cameron flinched. He lifted his eyes, expecting to see something ephemeral, shimmering, zooming just out of view.

Instead, he saw Santa Claus. A sidewalk Santa to be exact. One of those "Rent-a-Claus" types you see on street corners during the holidays collecting contributions for charity. Cameron had once used the phrase "Rent-a-Claus" in a *New Yorker* essay and it seemed quite apt here.

It was not a great likeness, however. This Santa was plump, but not Santa-size. He had the long, flowing beard, but it was as much gray as snow white. It was also scraggly and tilted slightly out of alignment with his chin as if the Rent-a-Claus had just dragged it out of his trunk and slapped it on his head without much care.

"Did you say something?" Cameron asked.

"I said, 'Is that any way to talk during the merriest time of the year?'" Rent-a-Claus had dimples, but they weren't particularly merry, nor were his cheeks rosy. His smile was broad, but gap-toothed.

"Sorry," Cameron said, not particularly sorry at all. "It's been a rough day."

"The holiday season can be hard on anybody," the Rent-a-Claus said.

Cameron took this to be a ploy for a handout. He fished into his pocket. All he had was a twenty, so he tossed it into the gold bucket.

"Merry Christmas," Rent-a-Claus beamed. He waved a green mitten grandly and said, "This charming community is awash in the holiday: Holiday World, the Santa Claus Post Office, Frosty's Fun Center, Santa's Lodge,

Lake Rudolph Campground, Frosty's Evergreen Forest. It's magical. Open your heart, friend."

Cameron smirked. "I already opened my wallet. I think that's enough openness for one day."

Rent-a-Claus tried to frown, but it was a struggle. "There's still hope, my friend," he said.

"I'm sure your charity will do very well," Cameron said, assuming that's what he meant.

"That's not what I meant," Rent-a-Claus objected, as if he'd heard Cameron's thought. "You've still got your family, you know. They still care."

Cameron started to ask how this gap-toothed, sidewalk Santa Claus knew anything about his family when he noticed something about the man; an indefinable something. He shook it off. "Yeah, whatever," he said as much to himself as anyone.

"Ho ho ho" the Rent-a-Claus enthused. Even if he didn't much look the part, the greeting sounded authentic. Give him that much. "Be of good cheer," he said, and waved.

Cameron fought the urge to wave back with just one particular finger. He wandered away. It occurred to him that "Santa" was only a couple shuffled letters away from "Satan." This could not be a coincidence.

Rent-a-Claus turned to the golden bucket and peered inside. He counted the assorted change. A lot of it was pennies, a few nickels, but there was a smattering of folding money. With Cameron's twenty, the take was pretty good. Both Rent-a-Claus's eyes twinkled full boar, a full-on Santa thing happening.

He watched Cameron shrug down the street, then reached into the fur-lined opening of his red coat. He pulled out a hand-held, electronic organizer, slid the stylus out of its holder, and scrolled through the contents of a file. The list was long. His eyes scanned it quickly. Yes, there was Cameron. He put a check next to his name. Good. Then he checked it twice.

Schnauzer lady tapped a couple crooked fingers on the glass front of her store and called out. "Hey, move along. You're blocking my customers."

"And a happy holiday to you, madam," Renta-Claus responded. It was the only correct response, if not the most satisfying.

Somewhere far away, jingle bells rang loud and crisp.

# DECEMBER 2

Lying in the dark underneath a decorated Christmas tree, looking up through the branches, the view can be enchanting. The blue, red, green, and gold colored twinkle lights reflect in the shiny ornaments, the beams of holiday cheer refracting through the boughs of the tree. The bright lights pull you in, pluck the strings of your senses and leave you with good will toward men.

That is, unless you are Dogwater Hunt, in which case the bright lights do pull you in, but instead of holiday cheer, they provoke flashbacks of torture, claustrophobia and seizures.

Dogwater Hunt was a multiple alien abductee. Most of his abductions had been of the classic maybe UFO/maybe weather balloon in the night sky, bright-lights-in-the-cornfield variety. He had a vivid recollection of the start of each abduction sequence, though nothing more. They always started the same. He would get chills, feel a vibration within the marrow of his bones and get plucked out of his car, his bed, off the meat packing plant assembly line, and the next thing he knew he was inside the ship.

Every time, he was treated upon his arrival to an amazing light show. Blues bluer than the Caribbean Sea; brilliant green; and rich purple hues. Portions of the color spectrum not ordinarily visible to humans stretched out before Dogwater, entrancing and blinding him simultaneously.

And then the torture would start. This is usually where Dogwater blacked out.

Ever since the abductions started, at age ten, he had experienced visceral reactions to bright, colored lights. It's not like he lived in the dark like a morlock. He simply quivered at the sight of a fireworks display, any sort of presentation involving a laser pointer, and, naturally, holiday lights. He sweated, seized, and, once, on a date at a rock concert, wet himself. He never got a date with that girl again. Stupid glow-sticks.

After doing laundry that night after the fateful date, Dogwater Hunt devoted himself to the alien abduction cause; to ease his laundry bill, if nothing else.

On this morning, he sat cross-legged on the living room floor. A massive snarl of holiday lights spooled out of a large cardboard box to his left, down the side, over and under Dogwater's legs and on the floor. The other end of the tangle was plugged into the wall socket and the functioning bulbs twinkled. It was one of those strings where one bad bulb causes a whole section of the string to cut out, but leaves the rest alone. A section of pink and green bulbs were reflecting in the finish of the oak floor. He was methodically checking each bulb, pulling out each dead one and replacing it with one of the bulbs from the pile on the floor of leftovers cannibalized from old, worn-out strings.

The Christmas tree was not in place yet, but Dogwater, anal retentive that he was, couldn't stand the jumble of wires sitting in the middle of the floor. He was making good progress on the mess and so far his crotch was dry. It might be a happy holiday after all.

Dogwater Hunt, an enigma for many reasons that had nothing to do with his name, met Cameron Jones when Cameron was doing background research for book number two, *The Deadman's New Hat*. Cameron was looking for a guy who could tell him all about conspiracy theories, especially the Kennedy assassination. One of the prominent characters in *The Deadman's New Hat* was the ghost of JFK, or at least something that the protagonist perceives to be the ghost of JFK. Dogwater Hunt was the man in Indiana to ask about such things.

When Dogwater wasn't running the local "Speedy Stop" gas station and video palace, he operated a conspiracy theory website called *Dark Matters*. Along with classic fare like the JFK assassination, Area 51, and the like, were more contemporary alleged conspiracies surrounding the war in Iraq. Once per month, he put out a print issue for the less technologically savvy among his readers. The headline in the most recent print issue proclaimed: "ALIENS GUIDED U.S. TROOPS," and a sidebar suggested that the governing council assembled to run Iraq after the fall of Baghdad included, at a minimum, three extra-terrestrials.

*Dark Matters* gave a voice to the disenfranchised conspiracist everywhere. Dogwater had great respect for anyone willing to stand up and say what no one else would—even if it was so whacked out that even *he* didn't believe it.

Dogwater Hunt had moved to Indiana because he dug the whole "screw daylight savings time" attitude of most of the state. It was a sign of the vibrant wackiness surging beneath the state's bland, Midwestern veneer. He wasn't much of a Midwesterner at heart, in attitude, or in appearance, but it was better to hide among the sheep than stand out someplace like New York where the government wolves were just waiting to pick off a good conspiracist.

With three bulbs left on the light string, Dogwater paused. He heard something. A creak. A shuffling sound. Dogwater cocked his head, reached over and plucked his gray fedora off the straight-backed chair, putting it on. For years, he had believed he could hear better with the hat on.

The sound was getting closer. Footsteps moving slowly. Coming down the stairs. Any moment now he would face...something. Was this another abduction? Usually, stress-induced paralysis preceded the attacks, but not this time.

He looked toward the stairs, bracing for what was coming.

A soft glow from upstairs was the only light. The being moved slowly down the stairs. Dogwater had left the lights off in the living room—all the better for holiday light testing. He couldn't make out the being's features; the being probably didn't even *have* features.

After the last abduction, he was convinced the next would be the last; the final showdown. And now, the time had come. And he'd wasted last weekend on Christmas shopping. Dogwater steeled his nerve and braced for his destiny.

The figure stepped off the downstairs landing and flipped the light switch. Dogwater was momentarily blinded.

"What the hell are you doing in my house?" Cameron said.

Until this moment, Dogwater wouldn't have thought it was possible for someone in such a fuzzy, slightly effeminate, terrycloth bathrobe to look so incredibly pissed.

Dogwater stood in a tangle of holiday lights. "Dude, you left the door open."

"It's five o'clock in the morning," Cameron grumbled.

"Yeah, and in Iraq, it's like, supposedly one in the afternoon," Dogwater scoffed. "So they say."

"Did you at least put the coffee on?"

"Of course. Hey, you know, you should be more careful. This is a dangerous town."

"It's Santa Claus, Indiana," Cameron said, turning toward the kitchen. "The greatest danger here is boredom. I knew I should have moved to Christmas Lake Village. They at least have guards against people like you."

"You're a celebrity," Dogwater said. "You gotta be careful."

"I *was* a celebrity. Now I'm a freakish quasi-celebrity."

"Yeah, but you've got some of the biggest coffee grounds I've ever seen. Like rich people jumbo java or something."

Cameron nodded, assuming that was some sort of a compliment; something like having big *cajones*. Then realization struck. "You did *grind* the coffee beans, didn't you?"

Dogwater laughed. "Yeah, *that's* gonna happen."

"Clean this stuff up," Cameron said, motioning to the festive clutter. "I'm not doing Christmas decorations."

"Why not?" The string of lights drooped in Dogwater's hands, as if disappointed.

"Too many ghosts."

"Man, you're not...hearing the voices again are you?"

"No, not exactly," Cameron said, not looking back as he walked through the kitchen door.

Barely clearing the tangles of holiday cheer at his feet, Dogwater hustled into the kitchen. "Did you say *not exactly?*"

Cameron turned from his hunched posture over the counter, coffee cup in hand. He handed a second, empty cup to Dogwater and motioned toward the coffee pot, nonverbally directing Dogwater to correct the desecration he'd wrought upon his appliance.

"I'm taking the meds, usually," Cameron said. "I do the therapy. I don't drink... much. I don't exactly *hear* voices anymore. It's more like a constant murmur just under the level I can hear at; like the voices are in the audience at a concert and don't want to piss off the conductor."

Cameron was, he often thought, a poster child for the miracles of modern pharmacology. Thanks to a rigorous regimen of antidepressants, a cornucopia of other drugs of various shapes and colors, including Thorazine once on a dare, he didn't really hear the voices anymore. It was a wondrous array of psychological bon bons. Pour all the pills out in a bowl, and they'd look like a sugary kid's cereal.

Cameron had been through enough therapy sessions with high priced doctors who liked to use big words as if they got paid more for them (and probably did) to guess that he was a borderline schizophrenic. Unless he wasn't. He had a mild mood disorder and a depressive disorder with mixed features. The treatment featured intense therapy, and a number of anti-depressants and scary antipsychotic drugs. He was gradually weaned off those drugs in favor of lithium once the worst of the symptoms subsided. Of course, when he asked the doctors directly for a diagnosis, they just patted the famous author on the shoulder and said, "You're just stressed."

"You sure all those pills are a good idea?" Dogwater asked, not for the first time.

"Not this again," Cameron groaned, sinking into his mug.

"Antidepressants, mood elevators, mood levelers, tranquilizers; it's all thought control. The government uses that shit to keep us docile, unthreatening."

"Yes, you've told me."

"Why don't you go see my herbal guy?" Cameron asked.

"Isn't he in prison?"

"Nah, he bonded out pending trial."

"Oh, that's good," Cameron said in a tone clearly indicating no intention whatsoever to see Dogwater's herbal guy, except maybe on a breaking news alert. Again.

The time-worn hands were rock steady as the old man glided the piece of wood through the whirring jig saw. Milo Vestibule then tossed the finished piece into a bin with several other similarly cut boards.

"Gonna get us a bumper crop of birdhouses this week, ain't we, Sally?"

The disgruntled cat, put out by the sawdust lining the garage floor, was too busy cleaning a paw to respond.

Milo's ears were still sharp for a man in his seventies—"Once in Korea, it was my good hearing that saved my buddy from dyin' on the crapper when

I heard that ol' commie sneakin' up on us," Milo liked to brag. He heard a familiar sound out front, hustled over to the garage door opener and pressed the button, patting down his hair with his other hand.

Sure enough, when the door opened, Cindy Lew Woo, the college co-ed who delivered Milo's prescriptions, was there waiting.

"Hi, Milo," the attractive young woman said sweetly. "You look busy. Are the kids coming again today?"

"Yeah, but not for a couple hours," Milo said, taking the paper bag from Cindy. "If you want to hang around..." He winked.

"Milo!" Cindy Lew Woo said in mock indignation.

Milo rummaged around in his pharmacy sack. "Oh, wait. Better take a rain check. I didn't get *that* prescription refilled this time, I guess." He grinned mischievously.

Cindy laughed and drove away.

"Oh, well. Guess I'll go have a beer."

Sconces illuminated a tasteful Old World style office. It wasn't spacious, but had a comfortable, cozy feel. Pieces of parchment littered the oak desktop. A quill pen extended from an inkwell, which itself rested on a closed and, clearly little used, laptop computer.

Rent-a-Claus lowered his wiry frame into the high-backed leather chair behind the desk, tossing his Santa suit coat and hat on the desk. He instantly inflated like a life raft. His waist thickened, his stomach rounded. Where mere sinew and muscle had clung desperately to bone on his arms and legs, flab now appeared.

He reached into a drawer and pulled out a hand mirror. He studied his features and removed the blackening on his teeth revealing a fine set of choppers arrayed in a stunning grin. He crinkled his eyes over his rapidly rosing cheeks. The hair on his head and beard became more bushy, full, and pure white. Within seconds, Rent-a-Claus was gone and Kris Kringle stared back at, well, Kris Kringle. He was grinning, happy with the results of his latest yuletide covert reconnaissance; secret forays he made periodically throughout the year to check up on things in the real world. He really got a buzz off it.

But then, the dimples fell, the eyes closed. The weariness came back. This all got harder every year. So much harder. Being Santa Claus was not what it used to be.

There was a time when he got millions of beautiful, handwritten letters from boys and girls all over the world. They would flow on and on. There'd be pages of "I love you, Santa," "Bless you, Santa." Pen, pencil, crayon, sometimes paints. Whatever the medium, the message was always the same: I love Christmas, I love my family (including, frequently, the family pet), I love you, Santa. Then after all this heartfelt sentiment, they would mention a few items that they would like for Christmas, if it was okay and if they'd been extra good—or at least tried real hard to be good.

He still got these kinds of letters, but not as often. Now, even if it was handwritten, it was more likely to be short on love and long on lists of stuff they wanted—pages and pages of stuff. He usually didn't even get handwritten letters anymore. It was emails. Or letters typed and printed on cold, sterile printers. And sometimes kids did still ask for things for people other than themselves—good health for relatives, save grandma's home; but those letters were coming less and less often.

But really, he wasn't down on the kids. He loved the kids. But he was tired, very tired.

"Does Christmas spirit really exist?" Santa said to the mirror. "Do *I* really exist?"

That was the one that kept him up at night. He really didn't know if he even existed. There was a clear division, everyone at the North Pole knew, between the imaginary world they occupied and the real world, but Santa had been a real-worlder once, hadn't he? And now he traveled between the worlds. Yet, no one in the real world saw him. If they did, he wasn't supposed to leave any presents. That was the rule. So what kind of existence was that? As he strolled through the reindeer stable, watched the elves at work, gazed across the breakfast table laden with sugar cookies and hot chocolate at his adoring wife of all these eons, he wondered: Who lives like this? Is any of this real? Am I really here?

Santa's children—meaning the children of the world—pretty much universally believed in him from the time they were old enough to reason such thoughts. He was generally regarded as a Christian creation, but he had a presence in some fashion pretty much around the world. But just as there was unfailing acceptance in youth, with age there inevitably came the time when they stopped believing. He stopped existing for them.

And maybe that was right.

He'd given this a lot of thought. He tried convincing himself that if anyone didn't exist, it was the real-worlders. They were the imaginary ones. That would seem to be more rational than seriously debating your own existence. However, he couldn't ignore the circumstantial evidence. He did an awful lot of miraculous things—sliding up and down chimneys, the flying sleigh, delivering toys all over the world all in one night.

No real person could do these things, could he?

And, how did he know what all those boys and girls were up to? How could he watch all of them? He saw them sleeping and when they were awake. He knew if they were bad or good. He didn't know how he knew, but he did.

Also, he hung around with elves. They were great. Santa loved them dearly, but, you know what, you never see elves anywhere other than the North Pole. Why is that? Maybe they weren't real either. It seemed to Santa that having imaginary friends that seemed like flesh and blood to you probably meant that you were imaginary too.

And another thing: what did he do when it wasn't Christmas? Where did he go? Santa didn't know. He couldn't remember. His only frame of reference was Christmas.

People talked about Santa a lot, but it was always Christmas-related. His likeness was everywhere. Usually, he was depicted in the red suit in a sleigh, or by a Christmas tree or something. Sometimes, though, he was shown playing golf, on the beach, fishing, being a doctor, barbecuing, even scuba diving. Santa, though, couldn't remember ever having done any of these things.

Maybe that was because he never *had* done any of these things. Maybe his existence was no more real than that of the Santa in all those snow globes they sold in Christmas-themed stores; a mere likeness of life, a facsimile of reality that could be manipulated for fantasy or profit.

He was about to send for a cup of hot chocolate—double marshmallows—when Mrs. Claus walked in. She was not soft and plump and grandmotherly-looking as Mrs. Claus is usually depicted. This Mrs. Claus was buff. Yet, she carried herself in the dignified matronly way that befit the wife of Kris Kringle.

"Hello, sweetie," she said, pecking Mr. Claus on the cheek.

"Hi, hon," Santa said, keeping his chair turned toward the window behind the desk. Outside, he could see a number of elves frolicking in the fresh snowfall on a break from holiday preparations.

"Enjoy your trip out to the real world?" Mrs. Claus asked as she stood, arms folded on the back of Santa's chair.

"Who am I, dear?" he asked in response.

"Is that a riddle?" Mrs. Claus asked, not missing a beat, though she had heard this question many times, in many forms.

Santa Claus arched an eyebrow. "Not today, please."

"Okay, then, you're Santa Claus."

"No, I mean..."

"Kris Kringle; that's a good one..."

"But who am-"

"Also St. Nicholas—though that one's a little pretentious."

"Dearest..."

"Do you prefer Weinachtsmann?

Santa chuckled a muted "ho, ho, ho."

"How about: Père Noël, Father Frost, Father Christmas, or Joulupukki?"

"Point well taken," Santa said.

"All over the world, children speak your name in their own languages with awe and wonder," Mrs. Clause said. "Yet, you haven't been very jolly this holiday season."

"After fifteen or sixteen centuries aren't I allowed an off year?" Santa said, in a tone somewhat sharper than he intended.

"No," Mrs. Claus said flatly, crossing thin, but deceptively powerful, arms.

At first, Santa was taken aback. Then he realized, "Of course, you're right, dear. As always."

Santa met Mrs. Claus somewhere around 400 or 500 A.D. She was reluctant to marry him. This was an age where pretty much all women did was get married and take care of their men. The future Mrs. Claus, however, was a very non-traditional woman. But there was something about the doughy, white haired, merry man that was irresistible. So, they married quickly.

For a while, they had counted anniversaries, but after a few hundred it got to be difficult to come up with good presents, even if you are Santa Claus.

It was a fantastic marriage in every sense of the word. How could it not be an amazing existence? Santa and Mrs. Claus prepare and distribute toys to children all over the world. They consort with elves and flying reindeer. They live largely on a diet of hot cocoa and cookies, but are in perfect health and enjoy apparent immortality. The word "fantastic" barely covers this existence.

But to Mrs. Claus, the marriage worked because of the man—Nicholas—himself. He was jolly—with the "ho, ho, ho" and all—but he was also seriously passionate about his need to help others. He was a student of culture—he made a study of the needs and wants of the children around the world and how they differed from country to country. He was also a student of art and a lover of nature. His care of the reindeer—flying and earthbound—was unparalleled. He also turned the elves from a greedy, war-faring people into the gentle, fun-loving, hard-working, generous makers of toys and Christmas magic that they were now.

Santa loved his work and she loved him for it. She could only remember a handful of times in the past millennium when Santa had lost his merry demeanor. Once, about three-hundred-fifty years ago, the most senior of all the elves, Dalor, died. She was there when Santa got the news.

"Santa, I have terrible news," Teelor, the second-elf, said to Kris Kringle, standing timidly before the great man that day.

Santa looked up from his workbench where he was carving a wooden ship. In the old days, before the elves, he made the toys himself. As time went on, he did less and less of the "hands on," but still got his hands dirty now and then.

"What is it, Teelor?" he asked in his genially booming voice.

Teelor shifted from foot to foot. She had never delivered bad news to Santa. In fact, to her knowledge, no one in Santa's village ever had. There never *was* any bad news at the North Pole, until now.

"Teelor?" Santa asked patiently.

"It's Dalor, Santa..."

"Dalor? He's down with the real-worlders gathering information. What about him?"

The "real-worlders" were the people outside of the North Pole Complex's imaginary world, including the people in the various countries who believed in Santa and received gifts from him each Christmas. Over the centuries,

Nicholas, later Santa, had changed from a mysteriously anonymous small-time gift-giver, to an international, mythical one. True, in those days international borders changed almost daily, but still his legend grew and more or less ignored those boundaries. In light of this, Santa did less fact-finding himself and would send out the elves under cover of darkness to scout out the needs and wants of the world's children and report back to the workshop, as well as add data to the naughty or nice list.

"The rest of the party returned today without him." Teelor barely squeaked out the next part. "They say he's dead, Santa."

Santa took off his spectacles. "Dead? How?"

"A snow storm came up. The group became lost and disoriented. They sheltered for the night in the woods and were set upon by wolves."

"How could this be? The elves are so...so in tune with nature. They love all animals and loved by them." Santa sat at the bench, the unfinished ship clattering to the floor.

"What do we do, Santa?" Teelor was scared. Dalor was old and frail. Since coming to the North Pole, Santa knew many elves had died from old age— extreme old age—but none had died like this so unexpectedly.

"Did they bring back his body?"

"Yes, Santa."

Santa nodded. "Then he shall have a proper burial. Now, please leave me." The tone was sharper, the speech unnaturally clipped.

"Thank you, Santa." Teelor moved briskly from the room.

The sobs emanating from this great, jolly, old soul shortly thereafter shook the walls, tearing at every yuletide spirit, none more so than Mrs. Claus, who slept no better than Santa that night, nor for many after.

Now, sitting there in Santa's office this early afternoon, three-hundred-fifty years later, as the deer pranced and the smell of lunchtime gingerbread hung in the air, the light streamed through the stain glass windows and glistened off Santa's brilliant white hair. Mrs. Claus loved her husband as much as she had all those centuries ago, even now as he sat slump-shouldered and forlorn. Maybe even more so.

Over the centuries, Santa had come to learn that things change: seasons pass, people—and elves—die, and children stop believing in Santa. But Santa still had trouble with the last one. Much of a person's psyche is formed by the faith and love of those around us. This is especially true for someone who exists directly as a result of love; someone who is an immortal legend beloved by children and remembered wistfully by adults.

As Santa read more and more letters from frustrated children claiming not to believe in him, Santa cut way back on his incognito excursions to the outside world. He seemed not to want to face the very children he loved. This was bad enough, But then, after Dalor died, the Christmas-y twinkle left his eyes. It was a frightening moment. A global blackout would not have been scarier. A chill permeated the North Pole castle where previously holiday warmth and good tidings pushed back the winter climate. Mrs. Claus had never been so scared for her husband or for the fate of Christmas as the world had come to know it.

Until now.

# DECEMBER 3

Holly berries are poisonous, but we use them for decoration. Romantics are encouraged to stand under mistletoe in expressions of love and affection. It's toxic too. Seeming contradictions like these occupied the larger percentage of Cameron's brain these days. And it really pissed him off.

There was a time when Cameron would sit up all night with a mixed bag of writers and celebrities debating issues of politics, art, and science; a time when he could write twenty, thirty pages—good pages—of a novel in one sitting; a time he spent hours alone pondering the mysteries of the universe. One of his favorites was this: if the universe, the embodiment of all that is, is expanding, as the physicists tell us, what is it expanding into? Cameron Jones was, in every sense, a pseudo-intellectual, once upon a time.

Now, focused thought for any appreciable length of time brought anxiety and dread. His mind would wander. And that's a bad thing because that's when the hallucinations and delusions start. A stray thought could lead to an internal monologue. That, in turn, could lead Cameron to talk to himself. From there it was a short leap to hearing the voices.

That's why Cameron enjoyed television commercials. They were short and required little depth of thought. When he thought about resurrecting his writing career, he sometimes thought about becoming a commercial writer. Cameron liked the Internet too for its short-attention-span qualities.

So now, this wealthy, bestselling author sprawled in the middle of his living room floor. He sank low in an oversized bean bag chair. He had taken to bean bags after his last hospital stay. They appealed to him because, though they did qualify as "chairs," they were amorphous. What they really were, were formless blobs to which someone had assigned the designation "chairs."

Similarly, Cameron thought he was a formless blob assigned the designation "writer," or—some days—simply "human." Those titles were as much a deceit as calling the bean bags "chairs." Bean bag chairs didn't even really have beans in them. The lie perpetuates itself.

*Quality, Not Quantity, The Dead Man's New Hat,* and *Sandstorm,* along with miscellaneous essays, a few short stories, and derivative works, had, in total, made an obscene amount of money. Even if he had the drive to work again, he really didn't need to. He had a fourth novel in the works; had had it in the works since before his stints in the clinics. It was called—at various times—*Blight, Cruel Existence,* or *Eternal Blackness.* Cameron had no idea what the book was about ("About 450 pages," he chuckled to himself) or what motivated him to write other than writing is what he does. Or *did.*

Mostly what Cameron did these days was think about his daughter Holly; actually, one particular day in his life with Holly and ex-wife Susan Wentworth Jones—back when she seemed happy to be known as "Susan Jones," even as she planned to leave. Even names concealed lies.

Like many family holiday gatherings, that Christmas Day had been a stressful odyssey of Noel-fueled torture. If Cameron had had a Yule log, he might have beaten himself with it.

Baby Holly, routinely up by 5:30 a.m., was well-past hungry and cranky when Susan's parents, Myra and Earl, arrived at ten for brunch that Christmas Day. Holly's Christmas outfit was streaked with dirt. She had stealthily discovered and probably ingested a fair amount of dirt from a tipped poinsettia plant in a brief moment when both Holly and Cameron were occupied with things other than her.

The debris field around the tree was impressive. Holly was far too young to grasp the concept of gift receipt and exchange, but was down with the concept of ripping paper. Cameron was a ripper too and it was evident he helped Holly open her presents.

When Myra and Earl arrived, an impressive array of breakfast foods—muffins, eggs, fruit, pancakes, various juices, multiple cappuccino options—awaited them on the dining room table. Myra and Earl, however, had grabbed an egg sandwich at the airport before picking up their rental car. They just asked for toast and black coffee.

"You look tired, dear," Myra said to Susan over breakfast.

"Holly works on her own schedule, Mom," Susan said.

"And what have you been up to?" Myra said to Cameron as if she were speaking to a very young child.

Cameron started to describe the book he was writing, and the book fair he had been invited to present at, and the interview he'd just done for a major national publication when Susan jumped in. "Mom, it's Christmas. Let's not talk about all that. Anyone want more coffee?"

It was a weird and weirdly non-responsive answer, Cameron thought. Why *shouldn't* they talk about it? Or maybe, he was overly sensitive. He was irritable most of the time now. A couple times, late at night especially, he found himself swinging between rage and weeping. He also had a hard time focusing, so he thought maybe he hadn't heard Susan correctly.

"Well, I do have the new thing..." he ventured, almost apologetically.

"Later, Cameron," Susan said, sounding like she was addressing the same child Myra had.

"But the new book is good," he said.

"Later, please. Let's open presents," Susan said, getting up from the table.

Myra and Earl shuffled after her. Cameron remained at the table and distinctly heard Earl whispering to Myra, in an unintentionally loud stage-type whisper, "Is he okay, yet?" Myra responded with a "Shhh."

Cameron and Susan sat on the oversized couch with Holly between them. Cameron was in a funk inspired first by the simulated, wood grain gun cabinet Earl and Myra gave them as their Christmas present. Out of politeness, Cameron had once commented on an identical cabinet in the Wentworth's living room. He had never owned a gun in his life, nor did he have a desire for one. But his mood was also inspired by the complete lack of physical contact that occurred as he and Susan sat on that couch—Susan actually jumped if even elbows brushed. Finally, the way he was increasingly treated like an infant—the slowed speech and exaggerated gestures—was grating. What was next? Diaper changes?.

Myra groused that Cameron and Susan spent too much on the leather-bound collection of Shakespeare's works that Cameron picked up on the *Sandstorm* book tour in England. Earl just shrugged. He wasn't much of a reader.

Throughout the afternoon, Holly napped; as did Earl, for which Cameron was grateful. Earl was not much for conversation and Cameron had never found a topic on which they agreed anyway.

With about three hours until Christmas dinner, Susan suggested a game of Scrabble. Earl wasn't overly enthusiastic, but Myra coaxed him. Cameron's eyes glowed. This was his game. He was a writer, after all, and a devout Scrabble player. He'd even placed third in a national tournament. This was going to be good.

The first few turns were predictable: Susan's words were good, but she was not a very aggressive player –she didn't maneuver to grab double and triple word scores or to grab a prime spot before another player did; she was more likely to just go wherever she happened to see a spot without using much strategy. Myra dithered over her letters, half the time not even realizing it was yet her turn. Earl grumbled, misspelled half his words, and delayed the game several times when he got up to get more beer.

Cameron's first few words—"aggregate," "zeppelin," and "quiche," gave him a very comfortable lead. He decided a bold move was in order to put this game away.

"Cameron, it's your turn," Susan said.

"What's the score?" Cameron asked.

"Um, Mom—95, Dad—87, I have 135, you have 197."

Cameron rubbed his chin. This would be easy. He shifted the position of the first two letters of the seven on his rack. Then he moved the letter on the left end to the right end and back again. The middle letter moved to the third position. He smiled. Yes, this was the word he wanted. He picked up his tiles and placed them horizontally on the board, playing off the "r" in Earl's word "bear," Cameron laid down the following:

"r-i-s-t-f-e-r-n"

"All seven letters used, that's a fifty point bonus," Cameron said, clearly proud of his brilliant play.

"What's that?" Myra asked.

"'Ristfern'?" Susan asked.

"Yeah, write it down," Cameron said, reaching for his replacement tiles.

"Honey, what does it mean?" Susan asked.

"What?" There was an edge to the word. Cameron hated being questioned about anything these days. Besides, it was disrupting the flow of the game.

"'Ristfern' isn't a word," Susan explained.

"Beer, anyone?" Earl said, heading for the kitchen.

"It is too," Cameron exclaimed, a bit louder than intended, but he owned it anyway. "Ristfern. You know...RISTFERN." Everyone knows in an argument it helps if you yell. This was the strategy Cameron went with.

"Honey, please, let's just-"

Cameron banged the table. The tiles jumped. So did Myra.

"Cameron!"

"Fuck this," Cameron muttered, pushing back from the table. He left the room.

"Well, I guess the game's over," Myra said.

Susan and Myra spent much of the rest of the afternoon in a battle of wills over the precise temperature at which to roast a duck. Cameron, who had fled to the train room—a room in the house filled with Lionel model railroad trains—emerged, somewhat relaxed, but dinner was a wordless affair. Myra and Susan made a good show of polite dinner conversation. Earl was content not to say anything.

When, mercifully, dinner was over, the last of the wine had been drunk (mostly by Cameron, but Earl was a close second), Earl and Myra called it a day and retired to the guest wing. Cameron was long gone, having bailed before desert. It was Susan's mother's strawberry-rhubarb pie anyway, so it was no great loss.

Cameron sat in his writing studio listening to an entire CD filled with nothing but versions of "Blue Christmas," sung by various artists. His favorites were the Elvis Presley and Porky Pig renditions. One afternoon he'd been working diligently on his fourth book, with the working title *Ambition*; next thing he knew, three hours later, he had in front of him a newly burned CD with fifteen renditions of "Blue Christmas" culled from his extensive holiday music collection. He had no memory of creating the disc. It was just there. For the next two weeks, he listened to it constantly. It was soothing.

Cameron still could not believe it. After all this time, all the hours together, the deep conversations, how could Susan still not get how he was the Scrabble master. How could she question him? More than that, how could she question his skill in a word game?

Track Seven came up, meaning Freddy Fender was just about to start having his blue Christmas when Susan came into the room. Cameron straightened in his chair and refocused on the monitor in front of him.

"Writing again?" Susan asked.

"Yeah. It's going great."

"The book?"

"Yes. I'm just finishing the courtroom scene. Finkler just broke down on the stand."

Susan looked over Cameron's shoulder. On the screen were snippets of dialogue between Finkler and the other characters in that courtroom. Most of the narrative at first looked pretty okay. A few lines down, however, interspersed with the sensible parts were odd bits. In one paragraph, there was nothing but "er" repeatedly without pause for six lines. In another section, were a series of variations on the name "Finkler"—"Thinkler," "Sinkler", "Finkelstein." "Finklerstein", etc.

The last paragraph on the screen read:

Finkler sat alone, pondering the fate he was destined to and for which only he was to blame. Fate was a concept with which he had long been obsessed. It haunted him; cursed him. Stinky Walters, his childhood friend, always told him, "Fate is what you make it." But Finkler didn't believe it. There were many things Finkler didn't believe. Stinky was one. Fate was another. Fate was a haunting, cursed thing. It haunted and cursed him. Stalked him. Followed him. Haunting. Cursing. Fate did that sort of thing. Fate. Bad fate. Rotten fate. Fate, fate, fate, fate, fate, fate, fate, fate, fate, fate, fate, fate, fate, fate, fate, fate, fate, fate.

Susan scrolled down further, skimming seven more pages on the negative properties of fate. Roughly two-hundred pages of the manuscript dealt with this issue. Another ninety covered the concept of existentialism; seventy-five pages on tapestries around the world; and a dozen pages on the Finkler character—his favorite foods, the word-for-word-recitation of his master's thesis (in medieval literature), and an annotated family tree going back fifteen generations. Number of pages devoted to furthering the plot of *Ambition*: two.

Susan knew this already. When Cameron had really started to lose it, about two months earlier, she had started monitoring his writing secretly. She had to. Whenever she asked him how it was going, he'd simply say, "Great. Finished another chapter." He'd be locked –literally, she'd tried the door— in his writing studio for ten, fifteen, sometimes eighteen hours at a stretch. Long periods of silence would be interrupted by great bursts of keyboard clickety-clickety. On the rare occasions when he went out and didn't lock the door behind him, she slipped into the writing studio and read through his various drafts. It took two weeks to get up the courage to do this the first time, but after she read stuff like the above—and some of what she read was even more manic—and because he rarely talked to her anymore, she needed some insight into what was going on in his head. Then when she found out, she wished she hadn't.

"Holly liked the play set," Susan said, attempting enthusiasm.

"Hmmm?" Cameron said, fingers racing across the keyboard.

"Her present. She liked her present."

"How do you spell 'miscellaneous'?" he asked.

Susan sighed. She did that a lot these days. Then she decided it was time. "I'm leaving," she said.

"No, it's okay," Cameron said. "I'll just use the spell check."

"No, Cameron, I said, I'm going. I mean I'm leaving you."

No response. Then across an echoing chasm, Cameron traveled the great distance back to the land of the rational. "What?"

"I can't do it anymore."

Cameron kept typing.

Susan turned Cameron's chair toward her and away from the computer screen.

"Do you hear me?" she asked.

"Maybe I'll just abbreviate it—m-i-s-c-period."

Susan knelt by the chair. "Please hear me. I can't do this anymore."

"I'm almost finished. Ten more chapters. Maybe fifteen. Twenty, tops."

"Cam, what's wrong with you? Why won't you see a doctor?"

"Why...?"

"Don't you see how strange you're acting?" Susan said. "You need help."

"No, I mean why are you leaving?" Cameron said, sensing something was amiss, but still not quite locked in.

"Because of this," Susan said, gesturing at the computer screen. "You sit in here all day and most of the night writing this shit. Then, when you do come out, you hardly say anything and when you do talk, it's nonsense. What *is* this anyway?"

Cameron looked at the screen. "Well...well. It's my book. You know that. You know how successful *Sandstorm* was. It's going to be hard to top."

"You've changed. Do you see that?"

"How?" he asked, sounding more curious, than anything else.

"Every day. Every day, I ask you to go to the doctor. You need to see someone about these weird mood swings, about how you ramble on and—honey, I'm sorry—you sound ridiculous, making no sense. I tell you this every day. And then, every day, you barely look at me and when you do, you yell like a crazy person."

Cameron's head snapped up. Then he opened his mouth. And immediately closed it again.

"Listen to me, you're obsessed with this thing," Susan said.

"It's a thriller. The plot has to be tightly woven..."

"Cameron!" Susan grabbed him by the arm. "It's nonsense! Look at it." She gestured frantically at the screen.

Cameron looked. It was his manuscript, page 741. Then he read. Finkler's saga burst off the page. It was obvious. "The trial of the century" was a phrase made for this book.

But then he read more closely, actually inching closer to the screen and squinting a little. The manuscript was a *little* long. He did include a lot of description and background. His own name appeared quite a few times. But still...

It was all wrong. He knew it. He felt it. But he couldn't control it. He came to this same realization daily and then he would climb back down into the abyss. Already he was tiring of this conversation.

"I've packed a few things—mine and Holly's—and we're leaving with my parents tonight," Susan said.

For no reason, an image of Earl trying to do the quarter-behind-your-ear trick with Holly and failing badly, dropping the quarter, flickered through Cameron's mind. Susan's words, however, barely registered. He turned back to the desk and picked up a sheaf of research papers.

"I give up." Susan said, throwing up her hands. She turned and left the room. Within the hour, Susan, Earl, Myra, and Holly were gone. Cameron never moved from his desk chair. He did, however, get three more chapters written.

He stopped eating or bathing, drank only coffee, and almost never slept. A week later, Dogwater took him to the emergency room nearly catatonic and he was admitted for psychiatric observation. Cameron's life, such as it was, both ended and started again that day.

Sitting there now, four years later, in his bean bag, Cameron remembered all this with the detachment of someone recalling a story he was told once about some guy he didn't know. It's hard to get worked up about the plight of a stranger.

Still, that's when Holly went away. That, he did feel personally.

Cameron's cell phone chimed. He lifted his head from the bean bag and pondered where it was. He struggled out of the bean bag and stalked around the room. His pulse elevated slightly like, well, like someone in anticipation of finding and answering a ringing phone. He found it and ended the chimes.

"Hello," he said evenly.

"Well, yes, hello, Cameron, how are you? It's Everett Franken."

"I'm not sure I should talk to you. You never call with good news." Cameron was only half kidding.

"Well, now, it might not be that bad."

"*Might* not?"

There was silence on the other end.

"Well, maybe it is."

"What?"

"Well, Mr. Bass has filed a motion with the court asking that all your visitation between now and our December 26 hearing be supervised."

"Why?"

"They say you're unstable, a danger to Holly's safety." He quickly added, "I've prepared a resistance and requested that it be set for hearing."

"So what do we do?" The voice was still steady, still slightly disconnected from all this.

"We go to court in three days. And we stay on our best behavior. You were a little short with Ms. Wentworth Jones at the courthouse before. That doesn't help your case."

Cameron ignored this bit. *Susan just brings out the best in me* he thought. "If I lose, then what?" he asked.

"Well it might be that the judge would let your visit go ahead, just appoint a third-party to supervise."

"So a social worker will follow Holly and me around like I'm some sort of pervert?"

"No, nothing like that," Everett assured. "More likely a trustworthy friend or family member. Maybe a pastor or something like that."

"Am I going to lose?"

"I don't know."

Mrs. Claus pensively watched all this in the magical North Pole way. The spell that allowed this was elaborate and tricky and it was amazing she'd gotten it to work at all. The silence that followed the end of the phone call was oppressive. She could almost hear the snowflakes hitting the ground outside the castle window. Cameron Jones was in a bad way. Officially, it was North Pole policy that once a child stopped believing in Santa for good (some of the newly non-believing were occasionally redeemed, but it didn't last forever) they were taken off the list for naughty/nice monitoring. I mean you can't watch everyone. Unofficially, though, Mrs. Claus still kept tabs on a few.

Inside Santa's castle, the situation wasn't much better. Santa stopped Christmas Eve preparations altogether. He just sat in the office going through the reject pile. The "rejects" were letters from kids who rejected the idea of Santa Claus so strongly, they actually wrote to him to let him know that they didn't believe in him. That was actually how Mrs. Claus came to be familiar with Cameron Jones. The United States Postal Service—sometimes intentionally, sometimes by magical holiday intervention—routed all the letters addressed to "Santa Claus, North Pole" and any other address kids put on the envelope through the Santa Claus, Indiana Post Office. All the letters from kids in the United States got to Santa through that office. One negative letter was overwhelming to Nicholas. Two were breeding grounds for despair.

Mrs. Claus turned from the window. It was cold in the castle. All the fireplaces were ablaze, the candles lit, but still there was a chill. The chill wasn't a temperature issue. The holiday warmth that for hundreds of years had resided within these walls was gone. Holiday music from around the world still flowed through the castle's sound system. Elves still bustled over the elegant wood floors moving from toy room to toy room making preparations for the holiday now three weeks away. In many respects, everything was much as it had been in years past for nearly a millennium. But, in the pause between chorus and refrain in the music, the heavy sighs of the great man could be felt, if not heard, throughout the castle.

Though the elves' holiday cheer was there, it was muted. For the first time ever, they actually whispered fears about the future of Christmas as it had been known all these centuries. Santa just didn't have it anymore.

Mrs. Claus walked from room to room in the grand castle. Ornate carvings surrounded sparse furniture—much of it built by Kris Kringle himself centuries earlier. The entire castle was a collection of now priceless antiques, had the Clauses or the elves cared about money, which they didn't.

Near the arboretum, Mrs. Claus came upon Chief-of-Staff Flifle, a first-rate elf with a death grip on his clipboard at all times.

"Flifle?" Mrs. Claus said, startling the enchanted little bureaucrat.

"Ma'am?" Flifle said with a jerk of his right hand, smearing a swath of ink from his fountain pen on his purple vest, but seeming not to notice.

"How are the Eve preparations coming?"

"Great," Flifle enthused.

"Are you lying?" The tone was playful, but not completely.

"Uh…" Flifle was unsure how to answer. He thought she was joking and didn't want to be accused—again—of being humorless. Still, he couldn't be sure.

"Never mind," Mrs. Claus said. "Tell me honestly." She took a deep breath. "Do you think Mr. Claus is all right?"

Flifle shrugged. "He's Santa." The elf was confused.

Mrs. Claus grinned and finally let her breath out. "Of course. Of course. Please go on about your business."

"Thank you, ma'am," Flifle said, brow still creased.

Mrs. Claus nodded and walked away quickly.

What was that all about? Flifle thought.

Maybe the pallor of the holiday this year was just inevitable, Mrs. Claus decided. Perhaps it was a cumulative effect of centuries of her husband evolving from an anonymous gift giver—a man who anonymously and with great humility brought food and shoes, and occasionally toys, to those most in need into what he was today; an icon who shared his goodwill toward men and women with all the world. He was far from anonymous.

Fame engendered love around the world, but also extreme isolation and loneliness. It wasn't like Kris Kringle could stroll through Central Park in New York, or sit in a sidewalk café in Paris, or any of countless other activities he once enjoyed. Even if he could, he certainly couldn't do so in, say, June or March or October. Father Christmas was only expected to be seen during the holiday season. If he showed his face other times, he would be besieged by children and adults alike who wanted to take advantage of the opportunity to make their Christmas requests earlier. Santa loved the people, but when you're known to millions, this can be exhausting.

What her husband needed, it seemed to Mrs. Claus, was some renewed inspiration. Reading the "fan mail" from the children wasn't doing it. Tinkering in the toy shop or grooming the reindeer wasn't helping either. Santa was far from finished filling his last stocking hung by the fire with care, but he was also very old and very tired. Surely, there must be something that could be done to recharge his yuletide spirit.

Moments later, like the glow from the Yule log, a tiny flicker of a plan sprang to life and began to grow...

# DECEMBER 4

Indiana, being a big, flat, rural state with lots of open fields, is no stranger to crop circles, UFOs, strange lights, and animal mutilations; all indicators of extraterrestrial activity. Coincidentally, Dogwater Hunt was also drawn here. There has been no verification whether these items are related or merely coincidental.

With the exception of the convenience/video store, the *Dark Matters* website was pretty much all Dogwater had going for him. Not that this bothered him. As he rationalized once: "Who needs women, money, or a productive future when you have a chance to take down shadow governments, expose fraud in corporate America, and finally prove that Teddy Roosevelt and Franklin Delano Roosevelt were in fact the same person?"

Dogwater was extremely open to a host of concepts, from the traditional conspiracy to the supernatural to the paranormal. Got ghosts in your breakfast nook? Dogwater would believe it. Did the devil decide to do a standup routine at your church picnic? Dog accepted that possibility. Is an alien parasite devouring Aunt Louise from within? Dogwater Hunt would be there with a video camera and an antacid. He didn't take much convincing to buy into any of them.

Despite all that Dogwater Hunt had seen, or read, or been told, or imagined in a probably illegal-substance-induced-haze, there was one oddity of human life which had not been adequately explained, even to Dogwater's extremely open mind: the purpose of fruitcake. What sinister other-worldly force came up with this?

At this moment, sitting in the kitchen, Dogwater was deep into his investigation of this phenomenon. It was a little frightening what he had to do to find the truth. Dogwater looked around and saw evidence of fruitcake spread abundantly around the room, along with vast quantities of fruit, sugar and flour.

It occurred to him that one purpose for fruitcake might be to allow bakers to get smashed in the service of Noel. Multiple empty rum, brandy, and sherry bottles littered the counter and floor of the spacious, modern gourmet kitchen. A fine layer of flour covered them and most everything else.

"Did Emeril wind down from a weekend bender in here?" Dogwater asked.

Roberta Evans, Dogwater's sister, turned from the stove, her face smeared with flower and currants. "Bite me," she said.

"Ho, ho, ho."

"As long as you're standing there, hand me the candied cherries."

"How do they 'candy' stuff?" Dogwater asked, passing over the fruit. He hesitated a moment before doing so, concerned he might be assisting in a crime against the people. Maybe he was opening a gateway to invasion by some sort of superior alien race along with, of course, the obligatory enslavement of the human population who would live out their remaining days on Earth in the service of fruit cocktail. He sighed over this fate, then handed over the fruit.

"I have no idea how they 'candy' stuff," Roberta said. "It's sometimes best not to ask so many questions."

"What are you doing?" Dogwater asked looking at the brown mash Roberta was fondling in the bowl in front of her.

"Making fruitcake."

"Yeah, but why?"

Roberta stared into the raisin-allspice-ginger mixture in the bowl, but did not answer. Why indeed?

Dogwater could not take his eyes off Roberta's hands working the fruitcake mixture. The most gruesome alien autopsy video he owned was nothing compared to this spectacle.

"Because it's a nice thing to do," Roberta finally answered. She shook the now empty brandy bottle to her left. "Is there any more brandy?"

"How do I know?"

"Look in the cabinet over the refrigerator," she said.

Dogwater shook his head and searched for the brandy. "How about scotch?" he asked, from atop a stepstool, digging through the cabinet.

From the kitchen doorway, Cameron said, "Stay away from my scotch."

"Whoops," Dogwater said, quickly climbing down.

"What have you done to my kitchen?" Cameron asked, looking around at the carnage.

"Surprise!" Roberta offered.

Cameron walked slowly around the room, taking in the disaster, the flour crunching under foot. Occasionally, he stepped on a currant, which was more of a *plllt* sound than a *crunnnnchhhh*.

"You know, you do have a kitchen of your own," Cameron said. "Remember the trailer?"

"Actually, we had to move," Dogwater said.

"Conspiracy-boy got us evicted," Roberta said.

"Why?" By now, Cameron knew better than to ask about such things, but when he was bored he sometimes did anyway.

"He howls," Roberta said while trying to coax some candied apricots out of a jar into the fruitcake mix.

"One time," Dogwater objected defensively.

"Every night for two weeks, Dog climbed up on the roof of the trailer and howled at the moon."

"I wasn't really howling," Dog objected again.

"So, what were you doing?" Cameron asked.

Dogwater sighed. His work was so important, so vital to the future of this planet, yet no one ever understood. He was sure this time would be no different.

"At certain latitudes on Earth at the right time of day, you can ..." he started to explain, then paused. Should he continue? What the hell. "You can communicate through a howling-type noise with particular species of aliens already present on Earth. That is, if you can hit the right pitch. The sound carries on the wind. This race of alien has an amazing sense of hearing."

A silent beat passed.

"And were you successful?" Cameron asked. He'd gone this far. May as well see it through.

Dogwater scowled. "No. Apparently, I didn't have the pitch quite right."

"We got the 'notice to vacate' the next day," Roberta said.

Cameron's blood chilled. "You weren't planning on staying here, were you?"

"No thank you, Mr. Scrooge. We've made other arrangements," Roberta said. "I'm staying with my friend Cassie and her whiny kids."

"And I'm staying in the *Dark Matters* van," Dogwater said.

"The what?" Cameron asked.

"The van I use to haul my equipment; computers, GPS, sonar, and a metal detector."

"What's the metal detector for?"

Dogwater shrugged. "When I'm bored I like to go down to the park and look for loose change."

Perhaps in a twinge of holiday conscience—from which not even Cameron Jones was immune—he considered extending an invitation to let Dogwater sleep on his couch. Then he thought better of it. It was likely he would end up there eventually anyway. By simple force of will he would gradually encroach upon Cameron's home (he already had the refrigerator and the TV) until the couch was his. Still, it was Christmas. So, Cameron said...

"So how's the fruitcake coming?"

Roberta started to explain the intricacies of mingling allspice and rum when Dogwater jumped up from the table, bumping it. A plastic colander of currants bounced and fell to the floor.

"Son of a bitch!" he shouted, presumably not about the currants.

Dogwater dug into a backpack parked on a straight-backed chair near the door to the living room. He pulled out a sheaf of papers and spread them out on the table. Each sheet was covered in dots labeled with names or numbers. Cameron recognized them as star charts like an astronomer might use.

"Milky Way, Sirius, Cassiopeia..." Dogwater muttered to himself and trailed off. He beat his fist on the map, causing the newly regrouped currants to bounce again. Roberta grimaced and moved them to the counter.

"What's up?" Cameron asked.

Dogwater's head snapped toward Cameron, mouth open as if he intended to launch into an explanation. Then his brow furrowed. Cameron was a skeptic and skeptics just don't get it. But then, he couldn't contain himself.

"The Santa Claus," Dogwater said excitedly.

"Uh, the Tim Allen Christmas movie?" Cameron asked, trying to understand.

"No, the Santa Claus E.T.," Dogwater said, as if that explained everything. "E.T. It means 'extra-terrestrial'."

"Yes, I know. Go on."

"'Santa Claus' is a code name—lunar astronauts used to use it all the time—to refer to aliens they sighted on their flights."

Surely by this point, Dogwater knew from experience, Roberta and Cameron would leave the room. Everyone else did. But they stayed and Dog went on.

"In 1927, Lars Heimdal, an astronomer in Greenland, proposed a theory that Earth is visited regularly every December by alien explorers."

He paused, but his audience didn't move, so he continued.

"He tracked the movement of the Christmas Star and coordinated that with global alien sightings. There was a strong correlation. And here's the thing; the frequency of sightings was increasing around the world, but mostly in December. And those sightings were always on the same path in the night sky. It was like a shooting star that repeated itself over and over following exactly the same path."

This was clearly impressive stuff to Dogwater, but Roberta and Cameron merely blinked back.

"He found," Dogwater said, "that the same flight path repeated itself year after year, always culminating on December twenty-four when thousands of people around the world all reported seeing the same thing at the same point in the sky right above the North Pole."

Now Cameron's brows furrowed. "Do you mean..."

Dogwater was shaking with excitement, face flushed. "Yes! Lars Heimdal was on track to prove the existence of Santa Claus—or at least an astronomical phenomenon that followed Santa's flight path." Dogwater shrugged. "But then he died."

"Santa!" Cameron said in mock horror. "I never knew he was sick."

Dogwater scowled and shook his head. "It's not just that. Every year, millions of people report seeing the sleigh flying over head. Hundreds, thousands maybe, report actually seeing the man himself—red suit, white beard, and all."

"Dog..." Cameron started.

"Sure, a lot of those witnesses are kids, but a lot of adults too. In 1938, the entire town of Wilshire, England—all forty-five of its citizens, young and old—reported seeing and talking to Santa on Christmas morning. They said he warned them that war was imminent.

"In 1951, Betty Lou Wainright of Sherman Oaks, California, said that Santa Claus awoke her on Christmas Eve and told her that her husband, an army sergeant in Korea, was okay.

"In 1971, Santa Claus was photographed leaving gifts in a pediatric ward of a small hospital in southern Russia."

"Photographed?" Cameron asked.

"Yeah. Unfortunately, the Soviet government buried the photo in its archives."

"Why would they do that? Seems to me Santa Claus is all about giving to everyone equally. Isn't that a communism thing?" Cameron asked.

"I don't know. I guess they saw Santa as a threat to their way of life. Give a child a toy truck and he might want another. Then he might want a real one. Then a bigger one. Then a house with a garage to store it in..."

Cameron shrugged. "I suppose..."

"Anyway," Dogwater said, "many individuals and agencies that advocate for full disclosure of alien and other conspiracies—*Dark Matters* included—have called for the release of that photo and other documents from many of the world's governments; with not much success, I might add. The list of encounters—some more credible than others, of course—spans, well, seventeen-hundred years. For as long as the 'myth' of Santa Claus has been around, people have reported this stuff. The government—all governments—know this. It's time someone brought this into the light."

"So there's a conspiracy to hide the existence of Santa Claus?" Cameron asked. "The most famous holiday icon of all time and nobody knows who he is?"

"I think there's a conspiracy to hide the existence of aliens that we call 'Santa Claus', yes. Maybe the man himself. NATO, the WTO, even organizations like Greenpeace, Salvation Army, and the Red Cross are in on it. As recently as six years ago, a summit of world leaders decided to suppress eighteen distinct satellite and reconnaissance photos of Santa's sleigh in flight and his village at the North Pole from public view."

"Why?" Cameron asked.

"Who knows?" Dogwater shrugged. "Maybe they're afraid of the world's people believing in a greater power than themselves."

"Okay," Cameron said noncommittally, by way of concluding this line of conversation. "Well, when is my kitchen going to be cleaned up?" Cameron asked.

"I've still got three more fruitcakes to make," Roberta said.

Cameron started to ask how that could possibly be true in a just and benevolent world, when Dogwater said, "Wait! You haven't heard the most amazing part yet."

"Is this where you reveal you're an elf?" Cameron asked.

"All the indicators point to this being the year that Kris Kringle finally reveals himself. And he'll do it right here." Dogwater could hardly contain himself; one leg bounced incessantly.

"Here? But I haven't had time to bake the cookies or buy the marshmallows for the hot chocolate," Cameron said.

"Not *here* here. His flight path this year, however, will take him right over the Midwest as the hour strikes midnight on Christmas Eve. With laser radar imaging, you can count the hairs on Santa's beard. A group of astronomy grad students is going to try and capture some photos. So am I."

"You've got radar equipment in the van?" Cameron asked.

Dogwater shifted uneasily. "Well, no. But I've got access to that stuff—never mind how—and I've got a telescope with a pretty good camera mounted on it so I'll be able to get something." He hesitated before saying the next part. "I've sort of got someone funding this."

"Who?" Cameron said, starting to get mildly interested.

All reticence was gone. "Bob Fencer—you know, the super-rich Silicon Valley computer guy. He's heavy into E.T.s and has got money coming out his ass."

Dogwater looked from Roberta to Cameron and back again, searching their faces for some sign of either complete scorn or, optimistically, a flicker of belief; these being the two responses with which he was most familiar.

Instead, he got blank stares. He must be on a roll.

"Those guys at NASA and the U.S. Air Force Space Command are sitting on a ton of awesome equipment for UFO hunting. And don't think they don't know it! Optical holographic filters, radar, infrared imaging, pole-mounted imaging, acoustic detection systems, airplane or helicopter radar detection, synthetic-aperture radar; ballistic missile early warning systems, for god's sake!" Dogwater finally paused to breathe. "Multi-spectral imaging, a ton of ground and space based imagery systems. All that shit's there and no one's coordinating it. This guy, Fencer, he's got it all."

"Suppose you do get a photo of St. Nick. Then what?" Roberta asked, finally weighing in.

Dogwater was stumped. What would he do? Money didn't interest him. Fame was deadly to a true conspiracy hunter. If you put yourself out there, you become a target. As a conspiracist, you're always on the edge—you need followers who believe in you, but not too many that you become famous; a threat to the forces in power.

"Well, I suppose I'll run a piece on *Dark Matters,* maybe put a piece in *UFO Hunter Magazine,*" Dog said nonchalantly. "Yeah, a big piece." He paused. Anything else? "Yeah, that's what I'll do. Make my findings known to the people. But not too well known." He looked around, nervously eying the rooster on one of Cameron's dish towels, not liking the look it was giving him. It could be wired.

"That's it?" Roberta asked.

"Yeah." Dogwater shrugged.

"No fame? No fortune?" Cameron asked. "Not even a guest shot on late night TV?"

Dogwater shrugged. "Who needs any of that? All I want is to conclusively prove that the governments of the world have been covering up the existence of 'Santa Claus' aliens. I will find them. They're mine. Hell, maybe I'll find Santa himself."

"But, Dog, why would Santa reveal himself to the world? It's not like he needs publicity," Cameron asked.

Dogwater responded with a shrug, "Maybe he needs a reminder that he's still alive."

Up at the North Pole, St. Nicholas sat straight up in bed, a thin sheen of sweat beading on the parts of him not covered in beard or flannel.

One downside of seeing everyone when they're sleeping and when they're awake, knowing when they've been bad and when they've been good, is that you're privy to an awful lot of disturbing stuff. Christmas magic did most of the work of compiling that naughty/nice list sort of like how your computer's virus checker completes its scans on its own, leaving you free to download your porn uninterrupted. But Santa, a magical being himself, could still sense moods; ebbs and flows of holiday spirit.

Along with knowing whether Johnny really deserves a pair of skates or whether Suzy should get that sled, Santa could tell when things were wrong in the world down below. Kris Kringle was not much for https and mp3 and urls and all of that, but Christmas magic was better than the best Internet server or a trusty old daily paper for knowing the mood of the world.

So, occasionally, Santa would wake with a jolt, or have to pause when working on the sleigh or whatever he was doing because of a knotting of his stomach. Waves of despair or naughtiness in the real world—like a war or violence—would do it. He also had that reaction whenever he personally was threatened. Sometimes the transition from childhood believer to adult nonbeliever was not just a smooth subconscious one. Sometimes it was chaotic and the youngster lashed out. Those who were sad and lost, especially during the holiday season, would take out their aggressions on him, curse him. And he could feel all of it.

And, once in a while, he got the sense that someone was not simply questioning him, but rather *looking* for him, seeking him out. That was something that wasn't supposed to happen. How many times around the world did mothers and daddies tell their children, "Santa can't come if you're still awake. You're not supposed to see him." But he was feeling it tonight. On top of a psychological complex that was either career insecurity or a midlife crisis, a stalker was not something he needed.

Kris Kringle shuffled out to the kitchen for a cup of cocoa to calm his nerves. He really was too old for all this. All he wanted to do was make the world's children happy, but now people were calling him a...a, what was it?...A space alien. He couldn't decide if that was worse than not believing in him at all.

"Ho, ho, me."

A doll?
No.
Tea set?
No.
A bottle of tequila and a box of smokes?
*Noooo.*

Another colored sticky note clung stubbornly to Cameron's middle finger before fluttering to the floor to join several of its friends, each one with the name of a possible Christmas present for a little girl scribbled on it and then scribbled out.

He had to come up with something good. No, something really good, to give Holly for Christmas. The kind of gift that says, "Hey, your pop may be a loon, but here's something electronic."

Do girls play video games?

DVD's? Kids were a little more sophisticated than in the days of 1960s and '70s Disney-fied cinematic innocence. So were movies for that matter. He had no idea what he would get that would be age-appropriate.

When Cameron was a kid, Christmas was a simple affair. Well, simple except for the excruciating torment of never knowing if or when St. Nick was going to cure the agonizing wait for Christmas morning. Right around Thanksgiving each year, he turned into a one-kid search-and-destroy team. No closet went un-rifled, no furniture un-moved, no doghouse un-ransacked in the search for some clue as to what he was getting for Christmas.

One year, it was a bicycle, which Cameron's mother—who always managed to be one step ahead of her son—hid at the neighbors'. Another year, it was one of those junior archaeologist kits. He spent weeks exhuming things like loose change, army men, and a dead goldfish from a shoebox full of dirt.

The year after that, he got a camera that was taken away from him within four days of going back to school at the end of the Christmas break after an incident involving the principal, the substitute teacher and a memorable field trip to the zoo. After "the emu affair," Mom hid the camera in her own underwear drawer. Experience had shown that Cameron had no problem with going into his sister's underwear drawer, and, on one occasion, putting several pairs of her panties on the family dog. However, there was no way that Cameron—even at the height of his package hunting zeal—would ever venture into Mom's underwear drawer.

But other than these glitches, Christmas—from a gift-getting perspective—was easy as a kid. You tell Santa what you want, go to bed as if you were a good boy, on Christmas Eve, and when you get up the next morning, there it is. Sometimes, the next morning came around 1 or 2 a.m. Sometimes, the opening of gifts came quietly in the night, even the day before (followed by meticulous re-wrapping, often accompanied by bribing your little brother to keep quiet), but still, the idea was the same. There was no shopping of your own, no bills or holiday traffic, no worrying, no fuss.

But now, he was the parent and kids were different. *Very* different. Ten-year-olds lined up to buy CDs or download singles from music groups with lyrics reflecting very adult themes the kids couldn't possibly know anything about; performers whose on and off stage antics would likely get them banned from half the world's countries.

Holly was only five and already she talked of low-ride jeans and tube tops. She wanted her ears *and* nose pierced.

"Don't little girls play with dolls anymore?" Cameron asked aloud. "Or play house? Or dress up?" They did, but the house was on Sleezy Street and the wardrobe was vintage white trash jamboree.

Just as stunning, it seemed to Cameron, were the parents who encouraged this sort of thing; baby beauty pageants, talents shows where nine-year-olds sing bump 'n' grind ditties. Cell phones in grade school. What was next, pagers for preschoolers?

Cameron sighed. "And they think I'm crazy."

"Maybe just a gift card," Cameron said, writing on the sticky pad at the same time. "I'll get one to the mall. Whatever the hell she does with it then is between her and her mother." He laughed a little. One benefit, if you could call it that, of being divorced and not having custody is that a lot of the really bad shit about parenting could be foisted off on the custodial parent.

He grimaced and crumpled the paper. "That stinks," he sighed, referring both to the gift and the foisting. He wanted all that parenting shit. He wasn't up to custody, but a little more real dad time would be perfect.

Cameron didn't know about Holly's present, but he was pretty sure that—if Santa was fair and just—extra bottles of lithium and wine would be under his own tree.

# DECEMBER 5

Ron's Discount Cow Emporium was one of the worst kept secrets in the greater Santa Claus, Indiana area. The most faithful regulars kept up the appearance of secrecy. Whenever they told anyone about the Emporium, they always prefaced the recommendation (it was never a criticism) with, "Now, not many people know about this, but…"

The Emporium was one of those places that found an orange/brown, imitation leather, faux wood grain look in the 1970s that worked for them and saw no reason to change with the times. No one went there for the décor anyway. They went for cow. You could get a twenty ounce sirloin for $7.99 ($8.99 with mushrooms). A one-pound burger set you back $3.99. Midwesterners know a good meat bargain when they see it.

It wasn't just cows that were nervous. Cameron actually favored the pork tenderloin special; a dinner-plate-sized loin served on a regular size bun with waffle cut fries. When the strawberry pie was fresh, this was a meal just about fit for a king—a pudgy king, but royalty nonetheless.

It occurred to Cameron as he sat enjoying his lunch that if he was in Manhattan now, he'd be lunching probably in some cramped, trendy, expensive place dining on goat cheese pizza or some other snobification of what had been great food before the self-proclaimed elite messed with it.

Cameron's agent Wendy actually encouraged a move back to New York in weekly phone calls and daily emails. She thought if Cameron got back to the heart of the publishing world, went to editors' parties, hung out with other writers instead of video-hawking, conspiracy theorists, it might help bring him in from literary exile and resurrect his career. He actually might finish *Betrayal*, several years late, but still done.

Wendy had a point, Cameron thought. But the celebrity lifestyle no longer appealed to him. He was well-known in Indiana, of course, but other than compliments on *Sandstorm*, *The Dead Man's New Hat*, or, less often, *Quality, Not Quantity*, they pretty much left him alone, respected his space. He liked that more than worrying which party he should go to so that he made the right public appearance or fostered the right business connection.

Besides, all he needed was to show up at Random House or Simon & Schuster and start seeing talking butterflies or something in front of the entire writing community.

"No, I think I'll stay right here," Cameron said to no one in particular.

"Great. That'll give us a chance to chat," the voice said.

Cameron glanced up from his garden-themed-word-find placemat. Ben Steene glided into the seat opposite him.

"How's the meatloaf?" he asked.

"What do you want, Steene?"

"Meatloaf," he said. "Maybe some mashed potatoes with those little bits of garlic in 'em. Yummy."

"Fine. I'm outta here," Cameron said and started to stand.

"What. We haven't even talked about dessert."

"I already had dessert."

"Okay, then we'll talk about Holly."

"See ya."

"The new book?"

"Steene..."

"How about that stink bomb, *Dead Man's Hat* movie?"

"Steene, I..." but the words caught mid-trip up the larynx. The water in Steene's glass appeared to spurt up, the droplets coalescing into eyes and a nose, the ice cubes forming a toothy grin; a lemon wedge became the wagging tongue of an insolent child.

Keenly aware that he was sweating and pretty sure his eyes were bulging, Cameron said slowly, "I'm, uh, not up to this today..."

"Oh, come on. You're a media pro."

"Steene. Please."

Steene crunched a breath mint thoughtfully. "Yeah, okay. Answering a lot of questions upsets the digestion, doesn't it?"

The water image sneered.

Cameron smiled weakly through the droplets. "Yeah. I guess. I'll call ya."°

Steene wrote his hotel room number on the back of his card and handed it to him. "Enjoy your lunch." He got up from the table and followed a good ol' boy out the door. Cameron's eyes never left the water glass.

Cameron, with all the discrete compulsiveness he could muster, flicked the smiling fountain away. The booth seemed to spin uncontrollably for a few seconds as he breathed deeply and centered himself. He felt a little better. Some of Dr. Whipple's little tricks worked pretty well.

Perry Como had just launched into "Rudolph the Red-Nosed Reindeer" on the restaurant music system and Cameron took his first bite of pie (peanut butter fudge—no strawberry today) when he was startled by a woman's voice over his left shoulder; jerking with already frayed nerves.

When Cameron turned, he saw a red-haired woman in her early twenties. He saw her very well, as she was leaning over the back of her booth and over Cameron's shoulder.

"Hey, you are Cameron Jones, aren't you?"

Cameron nodded with a mouthful of pie.

"Told you," the red-head said to her friend on the other side of her booth's table. Red pulled a hardcover copy of *The Dead Man's New Hat* out of a festively-colored paper bag on the seat next to her. His picture was featured prominently on the back cover, a point that didn't thrill him much, especially the time he had an hour-long conversation with that photo—and the photo did most of the talking. The day after that, the doctors had increased his dosage.

"Would you sign this?" Red asked, passing over the book and a ballpoint, pretty much precluding any resistance. "We just bought it for our brother Wade."

"Uh, sure," Cameron said, still a tad embarrassed at the fan stuff, even after all these years.

Cameron took the book; a thin smile cracked the corners of his mouth and pushed them up slightly. This one had one of his favorite character creations, Webster Stanhope. Webster was a hard-drinking, talking goldfish with a penchant for pornography. Cameron loved the little guy. He was one of those characters who leapt off the page and barked instructions to the author on how to write him. As Cameron started to scribble on the title page of the book, "Best Wishes. Happy holidays," (He was a little out of practice with the autograph thing), he could practically hear Webster barking, "She's a pretty one, laddie. She's yours. Make her squeal."

"That's so awesome. Thanks!" Red beamed as Cameron handed back the book, blinking from his mind a fleeting image of carrying out Webster's instructions.

Cameron was about to say, "No problem," and make with some holiday pleasantries when he heard Webster say, "Aye, laddie, you could do her real good."

"What?" Cameron said to himself.

"She wants you, man," Webster hissed.

Webster Stanhope was *talking to him*. The goldfish's voice was in his head, but also outside of him.

To Red and her sister, Cameron said abruptly, "Enjoy the book. Please excuse me."

Cameron threw down a couple bills on the table to cover the check and a generous tip and hastily exited the Emporium, leaving the two women bewildered.

"Never liked his stuff anyway," Red said. Her sister agreed.

Webster Stanhope chatted at Cameron all the way home. His voice came in quick bursts of high-pitched, pornographic one-liners punctuated by long periods of silence.

Cameron tried not to respond. When he did, Webster would just shoot back with, "Oh, blow me."

Cameron marched inside his home, locked and bolted the front door, set the burglar alarm, and closed the blinds. He did not turn on any lights, but walked straight to the second floor studio, locking behind him any door or window that would lock and closing every blind.

Clearly the pills weren't working. This seclusion was the only way to keep the voices out. They, apparently, feared the dark more than he feared them. He sat in the middle of the floor, rocking slowly

This could not be happening. No way. Not now.

Mallard Mall was like any mall in Anytown, USA. Santa selected it more or less at random. It had two floors with a food court, a chocolate store, two book stores, three big name department stores for anchors, four shoe

stores, two men's clothing stores, a computer game store, a video store, two music stores, and a ton of women's clothing stores, as well as a novelty gift shop discordantly mingling risqué adult gifts with fun innocuous ones for the whole family.

Mallard Mall also had, as its marquee' proclaimed proudly, the only truly interactive Kris Kringle in the tri-county area. Their jolly old elf didn't just sit on a throne before the mass of good children making wishes and bad children making pleas for leniency. Instead, their Father Christmas wandered the mall; actually went to the children asking them what they wanted for Christmas, instead of making them wait in line to tell him. For neo-traditionalists who still wanted to sit on the old guy's lap during designated "Santa hours," the elves handed out pagers, like you get when you have to wait for a table in a crowded restaurant, and would beep the parents when it was Billy or Becky's turn on the lap.

You could also still get the obligatory photo with Santa for ten bucks. The photos were taken by an elf who followed Santa around with a digital camera.

Santa was aghast at this mall's Santa. The suit and beard were fine. This one wore spectacles when in reality Santa only wore glasses for reading, but that was okay. But this mall Santa didn't have the walk, the attitude. He looked bored. Christmas was many things, but it was never boring.

But he would save the dressing down for another time. St. Nicholas's plan here was to mingle with the children and parents incognito and take sort of a straw poll on his popularity; if a majority of the respondents believed in Santa, then Santa must exist, or so the thinking went. For his disguise, he chose a Yankees ball cap worn backwards, baggy jeans—difficult to pull off on a large frame like his—a long, gray pony tail and an earring. This last took some convincing by Mrs. Claus, but once committed, Santa wanted to go full out: eye patch and wooden leg to boot. It took a while for Mrs. Claus to explain the earring wasn't a pirate thing.

The last "mall" Santa had been in was a village marketplace literally hundreds of years earlier. That marketplace had many things for sale, none of which were lingerie or free body piercings with the purchase of jewelry.

When the young women standing by a display of vibrating recliners came up to Santa and said, "You look like you could use something massaged," Santa was about ready to call the reindeer and pack it in.

But as he so often told his long-time head-elf Teelor, "If you can eat a million or so cookies in one night without getting a single cavity, you can do anything."

Santa stood halfway over the threshold into "Barry's Bun Hut" and surveyed the scene. The mall was busy; not surprising being a Saturday just a few weeks before Christmas. It occurred to him that he really didn't know what to do now.

He rummaged in his pocket, feeling around for his wireless North Pole connection; a cell phone of sorts for reaching the elves and, of course, Mrs. Claus. He pressed the "activate" button and waited for someone to pick up.

"Merry Christmas! Feliz Navidad! Froehliche Weinachten!" and comparable salutations in every other language on Earth beamed from the wireless at a rate of speed only Santa could keep up with. The sound went directly into Santa's ears and was not broadcast to the public, courtesy of Christmas magic. "How may I direct your call?"

"Sylvinia," Santa chuckled. "How are you, my dear girl?"

"Santa!" Sylvinia squealed, as if anyone else would be calling. Everyone knows the Easter Bunny only sends egg-grams, the Tooth Fairy was addicted to email (especially those annoying chain letters), and Cupid, well, Cupid wasn't speaking to St. Nick these days. He knows what he did.

"Would you get Mrs. Claus for me?" Santa said.

"One moment please."

Santa hummed a holiday tune from the ancient world while he waited. Within seconds, his blushing bride was on the phone. Well, after fifteen-hundred years, it was more of a rosy-cheeked glow than a blush.

"Hello, dearest." Mrs. Claus's voice floated with a magical twinkle through the wireless.

"Ho, ho, ho," Santa said, in a softer tone than he used for his public performances.

"How's it going with the real-worlders?" Mrs. Claus asked.

Santa frowned. "Am I doing the right thing?"

Mrs. Claus knew that tone. "What's wrong?"

"Well, I'm...I'm afraid. It's one thing to think no one believes in you, but what if they say so to my face?"

"Who's going to dis Santa?"

"'Dis'?" Santa chuckled.

"I've been studying real-worlder lingo. That's right isn't it?" Mrs. Claus enjoyed dabbling in linguistics. She was the first and so far only person ever to write an entire elf dictionary. "I think it means 'criticize' or 'make fun of'."

"I see," Santa said. "What other words have you picked up?"

"I'm still working on 'jeepers', 'yo', and be-atch."

"I'm pretty sure that last one is a direct line to coal in your stocking," Santa said in the tone he reserved for naughty boys and girls.

"You might be right."

"Have you looked at 'fashizzel'?"

"No, not yet. How do you spell it?"

"I don't know," Santa said.

There was a long pause in which no one said anything.

"Nicholas?"

"Yes, dearest."

"You're stalling."

"You know, the elves were getting a little behind on the doll production. I'm not sure they're going to make the Christmas quota. Maybe I should head back…"

"*Nicholas…*"

"I know dearest. I know. I'm saying goodbye now."

"Good boy," Mrs. Claus praised. "North Pole signing off."

With a slight hiss, the connection was terminated.

Santa Claus was alone. He looked around. The first store he laid eyes on was "Linda's Lingerie." Santa decided, prudently, perhaps that was not best store to go into to. His naughty/nice meter might explode.

Across the walkway, past the "Pretzel Fiesta" and a stand that sold sunglasses, a group of three girls and a boy stood outside a video store. The boy, who had a ring in his ear dragging his lobe to his knees and a stud in his lip was balancing on a skateboard as if it were a surfboard, much to the amusement of the girls. None in the group could have been more than twelve or thirteen. One of the girls had a ring in her eyebrow that looked exceedingly painful; the other was wearing a shirt much too light for a day like today, and much too revealing for any day.

This was not Santa's strongest demographic, but if they believed in him—or if he could win them over—well, that would… rock (another colloquialism courtesy of Mrs. Claus).

Santa took off his hat, finger-groomed his thick white hair and put the hat back on. Then checked to make sure his trademark Santa beard was smooth. His round little belly shook, but he wasn't laughing and it wasn't at all like a bowlful of jelly. It was more like a large hibernating mammal tossing and turning from a nightmare. Here goes.

Santa's first step across the mezzanine echoed, ominously. He strode as much as a large, fat man can. He hoped he looked both confident and steeped in the yuletide spirit.

"Ho, HO, ho," he muttered to himself. "Ho, ho, HO," he tried again. "HO, ho, ho,"

Well, maybe it would come to him in the moment.

Santa watched the crowd. The real-worlders were so different from the elves. Taller, certainly, and more conservatively dressed. But they were also less, well, *merry*. They plodded along, stern looks contrasting with the brightly wrapped packages many of them carried. Very few met smile after smile, there was nary a "Merry Christmas" to be heard.

As Santa turned to get the view in the other direction, he collided with the mall Santa—this establishment's Rent-a-Claus. "Ho-ho-ho to you, sir," Santa said.

The mall Santa, beard slightly off-kilter and polo shirt peaking out from under the imitation Santa-type jacket, looked the real Santa up and down, sniffed, and grunted, "Yeah, sure." He turned without further word and stomped off, hopefully not, Santa thought, to spread his brand of holiday joy to children. If so, there would be plenty of crying babies in the food court today.

Santa shuddered at the dishonor of the uniform perpetrated by that particular Rent-a-Claus and refocused on his task, shoring up his base of support: the children—specifically the "tweens," the ones who were too old to be unquestioning believers, but young enough that they could maybe be brought back from jaded disbelief.

He considered his opening. "Hey, kids, full of the joyous spirit of Christmas?" No, too "square." "Yo, homies (courtesy of Mrs. Claus) you down with Noel?" Maybe. "Peace on Earth, Dawg." Hmmm.

Santa was passing the Pretzel Fiesta now. No turning back. The boy had stopped his skateboard tricks and was now trying to balance an empty plastic cola bottle on an index finger. The girls were not as impressed with this.

Dispensing with the ho-ho-ho's altogether, Santa said, "Hey, children."

Most of the group barely glanced at him. "Perhaps they don't know I was talking to them," Santa thought optimistically. This was hard. He was used to a HUGE reaction when he talked to children. Of course, that was usually four-year-olds.

"That's a nice skateboard," Santa said. He didn't recognize it. Apparently, it wasn't one of his gifts.

"Thanks, man," the boy said. With a wink to the girls, he added, "You wanna try it?" He rolled the skateboard a little ways toward Santa.

Santa looked at the boy, The name, Randy, and age, twelve, came to him in moments, followed by his naughty/nice rap sheet. He was clean, more or less, except for a playing with matches incident at age eight (no damage) and talking back to the teacher at age eleven when he was running in the hall. He had been offered methamphetamine a couple times, but had refused. Piercings were distasteful to Nicholas, but Mrs. Claus had convinced him not to make that a "naughty" criterion.

"No, thank you," Santa said.

The girls laughed. One of them, a petite blonde (Brittany, age 12) said to another (Sophie, age eleven), "He looks like Santa." Sophie laughed, cupping a hand to her face, slightly embarrassed.

Santa's twinkling eyes turned to the girls. "Do you believe in Santa Claus?"

Brittany's was a pretty clean naughty/nice slate. She sang in the church choir, did well in school and was kind to seniors. She even volunteered at the Humane Society to walk the dogs and play with the kittens. She did get a bit of an attitude when her mom made her play with her little brother, but Santa could overlook that in light of everything else.

Sophie was bit more of a naughty/nice risk. She quarreled with her father a lot. She had tried alcohol at least twice. She was, however, very protective of her little sister in a wheelchair, protecting her from bullies who teased her in school, even if that meant fighting with other children. Santa didn't approve of violence, of course, but he appreciated Sophie's devotion to her sister.

The girls laughed again; the uneasy sort of laugh kids emit when an adult says something that kids are sure is supposed to be funny, but to them just sounds dorky.

"Have you told Santa what you want for Christmas?" he ventured.

"I dunno," Brittany ventured.

"Maybe a boyfriend," Sophie said.

Brittany giggled again.

"That fat old man hasn't ever done anything for me," the third girl said.

Elizabeth was twelve-years-old. With long, dark hair, faded jeans and oversized flannel shirt, her look was hard, but the appearance radiated bitterness rather than a tomboy quality. When she was four, she asked Santa Claus for a dollhouse. She got a gorgeous, hand-carved, three-story house courtesy of a team of seven elves. She played all Christmas day. The next day, her mother died in a car wreck. Six months later, her estranged father burned her family house down, along with her calico cat and the dollhouse.

Every year after, Santa made extra sure to bring Elizabeth something, though she never asked for anything. In fact, she routinely and vigorously trashed the idea of Christmas cheer and gifts. Since he didn't know what toys she wanted, Santa brought other things.

One year, Santa arranged for her stepfather to find an expensive lost watch (made by elves) so he could turn it in for a large reward that he used to buy food for a nice Christmas dinner for Elizabeth and himself. She refused to eat.

Another year, on Christmas Morning after his Eve run, he made a special trip back by Elizabeth's house. He often did this with especially tough cases. A young stray cat, almost a kitten, was shivering in the bushes near her house. Santa had an inspiration.

In a stark violation of Kringle protocol, he exited the sleigh in daylight on Christmas morning (it was barely dawn), scooped up the kitten—which, it seemed to St. Nick, mewed gratefully and burrowed into Santa's fuzzy coat—and went to the window sill of little Elizabeth's window. This was no small task. The snow was heavy that year in that part of the world and Santa, though a magical creature, struggled to move his bulk through the drifts. He rapped gently on the window, set the kitten on the sill and got out of sight.

Elizabeth stirred in the early morning light and spied the kitten on the sill. She sat up in bed, looked at the kitten and tossed her pillow at the window. The kitten bolted and Santa took her home to the North Pole (It's named "Cookie" and has been a great pet). Santa felt defeated.

Santa knew that Elizabeth talked to him every Christmas. She didn't write a letter, or sit on a mall Santa's lap, but he knew. She never came out and asked for anything, but she started to many times. Santa had a suspicion that he knew what she wanted.

A minute passed. Then another. Things were getting awkward. The kids were hoping the weird old man would go away, but Santa was just warming up. He decided to go for a little levity.

"Have you been good little boys and girls?" he said, grinning in a jolly manner. "Better not shout, better not cry. You don't want to get any coal in your stockings."

The kids emitted the nervous laughter again and exchanged looks. Santa also noticed out of the corner of his twinkling eye, that some of the adults around were starting to take an interest in him as well. This was not going well.

"Well," he said, deciding to bail, "I won't take up any more of your time. Merry Christmas."

Randy was engrossed in playing with a wheel on his skateboard. Sophie and Brittany muttered a "Merry Christmas" and quickly turned away. Elizabeth just glared.

As Santa passed by Elizabeth, he whispered under his breath, "Your mother loves you and is very proud."

Elizabeth's eyes darted. Rage faded into mere suspicion, which, in turn, faded into something like, but not quite reaching, gratefulness. A tiny, *really* tiny smile evolved from the eternal smirk on Elizabeth's face and became extinct just as quickly. Santa winked, said nothing more, and kept walking.

Santa had no personal knowledge of what went on the afterlife. That was outside his magical realm. He did, however, have well placed connections. Of course, now he owed someone a really big candy cane.

As he walked, his inner holiday glow became an outer one. Granted, he hadn't necessarily won them over, but at least no one said they didn't believe in him. Well, not exactly. His cheeks had never been rosier; his eyes never more twinkly. Finally, he could contain himself no longer.

Santa stopped, looked around, and bellowed, "A Merry Christmas to all and to all a good night!"

Randy flipped a bird that was definitely not a partridge.

Holiday shoppers were stunned. Santa was undaunted, however. He stuck out his hand to a middle-aged man and then a thirty-something woman, hoping they would shake it in season's greetings. They just averted their eyes and hastened away.

For a man of his...presence, Kris Kringle moved quite lightly on his feet; more so now that he'd brought the encounter with the teens in for a successful landing, even if the engines were smoking a little. He was so happy that when he spied a little boy of three or four standing with his mommy at a pizza-by-the-slice place, he bounded over to him, ruffled the boy's blonde hair, and boomed, very Santa-like, "HO, HO, HO!"

The little boy shrieked and clung to his mother's leg.

Mom, to her credit, tried to apologize, clearly recognizing that Crazy-Santa-Claus-Man meant no harm, even if little Wembley (yes, Wembley) didn't grasp that. This, of course, played out in the middle of the food court which has the highest ratio of children to square foot of mall space in the mall. As Santa slunk away (as much as a six-foot tall man of three-hundred-fifty pounds can slink anywhere), children throughout the mall clung to their parents and siblings. Several cried, but most just stared with eyes wide and mouths open.

A mall security guard came up to St. Nicholas and said, "Sir, perhaps you should leave."

"But I only wanted..." Santa began to protest.

"Sir, please," the security guard said in a polite, but firm, manner.

"Yes, of course," Santa sighed. "Merry Christmas."

"Sure," the guard said, pushing open the glass door that lead outside.

Well, there's always next year.

The Icelandic script of Lars Heimdal's journal was pushing Dogwater Hunt deeper and deeper into a funk. It wasn't the words—even though they veered alarmingly from Icelandic to English and back again—nor was it the shaky hand that the old man wrote in towards his last days.

The problem was the content. It made no sense. On one page, Heimdal described the patterns of the galaxies throughout the year in the northern sky. On another, he described vividly the various descriptions of Santa's sleighs recounted by the citizens of his small village. Some were positive it was a two-seater; others said only one. There was also disagreement over whether the sleigh had runners or simply hovered. All agreed, however, there were eight reindeer. No Rudolph.

On the next page, Heimdal laid out poetry—and not good poetry, either—about aliens that look like Santa Claus, including the following:

Up in sky, destiny awaits

I search for signs; my need is great.

St. Nicholas, are you there?

And, if so, why do you fear

Revealing yourself to me?

Is it because you have two tummies?

Dogwater laid his head on the table. Well, there was always next year.

# DECEMBER 6

Cameron's psychiatrist, Dr. Marjorie Whipple, hates to ski, but loves sitting in cafes enjoying the Alps. Every year, she and her Swiss-born husband, Jean-Pierre, spend a month in Switzerland over the Christmas holidays. A large share of the New York area that was under her psychiatric care was left to its own devices for that month, which explains an awful lot.

Cameron forgot this until about eight o'clock Saturday night after spending the entire day trying to convince Dr. Whipple's answering service that he MUST talk to her immediately. In their last therapy session, Dr. Whipple had specifically said that she would be out of the country. Actually, they spent twenty-five minutes of the fifty minute hour discussing dining options in Switzerland and how they compared to western Europe in general. To her credit, Cameron thought, in the therapy sessions, Dr. Whipple usually let him talk about anything he wanted. To his own credit, Cameron worked hard to talk about anything but himself. He *hated* these sessions.

But he needed them too; especially now after his little exchange with Webster Stanhope. He spent Friday night and all of Saturday locked in his study with the lights off, venturing out only to pee. He subsisted on a box of chocolates Wendy, his agent, had sent him as an early Christmas present. He neither shaved nor bathed and this Sunday morning, he hadn't done the crossword puzzle in his newspaper. He *always* did the crossword even before reading the paper (which he read meticulously from front page to singles ads on the back) In fact, he hadn't even picked up the paper and it was now noon. This was very serious.

Cameron considered calling Whipple's designated on-call fill-in, but he had talked to the guy before and he was a schmuck. He always wanted to talk about Cameron's *feelings* and his *childhood* and all that touchy-feely crap. Whipple did some of that, but she wasn't shoving the tissue in his face and telling him to cry like the on-call guy did. She'd just write a prescription.

He had to keep control, especially now that that reporter Ben Steene was dogging him. He could not get lost in the fog again. This time, more than just a mediocre book was at risk. He had to be able to convince a judge—if not Susan herself—that he was a fit parent. More than that, he had to convince his daughter Holly that he wasn't a freak.

This was no small task. Ever since the hellish visit a year previous, all subsequent visits—the ones that actually occurred—were at best icy and more accurately described as something like the first time Kennedy and Khrushchev sat down to chat, right down to Holly banging a shoe—a flip-flop, but still—on the table.

For example, on a visit in October close to Halloween, Cameron arranged to take Holly to a friend's masquerade party with the friend's kids, and a bunch of other kids belonging to still other friends. This activity served two very good purposes: (1) it would be a memorable, fun time for a young child; (2) it would minimize the one-on-one time Holly and Cameron would have, thereby decreasing the opportunities for Cameron to psychologically scar the child with one of his flip-outs.

Gretchen Morley, Susan's elderly neighbor, delivered Holly to Cameron's house that night since Susan was at a job interview and therefore unavailable. It was the interview for the job overseas that was now threatening to undo the final remnants of the family stability Cameron had.

"Hello, Mrs. Morley," Cameron said when he opened the door on the tall, wiry, white-haired woman with the granny glasses that she managed to give a youthful air, despite clearly being an actual granny.

"Hello, dear," Mrs. Morley said, handing Cameron a plate of chocolate-frosted rice crispy bars. There was always an internal struggle in Cameron's mind; hope that Susan herself would deliver Holly and he could see her, or hope for Mrs. Morley to deliver Holly and bring a plate of baked goods. Okay, it wasn't really much of a struggle.

"How is the book coming?" Mrs. Morley asked. Mrs. Morley was Cameron's biggest fan in Santa Claus, Indiana—near as he could tell—because she had strong-armed her book club into reading *Quality, Not Quantity*, *Sandstorm*, and *The Deadman's New Hat*. They even sprang for the hardcovers instead of waiting for the paperbacks.

"Good, good. Just a writing machine," Cameron said mechanically. It was his standard answer. Not a particularly good one, but if he was clever enough to come up with snappy rejoinders, he wouldn't be having so much book trouble.

Cameron could not see Holly. He tried to look around the tall, thin woman, but still no daughter. Cameron was alarmed, but composed, "Hey, uh, where's..."

Then, he saw her, inspecting a wooden crate with a kitten painted on the side of it that Dogwater had left on the porch. He used it for some of his alien-seeking equipment.

"Hi, Holly," Cameron said in what he hoped was a confident Dad voice.

Holly ignored him, tracing the outlines of the painted feline's whiskers with her fingers.

"Holly, come over here and show your daddy your new costume," Mrs. Morley said.

Holly, grudgingly, abandoned the artwork and hopped over to the front door. She stopped hopping when she saw her dad.

"Hey, sweetie," Cameron said. "That's a great costume."

It was, in truth, a pretty good costume. She had the brightly-colored, polka dot jumper, the floppy (if kid-sized) clown shoes, the neon wig, and that ruffley collar thing clowns wear around their necks. She did not, however, have any clown makeup, a point she felt, in typically five-year-old fashion, needed to be explained very deliberately and dramatically.

"I don't have any makeup," she said after Cameron had ushered her and Mrs. Morley into the entryway.

"I see that," Cameron said. He couldn't tell from her tone if she meant this as observation, objection, or apology. He chose, then, not to pass judgment on whether this was a good thing.

"If I had makeup, I'd look different," Holly said, studying the weave in the drapes on the window nearest the door.

"You'd look like a pretty clown," Mrs. Morley offered.

"But then I wouldn't be Holly anymore," Holly said, stretching out her name with several extra syllables. "I'd be someone else like Dad-" She stopped herself and shot a horrified look at her father.

Cameron forced a grin. What could he say to that? The kid had a point. For a while there, he had not really been himself.

"Well, she insisted on putting on her costume at nine o'clock this morning and has worn it all day," Mrs. Morley said, heading off an awkward moment before it became really awkward.

Holly hopped across the foyer and admired the scarecrow Cameron had placed there earlier in the day. Holiday decoration wasn't something he normally preoccupied himself with, but this was part of his "I really am a Dad. Really." campaign.

"Well, I should get out of your way. I'm sure you have a lot of fun things planned," Mrs. Morley said by way of exit.

"Oh, okay," Cameron said, not entirely sure that it was okay.

"Goodbye, dear," Mrs. Morley said, kneeling down to Holly with surprisingly little difficulty for a woman as seasoned as she.

"Bye," Holly said in that way kids have that sounds wistful and nonplussed at the same time, and hugged the woman.

"Have fun," she said to Cameron with a look he couldn't quite interpret before striding out the door with a young woman's confidence of foot.

And then they were alone.

Holly moved on –hop, hop, hop—to the basket of candy on the credenza. She poked at a mini candy bar and looked a silent request at her father.

"Sure, but just one. We've got a big party to go to."

The hotdog, milk, and carrot dinner (an odd combination, but the kid loved carrots) went quite well, actually. Cameron did an admirable job of asking the right open-ended questions about school, Holly's pets, and the finer points of finger-painting, a cherished activity for Holly. Holly was a talker when she got revved up.

Cameron did not ask about Susan. Cameron never spoke disparagingly about his ex-wife, but on these visits, he felt no compulsion to ask about her either. If Holly offered some bit of kid-gossip about home, he acknowledged it, but quickly moved on.

The ride to his friend's party went equally well. Holly dozed most of the twenty-five minute drive to Monty Winters' house. Even opening a car door was like a sleeping pill to Cameron's daughter.

Monty had a huge, old farmhouse outside of Santa Claus. He didn't farm himself—he was a website developer—but paid some guys to work the land for him.

When Cameron parked in the gravel drive, Monty's wife Sally bounded out the front door and down the porch, skipping at least two of the three steps. A polite buss on Cameron's cheek gave way to scooping the now waking child from the car. Holly was very popular in the Winters household. As much as Monty liked the child too, his wife's enthusiasm made him a little nervous that she may get it in her head to have another. The Winters had five children and Monty loved every one; but enough is enough.

Monty met Cameron at the door. Sally and the now fully awake and very curious child were already inside. Monty held in the right hand an open bottle of his own homemade micro-brew and with the left hand offered an unopened bottle of the same to Cameron. Cameron drank little because of concerns about messing with his medication, but it was hard to resist Monty's concoctions. In addition to website design, Monty was a well-known local brewer who supplied some very odd labels to local bars and restaurants. Beers with names like "Dirty Attic" and "Swamp Thing" were among the most popular.

"Hey, buddy," Monty said, shaking Cameron's free hand.

"Hello..." Cameron said, more than a little distracted by Monty's costume. Fat, balding men should not—under any circumstances, except maybe duress at gunpoint and then only if no else was around—wear tights.

"Nice costume," Cameron said. "What are you? Robin Hood after Little John dumps him and he binges on Little Debbies?"

"No," Monty said, a slight pout creeping through. "Sally wouldn't let me have a bow and arrow, even if the tips were rubber. I'm a non-specific figure from medieval times."

"Gotcha," Cameron said.

"How about you?" Monty asked, taking in Cameron's blue, denim shirt, khakis and officially-licensed professional ball team cap. "What are you supposed to be? Suburban, white guy?"

"Funny," Cameron said. "I opted to forego the costume this year. People with a history of hallucination should not intentionally pretend to be someone else. It just seems to cheapen the whole delusion experience." Monty knew something of Cameron's checkered psychological past, but Cameron opted not to mention the incident with Webster Stanhope at Ron's Discount Cow Emporium. With the visitation court case going on, it might not be prudent.

In truth, on his last trip to New York to see his agent Wendy, he had purchased a very cool Zorro costume for this occasion and had tried it on earlier in the day. He could not bring himself to wear it for the party though, because when he looked at himself in the mirror—saw the disguised man in the mask staring at him—the old shadows of paranoia and fear crept up. He had long since lost sight of whoever he had been once. He wore a mask all the time. Why reinforce that with a store-bought one?

He did, however, have the mask in his pocket. He didn't know why he'd done that, but that small act of defiance—bringing this "other person" with him voluntarily—made him feel more in control of the demons within.

The Winters' farmhouse boasted, among other quaint, country accoutrements farmhouses are prized for, a huge, walk-in attic. The writer-ly side of Cameron drooled every time he saw it. It would be a perfect writing studio. Monty Winters was not a writer, but he did use the attic for something just as important; he kept his pool table there.

This evening, the pool table was covered with an appropriate black and orange table cloth festooned with ghosts and black cats who were more comical than scary. On the table was a banquet of kid favorites: pizza, soda pop, popcorn balls, cupcakes, and even a few carrots, celery and broccoli (these last did not seem to be big sellers, but there were a few takers).

The party was intensively pre-school. An entire roomful of children wearing licensed-character costumes and hopped up on soda and caramel apples listened to "Monster Mash" roughly eight-hundred times. The center of the room was dominated by a throng of perhaps a dozen kids in costumes displaying various levels of intricacy; from store-bought to half-assed, thrown together to obsessively-constructed. Even though it was not a large crowd, it had the kinetic vibe of an impressive mob.

On one side of the room, a few kids were feverishly playing some sort of skateboarding video game. Others were playing a video game where you copy dance moves on the television. In the middle of the room, a few other kids were playing some sort of game that Cameron couldn't quite figure out. It seemed to be a cross between "Twister" and "Tic-Tac Toe." Around the edges of the room, little groups of parents huddled with slices of pizza, plastic cups of pop or, occasionally, beer. None of the parents, except for Monty and Sally Winters, was in costume.

Holly wasted no time joining the action. She was not into videogames, but was very much into anything that involved—or at least allowed for—hopping. This game going on in the center of the room, whatever it was, seemed to do just that. She quickly joined in. Although the kids in the group, except for the Winters' own children, didn't know her, they quickly took her into the fold in a way older kids never would.

Watching Holly laugh and play like this had a two-fold effect on Cameron. It warmed his daddy-heart to see his little girl enjoying herself. It also wrenched his daddy-heart to think that for so long he had been virtually oblivious to the existence of this beautiful child; oblivious really to anything of value, to anything that wasn't his own compulsions or delusions.

A little boy with Dracula teeth (the classics are still the best) bounded over to Holly as she waited her turn in the game. Cameron noted here that while he still had no idea what the game even was, Holly had already evidently mastered the rules. She may turn out to be nuts like her old man, but Holly Jones was still a smart one—and a fierce competitor.

With some oral difficulty owing to the plastic teeth, Dracula-boy said, "What are you s'posed to be?"

"I'm a clown," Holly said with an impressive amount of dignity.

"No, you're not," Dracula-boy countered, losing his plastic teeth, but swiping them back in with a practiced move of his right hand.

"Yes, I am," Holly said, mostly focused on the game.

"You don't have any makeup," the boy argued.

"So?"

"You gotta have a big red nose at least," the boy said.

"Why?" Holly asked, truly sounding as if she wanted to know.

Dracula-boy was stumped for a response, and instead settled for making guttural growling noises, apparently confusing Dracula with the Wolfman, but enjoying it nonetheless.

Holly looked the boy up and down. "And what are you?"

"Dracula," Dracula-boy said with all the theatricality of a seven-year-old.

"You don't have any bat wings," Holly sneered, and turned her full attention back to the game as it was now her turn to toss the little beanbag and bend into a pretzel shape, which seemed to be what the other kids were doing.

Dracula-boy was defeated. He shrugged and rushed off to see what some kids crowded around a card table were groaning about. Cameron cheered internally for his daughter's verbal skills and loved her all the more.

"Sally put gummi-worms in the gelatin," Monty Winters explained, tilting his head toward the card table and passing a beer over Cameron's right shoulder. "The stuff is black, by the way, in honor of the holiday."

"What, were actual worms too expensive?" Cameron asked.

"Don't say that too loud, she just might consider it," Monty said. "Sally is WAY into Halloween. Me, I'm more of a Christmas-man. Ho, ho, ho,"

The site of a fat man in tights going "Ho-ho-ho" was much more disturbing that any of Cameron's hallucinations had ever been.

Sally joined them. "Holly seems pretty happy," she said. "Have you talked to Susan lately?"

The muscles in Cameron's back clenched.

"We talk about visitation arrangements," Cameron said. "And she did actually call last week to say Holly won 'best reader of the week' by reading more minutes than anyone in class."

"She must have gotten that from you," Sally said.

"If she was my kid, she'd spend that reading time playing basketball," Monty said before filling his ample stomach with a swallow of beer.

"Say, guys," Cameron said, "Has a reporter been snooping around asking questions about me?"

"No," they said together. "Keep it that way."

Cameron watched his little girl, amazed by the intensity with which she competed with the other kids in the game. The wonder of a child was on full display. The way she devoted the adult-on-a-mission-to-save-the-world zeal to...well, whatever the hell that game was they were playing.

Cameron knew that he could never be that care-free. He had to be on guard all the time. If he wasn't constantly aware of his surroundings, every motion, every voice, he would slip. He would slip into the realm of the non-people—the voices in his head and the false images in front of his eyes. That could never happen again. Not ever.

But still, it would be nice to let go now and again. He remembered the Zorro mask in his back pocket. What was a mask really? A way to disguise yourself; become someone else. Cameron's big fear in life was that he would lose himself. What if instead of losing himself, he let himself go away for just an evening? Treatment or not, mental illness stays with you, but a mask you can take off. Hell, if Monty Winters could walk around unabashed in tights, Cameron could wear a mask for one night.

"Excuse me, folks," Cameron said suddenly. "I have to play with my little girl."

Cameron pulled a black Zorro mask out of his pocket and tied it around his head. In his best Spanish accent—which wasn't very good—he said, "My lady awaits."

He sauntered—for he suspected Zorro was a saunterer—over to the group of kids in the middle of the room. Holly was now at the end of the line, having just finished her turn throwing the little bean bags and doing something akin to hopscotch. She did not see her father approach, her mind focused on the drama unfolding in the game in front of her.

Cameron knelt down and, he thought very playfully, said, "Boo."

A couple of the kids looked in his direction, but were unimpressed. It was fair to say none of these kids even knew who Zorro was, but they were probably savvy enough to know that no mask-wearing superhero also wears khaki pants.

Holly, however, freaked. It was like she was over-compensating for the other kids' lack of enthusiasm by channeling their unused shock through herself. She shrieked, then screamed, then burst into tears.

"What, hey, it's okay," Cameron said. "It's just Daddy." He pulled off the mask. This made Holly cry even harder.

Sally bounded over to comfort the child. "What's wrong, honey?" she repeated several times. Holly allowed Sally to maneuver her out of the center of the room, but did not reply.

The other kids were stunned, complete with the dropped jaws that only kids can pull off without looking cartoonish. Twister/Tic-Tac-Toe was actually forgotten. That sound you hear is a party grinding to a halt.

Monty took action. "Hey, kids," he said. "Anyone wanna see a real, live zombie brain?"

Out in the hall, the situation was quieter, if not significantly better. Sally sat on a bench with the now mutely sniffling child on her lap. It flashed through Cameron's head absurdly for just a second that if Holly had chosen to go with the full clown makeup, it would be streaking by now. Sally was hugging the girl and telling her, "It's okay."

Cameron knelt by the bench, the mask in his hand. "It's just a mask, see?"

he said, not sure what else to say.

"No, it's not," the child insisted. "You're not Daddy."

"Well... sure I am," Cameron said. It seemed a silly thing to say.

Sally, however, asked, "What do you mean, honey?"

"He's somebody else."

"Who?" Sally asked.

"One of the other people," Holly said in a tone that betrayed her belief that this should explain everything.

"I don't understand," Sally said.

But Cameron did.

"He's one of those people Daddy talks to that isn't really there."

There it was.

"One of those people is gonna take my daddy away," Holly barely got out before a renewed round of sobbing.

"Oh, Holly, sweetheart, why would you think that?" Sally asked.

Cameron knew.

"It's just like last time, when Daddy went away."

The divorce. Holly and Susan moved away. The kid was only one at the time, but surely she felt the change in her little world; grew to feel it. Cameron took a, well, a *rest* to deal with the depression or schizophrenia or whatever it was that he had. He and Susan agreed to try and keep as much of his problems away from Holly, but he was, then at least, something of a celebrity. All the networks and most of the cable channels camped outside his home. Reporters go home and tell their spouses about crazy writers that they wrote about that day. Parents of other kids—Holly's friends for example—see the family drama played out on TV and the kids hear it. Then they talk on the playground.

Holly thought that one of Cameron's hallucinations—maybe one that wore a black Zorro mask—was taking him away. Again.

Sally looked at Cameron meaningfully. She understood too. Cameron motioned for her to turn Holly over to him, which she did. Holly protested a little, but relaxed. Cameron said a hasty, fairly awkward goodbye and carried the child out to the car.

Holly slept all the way home. Cameron struggled with how to broach the subject of his...his loopiness. They had never talked about it much. The child was only five. It didn't seem like such a good thing to lay on a little kid, but she clearly understood that something wasn't right with her father. For a man who made his living with words, however, he could think of no way to tell his little girl he was as scared of the monster inside himself as she was.

So, in the end, he said nothing that night. Holly did eventually calm down, but the rest of the visit was an uneasy one. It was an edgy, suspenseful time with specters lurking around every corner.

Perfect for Halloween.

As memories of "Monster Mash" melded into the dogs barking "Jingle Bells" on the radio, Cameron returned to the present and shuddered.

"Screw your bah humbug!" he shouted and was then very embarrassed for himself even though he was quite alone.

He would give his little girl the best Noel ever. This Christmas would be the happiest day this child had ever seen—*would ever* see. Santa Jones would kick Santa Claus squarely in the yuletide chestnuts. That old, fat man would pack up and go home.

Given that Kris Kringle had given up toy-making to spend his days downing shots of cocoa—hold the marshmallows—Cameron had no idea how prophetic his words were.

# DECEMBER 7

The Spencer County Courthouse in Rockport, about thirty minutes south of Santa Claus is, in many ways, like any other courthouse; an imposing granite gray structure with a clock on top. There's a split between how courthouses are portrayed in literature and what they actually are. How they're portrayed is as beacons of justice, hope, strife, and drama. Many legal thrillers—real and fictional—have played out in courthouses.

What courthouses are, however, is another matter. Courthouses serve many vital, but largely mundane, purposes. Most court cases settle out of court in a flurry of paperwork. Courthouses house administrative offices; you can often pay your boat license fee, your parking ticket, or register to vote in their halls. For the staffers, lawyers, and administrators who work in them, much of the day is routine.

For many of the visitors—the fee payers, for example—the courthouse is a utilitarian place on the scale of a run to the bank to deposit the check, or swinging by the video store to return the latest Ashton Kutcher vehicle.

There is one group of visitors to the courthouse, however, for whom the experience is not routine: moms and dads involved in family law cases. Families are built and torn down in the testimonies taken and papers shuffled in courtrooms and judges' chambers. To paraphrase an old saying, our legal system might be a horrible way to govern families, but it's better than the alternatives.

None of this, however, was going through Cameron Jones' head as he sat in an unused conference room. All he thought about was how his last, best tie to the real world was soon going to be taken away from him. The weary look in his eyes and defeated posture reflected the lack of quality sleep he experienced worrying about Holly being stolen from him.

Cameron was realistic; he knew he was unlikely to get expanded visitation, let alone custody. He had a shaky emotional and mental past and—if he ever got another book finished—he would spend weeks at a time on book tours and public appearances rather than being at home to take care of his daughter.

He knew all this, but still he had asked Everett Franken to try. He had to try. He had to have the opportunity to show the court and the world that he was a devoted father, even if he was loopy. If Susan succeeded in moving to Europe with his daughter, he would be lucky to see her once, maybe twice per year.

He knew Susan wasn't trying to hurt him. The purpose of today's hearing, however, made him angry. As if it wasn't bad enough that she was taking his daughter away, she now wanted to paint him as insane; a danger to his child. If she succeeded today, the last few visits he might have with his daughter would be supervised by some stranger as if he were a psycho or a pervert.

He tried to tell himself that this was just her lawyer's doing; a chance to take down a celebrity. He knew, however, that Susan was a strong enough person to not allow the likes of Wally Bass to lead her where she didn't want to go. Not wanting to hate Susan, however, didn't stop him from disliking Wally Bass. The man smelled funny.

The conference room door opened and Everett Franken came in. He had the grave look of a lawyer who knows he's about to have a conversation with a client that he doesn't want to have.

"Thought maybe you got lost," Cameron said.

"Sorry I took so long," Everett Franken said. "Mr. Bass is very long-winded."

"So what's the proposal?"

"Well, you know they're going to ask the judge to compel you to authorize Dr. Whipple to release your psychiatric progress notes and –"

"I've got nothing to hide," Cameron interrupted.

"It's very dangerous for things like psychiatrists' notes to be public. If there's anything in there—anything—that could be construed to say that you are not mentally competent, it's all over."

Cameron nodded. "The bid for expanded visitation?"

"The extra visits, the *current* visits, and, to be honest, your career."

"It's not your job to worry about that. My career is...well, it's fading anyway,"

Cameron said. "I just want you to make sure I don't lose my daughter."

"It's my job to make sure you are protected," Everett Franken said. "It's also my job to tell you what I think the judge will do."

"What's that?"

"Well, first of all, I think he's going to say that your mental health is relevant to determining if it's in Holly's best interests to have visits with you. The medical records will probably come in."

"Okay," Cameron shrugged.

"Secondly, I think that he's going to say your visitation should continue until the trial after Christmas. Mr. Bass doesn't have anything to compel a judge to restrict that."

"Good. So what's their proposal?"

"Well, we can avoid a hearing—and the uncertainty that's always involved when you leave things up to the judge—if you'll agree to have your visitation supervised."

"No," Cameron said.

"I'm not suggesting you agree to have a social worker supervise the visits," Everett Franken said. "But maybe you should think about letting a friend or relative do it. We could even negotiate who that might be."

"I know some of what I've done has been scary to Holly," Cameron said. "But I'm no danger."

"I know," Everett Franken said, in a tone that managed to betray both compassion and a bit of fatigue at having this conversation yet again.

"Who would I even get?" Cameron asked.

"Well, Mr. Bass suggested Susan's parents might be willing to supervise visits. They are apparently willing to fly in and stay in the area until the trial."

"No. They hate me," Cameron said. "Well, it's not so much hatred as it is loathing."

"I understand how there might be a strain with her parents," Everett Franken said. "If you had to do it, though, is there anyone you would feel comfortable with using?"

Who can you ask to do a thing like that? To sit with you, to watch you as you spend the few, precious, moments you have with your child like you're some sort of perverted freak who needs to be monitored? Since his fall from literary prominence and emotional stability, Cameron had severed or been shorn of many of the acquaintances he had before. The only person he could think of was Roberta Hunt, Dogwater's sister. Dog, himself, was too weird, but other than Dogwater and Roberta, Cameron couldn't think of anyone. Monty and Sally Winters were taking an extended vacation in Canada to visit Sally's family so they wouldn't be available for the Christmas visit. He told Everett Franken as much.

"What's going to happen, Everett?"

"Well, we know in family law cases there are no winners," Everett Franken said. "Beyond that is anyone's guess." He shrugged.

Cameron had never been a smoker, but he never wanted a cigarette more in his life.

Judge J. Donovan Collins had been on the bench thirty-five years. He had presided over countless trials and hearings. Thousands of those were family law cases, yet, he hated doing them. He believed in the court system, but did not believe that families belonged in it. He was bound to apply the law, but he didn't have to like it.

Family law cases weren't really about the law anyway. Sure, there was a framework—promoting the "best interests" of the child, calculating child support within legal guidelines, case law on property division—but ultimately, it came down to seeing to what extent Mom and Dad could tolerate each other. If they got along okay, settlements happened; if not, he, a judge who had never met these people before they were shuffled into his courtroom, would have to decide their futures, how their children would be raised. That seemed wrong, but then so many things about the law, on close examination, did.

"Margaret, I'm ready for them," Judge Collins said on the phone to the court attendant in the outer chamber.

Moments later, Wally Bass lumbered into the office, fixing his collar with one hand and holding a bulging, expandable folder in the other. He was followed by Everett Franken, whose gait was much more lithe, carrying a leather, shoulder-strapped briefcase.

"Hello, Mr. Bass. Mr. Franken, how are you?" the judge asked. "Please tell me you have an agreement."

"I think so," Wally Bass said, flopping into one of the two chairs positioned in front of Judge Collins' desk. Without prompting, he continued, "Mr. Jones has agreed that the upcoming weekend visit and the Christmas

Eve visit will be supervised."

Judge Collins looked over his half-glasses at Everett Franken. "Is that so?"

Everett Franken paused. "His position that it is unnecessary has not changed. However, in the interest of cooperation and, admittedly, concerns about making a big fuss and attracting even more publicity, we would consent to supervision of the next visitation—provided, however, that a suitable third party can be agreed upon."

"Any suggestions, Mr. Bass?" Judge Collins asked.

"Well, I'm sure my client's folks would be happy to fill in."

"That's not a realistic possibility," Everett Franken said. "Given the divorce and subsequent proceedings, there's substantial tension there."

"Then who would you suggest?" Judge Collins asked.

"Mr. Jones has a friend named Roberta Hunt. She's a responsible adult, known to both parties and to Holly."

"Who also lives in a trailer with a conspiracy-obsessed, alleged alien-abducted brother," Wally Bass said.

"I see," Judge Collins said. He brushed thoughtfully at his graying left temple. "Wait. Hunt. Is he the guy who spent a week outside city hall protesting...what was it? Hallucinogens in the water supply? No... he said the Parks Department was putting viruses in pollen. I think that was it."

"Both, actually," Wally Bass chuckled.

"I'm sure Mr. Hunt is harmless. And Roberta is very trustworthy," Everett Franken said.

"Perhaps," Wally Bass said suspiciously, "but I think Ms. Wentworth's Uncle Milo, would be even more trustworthy. He's a kindly, old gent. He's family. And, as far as I know, he has stayed out of jail."

"How's that sound, Mr. Franken?" Judge Collins asked.

"Cameron has not specifically vetoed this gentleman, but we haven't discussed him either."

"Any reason to think 'Uncle Milo' is not a fit, neutral third-party?" Judge Collins asked, his tone level, but with a tinge of a dare to challenge the idea.

"Well, not to my knowledge, your honor, but as I said..."

"Fine, then we'll go with Uncle Milo," Judge Collins said congenially, but firmly to stifle protest from Everett Franken. "It's only for a couple of visits. You're set to try this on the twenty-sixth."

"I guess I can convince my client to go along," Everett Franken said, not at all sure this was true.

"Fine, then," Judge Collins said, turning to Wally Bass. "You'll write up the order and get it to me this afternoon for signature?"

"Absolutely, Judge."

"Okay. Thank you, gentlemen." Judge Collins turned around to the other desk behind him where his laptop computer sat, effectively ending the conference. After the two lawyers filed out of Judge Collins' chambers, he released the tiniest of sighs, audible to no one. He hated these cases.

Audible to no one, that is, except the woman crouching in his empty ceramic mug, risking asphyxiation by orange pekoe.

Mrs. Claus peered over the side of the mug, studying the judge. Her husband could have made himself small enough to fit in Judge Collins' fountain pen, but she was not quite as skilled as he.

Judge Collins was a good man; he gave much and often to charity, raised wonderful children and was always fair with litigants.

Plus, he had given her the makings of a wonderful idea...

# DECEMBER 8

In all the many and varied stories of Santa and Mrs. Claus ever told there was never any mention of the fact that Mrs. Claus is a devoted, borderline obsessive, kick-boxer.

You may not know it to look at the pictures of her, but those are, after all, just pictures; publicity head-shots put out to feed the grandmotherly image of Mrs. Claus that sells. How else do you explain the lack of a first name? It's all part of the mystique.

Having just finished an intense workout that really ripped her abs, Mrs. Claus dabbed at the sweat glistening on rosy cheeks as she moved through the bright expanse of the arboretum, cris-crossing between the rows of—what else?—Christmas poinsettias of red, white, purple and nearly every other color of the spectrum except black. There was even a transparent one and another that only bloomed when the song "Santa Claus is Comin' To Town" played.

It was time to get Santa up off his ample butt and back on the Christmas sleigh. Countless boys and girls were counting on him. And now her visit to Santa Claus, Indiana (the name embarrassed Kris, but gave her a warm tingle) had convinced her of what she must do.

At the other end of the arboretum, Mrs. Claus activated the touch screen on the computer display in the wall. Except for a hand-held electronic organizer his chief of staff Flifle had brow-beaten him into, Kris Kringle was a traditionalist—quill pens and all that—but Mrs. Claus liked technology. She paged Flifle. A moment later, the bearded, weary face of the chief of staff appeared on the screen.

"Good day, ma'am," Flifle beamed, though he sounded fatigued.

"And good day to you, Flifle," Mrs. Claus replied. "How is production coming?"

"We're a bit behind on some units of...," Flifle paused, shuffled some papers on his desk and squinted at one. "...something called 'Ooze Mania'. We're not really even sure what it is. Have you any idea?"

Mrs. Claus frowned. Things were so much easier when children played with simple things like dolls, tea-sets, footballs and toy trains.

"Sorry, Flifle. I don't know. It sounds disgusting."

"Yes," Flifle said gravely, his weary eyes fluttering a bit. "We'll still be ready by the twenty-fourth as always."

"I'm sure you will."

"Now, then, what can I do for you, ma'am?" Flifle asked.

"Flifle, do you know where my husband is today?"

Flifle looked a little troubled. This look was only slightly different than the weary, pained expression he wore most of the time, but it was distinctive enough.

"Well, he was supposed to inspect the reindeer proving grounds, but..." Flifle suddenly became very interested in another piece of paper on his desk. He didn't want to look at Mrs. Claus when he said the next part.

"But what?"

"Well...Feebee says he hasn't left the Oval all day."

Mrs. Claus sighed. "Thank you, Flifle."

"Of course, ma'am." The screen went blank.

The Oval was a sanctuary to which St. Nicholas retreated at times of great stress or when there were matters of great importance that could not be dealt with among the elves. The latter happened rarely. What could anyone ever have to hide from an elf? If Santa was in the Oval now, things must be very bad.

Mrs. Claus had a plan to help her husband reconnect with the real-worlders and thereby regain his purpose. Now was the time to tell him. She asked one of her elf assistants, Deelay or possibly Meelay—it was hard to say since they were thoroughly identical twins down to the last hairs on their heads—to get her coat and boots.

Properly suited for the balmy North Pole, Mrs. Claus set out to the far side of the Christmas compound where the Oval sat.

The North Pole, of course, was ice and snow all year. But around Christmastime, it was magical; trite as that sounds. Mrs. Claus had that same thought every holiday season for centuries. Down below, the real-worlders would call such a notion corny or cliché, but who more than she was qualified to say—sans cliché—that this place really was *magical*?

In sharp contrast to nearly everything else in Santa Claus' North Pole complex, the path to the Oval is a somber one. There are no bright lights as in the main compound; no small, joyful elf voices singing. The only color is the white of the snow or—if you call that a color—the transparency of the ice, on the wagon wheel-rutted road. Santa rarely used a wagon or a sled anymore, preferring instead to make the trek on foot. And as for motorized transportation, it's not like Kris Kringle can stroll into Honest Bob's Pre-owned Vehicle Dreamhouse and pick up a minivan.

So, Mrs. Claus also made the trek on foot this day. She rarely came out here as it was tacitly understood that the only one who went into the Oval was St. Nick. It was where he went to clear his head in times of great need. Once, during the dark days of the bubonic plague, he spent a week in there. World War II brought three days in the Oval before he had to leave, unable to stand dwelling on the suffering any longer. How could he make the world's children happy when their parents were killing each other? Illness, even wide-spread illness, was one thing; but inflicting violence and death...

Mrs. Claus had understood Santa's sadness on those occasions. But this time was different. There was no clear outside cause. He had just given up. It had easily been two-hundred-fifty years since Santa last had such a "career crisis." That time, as the world's industrial revolution was heating up, he had been worried that he couldn't compete with real world toymakers. He thought he was out of touch, not "hip" enough—in those days, "hip" was not in the vernacular, of course, but it was still devastating.

Bad as that was, Santa never talked about hanging up his tasseled Santa hat as he was now. His recent behavior was as far from jolly as you can be and still call yourself sane. Mrs. Claus really didn't know what she would find in the Oval. Or how she would salvage the man she loved from it.

The Oval was simply that; a large, open-air oblong structure, like the center ring at Barnum & Bailey's. It was about a foot high, wooden, and had a diameter of maybe twenty-five feet. An invisible dome protected any contents from the elements.

As Mrs. Claus came over the last rise, the winter calm shook with the sound of *thwock/thwock/thwack/thwok!* As the Oval came into view, Mrs. Claus understood why.

Standing in the Oval's center, coat off, sleeves pushed up and sweating despite sub-zero temperatures, was St. Nicholas himself, tearing into a log with an axe.

*Thwockthwok-thwick!*

The log split in two and Santa cast the halves aside, grunting a little as he contorted his large frame to pick up and move the wood. He wore a look of intense concentration. A grim frown wrestled the color out of his rosy cheeks despite those being all the rosier from the exertion.

Mrs. Claus approached the rim of the Circle, but did not speak. She waited for Kris Kringle to notice her.

As he reached for the next log, she caught his eye over his right shoulder.

"Hello, dearest," he said simply. His voice still boomed, but it was uncharacteristically mirthless.

"You've been out here a long while, Nicholas," Mrs. Claus said. "The elves are getting worried. Flifle's dyspeptic again."

"They all know their jobs. They can get along without me," Santa said.

"Can they?"

"Of course. They've been at this as long as I have," Santa said, gripping the axe, but not yet chopping with it. "And they were toymakers long before I even became..." He paused. "Well, before all this." He motioned gently toward the North Pole Complex.

After about a thousand years or so, Mrs. Claus had finally learned to be direct.

"Do you mean to give up giving toys to the children?"

*THWOK THWOK THWOK!*

Santa sighed and put down the axe. "The children! Let me tell you-" he stopped, leaving that comment unfinished, gurgling in his throat. Instead, he said, "The children don't want me. Those young ones at the marketplace proved that." He picked up the axe.

"I think they call them 'malls' now, dear," Mrs. Claus gently corrected. "So that's what this is all about, is it? Those children made fun of you. But, Kris, they didn't even know it was you."

Santa drove the axe head into the log and turned to Mrs. Claus. "I know that," he said. "But they didn't have it. They didn't have the belief. The spirit of Christmas was dead in them."

"They were tweeners, weren't they?"

Santa scoffed. "Babies in longer pants. I've lost them."

"What about the little girl?" Mrs. Claus countered, remembering that Santa had told her about Elizabeth, the girl with whom he had shared a moment's mutual belief and love.

"She'll fade like the rest of them." Santa flexed his shoulder and stretched. Reaching out casually to his right with one hand, a cup of water appeared there. He took a sip, held out the hand again and let go of the cup. Rather than falling, the cup simply faded out of existence again.

"And what of you? Will you fade too?" Mrs. Claus asked.

Santa sighed again and crouched in a sitting position. A mammoth oak rocking chair appeared under him. To his right, first the glow of the flames and then the brick mantle and hearth of a fireplace around it came into being. For a long time, he didn't answer, just rocked gently.

Mrs. Claus tapped the invisible dome and the orchestral version of the song "Santa Claus Is Comin' to Town" began to play as swirls of color danced in time along the unseen roof. Santa irritably flicked it to a stop.

"Well?" Mrs. Claus persisted.

"I-" Santa started. What would he do? He wasn't qualified for anything but bringing joy to the world. And chopping wood, he supposed. But the real-worlders all had gas heaters and solar panels and microwave ovens for cooking. There didn't seem to be much need for the wood chopping . So that left only one thing. But...

"I just can't do it anymore," Santa said. "I'm tired."

"So take a nap! But in sixteen days, Christmas Eve is happening and if you're not there, there was be millions of devastated children around the world. Is that what you want?"

Another long pause.

"No," Santa admitted. "Of course not."

"Very well, then," Mrs. Claus said simply.

A "ho ho ho" rumbled low in Santa's throat, but by the time it reached the air, it degenerated into a mournful cry.

Mrs. Claus did the unthinkable. She entered the Oval. This had only occurred once before in the history of the North Pole Complex. The elf who had so horribly transgressed the unspoken rule that only Santa entered the Oval had stumbled into it during a game of "hurgle," sort of a variation on

American football played on snowshoes, blindfolded. The elf was so disgraced that he banished himself from the North Pole Complex for two weeks.

Mrs. Claus went to her husband, held his hand and said simply, "Let me help you."

Santa tried to smile; it was feeble, but there.

"Let us," a small voice from the nearby trees began. "Uh, that is to say, we would all like to help you, sir."

The voice belonged to Santa's Chief of Staff Flifle who stepped as quietly from the trees as he had gone into them. Stealth was a common, though little used, trait among the elves of the North Pole Complex.

"I have a plan," Mrs. Claus said.

Flifle's eyebrow lifted in some alarm. He had really just been expressing allegiance. He didn't know anything of a plan. He didn't like it. As Chief of Staff, he usually knew everything.

"Flifle, we're going to need your help," Mrs. Claus said. "My idea is a bit...extreme."

"Of course, ma'am," Flifle said, not having a clue what he was agreeing to.

"What do you have in mind, my dear?" Santa said, sounding both jolly and uneasy at once.

"Well, if it works, the real world will get its Kris Kringle back and some very nice real-worlders will have a merry Christmas."

"And if it doesn't?"

"Well, then December twenty-fifth should be very quiet, indeed."

"December twenty-fifth is gonna kick ass!" Dogwater Hunt proclaimed in ill-constructed, but heartfelt, hyperbole.

"Man, the twenty-fifth ain't gonna do nuthin' to your ass, man," Izzy Carmichel replied, not moving from the reclining, hat-over-the-face pose he had placed himself in twenty minutes earlier. "No, sir. Not a skinny ass like that."

The two men were sitting in the surprisingly spacious living room of Izzy's double-wide trailer. Except for the black plastic trash bag that served as a curtain on the living room window and the faux wood-grain paneling that had been outdated in 1980, it was not a bad trailer.

Izzy Carmichel, who was born Isaiah, but changed it at age fourteen because it was "too Biblical," was, it seemed to Dog, the physical specimen that the word "lanky" was meant for. Izzy lifted his long legs from the back of the recliner on which they were propped, pulled himself to a sitting position on the couch and said, "So, man, you gonna tell me what this Santa Claus shit is all about?"

Izzy was not just down on Santa, but the whole Christmas thing. He was a man adrift in a faith-less sea, drifting from island to island; Christianity, Judaism, Hinduism, Buddhism, Islam, but he found them all lacking in one respect or another. For good measure, he had thrown in skepticism about Santa Claus and Christmas. Besides, it got him out of buying presents.

The scent of stale marijuana smoke clung to everything in the room, including Izzy. On his website, Dogwater had run a few years earlier a six-part exposé on how the government used addictive drugs to control the poor, minorities, and anyone else they just want to keep a handle on. The government's "Drug War" with its "Drug Czar" was just a smoke screen to cover these machinations.

Izzy had no qualms about this and was quite content to be controlled by a shadowy, conspiratorial government if that's what it took to get stoned or high.

"It's not shit, Izzy. The Santa Claus alien is legit. I showed you the data," Dogwater said. He pulled from the torn canvas backpack leaning against his chair a sheaf of printer paper. He spread the pages out on the coffee table/ironing board in front of them. Some of the papers had streams of numbers, others squiggly lines, and still others had what appeared to be star maps.

"There is something moving in a regular path on track to enter Earth's atmosphere on the night of December twenty-four," Dogwater said.

"E.T.?" Izzy said, fishing through his pockets for something Dog guessed was probably a joint.

"We don't know what it is," Dogwater admitted, "But its flight pattern is way too regular to be a natural phenomenon."

"And you are the only one who knows about this?" Izzy had failed to find a joint, and decided to focus his attention on Dogwater; at least for the moment.

"Well, me and a few other believers," Dogwater said, shrugging. "But I'm probably the only one actively pursuing it."

"What you gonna do with it? The space bug. You know, once you catch it?"

Dogwater thought about this. Until now he had only been thinking about the chance to expose the truth that aliens walk among us, not about the possibility of actually *catching* one. What *would* he do with it?

Nothing. He realized that he would do nothing with it. A man who protested against animal cruelty and environmental degradation and human rights abuses could not be seen putting space aliens in thermoses (Dogwater's thesis was that the particular race of aliens traveling toward Earth were very small and preferred extremely cold climates.) Revenge was a seductive emotion, but he could never commit to it. He felt bleak about this for a moment, then shunted insecurity aside.

"I don't want to catch it," Dog said finally. "I just want to know what it is; show people they shouldn't be so arrogant. We're not alone in the universe."

Izzy laughed at that. He laughed a long time. He was still laughing as he went to the kitchen area which featured a breakfast bar and a mini-bar style refrigerator. He took out two cans of the cheapest beer you can buy and tossed one to Dogwater. Dog barely even looked up from his print-outs as he caught it.

Now Izzy stood, deep in thought, as he wiped away a bit of the carbonation-fueled spray from the now open beer that had showered his vertically striped, neon-colored t-shirt. He wasn't picturing extra-terrestrials in food storage containers. He was picturing them on "The Tonight Show." And seated next to them was Isaiah "Izzy" Carmichel in a tailored suit yukking it up with Jay Leno and Jay's other guests Lindsay Lohan, Jessica Simpson, and Martha Stewart. They were all drooling over him. That Martha Stewart was in the mix disturbed him a little, but there she was.

"And what do you want from me?" Izzy said as Jay thanked his musical guest and the credits rolled.

"If I'm going to track the Santas—that's what we're calling the aliens—I need equipment. Electronics. Some of the really pricey stuff you can't help with. But there's other stuff you can help with," Dogwater said, unable to contain himself. He was pacing now. "I need computers, GPS units, digital cameras, and high-quality photo printers."

Izzy groaned. Izzy Carmichel was an associate at Electronic Junction; had worked there for the past eight years. "Man, why should I steal for you?"

"No!" Dogwater said quickly, unconsciously looking around for Spencer County's finest to bust down the door. "Not steal. Borrow maybe. Take them out for a test drive. I'll return everything. I swear. I just need it for a while."

"I could lose my job," Izzy said.

"It's one night," Dogwater countered. "And it's Christmas Eve. The stuff will be gone and back before any of the other employees have finished their Figgie pudding."

Izzy squinted. "Don't you have a sugar daddy? That rich computer guy?"

Dogwater flushed. "He bailed on me. Said he wanted to give all his money to that cult that worships mustard instead."

"So what do I get out of it?" Izzy said.

"Well, I can't pay you, if that's what you mean," Dogwater said carefully. "But you get the pride of ushering in a new age of human enlightenment. You know what a giver you've always been." Dogwater grinned.

Izzy snorted. "Fuck you," he said.

And the deal was done.

On a kid-size table in her bedroom, five-year-old Holly Jones laid out six sheets of construction paper; two white, two red, one green and one purple. Next to these, she set out, with the careful deliberateness of a child at work, four crayons –blue, black, green, and red.

Holly had already had a busy morning of marking off another day until Christmas—her method was to glue a cotton ball onto the number representing that day's date on Santa's beard in a large picture hanging on her wall. After doing that each day, Santa would have a full beard on December twenty-four and you'd know it was Christmastime.

Not that Holly needed a fat man's follicles to tell her it was Christmas. Christmas was cool! Not as cool as Halloween maybe, but still pretty cool. She liked the toys, Grandma's Christmas cookies, and the way the cat, Meow-Meow, bounced around playing in the gift wrap and ribbons.

Mostly, she liked the lights. Every year, there were more lights on the tree than the last—twinkling red, green, blue and gold. Everywhere she went. There were more lights than she could count—probably like thirty or forty!

But she would think about those things later. For now, there was important work to do. She sat down and studied the four crayons. She had narrowed the choice down to either the red or blue to start with, when she had the sense that something was horribly wrong with Melvin Floppy.

Melvin Floppy was a large, overstuffed, pink bunny that sat at the foot of Holly's bed. At the moment, Melvin Floppy, who usually sat in a dignified, straight-backed position with a sophisticated air that was somewhat incongruous with the cartoon carrot design on his vest, was now sitting in a v-shape with his fluffy bunny derriere pointed upward.

Holly rushed over to him, righted him back in his spot, kissed both floppy ears and headed back to her seat. She stopped again as a sparkle of light from the other side of the room caught her eye.

She looked at the item that sat on the red dresser on that side of the room. It was an old, sixties-vintage music box, with a frozen pond skating scene on top. When it used to work, a miniature Santa, snowman, and a little boy would skate around a track on grooves built into the music box in time to the song "We Wish You a Merry Christmas" when you turned the key in the bottom to crank it up. Santa and the snowman were now frozen in place. The little boy mostly just stood alone next to the miniature cabin by the pond and occasionally skated back in forth a fraction of an inch every now and then.

Holly watched the box now. The sunlight from the window opposite the dresser filtered brightly through the sheer pink curtains and played off the silver parts of the music box. Holly thought maybe that's what she saw. But she wasn't sure.

She brushed the bangs out of her eyes and stared at the music box. A very small, but very precise beam of light seemed to come from the tiny window in the cabin by which the motionless boy stood. Holly watched it a long time.

Then, when nothing else happened, she shrugged the mystery off with the ease of a care-free child. She returned to her table, sat, centered a piece of the green construction paper in front of her, picked up the red crayon and thought.

"Dear Santa," she began, speaking to herself in a kid-intellectual voice as she wrote. She thought a bit more, then wrote:

Dear Santa,

My name is Holly Jones. I'm 5 years old. I like trains. And ponies I would like a train for Christmas. That would be cool! And a make up kit like Mommy's. But mostly I want a train And a pony. How is Mrs. Claus? Does she help you load the toys on the sled? I hope so. They're heavy.

Holly paused then as she pondered what to say next. She also took the opportunity to choose a different color crayon—blue now. After drawing a picture of a reindeer with antlers roughly twice the length of its body, she wrote:

My grandma wants fuzzy slipers. Grandpa says he just wants to take a nap.

And Mommy says she wants some purfum, but I think what she really, really, really wants is

DADDY (She drew a little heart next to this, then added ME TOO)

Say hi to Rudolph!

XOXOXOXO

*Holly*

Holly creased the letter a third of the way down the page and again two-thirds of the way down the page and then folded it over. In the upper right corner of the rectangle she drew a small rendering of a postage stamp. She addressed it to "Santa Claus—North Pole", took a moment to admire her work, then sprang from her chair and skipped out the bedroom door.

Over on the dresser, the little, near motionless boy on the music box ice rink did a pirouette and bowed. Santa and the snowman danced arm in arm around the frozen pond scene. And then, for the first time ever, snow fell on the skaters. A crisp, gentle Christmas flurry fell from non-existent clouds.

# DECEMBER 9

Milton "Milo" Vestibule, Susan Wentworth's uncle on her mother's side, was many things, including a retired grocer. "Vestibule's Veggies" was later taken over by Milo's son, Ernest, closed and reopened as the coffee bar "The Daily Grind," much to Milo's continuing chagrin. He was also a senior center billiards champion, and salsa dancer. Even when sober, which wasn't all that often.

And, as the whole neighborhood, the local fitness center, and the ladies' auxiliary could tell you, Uncle Milo was an unrepentant womanizer.

All of which makes one wonder why anyone, especially a family member who knows him well, would ever consider him a good choice to supervise visitation between a book author and his young daughter. For one thing, Milo was a TV man.

The reason was that for all of Uncle Milo's distasteful characteristics, many of which boldly crossed the line to faults, he was good with kids. Really good. Phenomenally good. Instead of being the crazy old man whose yard the neighborhood kids tried to avoid, Uncle Milo had all that he could do to keep the kids out of his yard. He'd lost more garden gnomes than he could count.

Of course, he brought it on himself. The man could bake a helluva good seven-layer bar. And, gruff as he was, none of the neighborhood parents worried about their kids eating them. It didn't even faze them (anymore) when Uncle Milo greeted the middle-aged ladies power-walking down the street with: "Why don't you lovely ladies walk on up to my bedroom," in a bellow from his front porch.

Around noon this day, Uncle Milo sat hunched in a lawn chair on the front porch in a parka and honest-to-God galoshes (though the weather was dry) which all covered an impeccable suit, even if it was forty-years-old. Most days, Uncle Milo wore a suit and tie, the hues of which became more vibrant as the week wore on. The only day he didn't wear a suit or shave was Sunday. He didn't want to be tempted to go to church for reasons that very few knew and, after so many decades, no one asked about any longer.

Uncle Milo nursed a buttered rum. Usually he stuck to beer or occasionally scotch, and usually he waited until at least three or four in the afternoon. Today, however, was a special occasion: Milo's seventy-eighth birthday. He had risen as usual at five-thirty, dressed and shaved, fed Sally the cat, ate a biscuit and sausage gravy breakfast, fed the cat the leftovers (after nine years of this routine, it was a really fat cat), read the paper, fielded calls from niece Susan and only son Ernest wishing him a happy day, and was pretty much out of things to do by eight-thirty.

Uncle Milo rose, shuffled into the house and stood in the small living room, unsure what to do next. He tossed the parka on the lumpy couch, left the galoshes in the middle of the room where he stood, and went over to the easy chair. He hit the clicker and a cable news channel flickered on. He took a sip of rum as he listened to the very attractive newswoman say, "When we come back from this break, we'll have big news from the world of science about the Big Bang."

"I got your big bang," Uncle Milo said into the opening of his rum glass.

Uncle Milo giggled the brusque laugh of a very old man nursing a dirty joke. Then, if it's possible, he heard two distinctly different sounds simultaneously, one in each ear as if coming from separate speakers: one was the soft voice of his late wife Evelyn singing "Happy Birthday;" the other was the sound of something that seemed to be...no, not really....yeah, maybe... jingle bells.

Shaking his head as if he could physically banish the sound from it, Milo raised the rum glass to his lips and drank. It was the last drop he would enjoy that day.

The glass dropped from his trembling hand and shattered on the already stained shag carpet.

Sally meowed indignantly, then went on licking the sausage plate.

In the catacombs below the North Pole Complex are two chambers; Annex A and Annex B. Annex A is the magic store. It's the place where Santa and the elves came up with some of the most wondrous facets of the modern holiday: the flying sleigh and reindeer; the ability to visit children all over the world in one night; the complex physics of sliding up and down all those chimneys and around the locked doors of the chimney-less; the bit about laying a finger aside of his nose; all of it. The magic store is a vibrant, happy place, complete with holiday carols. Unlike any given mall shopper by Halloween, Kris Kringle does not tire of Christmas music. Well, except maybe "I Saw Mommy Kissing Santa Claus." That one is a little embarrassing.

Annex B is a chamber secluded within Annex A. It's a dank, cobwebbed, desolate, and rarely acknowledged secret of the North Pole. Annex B is the home of the *dark* Christmas magic. Not all evil stuff really, just the devices, the spells, the tricks, that didn't turn out so well or had dubious origins in the early days of the North Pole centuries earlier; and a few things that worked all too well.

Annex A is a brightly lit, colorfully festooned (green, red, gold, and silver naturally) expanse reached from a wide staircase leading down from the upper level of the palace. The staircase features a banister strung with lights so bright Dogwater would have wet himself.

Annex B is a mausoleum of brick planted in the center of Annex A. In the early centuries, valiant attempts had been made to brighten it—faux snowflakes, ribbons, and banners were all tried. But the dingy, stained brick seemed to devour these like roasted chestnuts. No amount of decoration would hide the collective memory of what Annex B was, so they gave up. It was hard to mask the memory of dead elves with gay decorations.

Not long after Kris Kringle discovered his gift of giving to the world, he made the even more startling discovery that he had the gift of magic. He didn't age. He never seemed to tire even while carrying around all that... well, that bowl full of jelly. He could move silent as a mouse and nearly as nimbly, despite being nowhere near mouse proportions.

As his gift-giving prowess grew, the area in which he could disburse the toys, clothes and foodstuffs also grew. Word of Santa's anonymous deeds spread—even in those pre-Internet days. It became harder and harder to find secluded locations to make his treasures.

So he traveled north. *Way* north. He walked and walked and walked some more. This was a dubious virtue of his newly increased energy levels. On the long walk, he sang every song he knew. When he ran out of those, he made some up. It's a little know fact that Santa Claus was the original writer of "O 'Tannenbaum," only his version featured an oak tree, rather than a pine tree.

Eventually, Santa arrived at the North Pole and decided to stay. Why not? Everyone had to be somewhere. It was a vast, cold, desolate place, but to Santa it felt like home. It was the most beautiful place Kris Kringle had ever seen, if only for its vastness. The freedom to breathe deeply that open space provides washed over him. Quickly, though, the enormity of the entire journey he'd been on caught up with him. So he sat down on his ample butt. Right there on the ice.

*Now* he was tired. And also cold. A little anyway. Another facet of his increasing magical-ness was a self-regulating body temperature. Still, he set about building a shelter. It occurred to him there might be dangerous animals roaming around—polar bears and what not. He had a feeling he would be here a while **and would** like to put down his tools and his few possessions and needed **a place** to do that. It was time to make his home

Discovering **a paucity** of building materials, he settled on a snow fort, a wind break **really.** Kris Kringle settled down in his shelter and wondered what to do **next.** Eventually, he fell asleep and dreamed of being visited by a band of tiny people.

The next morning Kris Kringle awoke to a band of tiny people. Seven people, no more than three feet high peered at him patiently over the side of his makeshift snow fort. Some had beards, some didn't. Two were women in brightly-colored, fur-lined dresses. The men wore thick wool trousers and jackets, less brightly-colored than the dresses, but no less ornate.

And their smiles. That's what Kris Kringle really saw. These weren't toothy grimaces, nor were they lunatic grins. They were the expressions of those who are supremely happy, but somehow quite relaxed about it.

Santa looked at them wonderingly. They returned the look, but the smiles never faltered.

"Hello there," Santa said to the group. Without realizing it, he was communicating in their language fluently, despite never having seen them before.

"Hello," they said in unison, in perfect high-pitched voices. Santa thought their voices were harmonious peals of so many church bells.

"You're late," one of them grunted, clearly annoyed.

"Um, sorry?" Santa said, bewildered. "Who are you?" he asked.

"Elves," the being said.

"Okay," Kris Kringle said, not understanding, but not necessarily needing an explanation. If they were "elves" that was fine with him.

"Specifically," the elf continued, "my name is Teelor. These are my companions: Lizel, Thaler, Tomli, Bal, Stein, and Joy." Joy was the elf woman and she curtsied slightly as her name was listed.

"I'm overjoyed to meet you all," Kringle said, certain that this was true, though not certain why that should be as he had never heard of them.

"You're late," Teelor said again.

"Pardon me?" Kris Kringle asked.

Teelor looked up as if he were either studying the position of the sun or possibly trying to think of the precise word for what he was thinking. "We've been expecting you, sir," he said by way of explanation. "There is much to do."

St. Nick thought about this. He supposed that, yes, there was much to do. And these elves seemed to know *what exactly* there was to do, so it was best to get on with things. "Well, then, uh..." he stammered.

"Teelor, sir."

"Well, then, Teelor, carry on."

And with that, the legend of Santa Claus as we know it today began.

In the centuries since that first meeting, Kris Kringle learned much of the elven magic, but there was still much he did not know. Initially, he was little more than an observer, watching the elves scurry about mapping out the initial outlines of the North Pole Complex and creating the vast castles and roadways out of simple mounds of dirt and a few stray branches of wood and stone. Over time, as he grew to understand the magic—at least somewhat—he was able to actively participate as a designer and visionary. All he had to do was say something like, "If only we could do this..." or "It would help to have that..." and it would appear.

In the elves' initial plan, instead of eight flying *reindeer*, Santa's transportation was to be a flying boat. The idea was that a boat would have a larger cargo hold than a sleigh, but Santa pointed out that a flying boat would look rather silly (as if a flying sled made a lot more sense). The other suggestion—that Santa ride a flying polar bear—was similarly dismissed as unworkable once it was discovered polar bears are prone to air-sickness.

As the North Pole Complex progressed, and the needs of a global gift-giver became more evident, the magic necessarily became more complex. Not even the elves had considered when they committed to this man how you make it so that a man and reindeer can travel around the world, deliver millions of toys and return home all in one night. The wisest elders among the elves taxed their knowledge on that problem. Some even called upon the darkest elven magic, though when others found out, they were all quietly—and sometimes not so quietly—shunned.

All, that is, except for Teevo. Teevo was equal parts elven brilliance and instability. He knew more incantations, potions, and possessed more pure knowledge of countless subjects including biology, chemistry, alchemy, and metallurgy than any elf alive. He was also crazy.

Teevo would freely admit to being fond of drink and song and speaking in a language only he knew. He claimed to have invented an entire vocabulary and grammar structure for a language which he used quite often when talking to himself, but which he refused to share with anyone else.

Most of the elves whispered uneasily about Teevo—discreetly, of course. He was, after all, an elder, a brilliant one. His wild hair and uncharacteristically dark clothes were bad enough. But with his disturbing habits—muttering his gibberish, picking fights—physical, as well as verbal—most of the elves, with their cheery natures and delicate sensibilities just couldn't handle him.

Santa, on the other hand, put Teevo in charge of his laboratory.

To be a successful, anonymous (more or less) gift-giver, you have to be able to trust people; read them. And Santa could. Elves were a little trickier than humans, but Santa thought he had gotten pretty adept at reading them too in his time at the North Pole. Teevo was eccentric and sometimes off-putting, but Santa believed he could be trusted to do well for the cause.

Some of Teevo's early work cast doubt on this. The completion of each creation was heralded by Teevo with a succession of rapid elven cursing and greeted by everyone else with trepidation. He did create perpetual, self-renewing fuel sources so the North Pole Complex wouldn't have to worry about running out of wood or coal. That was good. But he also invented, for example, toy soldiers that came to life and fired steel-pointed candy canes ("because real world boys are so violent anyway," he said.)

Santa listened patiently to the elves complaints about Teevo, never becoming alarmed even as, over the years, the complaints became more frequent. He would gently admonish Teevo to play well with others, but that was about all.

Eventually, though, even Santa noticed that Teevo's inventions were becoming more, well, *disturbing*. One year, it was a herd of rocking horse-*heads*. Another year, Teevo synthesized an enzyme that would improve the reindeer's stamina and speed. Unfortunately, it also caused them to grow to four times their normal size. The effect, fortunately, was only temporary.

Finally, one year about nine days before Christmas, Teevo shaved off his flowing, unmanageable silvery locks and beard—virtual heresy among the elder elves—and barricaded himself in his lab with his latest device. This was, for the real-worlders, the height of the Industrial Revolution. The elves in many ways were way ahead of the real-worlders on issues of mass production. Teevo, though, thought they could be better.

The device was a small, black box about the size of an adult elf. It sat on a wooden cart, rendering it mobile. Teevo envisioned moving the device around the Complex. The device employed a combination of the steel machinery of the early-dawning industrial age and a fair amount of elven magic—*dark elven magic*. When activated, the device would emit a purple beam that would cause anyone in its path to work ten times faster. Productivity would soar. An entire Christmas worth of toys could be finished in a week. At least that was the idea. Teevo had not yet tried out the device on an actual elf, but he was itching to do so.

"But Teevo," Santa had said when he asked to do a trial run. "Making toys for the children is what we do all year round. Why do we need to finish it all in just a few nights?"

"I tell you, *St. Nicholas*," Teevo began (he had taken to referring to Santa by this particular nom de plume when he was feeling particularly truculent), "there is so much more we elves could be doing *besides making toys*." His nasally voice strained to spit out the last few words. Ironically, though he was Santa's production manager, Teevo was known as a world-class humbug with regard to the trappings of Christmas.

"Like what?" Santa asked, truly surprised that anyone could believe there was more to life than making millions of children happy.

Teevo started to answer. It was so obvious he was right. But he couldn't think of anything to say. Talking to a real-worlder was like trying to balance a *nervell* (elf bowling ball) on the head of a pin. Teevo was speechless. And he *hated* to be speechless. "Oh, bother," he grunted and lurched out of the room. The other elves gasped. For one thing, turning your back on someone in the middle of a conversation was the height of discourteous in elf world. Secondly, you *never* talked back to St. Nicholas. It just wasn't done.

"He's dangerous, sir," Flifle said to Santa when the dust had settled.

"He is...passionate," Santa agreed. "But I think that he has good intentions."

"Yes, sir," Flifle said, though not all that emphatically.

Meanwhile, out in the hallway, Teevo stomped, ran, howled, and cackled, his shockingly bald head flush with anger or manic zeal or both. The mirthless laughing sounds were odd coming from an elf, all high-pitched and frantic. On his tirade, he spoke little, but punched out two elves and kicked a dog. Finally, the rampage ended with the castle-shaking thud of the large door that led to his workshop in the annex.

For the next several hours, the brick-walled enclosure that was Teevo's private lab within the center of the toy-production area's annex remained quiet. This time of year, the castle was never quiet. Teevo was a stern taskmaster; saws and hammers were never still. Until today. All the elves sat, holding their collective breath, waiting for, well, whatever was going to happen.

Just before the dinner bell would call all the elves out of the toy workshop and off to dinner, the door to Teevo's private laboratory burst open. A shrieking Teevo emerged, followed by a billow of dark smoke. The tails and sleeves of his elven waistcoat were on fire and Teevo waved his arms and legs frantically.

Several of the other elves recoiled. A couple of the cooler-headed ones grabbed a tarp and buckets of water to douse the flames.

By then, smoke was pouring from the doorway and through cracks around the lab's windows. The room was dark. Four elves ran in to see what happened.

The explosion that immediately followed killed the four elves where they stood, blowing out the windows of the lab, but leaving the walls intact. The shower of colored glass injured several of the other elves who'd rushed in to help.

In the commotion, a badly-burned Teevo managed to sprint painfully out of the workshop, nearly colliding with Santa who was rushing toward the workshop with Flifle to find out what had rocked the entire North Pole Complex.

Santa grabbed Teevo, starkly staining his bright, crimson coat with soot and blood. Teevo shrieked, "Let go of me."

"Let me help you," Santa insisted, grabbing at Teevo and making him flinch as he made contact with Teevo's blistering arms.

"I don't want your help, old human," Teevo grunted, followed by something—probably cursing—in the elven language. He managed to slip from Santa's grasp, leaving him with only a portion of his blackened, shredded waistcoat. Teevo ran down the hall.

Santa made ready to go after him, but Flifle, hearing the commotion in the workshop, said "Sir, we need to see who else is hurt."

Santa, hesitantly, nodded. They entered the workshop to find a scene Santa could never have begun to imagine. Flames and smoke streamed from the broken windows of Teevo's workshop as the elves, assembly-line fashion, passed buckets of water to put the fire out. Around the edges of the room, elves tended to other bleeding and moaning elves injured in the blast.

Flifle immediately took charge of the team putting out the fire and designated his own deputy, Tula, to see to the medical care. He sent two other elves out to look for Teevo.

Santa simply stood in the center of the room and wept. He wept hard and bitterly. He didn't stop weeping for days.

Once the fire was out, the elves started poking around the remains of the lab and found the bodies. Apparently, Teevo had been working on his device when it caught itself and Teevo on fire and then exploded. The device was a charred ruin with its innards splayed around the room. The reason it exploded was never discovered.

The remains of the dead elves remained in the lab which became a makeshift mausoleum. The elf council decreed that they would not be disturbed as that would desecrate their memory and disrupt travel to the next life. It probably also had to do with the fact that no one really wanted to do the job of going in there to get them.

Teevo's body was eventually found nearly a mile from the Complex, burned, frost-bitten and very dead in the snow, the sickly smirk etched into his features.

Elf lore recorded all of this and passed it on from generation to generation, of course. But eventually, the horror of the event, if not the facts of it, faded from the elven consciousness.

Christmas, in fact, only occurred that year because Mrs. Claus accompanied her husband on his rounds, to keep him alert and focused. This is *never* discussed as it is a major breach of the Christmas code, not to mention a potential public relations nightmare, but there it is.

Santa thought about all this as he stood in a small storage room off the main toy workshop with Flifle and Mrs. Claus. This was the room where many of Teevo's inventions were stored. Most elves thought, or assumed, they were destroyed, and Santa did nothing to dispel the belief.

A big part of Santa had wanted to destroy these things, and it disturbed him greatly to mislead his elves like this. But, at the same time, there was much that could be learned, including the pitfalls of invention, the downside of progress.

"Dearest, are you sure this is necessary?" Santa said.

"Do you still intend to cancel Christmas and give up gift-giving?" Mrs. Claus responded.

Santa didn't need to answer that; didn't *want* to answer that.

"These real-worlders are good people, the child and the adults. But they've lost the spirit and the beauty of Christmas. You can bring it back."

"But..." Santa protested.

"You're Santa Claus," Mrs. Claus said firmly.

"You are, sir," Flifle shrugged.

Santa nodded. "Flifle, are you sure this will work?"

"Ye-yes, sir," Flifle said, though he wasn't sure if Santa was referring to the suit or the plan. Mrs. Claus had talked him into this crazy plan, but his orderly elf nature did not align itself comfortably with crazy plans.

The three of them were looking at an open, silver box. Inside was a neatly folded pair of long johns that appeared to have been made of spun gold.

"Well, there it is," Flifle shrugged and turned as if to leave. No such luck. Seeing the expectant look on Mrs. Claus's face—and the well-toned arms folded across her chest as she deftly moved to block the door, he sighed and gingerly reached inside the box, half afraid the sleeves would reach around his throat like arms and strangle him.

Flifle held the long johns out in front of him and Santa looked at them doubtfully. They were elf size, much too small for him. He said as much.

"The suit is woven with elf magic," Flifle explained. "It will conform to any size."

"I see," Santa said, not really feeling relieved.

"When you put it on," Flifle continued, "I will recite the spell to begin the joining. Your *kevloch* will join with the chosen one's." *Kevloch* was an elven term with no good translation; "soul" or "life force" was pretty close.

The suit had been an early Teevo invention from back when the elves were still trying to solve the problem of how exactly a mere mortal like Santa was going to get to all those homes around the world in one night. The idea was that Santa would not really go anywhere—at least not by walking or running. Instead, the suit would allow his *kevloch* to sort of jump from person to person around the world. Santa could then direct them to deliver gifts as he directed. There were a number of problems with this, not least of which was the issue of taking over innocent souls, even for the most selfless of purposes. The potential for misuse if the suit should fall into the wrong hands was too great and Santa had forbade it. Now, it seemed, the very thing that Santa had feared would undo his good work, might well redeem it.

"Well, let's get on with it," Kris Kringle said.

Flifle gave a look to Mrs. Claus that seemed to say, "Are we really going to do this?"

In response, she nodded firmly. Then she turned to her husband. "I love you greatly," she said.

"And I you," Kris Kringle said. Then he turned to Flifle. "Now, please."

Flifle exhaled deeply and closed his eyes. "*Lemargi!*" he said.

The suit twisted out of Flifle's hands and walked on nonexistent feet over to Santa. The suit raised its empty sleeves as if to give the much larger man a bear hug. It expanded and enveloped Kris Kringle giving off a shower of sparks of gold, silver, and blue.

"My goodness," Santa said simply, out of surprise, not pain. The vortex of sparks around him spun faster and faster, until the individual photons melded into one continuous streak of brightness. Mrs. Claus and Flifle instinctively stepped back to avoid being burned by the flickering shower, though the sparks actually were cool to the touch.

"*Heavem lenari ogash!*" Flifle said after a pause, having almost forgotten what he was doing.

The Santa Claus typhoon wound tighter, twisted faster. All at once Santa was consumed, lost in a shower of festive, twinkling droplets of light.

At that same moment, somewhere in Indiana, U.S.A., Milo Vestibule, seated in his worn recliner, dropped his rum glass, disappeared through a vortex of brilliant color, and entered the annals of North Pole history.

# DECEMBER 10

It took four emails, five phone calls, and an as yet undefined favor owed to someone named either Barty or Marty, but Cameron finally found the name and number for Dr. Whipple's hotel in Switzerland. So far this morning, he had left three messages. For good measure, he had also emailed the doctor's office mailbox four times. He put nothing in the text box, just the phrase "IF I ONLY HAD A BRAIN" in the subject line. He hoped the classic reference, coupled with the whimsical nature of his plea for help, would entice Dr. Whipple to break her vacation-imposed communication blackout.

Cameron was scared. He had known for a long time that he was not okay, of course. Mood swings, paranoia, and obsessiveness were not new. Even hearing the occasional voice was not all that unusual anymore—although Webster Stanhope, a fully three-dimensional, animated, visual hallucination, was a step beyond anything he had ever experienced before. He was reasonably certain that the DSM-IV, the commonly-used diagnostic manual for medical disorders, listed "seeing talking, floating, goldfish" among the symptoms of being "loopy."

But now things were getting serious. The visitation trial was barely more than two weeks away. If the judge thought he was nuts, there'd be no way he could keep Susan from moving across the goddamn ocean with his little girl.

And now he had a court-appointed visitation supervisor to deal with. True, it was just Susan's dirty old Uncle Milo, but it was still...wrong somehow. The celebrity news shows had had a field day with that development in the case, even the ones that were usually way more interested in Paris Hilton or Tom Cruise than dorky guys who wrote books. He had, per the usual, declined all interviews. There was no way he would call Ben Steene back. He took the man's card just so he could get out of that restaurant before Steene saw him throttle the neck or an imaginary goldfish—or throttle whatever they have in place of necks.

And while all this was going on, Marjorie Whipple was skiing the Alps, eating bonbons and Swiss cheese and then checking the time on one of those precision-tuned Swiss clocks.

While waiting for Dr. Whipple to come to her senses and call him back, Cameron decided he might as well try and work on the new novel, which he was now calling *Frustration*.

Back when the book was called *Inspiration*, it had been about a boy and his dog. Really. It wasn't a "Lassie" type story though. In his book, Cameron had intended to tell an inspiring (hence the original title), if somewhat far-fetched, story of a man who commits many sins and alienates many people. The man gets a shot at redemption when God comes down from Heaven in the form of a valet at the man's country club. God the Valet tells the man he's fated to die in a month from something which Cameron the author had not yet determined and that he must make his amends before he goes. To do that, God proposes that the man spend two weeks observing life from the point of view of a dog. It would be either a golden retriever or a simple mutt. Cameron had not yet decided.

In the book's present incarnation—*Frustration*—a grumpy old man shot the man/dog in the next chapter. Then ate him.

"All right, asshole," Cameron said to the computer in his study, though he was acutely aware that if anyone else were in the room, they would think he was having one of his hallucinations again. "Don't fuck with me this time."

Cameron knew he was serious about writing today because it hadn't even occurred to him to spend his writing session on the enclosed porch with the laptop computer. That's what he did when he was working, but wasn't all that serious about it. Mostly what he did during those sessions was sit there and stare out at the trees, half-heartedly tapping the keys now and then.

So, instead, Cameron sat now in his study, amongst dusty first editions of a bunch of books he'd never read, along with a few "good" books and many pulp novels and trade paperbacks that he had read. He tried as best as he could to summon up *the writer* as he used to be, banging out twenty pages (ten of which were good, ten of which were fair) before breakfast.

He needed to get on track, to write something good; really good. He needed to be a success again. Hell, he needed to be *something* again. He needed to show the world he wasn't a crazy person to be written off in the "where are they now" columns. And, most of all, he needed to show his little girl that her old man was a good dad. He wasn't really sure how writing a great book would do that last bit, but he needed to do it anyway.

Finally, he put his hands on the keyboard and typed: "The grumpy old man *tried* to shoot Conrad Brewster, now low to the ground in his canine form, but missed."

It was a promising start. He continued.

"And Conrad knew-"

The phone rang.

Fuck.

Cameron found the cordless phone off its stand under a tattered copy of *A Christmas Carol*, which he had tried reading the night before in a vain effort to incite some holiday cheer. However, the descriptions of Scrooge's hallucinations and hearing voices and dying cold, lonely deaths struck a little too close to home.

He depressed the "talk" button on the phone and said, "Hello."

"Cameron, dear, how are you?" Wendy the agent said in an impossibly deep voice.

"The book's not done yet, Wendy." Cameron's tone was equal parts annoyance and wit—as in "Ha, ha. Yeah, funny story about that. You know that book I've been writing that's years past deadline? Yeah, it's not done."

"Cameron, I don't *always* just call to hound you about your deadline, do I?"

Cameron wanted to say "Yes, of course you do, you relentless gnat," but that was too much. He liked Wendy. Instead, he said, "No, sometimes you just call to nag about life in general."

Wendy laughed. Her laugh was even huskier than her voice. "Seriously, hon, how is the book coming?" Now Wendy's tone was half-serious and only half-light. "I'm just asking just because...I mean, you sailed past your real 'deadline' like a year ago."

"It'll be done when it's done." Cameron was hoping this sound arty, but it probably just sounded like a dodge.

Wendy the agent sighed. "It'd be easier to wring you neck if we were in the same room. Really, Cam, why don't you just come back to New York? It's home."

Great an agent as Wendy was—the only reason he still had anything you could call a career was because of her—for the past ten years it had driven Cameron crazy the way she called him "Cam."

"Seriously, everyone wants you back. Hildy has been asking about you. And this town is so screwed up, you can't hail a cab without trampling seven psychiatrists. We can take care of you."

"Hildy is…" he wanted to say "a vampire" or "not Susan," but instead said, "a little much for my taste. And as for the rest of them, I'm sure they can talk about me a couple thousand miles behind my back more easily than if I was in the same room."

Wendy clucked peevishly. "Cam, you know everyone here loves you."

"The old me. The one that isn't crazy. The one that actually writes."

"Dearest…"

Awkward pause.

"'People' magazine called again," Wendy said, happy to change the conversation.

"No."

"Cam, you need to do some press. A nice little where-are-you-now profile. You're fit, you're healthy."

Was there a catch in Wendy's voice?

"Maybe talk up the new project," Wendy was saying.

Yes, there was a definite stutter on the word "new."

"Not now. Not with this thing with Holly going on," Cameron said.

"It might help. The doting father making a public appeal for his little daughter."

"It's exploitative and those stories are always pathetic."

"Well, if you won't do it for your child, then…" She paused. "Cam, sales are off. There probably won't be another run for *Quality, Not Quantity*. The *Sandstorm* movie project is being retooled."

Cameron sighed. "I'll think about it, okay?"

"A good family crisis story could help."

"Thanks for the wonderfully evil idea."

Wendy sounded wounded, but only superficially. "Cameron, you know I didn't mean it like that. I just want to see my favorite author back on top. I know the new book could be number one." She probably said that a lot.

"We'll see, okay? I better get back to work on my 'number one'."

"That's my boy. 'Bye, dear."

Cameron hung up the phone and went to pee, just as promised.

He came back to the study and sat. The idea of using his fight for Holly in any way that could be construed as a means to sell books was, of course, repulsive. On the other hand, CAMERON JONES—BACK ON TOP— headlining an article about the author's triumphant return to the literary world was seductive.

No, it wasn't.

Yes, it was. It *really* was.

No, he would keep this affair private. He was fortunate in that the local media were not all that interested in the case—a benefit of the cloistered, mildly repressed, Midwestern sensibility. The big media outlets rarely deigned to make the trip to a "flyover" state like Indiana just to cover what had been so far a pretty un-dramatic court case (for public consumption, not for the parties) featuring a washed-up, mentally unbalanced author. Now if he could just beat Ben Steene over the head with a frozen brisket and throw him in a dumpster, he'd be set.

He could take the idea of never publishing another best-seller. Hell, he'd gleefully print out the half-finished (okay, one-third) mess on his computer right now, burn it, and piss out the flames just to be free of it.

He could not, however, stomach the possible loss of his daughter. And to avoid that, he needed to show the judge (1) a viable source of income; (2) an absence of pissing in unnatural settings.

This also meant no more Webster Stanhope or anything else he couldn't reach out and touch. He could feel the psychotic little bastard, with his filthy verbiage and eerie fins that seemed to flap furiously as if independent of his body; the fins were practically tickling his ear canals from within his mind. Webster was waiting to spring out. Cameron wanted to jab a pencil into each ear and impale the thing.

Then, because he didn't know what else to do, he turned back to the manuscript. A pause to re-center and then:

"The grumpy old man *tried* to shoot Conrad Brewster in his canine form, but missed. And Conrad knew-"

The doorbell rang.

Fuck. Again.

Cameron flew down the stairs, determined to throttle whoever was at the door, even if it was his own mother—unlikely as that was, given she was dead. He crossed through the living room and trampled a mess of decorations Dogwater had not yet finished putting up. Two colored light bulbs which Dog had painstakingly vetted for functionality in preparation for hanging on the tree which wasn't yet there crunched under Cameron's left sneaker.

The doorbell was again in mid-ring when Cameron yanked the door open and glared out to the porch, only to find that he had to adjust his anger beams downward as the doorbell-ringer was shorter than anticipated.

Cameron stared directly into the eyes of a Dickens character. In fact, when the boy of nine or ten spoke, Cameron at first thought the boy had said, "God bless us, everyone."

Actually what the boy said, mumbled really, was "You wanna buy a wreath?" This was punctuated by half-heartedly holding up a plastic wreath about twelve inches in diameter with fake red holly berries glued at three and nine o'clock. "It's so we can get a class trip to Washington DC."

On this particular day, the boy could have said that buying that one crappy wreath would set about a chain reaction leading to the end of all cancer, and it wouldn't have swayed Cameron. Still, it was Christmas...

Cameron looked at the wreath.

Nope, still not swayed.

He looked at the boy. The boy picked intently at his right nostril.

Nope.

Is this what the holiday season had been reduced to in America? Kids schlepping crappy, tawdry decorations from house to house? What the hell kind of world was this anyway?

He was ready to unload his fury; fury at life, fury at the holiday season, and fury at the food channel on cable. He didn't quite understand that last one, but it infuriated him nonetheless.

Cameron looked at the wreath again.

He looked at the boy again.

Fishing into his pocket, he pulled out a bill and tossed it to the boy without looking at it.

"Keep your wreath," Cameron said, slamming the door.

The boy sprinted off to tell his buddy working the next block about the crazy man who'd just given him fifty dollars for nothing.

In the foyer, Cameron turned, marched back through the living room—taking out another bulb on the light string. He flopped down in an overstuffed easy chair in the corner and took advantage of a moment to sulk.

Absently, Cameron turned on the TV. The food channel—that bunch of bastards—was running a twelve-hour "Taste of Christmas" marathon.

CLICK

Channel 91 had one of those shows where a pop psychiatrist makes people cry with witty—but insightful—put-downs. It occurred to Cameron that it would be easier to get on one of those shows than to get hold of his own real psychiatrist.

CLICK

Channel 27 had a cartoon where, near as Cameron could tell, a village of good squirrels was trying to save Christmas from a group of mean squirrels; the mean ones indicated by the fact that their eyebrows were drawn on their faces in a "v" formation.

CLICK

On channel 82, Santa Claus was telling a group of children the "true meaning of Christmas" while feeding a carrot to a reindeer.

Cameron studied the jolly old elf. Doddering, stupid fool. What did Santa Claus know about the meaning of Christmas? Joy? Peace on Earth? Good will? None of that was what Christmas was about, Cameron thought.

Christmas is about malls full of whiny kids and short-tempered parents. It's about lame holiday gatherings that are the same every year, including the bitching about them the other eleven months of the year.

Christmas is about being alone. Alone and lost at the "happiest" time of the year.

But ultimately, Cameron thought, Christmas is about reinforcing what's already in your life. If that's joy and peace, fine. More likely, it's pain and torment. That, however, is probably not suitable greeting card material.

CLICK

The picture snapped out of existence as Cameron turned off the TV. "But what would Holly say?" he heard himself ask of no one.

Holly LOVED Christmas—Santa Claus, trees, candy canes, presents, the whole bit. And Cameron loved Holly.

Cameron was gripped by a great insight. He bolted up the stairs, the TV remote jettisoned across the living room.

In the study, he pulled open desk drawers, letting the contents fall to the floor until he found a large, black marker. He stood in the middle of the study, spinning in a tight circle, scanning the walls and floor. Finally, he moved to a poster of Tolstoy riding a bicycle with a flower between his teeth and wearing a party hat. He tore it down and wrote on the newly-cleared patch of wall in big, block letters:

HOLLY LOVES CHRISTMAS
CAMERON LOVES HOLLY
ERGO, CAMERON LOVES CHRISTMAS

There it was. True logicians my question the validity of the syllogism, but there it was. His addled mind dug syllogisms. Wenn diagrams, the little circles within circles were also awesome. For example: a small circle labeled something like "All door-to-door Christmas carolers" surrounded by a larger circle labeled "schmucks." This means all carolers are schmucks, but not all schmucks are carolers. Graphs were good too. Charts, not so much. Cameron tried to convince himself that IT, all of it—court battles, holiday-related anxiety, assorted mental disorders—that it was all answered by those three simple lines he'd written on the wall. It appealed to his new outlook on life.

Retrieving some fresh putty stuff used to hang posters from the one drawer he hadn't yet yanked out of the desk, Cameron hung the poster back on the wall, slightly to the left of where it had been so as not to obscure the syllogism.

He sat on the floor, back against the drawer-less desk. On top of a stack of magazines on the floor was a trade publication with a portrait of a cartoon Santa Claus on the cover and the banner "A Ho-Ho-Host of Writing Ideas Inside!" Cameron picked up the magazine with his left hand and scratched absently at a patch of auburn hair behind his right ear with the right hand. Then with that same hand, he balled the cover of the magazine into a fist, ripping it away from the staples binding the magazine in the middle. He tossed the balled-up Santa Claus portrait across the room where it landed inside one of the drawers formerly in the desk.

Climbing back into his desk chair with what sounded way too much like a middle-aged grunt, Cameron turned to the wretched Conrad Brewster, man-dog, living out his fate on the computer monitor.

"And Conrad knew," Cameron resumed, "that bullets would not puncture the heaven-sent beagle coat he had been given. And the eggs mixed with his dog food made the coat shiny too."

*God, this book stinks,* he thought.

The phone rang.

Thank God!

"What?" Cameron said when he picked up the phone.

"Cameron, it's Dr. Whipple," the voice said in a sleep-inducing lilt.

"Doctor, what a surprise," Cameron said, genuinely stunned. "Are you still in Switzerland?"

"Yes," Dr. Whipple said flatly, without so much as a "the weather is lovely" or "I'm having a glorious time," or even "wish you were here." Instead, she said simply, "My office tells me you've been rather distressed."

"Yeah, I would've talked to the on-call doc, but..." Cameron paused.

"But what, Cameron?" Dr. Whipple sounded mildly distracted. Cameron could hear in the background distinct clinking noises like either cups rattling during tea service or wine being poured and passed around some Swiss chalet.

"But I hate that guy," Cameron finished.

It was true. In fact, Dr. Whipple couldn't really blame him. Dr. Frank Pug, her on-call relief, was about one more corporate accounting scandal away from financial ruin and was, well, rather bitter about it. His therapeutic technique was along the lines of, "Yeah, well, you think you got problems...".

"Cameron, I only have a short time," Dr. Whipple said. "The party...er, I have an appointment."

Cameron stood and started walking around the room, cordless phone to his ear, ironically unsure what to say now that he'd finally got hold of his doctor.

"Tell me what's distressing you, Cameron," Dr. Whipple said.

"Am I going to lose my daughter?" Cameron asked with no preamble.

"Holly?" Dr. Whipple asked, pausing only briefly to conjure up the name of the child. "Has something happened?"

"The judge says I have to have a supervisor during my visits until the trial."

"I'm sorry," Dr. Whipple said. It sounded genuine enough to Cameron, but he could hear her whisper a refusal of more dessert. "Who's it going to be?"

"What?" Cameron asked, then remembering what he'd been saying, said, "Oh, uh, it's Susan's Uncle Milo."

"What do you think about that?" Dr. Whipple asked.

Before he answered, a thought occurred to Cameron. "Doctor?" he asked. "Are you on a cell phone?"

"No, Cameron, it's the phone in my hotel room," Dr. Whipple answered with the grace of someone used to fielding obscure questions from patients.

Cameron sighed, relieved from the suspicion of bugged cell phones Dogwater had managed to plant in him.

Dr. Whipple remembered Uncle Milo. He had driven Susan to the one session of couples therapy that Cameron and Susan had tried before the divorce was final. For the entire session, Uncle Milo sat in the waiting room reciting bawdy limericks to himself or blatantly ogling any women who passed by. Uncle Milo had inspired a pretty good paper that Dr. Whipple presented at the next psychiatric conference.

"So are you okay with this arrangement?" Dr. Whipple asked.

"I can't stand it," Cameron replied, feeling an increase in blood pressure as he thought about it.

"Have you had a visit yet with supervision?"

"No."

"Then how do you know you can't stand it?"

"Everything's just so hard," Cameron said. "The manuscript is shit. And then at the restaurant-" he started to tell the doctor about Webster Stanhope, angry goldfish of his dreams—but stopped himself.

"What happened at the restaurant, Cameron?" Dr. Whipple asked, then said to someone in the room with her either "My coat is over there" or "The goat is on my hair."

"Uh, I couldn't decide whether to order the lamb chops or the linguini," Cameron finished. "They both reminded me of Susan." It was ridiculous, but shrinks would buy just about anything.

"Have you talked to her about any of this?"

"Susan? Uh, yeah, I *don't* think so," Cameron said.

"Maybe you should."

Cameron barked a gruff, derisive laugh.

"Cameron, are you doing the relaxation exercises?"

"Yes," he said, which was sort of true. He liked the deep-breathing one. If you died it really fast, you could make yourself light-headed.

"And the sedatives and meds?"

"Don't like 'em. The tranquilizers make me sleepy," Cameron deadpanned.

"Ha. Ha. Ha," Dr. Whipple said. "Everything will be fine, Cameron. You know it will. Keep taking your meds. I'll see you in three weeks."

"Okay," Cameron said, not entirely sure that it was fine and almost certain he would not be taking any meds. "I guess...never mind."

"Is there something you're not telling me, Cameron?" Dr. Whipple asked.

Cameron thought again about mentioning Webster Stanhope, then thought better of it. The judge had still not said if he was going to let Wally Bass call Dr. Whipple as a witness to testify.

"Goodbye, Cameron," Dr. Whipple said and was gone.

Fuck.

Cameron turned back to the computer screen. "'Heaven-sent beagle coat' my ass," he said, talking to the manuscript. Hands on the keyboard, he had deleted his last line and typed, "He slammed one slug into Conrad Brewster's head—BLAM!—dead."

Somehow, Cameron felt better.

Several miles away, Susan Wentworth was in the living room straightening up in the aftermath of a fierce battle between the military action figures and the fashion dolls that Holly had staged. It wasn't clear who won, but the armed forces had taken major casualties, though they were stunningly accessorized.

Susan picked up Holly's purple school bag in which she kept her most vital kindergarten papers, spilling the contents thereof onto the floor because Holly had not buckled the latch.

As she was picking up the assorted, pasted construction paper crafts and drawings, she spied Holly's Santa Claus letter. Eager to get a tip on what her daughter wanted for Christmas, she scanned the sheet. Susan's eyes immediately found the crayon version of fourteen-point bold print: *And Mommy says she wants some purfum, but I think what she really, really, really wants is DADDY (ME TOO)*

Susan shook her head—silly girl—smiled and put the letter back in the bag, but she couldn't help wondering:

Was it possible?

# DECEMBER 11

Dogwater Hunt owned two pair of pants and four shirts. Yet, every rental he ever signed a lease on had to have a walk-in closet. Standard closets just didn't give him a proper night's rest.

Years ago, Dogwater, in a fit of paranoia induced by his most recent abduction by aliens, took to sleeping in his bedroom closet. They can see you *everywhere*. But the idea was that a small enclosure like a closet could be suitably camouflaged perhaps long enough for a careless government bureaucrat alien to overlook you.

When they lived in the trailer together, Roberta had not been shy about her thoughts on the stupidity of this. After the eviction, she had decided to go live with her on-again-off-again boyfriend, a middle-aged retired salesman and aging playboy. This was just fine with Dogwater.

When Dogwater searched for his new apartment, he'd worked hard to find one that had closets with ample leg room. The first thing he did when he finally moved into one, after conning the landlord into giving him until next month to pay the first month's rent, was put up aluminum foil in the closet. The foil would shield him from the alien scans when he slept. The oak in the sliding double doors of the closet, coupled with the foil, might provide just enough protection from detection, or at least allow enough time for his alien alarm to go off so he could flee to one of the safe zones strategically and discretely being built around the globe. They were disguised as coffee houses.

The alien alarm was basically a radio antenna tuned to the frequencies at which Dogwater and his fellow trackers suspected alien transmissions occurred. When aliens scanned the apartment, the signal would trigger the alarm. The alarm was just a cowbell on a string wired into the computer.

The computer was programmed to sound the alarm, which would trigger a switch that tugged on the string and made the cowbell ring.

In six years, the cowbell had barely moved except when the window was open. The cow bell and tin foil did not stop the abductions, but it was the only known line of defense.

The computer to which the alien alarm was rigged sat on a card table in the bedroom. Most of what Dogwater owned was in the bedroom except the couch with no legs in the living room and the box of fudge in the refrigerator. Dogwater Hunt loved a good piece of fudge, as evidenced by the still lingering traces of a significant case of adolescent acne.

A second computer sat on the table as well. This one was running a program that analyzed radio signals for signs of ordered patterns which indicated they were deliberately transmitted; in other words, alien transmissions. This computer also had an alarm; a bit more sophisticated one that simply made a dignified computer beep when it found something. The computer was pretty silent most of the time.

This evening, a gentle snow flurry blew around outside as Dogwater sat on the floor of the living room. The couch with no legs also had no cushions, but did have an ominous black, reeking stain permeating the material. The room did have one lawn chair, but no coffee table (which was just as well since Dogwater was trying—and failing—to get off coffee ever since the article posted on *Dark Matters* the year before documenting that coffee producers were part of a cartel of drug pushers seeking to addict people to the caffeinated goodness.).

Dogwater sat amidst an array of star charts and print-outs full of numbers anyone else would think were printer-inspired gibberish. Lars Heimdal's journal sat open on the floor next to him, the spine strained in a flagrantly abusive way that would have driven book-snob Cameron Jones nuts, sticky notes marking several of the pages. The print-outs were radio signal data the computer had been analyzing. Dog was excited about the repeated anomalous patterns that had been appearing the last couple weeks. There was definite alien chatter going on and it was getting stronger. He just couldn't figure out where it was coming from or what it meant.

Dogwater was looking for disruptions in the star fields. His theory was that even if you couldn't see the alien spacecraft, they would cause minuté disruptions in the star patterns that could be detected. Dogwater, of course, didn't have computers that could do that, but he knew people who knew people who knew people who did. Alien hunters are a persistent, but deeply underground, lot. Coming into the light would only mean mocking and ridicule. One day, though, he was sure all this secretive work would be vindicated. It had to be. It seemed sometimes his sanity depended on it.

Dogwater sat cross-legged in the pile of papers, wearing shorts despite the bitter temperatures outside and steady, sixty-five degree temperature inside. Alien-hunting being not very lucrative, it was best to avoid high heating bills. Dog tugged absently at the short hairs of his goatee under his chin as he examined a particularly intriguing piece of highly classified government data. Alien hunters who know people who know people who know other people willing to commit felonies are the luckiest people in the world.

The apartment door swung open, letting in a blast of the Midwest's finest chilled air, but Dog barely noticed. Izzy Carmichel came in holding a large pizza and a twelve pack of the cheapest beer available at the local mega-mart. He kicked the door shut with his left foot, leaving a slushy, dirty, rock salt encrusted footprint on it.

"Fuck, it's cold **out** there," Izzy said, by way of greeting.

"Hmm," Dogwater replied.

"What you doin'?" Izzy asked, setting the pizza box down on the nearest stack of printouts.

"Not there!" Dogwater shouted, kicking the box off the papers with his left foot. He grimaced at the pizza grease stain in the documents, not at all concerned that the grease was now staining the carpet. Ah, the freedom of being just a renter.

"Excuuuuuuse me!" Izzy said in his best, vintage Steve Martin. The two men had spent most of the day watching a "Saturday Night Live" marathon on the comedy channel. He set the twelve pack next to the pizza box. "I would put that in the refrigerator, but in this ice box you live in, I don't think it matters much." He took a beer for himself.

"Hmmm," Dogwater said.

Izzy shook his head and helped himself to a slice of the taco pizza. With the other hand, he started picking up a few of Dogwater's pages. Dog grabbed them back without taking his eyes from the page he was working on. Izzy was impressed to see him take a piece of pizza the same way, without losing a single bit of the toppings.

Izzy parked himself in the lawn chair and finished off the piece of pizza in his hand. "Want to watch the game?" he asked.

"No," Dogwater said.

"Whoa, an actual word."

"Bite me," Dogwater said.

"Two words! I'm speechless!" Izzy cried. "But also hungry." He took another slice of pizza.

A few more seconds passed.

"Son of a bitch!" Dogwater said.

"Hey, there's still a lot of pizza left, man. Relax." In truth, Dogwater had barely touched his first piece.

"Look at this," Dogwater said, clutching a sheaf of papers and struggling to a kneeling position next to the lawn chair, the piece of pizza that had been on his knee flopping—topping side down—onto the floor. He thrust the papers toward Izzy.

"The Galactic Center is moving!"

"No shit," Izzy said, nonplussed.

"It's simple. Why didn't I see it before? We're in the Milky Way Galaxy, right?"

"If you say so."

"The Galactic Center of the galaxy is at right ascension 17:45.6, declination -28: 56, okay? And the Galactic North Pole is at right ascension 12: 51.4 and declination +27: 07. That never changes. I mean, for epoch 2000.0."

"Whatever, dude. There any pizza left?"

Dogwater ignored him, but went on with his presentation. "Plus, the solar system completes one orbit around the galaxy every 220 million years, assuming 250 kilometers per second."

"Two-hundred-twenty million?" Izzy said. "That'd be a good number for the lottery winnings I'm gonna nail next week."

Dogwater still ignored him. "But this data shows that for one second each night—not even that, more like a fraction of second—the distance between Galactic Center and Galactic North Pole is..." he paused, hardly able to contain himself. "Zero," he finished. He shook his head.

"Zero? You mean the galaxy shrinks down to nothing for one second and then expands again?" Izzy was understanding this better than he would ever have guessed. He was clearly stoned. He never would have gotten it sober.

"Hell, yeah! It's happening every so often. No pattern to it, except that it always happens on Christmas Eve. Looks like it has been for as long this stuff has been recorded. Maybe longer."

"But why?"

"Well, the best way to travel a long distance is-"

"The Pontiac Grand Am," Izzy finished, chuckling to himself.

"No, man, the best way to travel is to not travel at all. You just bring your destination to you. Squish the galaxy down to the size you want, do your business, and put it back."

"This is that alien shit again, isn't it?" Izzy said, consuming half a slice of pizza in one bite.

Dogwater sighed. He'd been through this with Izzy many times, just as he had with countless others.

"How can you be so sure it's shit?" Dogwater asked.

"Martians coming down here and running around? It's stupid." Izzy gnawed on a pizza crust.

"Why?"

"Just is. Little bug-eyed fuckers shoving things up your ass and then disappearin'."

Dogwater bristled. That comment struck a little too close to home. "It's not, well, it's not like that. Not exactly. Not always."

Izzy laughed hard and loud. "I forgot, man. You been up in one of those spaceships ain't you?"

Dogwater chose not to answer. He had, of course, but an answer in the affirmative now would just fuel the mockery. Instead, he said, "With all the wonders in the world, never mind the hard science that I could show you... Think about Stonehenge, the Bermuda Triangle, UFO sightings, a species like human beings for God's sake. How can you still not believe it's possible?"

"You sayin' aliens made all that stuff? Maybe we're all aliens, man?" Izzy asked.

"I'm saying a lot of things. But, yeah, maybe life on Earth as we know it actually emerged first somewhere else."

Izzy really laughed at that. "Woo! Look at me. I'm an alien! I can shoot lasers out my asshole!" Izzy's laughter mutated into a coughing jag. He even dropped his pizza on the floor, then promptly picked it back up, brushed off a hair of indeterminate origin and took a bite. The "five second rule" assured that the food was not contaminated from the fall.

Dogwater smiled. He knew how to win this point. "So, if you don't have alien origins, then I guess you're one of God's creatures?" Dogwater asked in a calm that nicely countered Izzy's mirth.

Izzy took off his cap, smoothed his hair and put the hat back on, then asked, innocently enough, "What was that, man?"

"Well, if you're not descended from aliens, you must be one of God's creations, right?"

Izzy blinked and offered a mirthless "No."

"Well, then where'd you come from?"

Discomfort twinged just beneath the surface of Izzy's skin, making the surface heat up just a bit. He disliked the word "God" almost as much as the implications of "God." Even when he cursed, he always insisted that he used the word "God" in lowercase form.

"Evolution, man," Izzy muttered.

"Okay, but who or what put the first humans here?"

Izzy blinked. Glanced at the pizza box, then at his friend.

"Man, let's watch TV," Izzy said, picking up the remote.

Dogwater smiled and reached for more pizza.

After back to back episodes of a show on the science channel where people—mostly guys—blow stuff up almost randomly just so they can explain the science of it, Dogwater drifted back to his data and Izzy drifted into a third beer.

As Izzy lazily scanned through the channels, offering mostly negative commentary on the quality of the offerings, he suggested half-heartedly, "Want to play video games?"

Dogwater had, as it happens, one of the newest versions of a Japanese game console; a purchase made possible by the sale of the only article for which he had ever made any money to an obscure, underground government conspiracy mag that—amazingly—had funds to pay for such things—before it went belly up. The article was titled "Jabba the Hutt and Henry Kissinger: Switched at Birth?" and held the thesis that alien portrayals in movies and TV were often based on actual people which could in turn mean that people were based on actual aliens. Even Dogwater thought some of the data he used—not all, but some—was specious. However, the article netted him a cool two-hundred dollars. But he felt so guilty about taking money for his life's work, that he blew it all on the game console and a game disc, only to have his electricity turned off for a month for nonpayment of his bill.

"No, thanks," Dog said in response to the invitation.

"Aw, c'mon. We could play somethin' where aliens come down from Mars and stick stuff in your ass." This set off a new round of laughter, followed by a coughing fit. Izzy Carmichel's views on extraterrestrial life in the cosmos were pretty much framed by the potential of a life form to insert something in the anal cavity of another life form.

"Fuck you," Dogwater said.

The laughter sputtered to a tapered end. "Okay, okay. I'm sorry, man." Then, in lieu of a peace pipe, Izzy offered, "You wanna light up?"

Dogwater sighed. "I told you, not in the apartment. I don't do that shit and the cops watch this building all the time." He didn't elaborate whether that was because of him or the other tenants.

"Yeah, probably got the place bugged," Izzy said, presenting it as a joke, but not entirely sure it wasn't true.

A few more silent minutes of Izzy staring at the TV and Dogwater cursing at one anomaly or another in his data. Then inspiration struck Izzy.

"Hey, man, check it out. I wrote another haiku." Izzy was, to be fair, pretty well known for his haiku. Still, Dogwater was wary.

"This better not feature my ass," Dogwater warned.

Izzy swore it didn't. He sat up straight in the lawn chair, cleared his throat and recited:

Hey, there, aliens.

You, way up there in the sky.

Where you probing now?

"Guess I lied, man," Izzy laughed.

Dogwater beaned him with a crumpled print-out.

"Seriously, man, do you really expect to find anything looking at all these numbers and stuff?"

"He-it's out there," Dogwater said. "The Santa Claus aliens are real. I know it."

"More of that 'faith' stuff, huh?"

"I suppose it is."

"How much you think the press would pay for a picture of your 'Santa Claus'?"

Dogwater shrugged. "The so-called 'mainstream' press wouldn't touch it. Some papers might pay a few hundred, some maybe thousands. I know a couple websites that have raised donations and offer a pretty good reward for incontrovertible proof of the 'Santa Claus.' Mostly, though, people will probably just make fun of it. But someday, people will listen..."

"Thousands, huh?" Izzy said, becoming slightly more interested.

"Yeah," Dogwater said cautiously. "But I only said that 'cause you asked. I'm not doing this for money."

Izzy nodded slowly. Then grinned.

"And *you're* not doing it for the money either," Dogwater said, not liking that grin.

"Yeah, yeah," Izzy said with the air of someone who can't imagine that anyone would have a different impression.

"You are still gonna help me, aren't you?" Dogwater asked. "I need that equipment."

"Yeah, I know," Izzy said. "GPS, DVD recorders, telescopes, lights, blah, blah, blah. I got your list."

"Science is about sharing knowledge and truth with the world, not making money," Dogwater said, fully aware it sounded cliché, but unable to come up with a better response.

On the television, some heavily bearded guys in shorts welded sheets of metal onto a stripped down chassis of some sort of formerly moving vehicle. An announcer had just started explaining how the "Scream-mobile" was taking shape when the warehouse in which the guys were working and everything in it seemed to wink out into a black void of non-existence. Or maybe the TV shut off.

"Did you do that?" Dogwater said.

"No, man. The remote's over there." Sure enough, the remote was sitting on top of the now empty pizza box several feet away. Dogwater scooped it over to himself with his left foot and pressed the power button. When that elicited no response, he tried all the other buttons, which also did nothing to stir the blackness filling his television screen.

"Dead batteries?" Izzy suggested.

"No, I just changed them."

"Well, boy, looks like you got some dead air," Izzy said, cackling with amusement.

Dogwater grimaced. "Shit." He worked the buttons on the remote even faster as if performing some sort of electronic CPR. Izzy half expected Dogwater to start blowing into it. Nothing worked. He crawled over to the TV and played with the buttons on the set to no avail. An inspection of the outlet revealed it was working fine too.

"It's dead," Dogwater pronounced with all the solemnity of the doctors on the medical drama they could be watching if the television still worked.

"Guess that aliens-for-cash-money don't sound so bad now, does it?"

Dogwater sighed. "Izzy, go home."

"Might as well," Izzy shrugged. "You'll need some time alone to mourn." He stood, laughing again, and clapped Dogwater on the shoulder. "See ya, man." With that he picked up his parka and left.

Resolute, Dogwater tried to reanimate the dead television remote to no avail. Since electronics were such these days that it cost more to repair a broken item than to go out and buy a new one (*Dark Matters* had done a whole exposé on that little conspiracy), he supposed he would be doing a little shopping.

Shopping with what? Everything he made at the video store that he didn't spend on rent at Crapola Village or frozen burritos went to fund his research projects for *Dark Matters*. Besides, he had a long list of things he needed more than a television; a car for example. The van was on its last legs. Some furniture would be nice too. And a pair of pants that cost more than a quarter.

He could ask Cameron for some money, but would Cameron give it? Of course, he would. That's why he couldn't ask. Dog crashed into Cameron's life when Cameron found him on a research project and he just never left. Dogwater ate Cameron's food, slept on his floor frequently and borrowed his jeep dozens of times; once he even lost it for a couple days. The time that Dogwater spilled an entire bucket of alien genetic samples that turned out to be just mud—with a generous dollop of animal waste mixed in—all over the jeep's interior had not gone well.

At this particular moment, Dogwater did have phone service, though he had just come off a stretch without it because he was sure the FBI was tapping his line. He resisted, however, using it to call Cameron this night. He would get through his little financial rough spot on his own.

But how? Not by renting out copy after copy of the latest teen-centered bit of video-nothingness, that was for sure. And not by putting dark, blurry images of maybe-aliens, maybe nothings, on a free website that hardly anyone looked at.

What was he doing, anyway? Dogwater Hunt held degrees from the University of Chicago and MIT. Instead of working for any of the various think tanks or universities that courted him, or even the government, Dogwater Hunt had chosen to come back to Nowhere, Indiana and chase a quest that made him a pariah, if not an outright laughing stock, with very little to show for it, except a lot of student loan debt that he ignored almost completely.

Without any quantifiable reason why, Dogwater knew that he was close to capturing proof of the "Santa Claus aliens" this year. He had known this ever since the previous Christmas Eve. That year, a bad mixture of over-the-counter cold medicine and turkey loaf (Dog had a high susceptibility to tryptophan) had caused him to nod off while sitting on Cameron's roof, his prime viewing location. He awoke, positive he could still hear jingle bells in the night air and caught a faint glimpse of something that looked like the tail end of a shooting star, both telltale signs of the "Santa Claus" aliens. Cameron said it was probably just moon glow; the "moon on the breast of the new-fallen snow" and all that. Dogwater knew different, and this year he would prove it.

Underlying all of this was the certainty, however, that he would probably be abducted again before he made his discovery. There was no way the aliens would let him go public with this. If aliens wanted to be found, they would land on the White House lawn or at a television studio, or maybe start a blog. They wouldn't land in trailer parks and podunks like Santa Claus, Indiana. If they were here, it was only because they knew what Dogwater was doing. Yes, he definitely would be taken again before Christmas Eve. Cover your ass, boy, it could be a bumpy night.

Dogwater unconsciously massaged the inside of his left wrist as he considered all this. In his most recent abduction experience, the aliens had been very interested in the bones and veins in that wrist. He was sure they had implanted something there. He didn't know the purposes, but ever since they returned him, the lingering ache in his left ring finger that had been there since a childhood accident was gone. He supposed he could be grateful for that. You know, until the hand turned into an independent life form and started killing people like in some "B" movie.

He looked at the papers of streaming data piled on the floor. His entire purpose for existing—other than as an extra-terrestrial party favor—was tied up in the data, and he was no closer to his answer than he'd been that last, sleepy Christmas Eve and then he'd been no closer than the year before that.

Dogwater kicked one foot under the stack of papers and sent the pages floating like Christmas snow. He grabbed his MP3 player and headphones and went to his closet to sleep.

In the midst of Dogwater's hibernation, the alarms on both computers beeped discreetly; the cow bell moving, but just barely, and the other alarm chiming a couple times. The data-tracking computer had just finished analyzing a very strong, but short, burst of unidentifiable energy near the North Pole that occurred the day before. Something was moving up there; something not found in nature. The alien-defense computer was currently tracking something moving through the sky very fast, inbound for somewhere in the western hemisphere and due to land soon. *Very soon.*

Thanks to a combination of exhaustion and the headphones, Dog slept through both computer alarms. There were no alien abductions that night, but Dog did sleep through his clock alarm also, resulting in his being late for work and docked an hour's pay.

Whether it's from an alien probe, or from an employer, in life, you get it one way or the other.

# DECEMBER 12

Having gotten Conrad Brewster, man/dog, out of his predicament of being shot by the highly effective literary device of just doing away with the character completely, Cameron was now busily immersed in the twelfth chapter of the now-titled *Optimism?* He couldn't remember another novel title that ended in a question mark and this appealed to him. He could just see the reviews: "Buy this book! There's unusual punctuation!"

Cameron took off his glasses to give the bridge of his nose a respite from their pinching intrusion. He had foregone the contact-insertion ritual this day to get to the computer that much faster. He couldn't wait. He was really feeling it today. The Zen of writing was returning.

Then, the doorbell chimed.

Fuck!!!

Cameron opened the door and an old man stood before him in ever-present galoshes and what could have been a World War II surplus parka. He was carrying a duffle bag.

"Uncle Milo?" Cameron asked, trying to register at least a minimum of enthusiasm, and succeeding aptly at the under-achievement.

"Ho, ho-helllllo!" Uncle Milo said.

"What are you doing here?"

Uncle Milo seemed stumped by this question. "Er, well, I'm here about the visitation," he said with great care dripping off every word as if he was reciting drills from a foreign language textbook.

"My visit with Holly isn't until tomorrow, Milo," Cameron said, still not making any moves to invite Uncle Milo in. He was still a little uneasy about the duffle bag. He didn't want to give the wrong idea. During his days as an in-law of Susan's family, he'd heard plenty of stories about Uncle Milo drop-ping by for a drink to toast a new baby—with duffle bag—and not leaving until the kid had his high school graduation party.

"Well," Uncle Milo rebounded. "As long as I'm here, perhaps I could stay over? That would save the long trip tomorrow...for the visitation." Uncle Milo hesitated ominously on the word *long*.

Cameron said, "Ah, well, I don't know if that would be a good idea, Uncle Milo. Um, since you're the court-ordered supervisor, it might be a little odd if you were staying here." Cameron had a hunch maybe he should be calling Everett Franken, but, on the other hand, it was just Uncle Milo, how much trouble could this be?

Uncle Milo suddenly had an inspiration. "My house burned down," he said.

"Good God, Milo. Are you all right?" Cameron asked, having no reason to doubt this story, despite the out-of-nowhere quality of it.

"Yes, I'm slowly...becoming myself again," Uncle Milo said. As an after-thought, he threw in, "I'll be chasing the ladies soon," and immediately regretted it, being unable to deliver the line convincingly. "But for now, I really could use a place to stay."

There was something about Uncle Milo's demeanor, standing there on Cameron's front porch, that was a little, perhaps not off-putting, but just, well, off. Cameron didn't quite know what it was, but Uncle Milo seemed different somehow. Maybe that was just because his house burned down. It didn't really surprise Cameron that he had not heard of this before, being that he was no longer family. But still... it was all weird.

Cameron thought of something else. If he turned Uncle Milo away, that surely would get back to Susan, and worse, it would get back to her sleazy lawyer and would not help his chances in court.

"Okay, Uncle Milo," he said. "My home is your home." He regretted these last words as soon as they were out, but there they were.

Cameron ushered Uncle Milo into the front entryway of the house. Milo jerked and lurched as if his feet were not getting the emails from his brain about which way to go. Poor old duffer must really be slowing down, Cameron thought. He took Milo's duffle bag as the dutiful host. Uncle Milo, maybe from being relieved of the counterbalance, wobbled slightly.

"Uncle Milo, are you okay?" Cameron asked.

"Just a little...overwhelmed," he said in a display of massive under-statement. Then the deliberate tone was back. "I'd like to go up to my room for a while, if I may." Then, as an afterthought, he added, "Okay, dude?"

"Of course," Cameron shrugged. "It's not made up yet, obviously. I wasn't expecting you."

"No, no, don't worry. I'll take care of it. I'm an old sea dog, after all...aren't I?" This last part sounded a bit more like a question than perhaps it should have, but Cameron didn't really notice that.

Cameron led Uncle Milo up to the guestroom at the end of the hall on the second floor, the only spare room with a bed with bedclothes on it. This took a long while as Milo had an agonizing time getting one foot to step up onto the next step while the other balanced his weight.

When they finally arrived at the guest room's oak door, Cameron said, "Okay, Milo, here we are."

"Thank you, son," Uncle Milo said, winded a bit from the stair climbing.

Unsure what to do next—this whole thing was really weird—Cameron started to turn away, then thought of something.

"Did you call the insurance company?" Cameron asked.

"What?"

"You know, about the fire. Do they know what caused it?"

"Oh, probably just knocked over a candle doing some late night writing," Uncle Milo replied.

Cameron looked puzzled at this. Uncle Milo didn't look like the sort to have a lot of candles around, not being one for aromatherapy and such. Cameron nodded anyway, as if this made perfect sense.

"Have you talked to Susan yet?" Cameron asked.

"Oh, uh, about the fire?"

"Yes, of course," Cameron replied. The poor old guy was really slipping.

"Well, I don't want to bother her with this. She has enough to worry about of her own." Uncle Milo gave what he hoped was a meaningful look, but he really didn't know.

"Oh, of course, yes," Cameron said as if he understood completely.

Uncle Milo wobbled again, but covered it. "I'm very tired, Cameron," he said. "We, uh"—he seemed to count to himself, mouth moving slightly—seventy-seven-year-olds don't get around as fast as you young folks. Perhaps,

I should rest for a while."

"Yes, good idea. I'll just leave you alone, then. Uh, when you feel up to it, maybe we can have a drink later." Cameron remembered that Uncle Mile enjoyed few things more than a good drink in the late afternoon.

When Cameron was gone, Uncle Milo went into the room and closed the door behind him. A great sigh of seemingly impossible depth for the wiry old man erupted. This transfer was tough. Had Cameron opened his front door even a few seconds earlier than he actually did, he would have seen what, even for his unusual psyche, would constitute an odd sight. He would have seen a man who looked like Susan Wentworth's Uncle Milo Vestibule one moment and Santa Claus the next, wearing only the red pants, suspenders and white, cotton undershirt of his normal uniform. Further, Cameron would have seen this specter puking in the rose bushes that lined the front walk. The sight of an old man like Uncle Milo vomiting, is disturbing enough. The sight of Santa Claus vomiting would probably entitle one to many years of intense therapy. Cameron was already a candidate for this so it was just as well he didn't get to the front door until he did. As it was, when Cameron opened the door, the shifting images had settled and Cameron saw someone who was unmistakably, though palely, Uncle Milo.

A cleansing sigh and then three sneezes that came in rapid succession. All at once, reflected in the mirror of Cameron's guest room was Santa Claus wearing Uncle Milo's parka and old man galoshes. Kris Kringle frowned into the mirror, hair sagging on lowering jowls. This "Uncle Milo" business was going to be harder than he had thought. Not the least of the many problems was that St. Nick was extremely claustrophobic inside Uncle Milo's mind. Teevo's insane invention put the transferred party into the mind of the other body, and minds, unlike Santa hats, are not one-size-fits-all. Santa had assumed he would just become the other person. Instead, he'd arrived in a blinding flash of lightening that shook the poor Milo's house and terribly upset his cat. Not to mention that the far from instantaneous trip from his world to this one had left him shaky and nauseous, as Cameron's poor bushes had recently learned.

He'd spent centuries as himself and learning to drive another man's body was torturous. Santa had spent a day just learning how to talk for Milo, walk for him; studying Uncle Milo's house so he could become him. He'd even had a time figuring out how to ship Uncle Milo's cat, Sally, up to the North

Pole temporarily to get her out of the way (animals travel between the real world and the imaginary one much easier than humans; something about not having imaginations, ironic as that seems).

He'd even experienced flatulence for the first time in centuries.

And the really weird thing: Uncle Milo was still there, in his mind, but, for the time-being at least, was stunned into silence. It was like he was hiding in the corner watching Santa control his body. Santa could feel him watching, fascinated. Santa was very worried about what would happen if Milo woke up and asserted himself.

He was regretting, not for the first time, this whole idea. Sometimes Santa wished he was a little bit more forceful standing up to Mrs. Claus. Thankfully, she couldn't hear him say that.

As if on cue, a voice in his own head then said, "St. Nicholas, can you hear me?" The voice was Flifle's, his chief of staff.

Santa glanced around the room: bed, dresser, mirror, chair. No elves. "Great Scott," he muttered.

"Santa, are you there?"

Tentatively, Santa said, "Yes, I hear you, Flifle." He felt a little silly talking to air. "Where are you?"

"Look in the duffle bag," Flifle said.

Yes, Santa thought, Flifle might fit there. He did as he was told, expecting to haul out his chief. Inside the bag, instead of Uncle Milo's clothes or the elf, he found an old-fashioned short-wave radio that looked very much as you'd expect, except this one was bright red with a candy cane for a microphone and it was adorned with jingle bells.

He cautiously activated the candy cane microphone. "Hello," he said.

"Good, Mr. Claus," Flifle sounded relieved. "As you can see, I've provided you with this radio so that we can stay in communication. I trust that the transfer has gone well?"

"Yes, it has," Santa said, trying to sound confident, but not really succeeding. It's not like he really knew the signs of a "good" transfer or a "bad" transfer.

"Except," Santa said, "I did feel a bit nauseous."

"Yes. You'll find in the duffle bag a blue candy cane. If you eat that, it will cure the queasiness."

Santa rummaged through the bag and found the candy cane. He munched it gratefully and instantly felt better.

"One other thing," Santa said, mouth full of sweetness. "I think we have to burn down a house."

"Sir?" Flifle wasn't sure he'd heard his commander-in-chief correctly.

St. Nick explained about the cover story he'd use to finagle a room at Cameron's. Flifle said he would consult with the other members of what they were now calling "Operation Yes, Virginia,"—meaning Mrs. Claus and himself—and see what they could come up with. He thought one of Teevo's tricks would work; an illusion of some sort. The alternative would be to actually burn the house down. It would be bad public relations, though, for word to spread that Santa Claus had burned down some old man's house.

In the next morning's paper, Santa would see a short article about the tragic loss of a local man's home. Santa was at first horrified at the accompanying picture of the charred remains of the ranch-style bungalow, until advised by Flifle that the burned shell was an illusion and that the home could be fully restored once "Operation Yes, Virginia" was over. Santa didn't ask, and really didn't want to know, how the illusion worked.

For now, though, Santa signed off and stowed the shortwave radio under the bed. He realized that he was really quite tired and looked at the queen size bed, though he was doubtful that he would sleep at all. At the North Pole he had a custom-made featherbed that had a magical quality ensuring perfect slumber. Still, if he was to play the part of Uncle Milo, he would have to adapt.

He stowed the parka neatly next to the duffle bag with the shortwave under the bed. He removed Uncle Milo's old brown loafers; the galoshes having been parked by the front door.

As he laid there waiting for sleep to come, Kris Kringle suddenly realized that he had been here before. Not here, here, but here in Santa Claus, Indiana. In fact, he had given the town its name. It was, let's see, 1852, near Christmastime. The town was young and unnamed. Santa had paid a surprise visit to a town meeting—the topic for which, coincidentally, was naming the town. He couldn't really remember why he'd gone there. Probably just homesick for the real world. This was back in the days when the world's population was smaller and their communication methods not as good. It was unlikely anyone outside of the town would ever hear about his visit. He greeted the town's children and so charmed the adults that they named the town after him.

That was also at a time when nearly as many adults believed in him as children. It wasn't like today. He missed those days. The jaded disbelief of the real-worlders today was devastating. It was so bad, he was starting not to even believe in himself.

Well, that's why he was here, wasn't it?

Santa sighed deeply and closed his eyes. He enjoyed a sleep that rivaled any of the coziest he had on the snowiest nights at the North Pole.

Downstairs, Cameron stared at the kitchen phone. It was blacker than he remembered. He'd always thought of it, when he thought of it, as more of a navy blue with opaque off-white, perhaps vanilla, colored buttons. But really, it was a very black device with stark white keys. Interesting details, surely, but hardly useful at the moment.

Cameron willed the phone to ring and for the ringer to be Susan Wentworth so that he could tell her about Uncle Milo. It seemed like *someone* should alert the family what happened, since it didn't appear Uncle Milo had. Cameron just couldn't bring himself to dial.

It occurred to him that maybe he could call Everett Franken, who could then relay a message to Susan's lawyer, that slug Wally Bass, who would then tell Susan. But that would take too long. Besides, this message, technically, didn't have anything to do with the court case, so he, technically, probably didn't have to communicate through lawyers.

For obvious reasons—those being that he was crazy and Susan was not fond of crazy—Susan and Cameron rarely talked. Any communication required for visitations or to convey messages about Holly was done through the neighbor Gretchen Morley, or through Holly herself depending on the nature and complexity of the message.

Cameron continued frowning at the telephone. The problem was, in addition to being crazy, he was a coward. How do you carry on a conversation, even about a family emergency, with someone with whom you once shared center of the universe status, but to whom you are now a dead, burned out shell of a planet?

A hoarse, little whisper tickled Cameron's brain and slowly amplified into gruff laughter. Cameron realized what it was right away. It was Cameron's own imagination of his character Webster Stanhope, the talking goldfish from *The Deadman's New Hat*. Webster Stanhope appeared, swimming in a jug of apple cider on the counter.

"Aw ya chicken-shit. Pick up the phone," Webster Stanhope said, and then laughed again. The laughter made little air bubbles gurgle in the cider.

"Shut up," Cameron said, softly, but with feeling.

*Pfffft.* Webster Stanhope spit a long stream of cider toward Cameron and disappeared. Cameron recoiled from the liquid, but felt no dampness.

Cameron stared some more at the phone. In a sudden spurt, he dialed the number and put the receiver to his ear. The electronic tone of the ring on Susan's end took on a depth and sharpness Cameron had never before experienced in a phone call. A fleeting thought of doing a commercial for a telecommunications company—"Hello, my name is Cameron Jones. You might remember me as a famous writer before I went crazy. When I want to reach out and call the voices in my head, I use..."

The pitch was interrupted by a soft, sultry "Hello."

Cameron was stunned. *She wants me!* But then he realized, it was not breathy lustiness he heard, but simply the sound of a woman out of breath.

"Hello?" the voice repeated, sounding slightly irritated.

"Uh, hi, Susan, it's Cameron," Cameron said. "Are you okay?"

"Yeah. Uh, yeah. Just a little winded from hauling all the groceries in. Holly's having a tea party for some of her play buddies and insisted on the double chocolate cookies." Susan laughed a little laugh, more for window dressing on the awkwardness of talking to her estranged ex-spouse than for a genuine expression of amusement.

"Sounds nice," Cameron said, wondering how many tea parties, sleepovers, school plays, dates, weddings, and grandchildren he would miss out on if the court case went badly and Susan moved to London with their child.

"Yeah," Susan said, to fill time.

"Listen, Uncle Milo is here..." Cameron began.

"Oh, Cameron, the visit's not 'till tomorrow."

"I know," Cameron said, a little sharper than he intended.

"And Holly's already got three friends on the way over," Susan added.

"No, Susan, he's staying here."

"What?" Susan said, trying to remember if Wally Bass had told her that and deciding that he had not.

"He says there was a fire at his house. Did you know anything about that?"

"God, no. Is he okay?"

"He seems to be. He didn't really say much about how much damage there was or how it started," Cameron said, shrugging, despite the fact that Susan couldn't see it. He wondered if he was really the best person to judge whether anyone was all right. "I agreed to let him stay here. It'll be good. You know, for the visitations..."

"Yeah, I guess," Susan said.

Sensing a tone, Cameron said, "Unless you don't want him to. Or maybe your lawyer wouldn't like it."

"No, no, that's great," Susan said, thinking maybe it was. "I'll let the family know."

"Okay."

Pause

"Thank you," Susan added after a beat.

"Sure."

Pause

"So, uh, how are you?" Susan said, not quite sure how to end the conversation.

Cameron couldn't resist. "Don't worry, your uncle will be perfectly safe." He regretted it as soon as he said it.

Susan froze. "Well, then. Holly will be there on time tomorrow. Bye."

*Well*, Cameron thought as he hung up the phone, *that went well*.

Cameron shook; first his head, then both arms and finally the legs. Telling himself he was now relaxed, or at least what passes for it with Cameron, he turned his attention to his guest. What the hell was he going to do with the crazy old marine? "Get him some alcohol," Cameron muttered. "That'll keep him busy. Maybe have a couple cheerleaders do cartwheels on the front lawn."

As he considered what wine went best with week-old egg rolls, Milo padded into the kitchen. Cameron couldn't help but take note of Milo's "musty-fab" old guy look featuring wrinkled khakis and flannel shirt with a pair of spectacles dangling from a chain around his neck. The ensemble was offset by a bright red pair of socks. And for just a moment, Cameron thought he heard "Jingle Bells" coming from somewhere. Must have left the TV on in the other room.

"Milo," Cameron said. "Have a seat. I'll get you a beer."

Santa smiled uncertainly, but took a seat at the small table in front of the kitchen windows. Cameron set a tall, narrow pilsner glass in front of him and began pouring liquid from a dark bottle. He watched the amber liquid flow, the foaming head shrinking as quickly as it appeared. The sequence of bubbles appearing and disappearing; suspended, then floating reminded Santa of the "snow" in a snow globe a little girl had once proudly thrust at him one Christmas Eve when his cover was blown. All because of a dog. Man's best friend, perhaps, but not if the man is imaginary.

"Good boy," Santa remembered telling the pooch as he took hold of the other end of his toy bag. "Let Santa have his pack."

McDogal wasn't biting. More to the point, he *was* biting—on the bag's gold drawstring as he curled into an awkward ball in the corner of the living room behind the tree. And he wasn't letting go.

"Give Santa his pack and next year, there will be an extra snausage in your stocking."

McDogal shook his massive head and laid it down on his paws, drawstring between his teeth.

"Try this, Santa," a small voice from behind the big man said. Santa turned and a petite girl in pigtails placed a fluorescent green rubber ball into the green-mittened hand, the shades complimenting each other .

Santa was confused.

"Throw it," the girl said.

Santa gingerly tossed the ball a few feet across the room and it rolled a little further. It was enough, though, to dislodge McDogal swiftly, if not gracefully. Santa retrieved his bag.

"Thank you, my dear," Santa said to the little girl."

"You're welcome." The gap-toothed six-year-old beamed.

"Shouldn't you be somewhere? Santa reproached.

"Where?" the girl asked wonderingly.

"In bed maybe," Santa said.

"Yes," the girl admitted solemnly.

"Well, then," Santa said, tempering his tone with his gratefulness.

"I just wanted to give you this." She reached into the oversized pocket of her yellow bathrobe and handed Santa something.

He looked and saw the translucent curve of a snow globe. Flecks of color floated onto and away from a pair of kittens romping in a field. It was lovely.

"My dear," Santa said as the name came to him. "My dear, Anna. It's lovely. Much too lovely to part with." He started to hand the globe back.

"No, Santa. It's a gift," Anna protested.

"But..."

"Momma says Christmas is a time for giving. Like you do. Isn't that right?"

Santa smiled. Beaten by his own logic. "Yes, of course. Thank you, Anna."

Anna beamed. "Okay. Hey, shouldn't you be going?" She pointed at the clock and midnight was fast approaching."

"My goodness, you're right," Santa said. "Merry Christmas, Anna. Merry Christmas, McDogal." The big man had sprung to his sleigh before Anna could respond. McDogal just gnawed a rawhide and farted.

As he soared across the world, the night sky's splendor mingled like a large version of that snow globe. Light floated up and down silently unable to pierce the shell of darkness.

Drifting back across time and space, Santa emerged from the pilsner bubbles floating in his memory as the bubbles floated in the liquid. As he gazed into the beverage, from deep within, Milo perked up. The words "Yes! Surf's up," echoed in Santa's head.

Impulsively, he raised the glass and tossed the beer back. Before his eyes, colors and light exploded in spiraling bursts that had the snow globe kittens surfing on an intoxicating wave of beer.

Would eggnog have been more appropriate?

# DECEMBER 13

Santa woke with the sun. It wasn't the sunrise that stunned him to consciousness, but the silence. Santa was accustomed, after nearly a millennium, to his own "alarm clock." Every morning at sunrise, all the male elves in the North Pole Complex raise their horns and blast out an elven tune of welcome to the day. This came on the sleepy heels of the previous night's elven tune of farewell to the day that occurred late in the night. Santa was sure—well, reasonably sure—that the elves slept. He just didn't know when.

On this morning, as soon as Santa opened his eyes, he wanted to shut them again, which he did. By then, though, the damage was done. The room didn't spin as it had the night before, but it did wobble relentlessly.

Santa Claus was hung over.

When Cameron offered him, in his Uncle Milo persona, a beer, the still unconscious Milo had stirred in Santa's mind. Santa actually had the sensation of a slumbering bunk mate rolling over. It occurred to St. Nick that Uncle Milo would probably accept the offering. Santa had a vague familiarity with ale, but had not had any alcohol in centuries—all wine in the Complex was non-alcoholic on Mrs. Claus's orders, mostly in an effort to slim Santa down. Sweets were curtailed too—except at Christmas, of course, when the cookies rolled through the dining hall like, well, like cookies rolling through a dining hall.

At dinner with Cameron, Santa accepted the beer and truly did enjoy the first sip. The "low-carb" (whatever that meant) beer was not as full-bodied as the ale he remembered, but it was not all together unpleasant. Two sips later, however, he was ready to call it an early night.

Now, this morning, Santa was aware of everything; aching head, the bed covers holding in nauseating heat, and the cooler, comforting air in the room when he managed to—slowly, lest the room start spinning—free himself of the covers. His head pulsed (oddly, to the tune of "Deck the Halls"). The stale air in the room pricked at his skin and seemed determined to pick him up, flip him over, and shake him until he yakked in a very un- Father Christmas-y way.

With great care, Santa slid one leg from under the sheet and dangled it in the direction of the floor. Sadly, his leg was not quite long enough to reach from a prone position on the bed. With a groan, the other leg followed. Santa moved to a sitting position. His stomach flipped, but settled.

Before he could talk himself out of it, Santa stood up. He wobbled once and then immediately, miraculously, felt better. The hangover was gone. He was tingly, though, and wondered if elven magic was more at work here than his old gift-giver's iron constitution.

Santa made quick work of his morning routine. Shaving was tricky, how-ever, after centuries wearing a beard. Uncle Milo had a clean-shaven face. Santa was fortunate that Milo's shaving kit contained both an electric razor (which he set aside distrustfully) and a disposable one. He would have been even better off still with a straight-edge more akin to the shaving devices of old, but the disposable one was manageable. Santa maneuvered Milo's face with the razor, leaving only two cuts. Internally, he apologized profusely to the still slumbering Uncle Milo with whom he shared a mind—and pain receptors.

Santa put on yet another pair of Uncle Milo's khakis and a flannel shirt (these seemed to be the only articles of clothing, save the galoshes and a couple worn-out suits, that the man owned; not that a man who wore a red suit all the time could complain). He went downstairs.

Cameron, with sleep-tortured hair and wearing a bathrobe loosely over rumpled t-shirt and sweatpants, was already seated at the kitchen table clutching a coffee cup as if it was the source of all his power.

"Ho, ho-" Santa started, then caught himself. In his best Uncle Milo, he finished, "Mornin'"

Cameron stretched. "Morning, Milo. Sleep well?"

"Yes, thank you," Santa said. "'Twas kind of you to put me up." It occurred to Santa that maybe real worlders don't say "'twas," but it was already out there.

"No problem," Cameron said, evidently not noticing. "There are doughnuts on the counter and juice in the fridge." He nudged toward the refrigerator, much to Santa's relief as he didn't know what a *fridge* was. "You might want to nuke the doughnuts to take a little of the chill off. They just came out of the freezer."

"'Nuke'?" Santa said, alarmed. He had heard the term, even way up in the North Pole Complex. It was a very bad term for something that real-worlders could use to inflict suffering and death, not pastry.

"Warm 'em up in the microwave. They're pretty good. They're those 'Doughnut Magic' ones that the entire Midwest is clogging their arteries with glee over."

Kris Kringle stepped cautiously to the refrigerator and opened the door. The light came on inside, surprising Santa pleasurably. He closed the door, opened it again quickly and chuckled when it happened again. He made a mental note to check that out again later. Then he found the doughnuts, took one—with red and green sprinkles—and glanced at the microwave. It looked like a television to him and he didn't know how to work that either, so he bypassed it. He bit into the doughnut as it was and it was good. Santa Claus didn't know much about technology, but he knew a good chocolate doughnut.

Cameron went to the counter and poured another shot of coffee into his mug. He waved the pot at Santa. "Coffee?" he asked.

Santa beamed. Another thing he knew was coffee.

After the coffee was served, the two (or possibly three, depending on how you count), men sat at the table. For a while, Cameron pretended to read the newspaper as he turned its pages. Santa, too, read some of the headlines in the paper—his first ever—and was a little stunned by all that went on in the real world. In that day's paper alone there were stories about a murder, a suicide, an investigation into a school official with child pornography on his computer, and an article about how lots of people in rural areas couldn't pay their winter heating bills.

There was also a comic strip featuring a caricature of a dopey, grinning fool of a Santa Claus that Santa found typical of how he was usually portrayed. He shook his head in mild disgust. However, right below that strip was one that featured a hilarious talking duck. Santa roared at that one.

At that, Cameron grinned into his coffee mug and went for another doughnut. The old guy's house burns down one day, the next day he's eating doughnuts and yukking it up. In contrast, if Cameron so much as misplaced the remote, he went to pieces. The Greatest Generation, indeed.

"Well, today's the day," Cameron said after Uncle Milo had worked his way through the remaining comics on the page and was now scrutinizing the crossword puzzle.

"The day?" Santa asked. For him, "the day" was Christmas, but surely Cameron knew it was still too early.

"You know, the day you get to play visitation patrol, scrutinizing my time with Holly; rating my crayon skills—do I stay in the lines? Monitoring my roster of kid jokes." He sighed. "Making sure I'm not a creep."

Santa, however, was enthralled. Of course, this is why he was here. To bring this man and his little girl together. The man wanted it so badly. This would be his gift to this man. No question.

Santa grinned, the perfect teeth of his own dazzling smile (really, the man should do commercials) somehow twinkling in Milo's mouth and Kringle's eyes shining. "You're excited to see your little girl, aren't you?"

"Is 'excited' the same as 'freaked out'?"

Santa didn't really know, so he let that go. He settled on, "You'll do fine."

"Maybe, but with my...stress—you know the history—I just don't want to scare Holly again."

Santa did know the history. Flifle had compiled a dossier on Cameron Jones, Holly Jones, and Susan Wentworth with information culled from Complex spies, the Sandman, the Tooth Fairy, the Easter Bunny, and other lesser-known sources, some of whom were so anonymous, even Flifle didn't know who they were. These were the type of sources that, had he known about them, Dogwater Hunt would have wet himself with joy.

"Well, you're doing well now," Santa said. "You know what you want; to be with your daughter. And you're writing again."

Cameron was tempted to mention that he had, in the next chapter of the manuscript, re-painted himself into a literary corner by again reviving his banished protagonist, the man/dog Conrad Brewster, but then shooting him again. Cameron had taken, informally, to calling the book *Bookseller Poison*.

And then, of course, there was Webster Stanhope. Uncle Milo surely would be expected to report to the court on how the visits went. Including in that report that Cameron had conversations with a foul-mouth talking goldfish probably would not play well in the transcript of the court hearing. If he was lucky, he might get another visit with Holly at her high school graduation; and then only if he snuck in dressed as the school mascot.

"When will Holly be here?" Santa asked.

Cameron sighed. "After lunch. Kindergartners only go half days."

"What do you have planned?"

Cameron sighed again as he didn't feel particularly creative. "The movies. I've seen a lot of ads for some new computer-animated Christmas movie. It's playing in Jasper."

The movies! Santa was stunned. Talking pictures! He'd never seen one, but had wanted to for, well, for as long as talking pictures had existed. The endless stream of videos and DVD's (whatever they were) that kids put in their letters to him didn't interest Santa much. But going to the theater was something else entirely. "Sounds nice," he said in his best effort to be cool.

"I guess. Say, Milo, you're pretty good with kids..."

Amazingly, it was true. The crude, foul-mouthed geezer Milo Vestibule had long been a hit with virtually every kid he ever met.

Santa smiled a bit, revealing a couple of gaps in Milo's mouth that would have been filled in with a bridge if Uncle Milo had been wearing it when, well, when he took his *trip* with Santa. Instead, it was packed in Santa's duffle, but Santa didn't know how to insert it, so he left it out. Santa would study the thing later and try to figure it out. "I guess kids like me," Santa said, in a great understatement, but choking on it nonetheless.

"Well, do you think I'm up to this visit?" Cameron asked with a questioning shrug. "It's not like I'm one of those cool TV dads who always has the funny line or cool game to play. I'm a moody, has-been writer, who-" he stopped short of saying, "who hears voices." Uncle Milo may be family (sort of), but he still also was the court-appointed visitation supervisor. "Who hasn't been around much and wasn't a great dad to begin with," he finished instead, impressed that it covered his Webster Stanhope problem and also happened to be true. It might play well in Milo's report to the court.

Santa looked at Cameron with the trademark twinkle. "Why did you ask the...er, great council for Holly?" Santa asked, unsure of his terminology.

"Great Council?" Cameron frowned. "You mean the court, the judge?"

"Yes, that's it," Santa said.

Cameron thought about that. He'd be lying if he said a part—a small part, but a part nonetheless—wasn't motivated by a competitive urge to not let Susan take Holly away. Another part of him was frightened at the idea of Susan taking off with Holly to England. Which part was bigger depended on the day.

In answer to the question, Cameron said, "Because I can live without her and she can live without me, but there's no damn reason it has to be that way. And all sorts of reasons why it shouldn't be that way." It wasn't what he planned to say. He hadn't had anything to say. It just sort of came out that way.

"Well, there you go," Santa said.

Cameron nodded. "Thanks, Milo." He took his last sip of coffee and said, "Guess I'll go get dressed. Think you can amuse yourself for a while?"

"Of course," Santa said. He wasn't sure, but would find out. For one thing, he could take a little time figure out what, exactly, Mrs. Claus wanted him to do before he went home. Then he could work on figuring out if he *wanted* to go home.

Somewhere between the lather and repeat stage of Cameron's shower-time hair care, Cameron found himself remembering another shower.

It was Christmas, one year ago. Cameron had just completed the loofa portion of the shower. "Deck the Halls" warbled offensively from his throat.

But he didn't care. This is Christmas. The best time of the year. As his morning grooming proceeded, he moved on to "We Wish You a Merry Christmas" and even "I'll Be Home for Christmas," but that one brought him down a bit so he switched back to "Deck the Halls." It's impossible to be somber when you're falala-ing all over the place.

Finally, dressed in jeans, socks and a Purdue sweatshirt, Cameron sprinted down the stairs and turned on the lights on the Christmas tree, casting a multi-colored glow that crowds out the darkness. It was four-thirty. Christmas would be starting any time now. Got to be ready.

While he waited for Holly to awaken in her room at Cameron's house, Cameron busied himself checking that the bows on all the packages under the tree were perfectly positioned. He always placed them in the upper left corner of square or rectangular packages and it distressed him if any of them fell off. He set out fixings for hot chocolate, a plate of doughnuts (homemade—at Roberta Evans' home) and, in a nod to Holly's health conscious mother, strawberries.

He arranged, then rearranged, the remnants of cookie left on the plate set out for Santa the night before. It must look as if the jolly old elf gratefully bit into them, but—being very busy—had to leave some behind. The cookie remnants, complete with tooth marks, helps with the illusion of the visitor. It didn't occur to Cameron that he had no memory of having eaten the cookies himself. They were whole when he and Holly—who took great care selecting them, reasoning that Santa liked sprinkles way more than candy toppings—had put them out before Holly went to bed last night.

Between five-thirty and six, four-year-old Holly, clutching Melvin Floppy, her pink bunny, shuffled down the stairs. Cameron didn't see her at first, so intent was he on staging the scene of St. Nick's visit. The child's eyes immediately went to the brightly colored tree and the even more brightly colored packages beneath it.

Sensing the girl's presence, Cameron turned. "There's my girl," he beamed. "Merry Christmas." There was a muttered "Merry Christmas" in return as he scooped the child up, along with a sleepy hug.

"Santa came last night," Cameron whispered eagerly.

"Uh-huh," Holly responded. Of course he did. There was never any doubt.

Cameron showed the child the half-eaten cookies and empty milk glass. She was suitably impressed.

"Want some juice before presents?" Cameron asked.

Holly considered this with an apparent intensity that a child this age can only apply to a few things—one of them being presents. Finally, she nodded, though her eyes were still fixed on the twinkle lights.

Cameron got the girl a small plastic cup of orange juice. The two sat quietly at the kitchen table. The child drank her juice, legs swinging beneath the chair. The father tried to occupy himself with his coffee cup, but was too caught up in simply watching his daughter doing this simple act. Given that he got to see his child so rarely, even being part of the mundane event of sitting at the table drinking juice was something to be savored.

"Maybe later today we can make a snowman. What do you think about that?" Cameron asked. Earlier in the week, Mother Nature had left a good quantity of packing snow on the ground, very suitable for such an activity.

Holly nodded, yawning. The child's mental will for Christmas to come was not matched by the body's will to sleep.

Finally, the juice was done. "Can we see what Santa brought now?" Holly asked, getting right to the purpose of the day, in what Cameron thought was a very prim and proper tone for a four-year-old.

"Oh, yeah," Cameron said. "Race ya." He jumped up from the table and barely –just barely—arrived at the Christmas tree ahead of his daughter.

The next several minutes were lost in the typical flurry of Christmas mornings. Holly, like her father, is a package-tearer, not a wrapping-opener, seemingly fearful of damaging the paper in any way. Holly has no qualms about letting the stuff fly.

Holly started out conservatively enough, opening the contents of her Christmas stocking—mostly crayons, children's puzzles and games, and a few pieces of candy –with the care and ponderousness of an archaeologist examining artifacts. Cameron enthusiastically showed her each item, demonstrating some as necessary. Holly enjoyed them, studied them, but not boisterously.

As they moved on to the big-ticket items under the tree, however, the yuletide momentum picked up. With each gift, her exclamations grew. The muttered "thank yous" she dutifully uttered after every gift gave way to giggly shouts of "Cool!" and "Wow!" and "That's the one I wanted!"

Cameron was beside himself. The digital camera hardly had time to cool down. He made a mental note to thank Susan for the inside tips on Holly's preferences for this year, and another thank you to Monty and Sally Winters, veteran parents, for helping to round out his knowledge of what the pre-school set was into this year.

Finally, as Cameron was about to declare an end to the holiday carnage in his living room, he spied one more package sitting behind the Santa Claus doll decoration that was parked beneath the tree. The gift was wrapped in brilliant red paper, shiny as if satin, with an equally vibrant green bow. The wrapping stood in stark contrast to the cast of Christmas trees and cartoon snowmen on his own wrapping. He did not remember this package.

"Well, I guess Santa made one more delivery," he said, with no sense of the foreshadowing he has unwittingly unleashed.

"What?" Holly said, not really caring, distracted as she was by the intricacies of her new doll's wardrobe.

Cameron crawled under the tree and pulled out the mystery package. It was a box about a foot square. And heavy. He shook it gently and heard nothing. The name tag bore Holly's name in a festive, holiday calligraphy. It occurred to him maybe the Winters dropped off a package for Holly and he forgot it. That must be it. He shrugged and sets the package down next to his daughter.

Holly immediate set the doll down and stares at the package, fascinated. "Ooh, pretty."

Cameron agreed. It really was. You couldn't even see the tape holding the folds of paper together.

Holly looked eagerly at her father.

"Go ahead," he said.

Holly ripped open the last gift. When she opened the box, she jumped back in surprise as a small electronic dog's yip called to them from inside the box. All at once, the box tipped itself on its side and the lid slid off as a mechanical fluffy dog with white fur and pink bows in its ears strolled out. It turned its head toward Holly, emitted another bark, this one almost playful, and wagged its tail.

"Well, look at that," Cameron said encouragingly for Holly retreated somewhat toward her father.

The dog set to walking again, stopped, squatted and sat up as if begging for food. Another yip.

Holly, a little more confident now, moved a little closer to the dog. It did a perfect somersault and landed again on all four feet. Holy clapped appreciatively. The mechanical dog barked.

*What makes it run?* Cameron thought. *And who turned it on?*

The toy dog ran circles around Holly, tail wagging, much to Holly's delight. The dog was amazingly realistic, complete with twitching ears and blinking eyes. Cameron even started to think maybe it was real. No, surely not, all boxed up like that. Plus, he could hear the faintly electronic tone in its bark. It must just be a very good robot toy dog. And probably very expensive.

Surely Monty and Sally would have said something if they were giving her a present like this. Mesmerized, he reached for the dog.

As Cameron reached for the mechanical pooch while it was shaking hands with Holly, the dog's head turned toward him. The bright, shining eyes went dark. The ears lay back. The small poodle-like thing displayed two rows of very sharp teeth. A low growl rumbled in the dog's throat and it did *not* sound at all electronic.

Cameron hesitated. "Easy boy," he said, as if that will help with a toy dog.

Holly went on playing and clapping, seemingly oblivious to all this.

"Just hold still while I..." What? Go for the power switch? Ring your neck? Cameron didn't know. He just needed to see if this thing was *alive.* He reached toward the artificial pooch again.

The dog stopped rolling over mid-roll, sat up, bared those deadly incisors again and *spoke.* Real words. "Bite me," the dog growled.

Cameron just had time to think about the old joke about how "man bites dog" when he saw those toy canine eyes darken again. The dog leapt. Holly was still clapping even as the poodle sank his teeth into Cameron's left arm.

Cameron cursed—"Damn you, you piece of shit!"—and swung out with his right arm instinctively, connecting with the left flank of the toy beast. It felt hard, beneath the thin layer of fake fur, and Cameron was sure he could hear the sound of plastic cracking.

The toy poodle sailed across the room. Holly screamed. So did Cameron for that matter. In fact, Cameron was sure he could hear the *fake dog* scream as well. The dog plummeted to the floor, half bounced, and laid still several feet away.

Holly was crying now. Cameron clutched his left arm where he could still feel the pierce of the fangs. He looked at it to assess the damage and saw nothing. He pushed up the sleeve of his sweatshirt. Nothing there. No blood, no pressure marks, not even doggie saliva.

At that point, Cameron realized his child was shrieking. "Honey, honey, it's okay."

She pushed him away. "No!" She sprinted up the stairs and slammed the door to her room, despite its heft.

Cameron shivered. Well, at least he protected his little girl. Right? He looked at the toy dog lying in a very non-threatening position balanced on its snout, butt up in the air, with four legs sticking upwards. He crawled over to it. It still looked like a toy. Even the liquid, real dog eyes had been replaced with plastic, unmoving blue ones. A cautious finger poked gently at the dog's belly. Nothing happened. Cameron noticed then the on/off switch on the dog's underside. It was now in the "off" position. Cameron decided to keep it that way. If only his psyche had an on/off switch.

Christmas that year ended for Cameron not much later with an urgent call to Susan at Earl and Myrna's. Earl and Susan drove to Cameron's house at once to whisk Cameron's only child away from him at a point on Christmas Day before most people have even finished their pre-gifts coffee. Earl, per the usual, said nothing, looking more bored than anything else. Susan, after asking, "Where is she?" said nothing either, just fixed Cameron with icy stares. The child, who thankfully stopped shrieking, had a tear-stained face and was still wearing her pajamas when Susan hastily bundled her into her coat and mittens. Earl got back behind the wheel of his car and Susan and Holly climbed in. They drove away, no one waving goodbye; no one even saying "happy holiday".

It was at this point that Christmas, which for so many of Cameron's thirty-odd years has been on life support, finally flat-lined.

Or so he thought. Standing in his bathroom on this day so close to Christmas just one year later, debating whether to shave or not and ultimately deciding yes, Cameron couldn't help thinking of all this. He wasn't yet back up to overnight visits, but Susan was starting to allow more visits—despite the court battle—and Holly seemed to look at him less often as if he were the boogeyman.

Cameron smiled at that, remembering another overnight visitation when Holly was three. Shortly after bedtime, Cameron had been in the living room watching a ball game when Holly called from upstairs for him. When he went to check, she had claimed there was a monster under the bed—a classic kid complaint. Cameron dutifully investigated under the bed, the closet, the drapes, suitably convinced his daughter the room was safe, got her a drink and snuggled her back in bed with a kiss.

He felt good doing that. No matter how much more time his ex-wife got to spend with their child, she could never chase away the ghosts, monsters, and general bogeymen like he could. That was a *dad's* job.

Cameron wondered if maybe one day, if he asked real nice, Holly might come and chase his bogeymen away.

Around twelve-forty-five, Santa dozed contentedly, having discovered the seductive powers of both naps and recliners. At the North Pole Complex, especially this time of year, Santa worked sometimes twenty hours per day on one toy, food, or other general world-joy task after another. This concept of relaxation was a new and not unpleasant one. Sugarplums danced in his head and he now finally understood what that old story meant.

The doorbell rang. Santa started in his chair and Cameron froze in his study.

Disoriented and uttering an impressive old man grunt (a left-over from the still dozing Uncle Milo), Santa hoisted himself from the chair and, after realizing that the chime he heard was a door chime, and not, in fact, the heralding of Christmas morn throughout Christmas village at the North Pole, headed toward the sound.

When he opened Cameron's front door, he was met by the joyful face of someone he'd never met, but who seemed truly excited to see him.

"Uncle Milo, how are you?" Susan squealed in that high-pitch reserved for greeting people you haven't seen for some time. She moved in for the familial hug before Santa barely had time to shake off his slumber and remind himself that, for now, his name was Milo.

"Fine, fine, my dear, and you?" he said.

"Are you sure? Cameron told me about the fire. Milo, why didn't you call anyone?"

"Er, well, I'm fine, really. I didn't want to be a bother."

"Milo," Susan said, in a mildly reproachful tone. She hugged him again.

Then Santa noticed the little girl standing behind Susan staring intently at some ice crystals on the porch railing.

"Well, hello, Holly," he said. "How are you?"

Holly turned away a bit reluctantly from her ice crystals and looked at her great-uncle Milo.

"Santa!" she cried.

Santa's heart, which had beaten steady and true for centuries despite a perpetual diet of milk and cookies nearly stopped dead. A look of horror registered on his own face, though he did hope that it came out as mere confusion on Milo's face.

"Silly girl," Susan said. "You remember your great-uncle Milo, don't you?"

She put the right amount of emphasis on the question to convey that the child did, in fact, remember Milo.

Holly repeated the exclamation—SANTA!—this time holding up a piece of pink construction paper as she did so.

Susan laughed. "They did a little Christmas activity at school today," she explained. "Holly, do you want to show your great Uncle Milo what you drew?"

Without really indicating if she wanted to or not, Holly handed the man the pink paper. Santa beamed, with not a little pride, as he saw that it was a rendering, a pretty good one in fact, of himself. He was depicted feeding Rudolph the Red-Nosed Reindeer something that was either a carrot or some sort of sea creature. Although Rudolph's place in the Christmas hierarchy is complicated due to a myriad of factors, including a long-running feud with Comet over participation in reindeer games—the picture was still very well done.

"Well, bless my soul!" Santa exclaimed. "It's beautiful!"

Now it was Holly's turn to beam.

Susan, for her part, was a bit shocked to hear "Bless my soul" come from the kind, but typically profane, mouth of her uncle.

"You can have it," Holly said, shyly, but with also a little petulance. She invited herself through the doorway into the house.

"Holly's a little down on Santa," Susan said with a confiding tone. "You know how it is. Seems like Christmas will never get here and she isn't going to get what she wants anyway."

Santa nodded. He did understand, more than he could ever say.

Inside, Holly was admiring an impressive rendering of a snake on black velvet. The hideous thing had been a gift from Dogwater in appreciation for all of the favors—usually monetary—that Cameron did for him. It sat now, as it had for the past 18 months, leaning against the wall behind a large, fake palm tree in the hallway. The palm tree was something Cameron had acquired from the editorial assistant who worked on *Quality, Not Quantity*, ostensibly also a show of appreciation, but really, Cameron suspected, an effort to get rid of the damn thing. Cameron's decorating philosophy was way beyond feng shui. It wasn't just a matter of choosing pieces that created inner peace, it was a matter of not choosing pieces at all, but rather just letting them come to him. At least, that's what he told people.

About this time, Cameron came down the stairs. He got within about three steps of the bottom before he saw Holly and stopped, his left foot frozen in mid-step. He watched her for a few seconds. She had grown. It was a cliché thing to think upon seeing a child for the first time after a long absence, but it was true. Her hair was darker too; not a lot, but definitely some. Was Susan dying it? No, probably not.

Cameron decided he had to say something if this visit was ever to get started. The idea of spending the whole afternoon right where he was on the steps was not unattractive, but it was also not the way to win Father of the Year.

"Hello, Holly," he said to himself, mentally checked it over, and decided it was worthy of verbalization. "Hello, Holly," he said out loud, noting that his voice only quavered slightly.

Holly, in true horror movie fashion, spun around to face the voice, eyes wide. Cameron, the author, half expected to see lightning flash and thunder rumble on cue.

To her credit, Holly recovered quickly. "Hi," she said, politely enough, if a little cautiously.

The dad and the dad's daughter stood this way, Cameron on the steps, Holly ten feet away, studying each other.

Susan and Santa took in the scene. Susan looked at Cameron and now it was his turn to do the monster movie turn.

"Hello, Cameron," Susan said in a tone she hoped was light.

And instantly, it was four years earlier, only instead of saying, "Hello," she was saying "goodbye" and taking their daughter and leaving him. And he, instead of protesting, was locked in his study, thinking gibberish and then typing it. And, really, had anything changed?

Cameron became aware that Susan was saying something else.

"You look good," Susan said. "Merry Christmas."

Instead of "You too" or "Happy Holidays," Cameron was tempted to say, "You look different too. I hardly recognized you without your lawyer," but resisted the urge. He settled on, "It's good to see you again." And it *was* good. She was stunning. The brunette dye job was a great improvement on an already excellent head of hair; not to mention the exquisite, and heretofore unexpected, thrill of her actually being in this house again.

Susan, too, was feeling a bit of déjà vu at being here again. It was equal parts pleasant and repellant. Every memory of special events or laughter was juxtaposed with visions of Cameron on his nonsensical rampages or locked in his study typing nonsense on his computer.

The inevitable awkward pause followed, after which Susan said to the room, as much as to her daughter, "Holly, don't you want to say 'hello' to your father?", never mind that she already had.

Holly didn't hear, or pretended not to hear, as she was way more interested in comparing her foot size to the size of Milo's galoshes parked on the mat by the front door. She was suitably impressed by the giant who must ordinarily inhabit them.

"Hollllly..." Susan said, drawing it out with is much lightness as you can muster while battling the sense that an awkward silence is becoming a vengefully sadistic void of nothingness.

"I already did," Holly mumbled.

"Holly," Susan said, more sharply now.

Finally, satisfied that the galoshes didn't really belong to a giant, but rather some dumpy old grown-up, Holly turned, blinked at her mother, smiled shyly at Santa, then looked at her father; really looked at him, not a cursory glance. Naturally rosy cheeks turned an even deeper crimson.

"Hi," she said again. It was an uncertain "hi," still tentative, but not—Cameron noted—unenthusiastic. Not completely, anyway.

"Hi, Holly," Cameron said.

Holly's eyes lingered on Cameron for another moment. Then they moved to Uncle Milo where they widened and brightened. She definitely knew this man.

"Santa!" she said again and three her arms around the gangly tall man's knobby knees.

Santa nearly let out with the standard "Ho, ho, ho," then caught himself. He laughed a nervous approximation of a geriatric laugh. "Well, I guess somebody's excited about Christmas," he said and patted the child's head.

"Silly girl," Susan teased. "That's my Uncle Milo, you kidder."

Holly laughed too, but it was clear from her eyes she didn't buy it. Santa could see that as clearly as Holly could see he was Santa. She went along with her mother for now because that's what her mom wanted. But for how long?

Santa was worried. Very.

Susan's departure went pretty well. She hugged her little girl, promised to come back promptly at seven and told Holly to mind her father. To Cameron, she said, "Good luck," in a tone that suggested she was trying to be wittily sarcastic, as if to suggest "she's a pistol, that one, watch out, Dad," but which actually sounded more threatening than anything else.

For a good minute or so, Holly was entranced by the tangled mess of holiday light strings Dogwater had left in the corner of Cameron's living room. They weren't plugged in, but Holly seemed intent on seeing what it was inside the bulb that made the string light up, and just as willing to wait patiently for that thing to appear. Adults consume themselves with work, taxes, the playoffs, and the latest victim to get voted off a reality show. Kids, on the other hand, can apply the same level of intensity to watching the grass grow. Anxiety-ridden Cameron was fascinated by that, though to an extent he could relate, having spent a recent extended, eight hour period meticulously cleaning the refrigerator.

Cameron decided he had to find something to say. He considered complimenting Holly on her pretty dress. Except she wasn't wearing one. Then he considered saying her sneakers were cool, but they weren't really all that interesting. This was hard.

Whether it was out of a need to help out, or whether it was his own excitement to see a real "talkie" motion picture, Santa broke the ice. With a spring in his step that Cameron thought was notably out of character for the old man, Santa went over to the little girl and said, "I think your dad has a surprise for you."

The little girl and the old man looked at Cameron expectantly, both sharing the Santa Claus eye twinkle.

At first, Cameron was stumped. Surprise? What surprise? What was that crazy old fool doing? Then he ventured, "Uh, want to go to a movie?"

The "yes" was quite definite. All around.

Movies are great time-fillers for awkward first dates, as well as awkward visitations. While Holly laughed at the antics of the anthropomorphic cartoon animals singing and jabbering on the screen in their quest to save Christmas, Cameron was studying his little girl, trying to figure out what was inside her—other than two kid-size fun packs of popcorn. What thing in her mind could he reach and use to win her over?

Santa, for his part, was mesmerized not so much by what the characters on the screen were doing, but the fact that they were there. In all his years, he'd never taken in a moving picture. And he loved it. He sat forward in his seat, head in hands, or with fingers tracing the outlines of the characters on the screen. The snacks were amazing too. Not being familiar with currency— every thing at the North Pole was free to whoever wanted or needed it—he'd fumbled with making change for his purchases from the bills in Uncle Milo's pocket. Cameron had mistaken this for Uncle Milo being broke and paid for him. His snacks alone were about twenty dollars—a sugary array of chocolate, caramel, fruit-flavored sweets, and, of course, popcorn. Santa didn't know if twenty dollars was a lot of money (in the fourth century— the last time he was a real-worlder, it would have been a fortune), but he was touched by Cameron's generosity all the same. And the snacks were good, even the rubbery, tart ones that looked like worms.

About half-way through the film, during one of the dramatic scenes where the council of wise elder-monkeys was speaking gravely about the crisis befalling Christmas in this particular film, Cameron saw one of the monkeys, an old grey-beard, looking right at him. The monkey's gaze actually compelled Cameron, who had been admiring his daughter with proud-papa wonder, to look away from her and look instead at the screen. He was stunned.

*Please don't let me flip out*, he thought. *Not here. Not in front of my daughter. Not again.*

Things were not helped when the monkey said, "You're a lousy father." Then, the toucan up in the tree overseeing the council meeting said, "And your book sucks too." If the animals really said these things, they would have sounded pretty silly in the midst of this serious scene so the audience would have laughed. Cameron looked around, his ears perked like a dog's— they literally seemed to rise up on his head—listening for the faintest titter. Nothing. Everyone was silent, except for the occasional cough or the crinkle of a candy wrapper—very likely, Uncle Milo's. Everyone was in stand-down mode, waiting for the next goofy scene, featuring some nutty comic-relief character, to guffaw at.

So it really was just him who heard the voices. Cameron nearly lost control of his bowels at that point. But then, just before going into full panic-mode, a thought occurred to him: he *knew* the animals weren't really speaking to him. Sure, he heard the voices, but he knew he was imagining it. That must mean he was all right. Right?

For the rest of the film, Cameron stared straight ahead at the seat back in front of him, not daring to move, as if he were an airsick flyer riding turbulence.

On the drive home, Holly chattered endlessly about the movie, more or less acting it out start to finish, singing abbreviated versions of the songs. Santa gleefully joined in on some of the choruses. If possible, he'd had more fun than her. Cameron rallied his senses a bit and scored a few points with a pretty good Dad-like impression of one of the great, lumbering elephants featured in the film. He even joined in on the final verse of the moving, if non-traditional, Christmas carol that all the animals of the jungle sang at the end of the film.

Dinner that night was homemade pizza. Cameron was widely known, at least among friends and family, as a pizza connoisseur. Santa had never experienced pizza either, and was quite enthralled—not movie-level enthralled, but still pleased. Cameron made his own crust and sauce from scratch. Holly eagerly helped her dad add the toppings, including extra mushrooms. The kid loved mushrooms. The two of them laughed and talked—about kid stuff mostly, a little about Christmas; Cameron trying to weasel hints for gifts and Holly not taking the bait. She saw no reason to drop hints. She had already written to Santa, of course. Christmas was taken care of. Little did she know...

Santa hadn't yet seen the letter—might never see it if he didn't get back to the North Pole, but he sensed she was a true believer and so obviously had written a letter. He also knew she had been good all year, more or less.

The pizza went over big all around. As it came close to time for Susan to pick Holly up, and after the pie was eaten (courtesy of Dogwater's sister Roberta, who had given up on the fruitcake), Holly came up with a question out of nowhere, as only kids can.

"I used to live here," she began, taking a good, slow look around the kitchen. "Am I ever gonna live here again?"

Cameron nearly choked on the pie crust crumbs he'd been picking off his plate with an index finger.

Santa watched the two of them closely.

"Would you...would you like to live here?" Cameron said.

Holly shrugged. "It's a nice house," she said fairly non-committally. "But you don't have a dog."

Cameron smiled. He had a sudden urge to run out to the nearest pound and get a dog. Or two. Or twelve if that's what it took. Unfortunately, at this time of day, the pound would be closed. Damn. Everyone was against him.

"Maybe I'll get one," he said nonchalantly, even though he wondered how long it would be before any dog he owned would start talking to him while it's head spun around three-hundred-sixty degrees.

"Okay," Holly said agreeably, her tone not betraying whether or not this would seal the deal.

When Susan came to pick up Holly, Cameron was a little hurt to see how excited his daughter was to see her mother. He was happy to get a polite, if not sentimental, hug (no kiss) from his little girl, but that was enough for now. He also got a very dry peck from his ex-wife. Perhaps she was just relieved he hadn't freaked their kid out.

As Uncle Milo and Cameron watched the SUV drive out of the circular driveway, Cameron was thinking of Christmas-yet-to-be.

For that matter, so was Uncle Milo. And, he thought, it would all begin with a little dog...

# DECEMBER 14

Mrs. Claus had never wanted a cigarette more in her life. Not that she had ever smoked one, of course. And she certainly was against smoking. But still, with all the pressures of the season, it was tempting.

Sitting now in the large, leather chair behind St. Nick's sturdy pine desk, she realized what an enormous job it was being responsible for the Christmas dreams of millions of children. Here it was, ten days before Christmas Eve and everything was a mess. The electronics elves were way behind on the new computer games. The wood toy elves were still grousing because requests for their stuff were down *again* this year. The reindeer were demanding more pre-flight carrots. And, of course, the love of her eternity, and the man in charge, Santa Claus, was not at the helm of this holiday voyage.

And nobody knew it.

Nobody except Flifle, of course. It had to be that way. If word got out that Santa Claus was not at his post, the world would be devastated. The elves were trustworthy (except for the one who had once leaked an unflattering photo of Santa in a Hawaiian shirt, prompting a trend of people selling likenesses of Kris Kringle in all manner of silly scenes; from the beach, to being a doctor, to dressed like Elvis. That was one elf who had gotten a HUGE lump of coal that year.) Still, it was hard to lie to these elves, these dear family members.

But it had to be this way. The elves looked to Santa for guidance, but more than that, they loved him. He was a father to all; a pillar of jolly good-natured strength. If word got out that Santa was having emotional problems, there would be anarchy. The North Pole Complex would be devastated. The world would follow. There'd be yuletide chaos.

"Yes, Virginia, there is a Santa Claus. And he's crazy," she muttered.

Mrs. Claus cupped her hands over her mouth as if she couldn't believe she had just said that. Kris wasn't crazy. He was, well, he was upset. "Stressed out," people called it. He just needed some time to clear his head.

Time, unfortunately, was in short supply. Maybe she shouldn't have sent him away. What was she thinking, anyway? Could he really show Cameron Jones and his little girl the true meaning of Christmas like in some real-worlder novel? And if he could reunite the two of them and the child's mother, would Santa bathe in the Yuletide spirit and come home ready to kick-start Christmas?

Basically, would the morose lump that was her husband be gone forever or would he return in time for the holiday? Would he return at all?

Again, she cupped her hands over her face. How could she think that? It was true: Christmas was failing this year. And it hurt her to see her joyful husband so beaten and down. A part of her did think, with a little luck, she could get the toys together faster without Santa moping around the workshop. In fact, Flifle should be back anytime with a report on production progress.

Mrs. Claus turned in Santa's chair and gazed out of the double-pane, energy efficient windows at the glowing snow outside. This year's Christmas weather report was iffy. There was potential wide-spread blizzard activity along Santa's flight path. The next few days promised to be blustery, threatening to put a damper on reindeer practice maneuvers. That was bad. The team was breaking in a new recruit this year—Donder wasn't as young as used to be and was making noises about sitting out this year. No one believed him, though. He was too dedicated.

Mrs. Claus smiled as she remembered when a much younger Santa had personally selected a much younger Donder to be on his sleigh team. That reindeer had jumped so high you could barely see him. This memory led to other remembrances of Christmases passed. So many happy times. And now, what did the future hold?

Flifle burst into the office as dramatically as one can while wearing jingle bells on his shoes and hat. The bells were a sign of rank at the Complex; only the Chief of Staff wore them. He hated the cursed things, but at least he had the rank.

"Mrs. Claus," Flifle said, clearly having run from wherever he had been. "Santa Claus wants a dog."

He said this with all the drama of a detective in a whodunit revealing the murderer.

"What?"

"I just received a communiqué from Mr. Kringle," Flifle explained, having taken to using the exotic "communiqué" when really he just meant a radio message. "He says he needs a dog for Christmas."

Mrs. Claus was at a loss. "Well, of course he can have a dog. He can have all the pets he wants." Santa and the Mrs. were both very much animal lovers.

"No, ma'am," Flifle said in a tone clearly betraying that it nearly killed him to correct her. "He wants a dog to give as a present."

"No!" Mrs. Claus said. This was amazing. In years past, Santa had occasionally accommodated requests from children for pets—once even managing to get a horse into the sleigh with him (an airsick horse unfortunately). But new policy directives, prompted by an unfortunate incident with a basset hound somewhere over Cleveland, had abolished that.

"It is a bit against policy," Flifle said, clearly nervous to be heard questioning his boss's judgment.

"Why does he want it?" Mrs. Claus said.

"He didn't say," Flifle shrugged, in a very un-Flifle like lack of knowledge. "He just said he had a plan."

"Where will we get a dog? We're not still making them, are we?"

Flifle looked at her blankly.

Mrs. Claus realized the oddity of her statement. "Sorry, I was thinking toy dogs. He does want a real one, right?"

"Yes, ma'am."

"What kind?"

Another shrug.

The North Pole had only two humans—Santa and Mrs. Claus, a bunch of birds, polar bears, seals, foxes, caribou, and, of course, reindeer, but did it have any dogs? Mrs. Claus didn't know. Before the no pets policy, a division of the workshop had actually raised and bred them. They were excellent, purebred pups. After the new policy came down, some elves had snuck the few remaining ones into homes of "late submissions" (children whose letters didn't make it to the Pole before Christmas), but never without clear assent from the parents, or took them anonymously to shelters dedicated to finding homes for stray pets and left them.

Mrs. Claus straightened in her chair, shook her head and said, "We've got time. We'll deal with that later. Give me a status on the workshop."

Instantly, Flifle stood tall and started, "Well, all divisions reported in this morning. Overall-"

"*Meeester Claus*," a voice called from the outer office. "I am looking for youuuuu."

Mrs. Claus and Flifle exchanged a horrified look.

"Doozil!" Flifle hissed to Mrs. Claus.

"Get rid of him!" Mrs. Claus hissed back.

Doozil was a long-time elf in the Complex. He was also a major butt boil (butt boils being a very serious, and sadly chronic, problem among the elves).

On top of all this, Doozil was a major gossip.

"What should I tell him?" Flifle asked.

"I don't care," Mrs. Claus responded. "Just don't let him come in here."

Flifle sighed, straightened his tasseled, jingle-belled hat and marched to the outer chamber of Santa's office, trying to look as bureaucratic—and therefore unapproachable—as possible. He wished he had a clipboard. As it was, he went out to meet Doozil unarmed.

"Greetings and good will, Doozil," Flifle said, giving, in a stilted fashion, one of the standard elf-to-elf greetings in the Complex. His tone was polite, but cool.

"And many pleasant days to you, as well, Flifle," Doozil oozed. "May I see St. Nicholas?"

Flifle's teeth clenched. He hated the way Doozil threw around the title "St. Nicholas." Elves did not subscribe to any human religion and it seemed wrong for him to use such terms.

"Mr. Claus is not available," Flifle said.

Doozil looked surprised. "Not available? Since when?"

"He's studying the Christmas Eve flight path," Flifle said, this being the only thing he could think of. It was a terrible lie. For one thing, it was still ten days away from Christmas. For another, the man had been flying the same route for centuries. He could fly the route—or more to the point, the reindeer could—in his sleep; and had on one occasion around the time of the French Revolution when he was suffering from a head cold. Still, that's what came out of Flifle's mouth. He was stuck with it.

"It will only take a minute," Doozil persisted in a tone suggesting it would take far longer. Doozil never took only a minute to do anything he could spend ten minutes doing. That elf could talk.

"Well, tell me what you need, and I will pass it along," Flifle said, gently trying to turn Doozil and usher him out of the room. This was also unusual as elves very rarely touched one another for any reason.

Doozil eyed Santa's chief of staff carefully, reading him. Flifle felt distinctly awkward and wished he would stop.

All the elves had bright, clean, rosy-cheeked faces, but Doozil's had something more: a look of horrible purity. He looked like an elf who could be featured in a happy toddler's picture book one minute and ripping your throat out the next.

Flifle was dragged from this image by the sound of Doozil's starkly high-pitched voice (even by elf standards) saying, "I need to ask the old gent about the project."

"Not this again," Flifle groaned. "*Mister* Claus made it very clear that, while he appreciates and is grateful for any suggestions, he was not interested in pursuing that at that this time." The "mister" was a bit unnecessary— everyone in the Complex called him "Santa" or some similarly informal title. Flifle thought, however, it was important to reaffirm the power structure for this particular elfish bug.

During the previous mid-summer dead time, well before the Christmas rush started to ramp up, Doozil had taken advantage of one of the many gatherings of elves and the Clauses, this one for business rather than play, to make a proposal.

"Time clocks," Doozil had said in his self-important way in response to Santa's request for ideas to make the upcoming Christmas campaign run even more smoothly than it already did after more than a millennium. His tone, coupled with the superior gaze he leveled at his fellow elves, clearly conveyed this was to be perceived as a brilliant idea.

Elves rose with the sun and slept when the sun slept. In between, they worked—or sang or did cart-wheels and somersaults. There was not a lot of scheduling involved which necessitated "clocks".

Santa mentioned all this, then said, "Well, Doozil, I don't know that we really need ..."

"It will make the elves much more productive, Santa," Doozil had said, oozing with, well, with that annoying quality that makes you hate your co-worker simply for existing. "If the elves have start and stop times—and detailed daily schedules—they'll know what to be working on and when to be working on it."

Santa's round belly shook with laughter. "Doozil, that's not necessary. The elves work when there's work to be done." This was met with affirmative cheers from the elves. Santa continued, "And the elves play when it's time for play." His eyes twinkled merrily. The cheers were longer and deeper for that.

"You see this reaction?" Doozil asked, voice squeaking at an even higher octave. "That's what I mean. The elves would rather play. But we must work. We need structure. The world population of human children is growing. We need more toys built than ever. Those computer games, especially, require a lot of time to learn." It was true, elves, admittedly with a bit of help from magic, learned all the games and built every single game disc by hand.

"Well, I'm sure we could find more work for you, Doozil, if you need some. Couldn't we everyone?" Santa said jovially. The group laughed.

Doozil's pink cheeks went crimson and the elven eye twinkle darkened momentarily. "Well, I'd at least like to study the idea," he said with as much dignity as possible, but it came out petulant.

Santa had agreed to let Doozil study the matter in the hopes that eventually he would give up on it. He didn't, however, and since that mid-summer North Pole day (not demonstrably different than a winter North Pole day), he had periodically demanded time with Santa, like today, to discuss it.

"Is he in?" Doozil asked pointedly. In a thousand years, Santa had never been not in—except on Christmas Eve.

"Of course," Flifle lied. "But at the moment, he's not available."

"And why not?" Doozil asked, peering over Flifle's shoulder in a semblance of nonchalance, but this was difficult as Doozil was short, even by elf standards and Flifle was unusually tall.

"Because," Flifle began and paused. "Because he and Mrs. Claus require some...private time."

Doozil's single, fuzzy eyebrow rose. "Oh, I see. Well, don't let me disturb them," he said slowly, still peering over Flifle's right shoulder. "Perhaps I'll come back later." With that, he turned slowly on the curled up ends of his shoes and marched out.

Flifle blew out a breath, then winced. It was no wonder Doozil had retreated so **quickly.** "**Pri**vate time" was essentially code for...well, it was just code.

Santa better come back soon. Flifle didn't know how long he could handle this. He turned and went back into the inner office.

Mrs. Claus was making notations on the naughty/nice list with Santa's favorite quill pen and didn't look up right away. After a few seconds, while pondering the fate of Stevie J. in Wichita, she glanced up.

"Is he gone?"

Flifle nodded, growing pinker.

"How'd you get rid of him?"

"Well, I just said you and Mr. Claus were...busy with something personal."

"And he accepted that?"

"I really don't think he wanted to press it," Flifle said, true enough.

Santa's Workshop, the nerve center of the North Pole Complex, is, put simply, huge. You might be able to fit it inside a professional football stadium, but just barely. The front chamber of the Workshop, however, is smaller than the rear. It's the gray, vaguely castle-like, torch lit room with the long workbench lined with busy elves, that you always see in holiday programs and commercials.

The elven alchemists and computer programmers tended to hang in the larger chamber of the Workshop. The front room was, in the modern age, more for the old-timers; the wood-toy types. Some parts of the world still got into the occasional wooden rocking horse or race car. In a nod to modern times, the "some assembly required" types hung out here too. One of the benefits of Santa bringing your kid's gifts is that they come fully assembled. And the elves never have mystery parts left over or have to read the instructions. Plus, they actually have that one tool—whatever it is—that you realize you need but don't have until too late on Christmas Eve to go get it so that you can put Junior's toy together.

Over the centuries, the demands on the elves had increased and varied. While fruit, candy and wooden toys were fine at one time, demand was up for books, dolls, "extreme" sports equipment, bicycles, action figures, board games, CDs, and computer games. In the Days Before Time when the elf elders were developing the fundamental science of elf spells, it's safe to say they never anticipated today's kids who are—with all love and affection –greedy an possibly insane.

When Mrs. Claus and Flifle surveyed the troops in the front chamber this morning, it was a highly kinetic place. A couple elves were assembling a mountain bike. Another was tinkering with a portable CD player, trying to get the mechanism that opened the door to work. A fourth elf was jumping up and down on a pad that lit up in different spots to signal the player to do certain dance moves while some sort of cacophonic human music played. Through the open door to the larger chamber, the sound of some extremely violent computer game under construction could be heard. A good intellectual property lawyer would make a killing on infringement suits against Santa Claus. Except of course, he has no money. Plus, all the lawyers of the world need is to feed the mob of lawyer-bashers by suing Father Christmas. Maybe the lawyers could ask Santa to put writs of habeas corpus in their Christmas stockings.

"We've got fifty-thousand units of superhero action figures ready. A quarter of those are included in playsets. Also, assembly of the..." Flifle paused in his report, as if choking on his words, "*Lord of the Rings* items are going well." Santa's elves were ordinarily a supremely tolerant bunch, except when it came to portrayals of elves in film and narratives.

As usual when a North Pole elf was in a dark mood, it passed quickly and Flifle more energetically said, "We even managed to get a compact disc recording of 'Dead Skin,'—a brief, repulsed shudder—"the popular human music group."

Mrs. Claus grimaced. Music at the North Pole, provided by the elves, was beautiful; flutes, drums, harps. Santa would join in occasionally on the violin. It was peaceful and serene. The real-worlders were way more...what? Violent? Brutish? Neither word seemed quite right to Mrs. Claus, but the real-worlders were *different*.

Mrs. Claus heard one old, nearly ancient elf, sanding a child's toy, wood block at the end of the table say to another old elf gent, "Those humans have become *vespla*," using an elfish word that was far from complimentary. With all the news from the real world of wars and poverty and turmoil, Mrs. Claus had to agree.

The elf had been working that block of wood for days, intricately carving a letter "C" into several of the sides and various kid-friendly animal portraits into the remaining sides; not necessarily because a kid in Glasgow, Saipan, or Rochester, Minnesota had asked for it, but because that's what he did, what he'd always done. He'd already completed "A" and "B" and intended to do the whole alphabet, though it seemed there was no way he'd have it done by Christmas. It didn't matter. In the minds of some elves, children would always be children and always like the same things, no matter how much the real world changed or how fast kids nowadays grew up.

Really, though hadn't humans always been at least a little *vespla*? Was that so bad? And weren't children still children, after all; just as bright, and honest and good as always?

The truth was, Mrs. Claus believed deep down, children weren't the same today. She would like to have encouraged the elf's wood-toy making over the video games, but knew the reality of the Christmas market. Children saw more of the darkness of the world than ever. It was not an exaggeration to say they grew up faster than ever too. Innocent toy blocks and rocking horses would work for the very, very young—briefly—but it wouldn't last long.

The window during which faith in Santa Claus was strongest was narrowing. This was the source of Santa's current crisis. And if he was going to do something about it, Mrs. Claus needed to jumpstart his own Christmas spirit. Otherwise, that narrow window would close completely.

From within this internal monologue, Mrs. Claus became aware of two things: the first was Flifle furiously scribbling notes on his clipboard; the second was a tug at the hem of her long skirt, which was red with white fringe to match Santa's suit, of course.

Mrs. Claus looked down to see a small, young, wide-eyed elf with long flowing hair streaked with blue and silver seated at the work table. She was, even among the physically spectacular North Pole elves, stunning. Mrs. Claus saw that the little elf was holding a wooden mallet in a hand that seemed much too small to hold it. She had evidently, been putting together something that looked like it would be a dollhouse when it was finished. She was looking up at Mrs. Claus expectantly.

"Oh, yes, dear. What is it?" Mrs. Claus managed to say.

The young elf flushed furiously. "Well, it's just that...well, I hope Santa is okay."

Mrs. Claus was alarmed. "Why would you say that?" She hoped this sounded casual, but thought it probably sounded panicked.

"Well, Doozil told us Santa was indisposed."

The other elves nodded in confirmation.

"He'll be okay soon, right?" she asked. Now all sets of eyes at the table were on Mrs. Claus. Flifle stood behind her, saying an elven prayer to himself.

Mrs. Claus laughed. It sounded horribly fake in her head, but the sound seemed to relax the elves. "Of course Santa is all right. He's Santa, you know. He's just very busy planning the flight path for this year." While inspiration had failed to spruce up this lame cover story for Flifle, Mrs. Claus was relieved to suddenly think to add, "They're breaking in a new reindeer this year and Santa wants to make sure she's up to the challenge of the Christmas Eve run."

The old elves shrugged, not caring particularly about this. They were craftsmen and couldn't care less what happened to their toys once they were done with them. The young elf, though, smiled brightly. "I'm so glad," she said, then added, "I've only been in the Complex a short time. I can't wait to meet him." The flush was there again.

"And he's excited to meet you too," Mrs. Claus said. It probably wasn't really a lie. Santa loved all his elves and surely would want to meet her.

A small, almost imperceptible grunt bubbled up from the old elf with the wood block, signaling his old-timer's cynicism. He'd probably dined with Santa hundreds of times, if not thousands and long since forgotten the thrill of the first time.

The young elf, Shivla—Mrs. Claus suddenly remembered her name— laughed, however, and happily went back to putting the interior walls of her dollhouse in place, singing a happy elf tune softly to herself.

The inner chamber of the workshop was where the bulk of the toy stock was kept and where most of the toy production took place. On this morning, most of the elves were in the production wing trying to figure out if it was possible to build a bicycle with a built in DVD player and snack bar dispenser, in order to fulfill one little boy's request.

Over the sounds of hammering, Mrs. Claus could hear the elves singing:

*Santa came from far away.*
*To make gifts and toys all the day.*
*We love Santa; he is our king.*
*His good work is what we're doing.*

The song made Mrs. Claus's heart flutter. It was one of the regular work songs the elves sang, but under the present circumstances it was especially poignant.

Mrs. Claus and Flifle continued to take stock of the toy inventory. Flifle was counting the basketballs on a rack that extended forty feet up to the ceiling. It was one of fifty such racks on the workshop floor.

"Flifle," Mrs. Claus asked, "Do you think we're doing the right thing?"

Flifle held up the finger of one hand while drawing hash marks on the pad on his clipboard as he mumbled numbers to himself and stared at the rack of balls. Finally, after several moments, he said, "Two-hundred-twelve-thousand-forty-seven." He drew a large check mark next to that item on the inventory. "I'm sorry, ma'am. What did you say?"

"I said, do you think we're doing the right thing?"

Flifle looked blank for a moment, his mind still mostly focused in inventory. "About what?"

"Sending Mr. Claus away. Do you think Christmas is lost? Do you think *he* is lost?" Mrs. Claus asked in a rush of questions.

Flifle shrugged and considered his response carefully. "I don't know," he said. "But I do know that you did what you had to do and now it's real important that we carry on as if he was still here."

Mrs. Claus nodded. "I suppose you're right. But lying to the elves..."

"Ma'am, don't worry. It will all work out," Flifle assured her.

She hoped he was right.

After a couple more hours of counting and Flifle providing Mrs. Claus with a crash course in Christmas production, the two made their way out of Santa's workshop, dodging several more inquiries about why Santa wasn't personally inspecting things as he usually did. Mrs. Claus made a decision that she would limit her visits to the Workshop until this crisis was over.

Back in the long, cavernous hallway outside the Workshop, Mrs. Claus sighed. "It's going to be a long ten days," she said. Flifle nodded sympathetically. The two of them walked down the hall, headed out to talk to the engineers about the progress of a refit on the sleigh.

As their footsteps echoed down the hall, an orange tasseled hat floated up from behind a small, gold Christmas tree, one of dozens scattered around the castle. Doozil's perpetually smug and preternaturally, ghostly smooth face appeared below the hat. He was grinning, half with shock and half with wicked glee, not quite believing his pointed ears. He had heard Flifle and Mrs. Claus talking in the inner chamber and had watched them intently since then—from behind the basketballs, under the action figure conveyor belt, and once from in the middle of a pile of designer jeans. Was Santa really gone? Doozil didn't know how or why, but if this was true, it was good news.

Very, very good news.

# DECEMBER 15

As the sun rose, not permeating Dogwater's bedroom thanks to the heavy-duty trash bags over the windows, Dogwater Hunt re-endured a horrible event from his past. Lying in a fetal position in the foil-lined closet, which was the only position he could comfortably lay in, he dreamed of a night five years earlier...

It was a humid summer night. Dogwater dozed outside the trailer he shared with his sister Roberta in hopes of experiencing some sort of breeze that wasn't getting into the sweat box. Sleeping outside would seem to be a dangerous thing for a multiple abductee to do, but, really, intelligent life from other planets can find you anywhere (anywhere without tin foil), so you might as well sleep comfortably while you can, where you can.

As he laid there half sleeping, half wondering if he'd get busted for indecent exposure if he removed his sweaty, clinging skivvies, the wind picked up. It wasn't a cool breeze, just a hot churning of the night air.

The Dogwater having this dream paused here a moment to reflect on the existential coolness of how he was sleeping and dreaming about himself sleeping.

Back in the dream, as the wind blew more forcefully, leaves floated down from the trees. Lots of them. They tickled his bare legs and chest, causing him to swat at them limply in his sleep. He stirred, too, from the change he detected in the air. It was getting cooler.

The humidity evaporated—no, make that *froze*—with the temperature change. If he were awake, Dogwater might have seen little humidity droplets falling to the ground as frost. The formerly clear night was shrouded in wispy clouds; the moon obscured. Even the lights of the trailer park could not punch through the blackness.

Dogwater shuddered and awoke. His first thought was that he should have brought a blanket out here with him. His second thought was that it had suddenly gotten very dark, the few lights in the park now non-existent. His third thought was that this was very, very bad.

Then, he stopped thinking. Utter terror conflicted, but ultimately mingled, with a resigned acceptance of this familiar routine. Though his heart pounded, he leaned back in the lounge chair. He was not paralyzed—contrary to many alien abduction reports—but could not compel himself to run. What was the point? If they want you, they find you. He closed his eyes and waited.

The next period of time—Minutes? Hours? Days?—was a disjointed jumble of images; long periods of numbness and lack of any sensory input interspersed with momentary bouts of searing pain. He was being experimented on, of course. That's what the aliens always do, isn't it? It's not like they ever invite humans up for beer and billiards. He never really saw them, his captors, but the Dogwater reliving this experience in his dreams remembered that sometimes, if he thought real hard, he could almost recognize them, but when asked to describe them later, he could not. He knew that this hurt his credibility when he recounted his tales and that frustrated him so much, he could feel the taste of that bitter disappointment like so much unsweetened baking chocolate.

In between the procedures, Dogwater's attention drifted and lingered on the multi-colored lights above him, twinkling in seemingly random patterns, much like Christmas tree lights, the source of his near pants-wetting phobia of holiday decorations.

Dog slammed down hard from a jolt of pain, caused, he thought, by an alien removing and then reattaching all of the toe nails on his right foot. The aliens don't use sedatives or anesthesia. He just experienced the whole thing in a sensation-dulled (but not killed), floating limbo. As he laid there catching his breath, he smiled and thought, "Hey, I remember you," while looking at an alien preparing some sort of stainless steel, pointed instrument. He started to say this to the alien captor. The alien stared blankly back, not making any facial expressions, or not able to. Dogwater was sure he had seen that one before. Yes, definitely. Though, if you've seen one metallic blue-hued, glassy blank eyed alien, you've seen them all.

As usual, the aliens poked at his ears. The aliens *always* do that. They were especially fascinated by the outer ears. Maybe this was because the sides of their own heads are smooth. At least, Dogwater thinks they are. Of course, sometimes he also thinks the sides of their heads have horns. It's hard to say.

The alien calmly, but firmly, ripped Dogwater's left ear from his head in a tearing of cartilage and a shower of blood drops plop-plopping on the metallic floor.

Dogwater screamed, begged them to stop. He was not sure what they were doing, but it hurt like a son-of-a-bitch. Sometimes during these abductions, he saw blood; his own, and often a lot of it. No matter how many times they abducted him and let him live, he was always sure he was going die. He probably did a couple times, but the aliens brought him back. Angels. Bastards.

Dogwater heard a snap then moaned, yelling at the stupidity of the torture, the lack of creativity, not necessarily the agony. He just had time to conclude that his right arm had been shattered before he passed out.

Still in the dream, Dogwater awakened to find himself back on the lounge chair outside the dilapidated trailer in which he lived with his sister Roberta who was probably sleeping in sweaty coziness inside. The moon was back out and the air was familiarly humid again. Dogwater automatically rubbed his right arm, but knew that it was fine. No matter what the aliens do to him, they always return him physically whole. Occasionally, he had tiny scars or bumps, strongly suggesting that by this point in his life he is riddled with alien implants, but essentially he was okay.

The Dogwater having this dream felt a bit anxious as he remembered that in the shower the morning after this abduction, he became convinced he was missing a testicle. The fact that for three days subsequent to the abduction, he peed blood only solidified this belief. But did he go to the doctor? Sure, he said, "Hey, doc, I think a space alien ripped out one of my balls. Got any good drugs for that?"

No, he didn't go to the doctor. His urine returned to normal. But it did make one hell of a first-person account for the Dark Matters website.

Unlike dream sequences on television, this one did not slowly fade to black. Instead, Dogwater was jolted awake by a crazy woman ripping open the sliding closet door of his bedroom and shaking the sleeping alien hunter.

"Jesus," Dogwater shouted, suddenly very awake; reflexively protecting his groin area. As his eyes focused, he realized that the alien that had awoken him was his sister Roberta. In a cocktail dress.

"Get up. Get up!" Roberta shrieked, trying to drag Dogwater from the closet by his right ankle.

"What, what?" Dogwater struggled to his feet, more or less under his own power.

"I've got to tell you what happened," Roberta said.

"What are you wearing?" Dogwater noticed that the little black cocktail dress was capped off by pearls and a hairdo that was probably quite sophisticated (for Roberta) the night before, but by now was rather askew. The cut of the dress almost, but not quite, obscured the tiny pink flower tattoo between her breasts.

"Danny and I went to a thing last night," Roberta said, irritated and clearly eager to get to her news.

Danny was Roberta's on again/off again boyfriend. Danny was a former executive with a big manufacturing company who had taken early retirement mostly because it allowed more time for drinking. He was a pretty good guy, but an even better drunk and a good twenty years Roberta's senior. Roberta knew all this, but still found the man so damn charming.

"Last night? You're still wearing the dress," Dogwater persisted. Someone inside him, a way more brave version of himself, got ready to assert his prerogative as the protective brother to kick Danny's ass for keeping his sister out all night.

Roberta grinned. "It was a really good thing."

Dogwater grimaced his disgust.

"Anyway," Roberta said, "Dog, listen, I was staying over at Danny's and-"

"Ewwww," Dogwater said, covering his ears and shuddering. "Danny and my sister. Ugghh!"

"Shut up. I've got a scoop for that stupid website."

As Roberta hoped, this worked. Dogwater immediately snapped to attention. This must be important. Roberta had only called it a "stupid" website. Usually she referred to that "Internet shit-a-thon."

"What?" Dogwater asked.

Roberta took a deep breath. "I had a psychic vision."

Dogwater groaned. "Again?" He sat down on the floor and threw up his hands. "Did anyone call the cops this time?"

"No, really. It's not like last time."

Two years earlier, Roberta had made local headlines when, during annual Fourth of July fireworks, she had stood up the middle of a crowd of oohh-and-aah-ers and started screaming in tongues. She then ripped off her sundress (bonus: she was going sans skivvies this day), and started running across the field, bathed in the rockets' red glare.

Later, she told the police that she did it because she was overcome by a vision of the governor riding a donkey. It turned out her "vision" was a memory of a photo that had appeared in that day's paper that did, in fact, show the governor of Indiana sitting on a donkey for some sort of photo op to benefit something or other. It also turned out Roberta was very drunk.

"So what was it this time?" Dogwater asked. "Did you have a vision of me sleeping in the closet? Or maybe after you watched a "M*A*S*H" rerun you had a vision of Hawkeye operating on someone?

"Why don't you ever believe me? You spend all your time in your dark, little room, writing on your computer about aliens and conspiracies and, I don't know, the evils of dating because girls have cooties. Yet, you don't believe that I'm psychic."

Instead of answering that, Dogwater said, "I'm getting coffee. You want some?" Dogwater turned and shuffled down the hall. One sock had slid down his ankle and partly off his foot during the night. He kicked it off now and abandoned it in the hallway. The other sock, also off the toe slightly, but still mostly in place, waved back at its lost companion.

Roberta followed Dogwater down the short hallway, through the living room, to the small, galley kitchen. "This one was different. I had the tingle."

"Hey, what you and Danny do, leave me out of it." Dogwater took the bag of coffee from the cupboard, did a cursory check for bugs and measured out enough for a full pot.

"No, the tingle, like when I'm about to have a vision. And I got the chills. My mind was cloudy, but also clear...you know?"

Dogwater tore his eyes from the pot filling up with fresh brew and said, "No, I don't. Psychic phenomena, except among abductees in very rare cases, do not exist. For everyone else, it's a scam by TV spoon benders and snake oil salesmen who want to make a buck." Dogwater was really wound up now. "Only the more evolved life forms of other galaxies have developed the power to communicate mentally and receive images. Sometimes they pass that on to humans in their experiments. *But you are no abductee.*"

Roberta gulped. "What about David?" she asked.

Dogwater had been stirring copious amounts of sugar into a green alien-shaped coffee mug and stopped short, still holding the spoon submerged in the cup.

When Dogwater was ten and Roberta was fifteen, they had been on a trip with their parents to see a basketball game. Their older brother, David, was eighteen and had opted to stay home and work on his car (also Cindy, the girl—literally—next door.)

Halfway through the second half, Roberta had been seized by the conviction that something was wrong with David. She had a vision of him lying in the street in front of their house dead. She wouldn't stop crying and screaming. Even though their parents didn't believe her, they rushed home just to calm her down. They arrived home to a crowd of police cars, an ambulance and other assorted emergency vehicles. David had, in fact, collapsed from what was later found to be an undiagnosed heart defect. Ironically, Cindy, the neighbor girl David lusted after, had been the one to call 911.

Dogwater looked like he'd been slapped, and, mentally perhaps, he had. At the time, Roberta had claimed she saw their brother collapse. And about the time she first said it probably was about the time it actually happened. But still...for her to bring up that horrible, wretched day. The family *never* spoke of David again. It was too painful.

Standing there now in the apartment, years later, Dogwater hated his sister for bringing all that up again. He wanted to do something. But what? He could hit her; wrestle her to the ground like when they were kids. But now, he was a lazy, soft weakling and Roberta did Pilates obsessively. There was no doubt that as adults, Roberta could kick Dogwater's ass.

"I'm gonna make sure Santa puts a big-ass piece of coal in your stocking," he said when he couldn't think of anything else. "How dare you say his name."

Now Roberta looked wounded. "I'm sorry," she said in a small voice.

The moment passed in a stereotypically Midwestern repressed manner. Almost instantly, Roberta was back up bouncing on her toes, eager to share her vision.

Dogwater took a jolt of mud from his coffee mug and savored it before saying, "All right. Tell me what you saw."

Roberta took a deep breath. "You!" she shouted.

Dogwater's eyebrows ascended. "Me?" he asked. "Actually, I meant tell me what you saw before you broke in and woke me up."

"No, no. I mean a saw a vision of you. You were standing in the park—or, at least, outside anyway—looking up at the sky and it was snowing. Not like a blizzard, just a light snow. In one hand you had a gun—I don't know, a pistol or something—and in the other hand you had a giant candy cane. It must have been two feet long. And...and a deer head at your feet."

"You saw me holding a gun? *I hate guns*," Dogwater said. "The government seizes guns from criminals then slips them back on the streets as a tool to kill off minorities and poor people. And you know I throw up if I so much as step on a worm."

"No, this was a real vision," Roberta insisted. "I saw you. You were wearing that stupid red hat with the flaps you like. It was like I was *there*. I could feel the snowflakes. I heard the snow crunch beneath your feet. And...and there was blood on your coat."

"Of course there was," Dogwater said. "Well, thanks for sharing, but I have to go to work now." He started ushering Roberta toward the door.

"Wait. What do you think it means?"

"That at some point in the future, I'm going to get drunk in a snowstorm. Actually, that's not a bad bet." They were at the door now. "It really doesn't even have to be snowing."

"You had a gun. What were you doing with a gun?" Roberta actually seemed a little worried, as if her brother was standing there right now holding a .357 Magnum.

"Paperweight? Winter Wonderland squirt gun fight?" Dogwater shook his head. "Roberta, it's not going to happen. Go home."

Roberta stared at her brother. "Just be careful."

Dogwater frowned. "Careful with what?"

Roberta shrugged. "Everything." Then she left.

Dogwater turned and shuffled back to his coffee mug. "Psychic vision, my ass," he mumbled into the brew.

In the entire history of Christmas, all the way back to the original tannenbaum of "O Tannenbaum" fame, no one has ever gotten a Christmas tree to stand up straight on the first try. Lovely as its branches were, even those determined Germans couldn't get that tree to stop leaning.

So it was no surprise that in modern times, Cameron Jones was having his own tree troubles. Cameron had decided that if his next visit with Holly was going to be perfect—or at least something that would not cause undue embarrassment to perfect—he needed a tree. Besides, ever since Uncle Milo had moved in, a relentlessly annoying and alien holiday spirit he couldn't explain had been knocking on his mental door no matter how quiet he tried to stay.

Plus, needing to obtain and decorate a tree was an excellent excuse to get away from the novel he was working on, now under the title *A Giant Mess of Literary Crap*.

Cameron had opted for an artificial tree. He did this for two reasons: first, his ex-wife Susan was an ardent environmentalist with issues against the death of trees for people to put in their living rooms and then toss out; second, Uncle Milo was deathly allergic to pine. At least, he thought he was. Cameron had a vague recollection of Susan telling him this once during their marriage. When he had asked Uncle Milo to confirm this, all he had said was, "No, I don't think...Yes! I am...aren't I?" Poor old guy was really losing it.

The vaulted ceilings in Cameron's living room allowed him to go with an eight foot tall blue spruce. Cameron thought it looked magnificent standing there in the corner of his living room, now that he had finally managed to get the thing straight in its stand. But now there was another problem. The tree was naked.

"Shit," he said to Uncle Milo. "I don't have any decorations." There was the old string of lights Dogwater had dug up and he vaguely remembered a box of mostly broken, blue and green ornaments from his college days that might still be around, but Susan had taken all of the "good" decorations in the divorce settlement. Not that it had mattered to him at the time. When would he ever need a little Christmas again?

Today, that was when. What would he do? He could go buy more, of course, but that meant going to one of those big discount stores. Ick. Or to the mall. Double ick. Santa Claus had a fine, small shopping district of course, but frankly he avoided going out too much in town. Everyone knew him here and he tired of answering—read lying—about how well his next project was going and how much fun he was having writing it. And what would he buy, anyway? As a famous local person, he felt all sorts of pressure— real or imagined—to buy stuff even if he didn't really want it. Maybe this had been a bad idea...

"You know," Santa Claus said thoughtfully, "I might have seen a big box marked 'X-mas stuff' in the basement."

Cameron was bewildered. "Really?" he asked. "Are you sure?"

"Yes," Santa said. "On the bottom of the shelving unit on the..." he screwed up his face in concentration, "on the east wall."

"Hmmm," Cameron said, before shrugging and heading to the basement. Maybe Susan had left one box behind. A satisfied glow, small but perceptible, flared briefly in his heart.

Santa smiled to himself a mischievous grin.

Cameron pulled the chain on the light at the bottom of the basement stairs, crossed the large, concrete room, tripping over the same old tool chest he always tripped over, but never moved, and arrived at the east wall.

As promised, on the bottom shelf sat a large cardboard moving box with "X-MAS STUFF" stenciled in the front in old-style red lettering. He didn't remember Susan being schooled in calligraphy, nor was he. He shrugged and grabbed the box—which seemed impossibly light for its size—and headed back upstairs; tripping over the tool box again.

"You were right," he told Santa as he set the box down in the living room. "Here it is, but I sure don't remember it."

The flaps on top of the box were folded together in an overlapping pattern to hold them closed and as Cameron worked to open them, Santa nodded gently and slightly waved his right hand in the direction of the box.

Crouching on the balls of his feet as he opened the box, Cameron was nearly bowled over as he opened the flaps. He heard, or thought he heard, the Vienna Boys Choir singing "O Come All Ye Faithful." The brilliant shimmer of blues, reds, greens, and golds soared from inside as the colorful decorations grabbed hold of the sunlight from bay window in that room and used it to their full advantage.

"Wow," he said. There was no other way to describe it. As he looked inside the box, he saw ornaments of every shape and size; some were smooth, others were ornate designs. Still others had moving parts; twirling baubles, dancing wooden soldiers. One ornament featured a parade of dancing toys that actually marched. There were also long strands of lights, ropes of garland, and bushels of mistletoe and holly. And, of course, candy canes by the gross. Some of them looked to be at least two feet long.

"I don't remember any of this stuff," Cameron said. "Maybe it's Susan's. She just never took it with her." He picked up a glass ornament with a scene in miniature in the center of it depicting a snowman dancing around a Christmas tree. Cameron could swear even the ornaments on the tree in this tiny scene were twinkling. "These things are amazing," he, the self-appointed Scrooge for modern times, said. He beamed at Santa.

Uncle Milo beamed back. "Shall we?" he asked with a nod of the head toward the still bare tree.

And so, this thirty-something, burned-out writer and possible crazy person, tackled decorating a Christmas tree with an enthusiasm he hadn't shown for such activity—or any activity—since childhood. Uncle Milo helped a little, but mostly he enjoyed watching Cameron. Cameron didn't notice, caught in the action as he was. He actually giggled—giggled!—at some of the more comical scenes depicted in the decorations, including one with poor Santa flopped down in a snow bank.

When, at last, Cameron stopped. He stepped back to admire the tree. "What do you think?" he asked Uncle Milo.

Santa thought it was the most beautiful tree he had ever seen; and this was a man who knew his trees. Every branch held a brightly colored ornament, some of which were moving, and one of which, somewhere, was playing "Silent Night." Boughs of holly flowed into long, winding paths of silver garland, which looped into strands of tinsel. The whole effect was staggering, even to an old Christmas veteran like him.

But there was still something missing.

Cameron saw it too and frowned. The top of the tree was bare. "Ideas?" he asked Uncle Milo.

Santa frowned too, but quickly smiled with inspiration. "Look in the box. There might be something."

Cameron shook his head. "I think it's empty," he said, but looked anyway. In one corner was a box, about the size of a shoebox, that he hadn't noticed before. Cameron opened it and gasped in a decidedly unmanly fashion.

Inside the box was a Christmas star of silver and gold. He looked at Uncle

Milo. "It's, it's just like one that we had when I was a kid," he said.

Uncle Milo smiled.

Cameron wondered if it could be the same star. It looked like the one he remembered, but it couldn't be the same one. Surely that one had been lost in the fire that gutted the family home when he was eleven.

Cameron sat cross-legged on the floor a long time, just looking at that star, a small grin of wonderment on his face, until finally Santa said, "Well, are you going to put it up?"

Without a word, Cameron stood, positioned the step ladder he'd brought in from the garage for just this purpose, and climbed to a point that put him within arm's length of the top of the tree. He reverently put the star in place and quickly climbed back down, eager to see how it looked.

The star promptly bowed the branch it perched on.

"Fuck," Cameron grunted and remounted the ladder, righting the star again.

"It's beautiful," Kris Kringle said.

"Yeah," Cameron sighed, blowing out a satisfied breath. "Just one more thing..." Cameron scampered—scampered! Cameron!—over to the tree and crouched down fumbling with the electrical cord for the lights and plugged them in. The tree came brilliantly to life. The colors twinkled and bounced off every reflective surface in the room. Cameron stepped back to stand next to Milo and admire the view.

"Good job, son," Santa said.

"Yeah..." Cameron agreed.

After a moment, Cameron stepped back toward the tree to adjust one of the shiny red, ball-shaped ornaments. He could see Uncle Milo grinning widely in the reflection on the ball. Except it wasn't Uncle Milo at all. Cameron blinked and looked again. Did he see what he thought he saw? Yes, it was. There was no mistaking it. Santa Claus was standing behind him, complete with long white beard and tasseled cap.

Cameron whirled around. Instead of a jolly old elf. He saw the same, smiling, old Uncle Milo in his ever-present khakis and flannel. He turned back to the Christmas tree ball. There was Santa again, complete with the eye twinkle and perfect teeth. Cameron's head whipped back around to the person behind him. There was Uncle Milo, slightly, but not completely, gap toothed (because of the missing bridge), still smiling, but it was a slightly more quizzical smile.

"Are you all right, son?" Santa asked.

"Uh," was the reply. He looked at the Christmas ornament again. This time, it was a headshot of Santa, but there was something else. Cameron squinted and wished for a moment he wasn't so vain as to prevent himself from wearing his glasses as much as he should. But, squinting, he could see standing behind Santa...no, couldn't be...Uncle Milo?

Again, Cameron whirled around, a full-body whirl this time. Still only one person, just Uncle Milo. "Did you see, um..." he began softly. "No, probably not. Definitely not." He started to walk slowly out of the room.

"Cameron?" Santa began.

Cameron turned slowly. "Yeah."

"It's a beautiful tree." Santa gestured at it. "Holly will love it."

Cameron smiled. Inside, he was freaking, but it was a freak wrapped in a warm blanket of joy. Holly *would* love it. It *was* beautiful. He had done it all himself. At that moment, it seemed all he needed was a good tree to win over his daughter. If other families were in on that secret, family court would be a much less busy place.

That resolved, Cameron prepared to hole up in his study, the normal remedy for his little episodes. There, he would purge the Santa vision in the ornament from his psyche. He hoped Uncle Milo knew how to cook because he probably wouldn't be out for a while and the old man might get hungry.

With a half-hearted wave over his shoulder, Cameron shuffled out of the room wordlessly.

Santa didn't know what to make of this, but he himself was basking in his own satisfied glow. He felt Santa-y again. But it was something more. He felt like *family*. Cameron was like a son. Even little Holly was the grandchild he never had. Sure, he dearly loved Mrs. Claus and the elves, and they him, but being here now gave him something he hadn't had in centuries. *Simplicity.*

Late that night, Santa pulled the old-fashioned, brilliant Christmas-red radio transmitter from under his bed. He had decided Cameron must be sleeping. He'd not heard a sound from his study in hours. He flipped a couple of toggles on the radio, blew into the microphone, said a couple of elfish magic words Flifle had given him, and waited for the connection to be made.

A few moments later, amid a crackle of static, Flifle's voice came through. Apparently, this elf slept even less than the others. "North Pole Complex. Mr. Kringle?" he greeted, still speaking elfish.

"Yes, Flifle. How are you?" Santa replied in Flifle's native tongue. They had decided before Santa transferred into Uncle Milo, that all communications would be in the elf language to guard against the unlikely event that the radio transmissions—beamed on purely magical lines, but still beamed, could be intercepted.

"Fine, sir. Are you well?" Flifle said.

Santa paused. How was he? He wasn't ready to go home. But he did feel wonderful. So that's what he said. "Wonderful."

Flifle let out a deep breath. This was a good sign. "Great, sir. So you'll be ready to return soon?"

"Well, I think I still have a bit to do here..." St. Nick said noncommittally.

"Of course," Flifle hastily agreed. A good chief of staff *always* agreed. "It's just that the elves are starting to ask questions..."

"Mrs. Claus can handle things. She knows the procedures as well as I do," Santa said, a slight tone in his voice, unintended, but still there.

"Yes," Flifle said hesitantly. "But Christmas needs its leader. The children love you. We all do, sir." Flifle put a small hand over his mouth. He was a bit out of bounds.

Santa didn't take offense; wasn't really even paying attention. Instead, he thought of the wonderful time he'd had at the movies—his first moving picture show. He could smell the popcorn, hear the "crkcrkcrk" of shoes attaching and tearing free of the sticky floor.

"I'll come back soon, of course," Santa said, with too little enthusiasm to suit Flifle, but he let it go.

"Good. I'll start working on the recall process," Flifle said.

"Recall?" Santa said with a tinge of alarm.

"Yes, sir," Flifle replied. "The transmitter is rigged with a recall device that will instantly return you to the North Pole Complex and return the human *kevla* to his body." *Kevla* was one of many North Pole words for "soul" or "essence."

There was dead air for several seconds.

Finally, Santa said. "Good then," still not enthusiastically. "Tell Mrs. Claus I love her. Good night, Flifle."

Flifle could hear something amiss in Santa's voice, and it probably wasn't distortion in the transmission. He hesitated then started to say "Good night, sir," but failed to finish before Santa closed the connection. Flifle set the microphone on his own radio down and sighed. "We're in big trouble."

Back in Santa Claus, Indiana, Santa felt a pang of guilt for not wanting to leave and give the real worlder back his body. But then he picked up a copy of the comics page from the newspaper he'd been reading earlier and saw that whacky duck. There were no newspapers at the North Pole. No funny pages. He looked at the comic strip and laughed and laughed...

# DECEMBER 16

Cameron awoke early the next morning, stiff-necked and groggy. At some point during the night, he'd drifted off sitting in his high-backed desk chair. The previous afternoon, he'd gone straight from his vision of Santa Claus to his study, locked the door and sat in front of the computer. He sat without even expending the effort for conscious thought.

At some point during the evening, he'd been seized by a compulsion to work on the book. He didn't want to do it. He *had* to do it. He wrote through the night, not stopping for food, bathroom breaks or even to rest his eyes, straining under so many hours of staring at that screen. Even when the words on the screen blurred and became unrecognizable, when his eyes did back flips in their sockets, screaming for relief, he typed on.

He had produced nearly half a ream of printed text, many pages of which he crumpled with hatred nearly as quickly as they came out of the printer, only to later regret it and smooth the pages out. He looked at them now. Among the representative samples of the night's work was:

*Mary had a little lamb.*

*What a bitch.*

Many of the pages made even less sense. None of it seemed to further the plot of the novel at all. Yet, as he wrote it, it had seemed to make the manuscript the stuff of Pulitzers. He'd wept during twenty of the pages in the middle that, Cameron saw now, were filled simply with repetition of the number sequence 2145 separated by two dashes.

What's more, Cameron had no memory of typing any of this. He remembered why he'd gone to his study, and remembered the typing, yet he didn't remember anything he produced there. He skimmed the pages as casually as a browser in a bookstore. Finally, satisfied that none of it was going to remain in the next draft of the book, he shrugged, tossed it all in the recycling bin and went to find coffee. He assuaged himself—tried anyway—with the writer's notion that a bad session at the keyboard was better than no session at all, except that he intrinsically knew there was much more going on here than a bad writing stretch. He lacked the energy to think about that right now.

Cameron crept down the stairs to avoid waking Uncle Milo. He paused on the way to the kitchen to admire the gorgeous Christmas tree that now graced his living room, though he avoided looking directly at the ornaments for fear of seeing any more rogue reflections. Then he paused to open the drapes on the bay window to look out on the new day.

The sun was coming up in the chilled, crisp tones of winter. A sleet/snow combination fell, but only half-heartedly. It occurred to Cameron to flip on the weather forecasting channel on the television to see if a blizzard or something was coming, but then it struck him that it really didn't matter. He had no plans to go anywhere this day.

In the kitchen, Cameron stretched, yawned, and fumbled for the coffee pot as if this was a typical morning and not the morning after a mental bender. While waiting for the coffee to brew, he went and retrieved the newspaper from the front porch. There was a stinging wind outside and it certainly felt as if more snow would soon be in the air, but, again, it really didn't matter.

He considered reading the paper, but tossed it on the kitchen table still rolled up instead. He took his coffee cup into the living room and flopped down on the couch, untucking the previous day's shirt from the previous day's jeans and undoing the first three buttons, as he sat. Then he settled back with the remote.

When he was working on *Quality, Not Quantity*, which featured an extended subplot involving a campaign for U.S. Senate, Cameron had become something of a political junkie and avid devotee of the cable news channels. He turned one on and saw a well-dressed, obsessively upbeat morning news show commentator blathering about something or other. Whatever it was— something to do with Medicare funding—it couldn't hold Cameron's interest this day. He changed to a channel airing a vintage Laurel and Hardy movie. Hardy had just split his pants and was making funny faces at the camera. Cameron laughed a hoarse, early morning laugh, softened by the quiet that coated this time of day. The bit wasn't that hilarious, but funny is funnier still when it pervades the stillness of an early morning. By the time long-time L & H foe Jimmy Finlayson got knocked off a roof, Cameron was outright chuckling. By the time the short ended, his sides hurt.

And then, for the next twenty minutes, Cameron Jones cried softly to himself.

"Bad news, man," Izzy Carmichel said after Dogwater completed a rental transaction at Video Voyages.

"What?" Dogwater asked.

"Becky ain't gonna loan me all that technology shit you wanted." Becky was the manager of Electronic Junction where Izzy worked, or at least where he picked up his check.

Dogwater tensed. Had someone in the shadow government gotten to Becky the Manager? "Why not?" he asked

"On account of, she fired me," Izzy shrugged.

"What? What happened?"

"Dunno, man."

"Did you sleep with her again?" Dogwater accused.

"No, man, really." Becky and Izzy had had a fling several months earlier that ended badly because (1) the district manager got mad over the violation of the no fraternization policy for management and (2) Izzy was an asshole who only called on Becky when he wanted a jump anyway. "Besides," Izzy continued, "if I *had* nailed her again, she'd be givin' me a promotion...and a big-ass company car. No lame-ass extra quarter an hour for me. I'd be livin' large."

"Keep your voice down," Dogwater hissed. "Gladys has a thing about cursing." Gladys was the manager of Video Voyages. Dogwater had certainly not slept with her (or anyone else according to Izzy) and was not likely to. Gladys was seventy-years-old, had brown teeth and was, by Dogwater's conservative estimate, nine-hundred-pounds. It's not fair to judge someone by their weight, but when you're fat *and* scary, that's a whole different deal.

"Anyway, sorry man," Izzy shrugged again.

"Great, I'm about to make the greatest scientific discovery ever and I can't even get a stupid camera to record it."

"You could buy the stuff, man," Izzy said.

Dogwater laughed. "Look around. This place doesn't hand out many stock options that I could cash in to fund this little venture."

Izzy, not being the greatest at taking in sarcasm, did look around. He saw a small, cheaply paneled shop with dingy windows. The rental shelves were filled, mostly with older titles rather than new releases. A lot of John Hughes stuff from the eighties.

"And my confidential government source says thermal imaging places an alien presence in the area," Dogwater was saying. He spoke barely above a mumble in case the walls had ears. He was sure the walls of his apartment did (The tin foil kept out aliens, but not the feds.), but was fairly confident they hadn't bugged Video Voyages.

"What government source, man?" Izzy asked.

"Well, if I told you he...or she...wouldn't be confidential would he...or she?"

Izzy shrugged. "Whatever, man. How much cash you need to buy this stuff?"

Dogwater thought. "Three thousand would probably be okay. Five thousand would be better. Are you gonna loan it to me?"

"Yeah, no problem," Izzy said. "I'll go home and pull it from under my fu-...er my *freakin'* mattress. Be right back."

They both laughed.

"What about that rich writer dude you're always hangin' with?" Izzy said.

Dogwater folded his arms. "Cameron? No, I can't ask him."

"Why not?"

Dogwater was momentarily distracted by a couple kids, aged ten or eleven, hovering around a bin of licensed character toys near the "Christmas Picks" video shelf. The shelf itself had only two videos on it, both of which were ancient when Dogwater himself was a child.

"Hey, you guys gonna pay for those?" Dogwater asked in an elevated tone. One of the two kids, a red-haired, freckle-faced specimen of youth, looked sharply at Dogwater then jabbed his friend in the arm. The friend, a dark-haired boy who looked way too sinister for someone his age, tossed the superhero figure he'd been holding near the pocket of his parka back into the bin. The two boys hastily exited the store without a word.

Dogwater turned back to Izzy. "Cameron is my friend. I can't go to him for a handout."

"It's not a handout. Tell him it's an investment. When you sell your little alien to the highest bidder, you can pay him back. With interest."

"I told you," Dogwater said, "I'm not doing this for money." It didn't come out of his mouth sounding nearly as convincing as it had before his television blew up and Izzy lost his job.

"Yeah, yeah," Izzy said dismissively, not buying it. "Rich folks like that are just dying to put their money in schemes like this. Plus, this guy's a celebrity. Lived in New York and all that. He probably ate lunch with movie stars all the time. You know how those people are. You watch the celebrity channel on TV don't ya?"

Dogwater thought about pointing out that he doesn't watch much of anything these days, but let it go. Maybe he should talk to Cameron. It really would be a loan. He'd pay it all back. Someday. Somehow. His data was good; worthy of Lars Heimdal himself. If there was ever going to be a chance to prove alien contact with Earth, this was it.

"All right," Dogwater said. "We'll go talk to Cameron after I get off work."

"We?" Izzy said.

"Sure," Dogwater replied. "With those puppy-dog eyes, how could anyone say 'no' to you?"

Despite the fact that about the only game Santa Claus had played in centuries is chess, games of which he lost to Mrs. Claus on a fairly regular basis, Kris Kringle was proving quite adept at cribbage. This card game utilized a peg board and arcane scoring procedures involving taking turns laying down cards in sequences of fifteen, though, for reasons mysterious to Santa, you get only two points every time you do so. Nevertheless, he was proving quite good at it.

After the previous night's odyssey, Cameron had been unable or unwilling to go into the study at all today, even to the point of asking Uncle Milo to retrieve his reading glasses for him. So, the two men had spent the afternoon playing cribbage.

Santa's success on the cribbage board was particularly remarkable given the impressive headache he was experiencing. Generally, Santa experienced not so much as a fart at the North Pole, but down here in the real world, stomach aches, hangovers, and headaches seemed to be the norm. He blamed it on the body he was inhabiting.

But there was something else. Uncle Milo's *kevla* seemed to be growing restless in his mind and the strain of sharing a body with another soul was tiring.

*Well, no matter,* Santa thought, *I've got a job to do.*

"How are you feeling today, Cameron?" Santa asked as Cameron was shuffling the cards.

"Fine," Cameron shrugged.

Santa knew he was lying, but, then, he was Santa. "Really?" he asked.

"Really," Cameron repeated. He tried to look the old man in the eye, but only saw the jolly old elf in them, so quickly cast his eyes back down to the cards he was dealing.

Santa looked at the man across the table who was counting to himself as he dealt the cards, making sure they got six each. When the dealing was done, he looked *into* the man. Santa saw a five-year-old Cameron waking on Christmas morning to find he had gotten the toy he wanted—not a Santa delivery, a parental one—except it was broken. He looked a little more and saw a six-year-old Cameron who's Christmas puppy died two weeks later; a nine-year-old who was so ill with chicken pox that he spent Christmas in his room; an eleven-year-old who experienced his house burning down right before Christmas; a sixteen-year-old who's best friend, and newly-minted driver, died a month before the holiday; and the nineteen-year-old who's father died.

It occurred to St. Nicholas that in all the stories and legends of, well, of him, the focus was always on the children of the world. Santa loved them all; did what he could for them. He knew they grew up and that could be sad. It was especially painful to see their torment as they transitioned from believing to not believing—lost sight of the magic and love of the Christmas holiday—and foundered in adulthood without their Christmas spirit. It killed a little piece of Santa every time. But they all did it. After all, it wasn't like he could find a kid who was turning seven or eight and teetering on the brink of nonbelief, knock on his door and say, "Hey, buddy, I'm still here. Got any milk and cookies?"

The thing was, Santa now realized, once the children became non-believers, he typically lost track of them, at least until they had children of their own. Then the cycle would begin again with the next generation.

By then, of course, the former children were now focused on more "important" things than toys and games. Santa was a toymaker and a gift-giver. He delivered stuffed animals, dolls, and games to children. What, really, could he do for the adults? It's not like he could pay off their mortgage or give them back their old hairlines. And when they got old and frail, he couldn't comfort them.

Even some of his least-naughty children had bad problems as adults; drugs, alcohol, other wickedness. Santa had always ignored all this. But maybe if he'd been there more for Cameron and the other children who became adults, things would have turned out different. Throughout his childhood, Cameron experienced one bad Christmas after another, yet he still believed in Santa just as long as any other kid. And then, when Cameron grew up, how did Santa repay those years of loyalty? He moved on to the little ones, the "true believers". And that seemed wrong now.

Well, now was his chance to put things right; for Cameron and for his daughter. Ho, ho, ho.

The "ho, ho, ho," had almost been audible until Santa quickly stifled himself. Instead, something that sounded vaguely like a cough came out.

"You okay, Milo? Want some water?" Cameron asked.

"What? Oh, no, no, my boy," Santa said. "Thanks."

"Okay," Cameron said, not entirely convinced. Uncle Milo was no kid anymore. All Cameron needed was for the old guy to catch a cold, then pneumonia. What would it do to the visitation case if his ex-wife's uncle died in his house?

"Well, I dealt, so you start," Cameron said.

Before Kris Kringle could lay down his first card, the doorbell rang.

"I'm not buying another box of Christmas peanut brittle," Cameron muttered. Cameron had barely stood when whoever rang the bell let himself in.

"Hey, Jones, you here?" Dogwater's voice called from the living room.

"Dining room," Cameron called back, recognizing the voice.

Dogwater and Izzy Carmichel came into the dining room (Dogwater flinching reflexively at the sight of the Christmas lights—so like the lights of the alien labs he experienced in his abductions). The men strode briskly, shoulders hunched and blowing on their hands for warmth.

"Yo, man, jack the heat. You're rich, ain't you?" Izzy grunted.

Cameron turned to Dogwater with a bemused smile, expecting an explanation..

"Jones, this is my buddy Izzy," Dogwater quickly interjected. "Izzy, this is the great author and celebrity-type-person, Cameron Jones...and some guy I've never met before."

"Sorry, guys, this is my...er, my ex-wife's uncle Milo Vestibule. He's, uh, staying here for a few days." It occurred to Cameron in that moment that he had no real idea *how long* Uncle Milo intended to be with him, but it also didn't really bother him. It was fun, no *comfortable* having him around; like the entrenched butt prints in your favorite easy chair. "And as far as the heat, my guest likes it cool."

Santa shrugged apologetically. You can't fight more than a millennium of acclimation.

"Want a beer?" Dogwater said to Izzy. Izzy shrugged and Dog headed for the fridge. Cameron didn't even blink at the apparent boldness of this guest. Santa was amazed.

"Anybody else want one?" Dogwater called from the kitchen.

"Yeah," Cameron called back. He raised his eyebrows to Santa, who emphatically motioned that he did not. Santa had learned that lesson on his first night here. He winced and massaged his temple at the memory.

"Have a seat," Cameron said to Izzy, somewhat unnecessarily as the man was already perching, but perhaps Cameron needed to reassert his prerogative as the true owner of the house. Izzy shrugged again.

Dogwater returned with three bottles of beer, two frosted mugs and a pilsner glass. He knew that Cameron always drank beer from a pilsner glass, regardless of whether it was a pilsner beer or not. He sat next to Cameron, slapping him, guy-like, on the shoulder as he sat.

"How you been, guy?" Dogwater asked.

Now Cameron shrugged. "Still kickin'."

"How's the book?" Dogwater asked.

"It's there," Cameron said, tight-lipped.

"Hey!" Izzy blurted in a sudden burst of realization. "You're that writer dude. You wrote that book....uh..."

Dogwater offered "*Quality Not Quantity?*"

"No..."

"*Sandstorm?*" Dogwater said.

"No..."

"*The Dead Man's New Hat,*" Cameron said, since that was the only one left that he had published. He was pretty sure Izzy wasn't referring to the piece of shit fouling his computer at that moment.

"No, man, you know, the book about the secret code in that cat DaVinci's paintings and shit that leads to God or something."

Cameron smiled. "You mean *The DaVinci Code?*"

"Yeah, man! That book was number one forever, man."

"Did you read it?" Cameron asked.

"Sure, man."

"Screw you, man, you did not," Dogwater said.

"Yeah, well, I meant to."

Cameron thought he really should tell this young man that actually Dan Brown, not Cameron Jones, wrote *The DaVinci Code,* but he just didn't feel like it.

"Do I understand you write *books?*" Santa said, partly in wonder, partly to be part of the conversation.

The other three seated at the table glanced at the old man, smiled politely, overlooking the man's apparent obliviousness, and then Cameron said, "So what are you boys up to?"

"Funny you should ask," Dogwater said and coughed nervously.

"Uh-oh. What's it gonna cost me?" Cameron asked.

For a moment, Dogwater hesitated. How did he know? Was he psychic? Unlikely, as the aliens usually only put those implants in Pacific Northwesterners. They usually reserved Midwesterners for intestinal experiments.

"Well, like I said, funny, that is that you ask..." Dog trailed off.

"The man needs cash for his alien hunt," Izzy offered.

Cameron frowned. "Is this the 'Santa alien' thing you told me about?"

At the mention of 'Santa alien' the real Santa Claus did a near perfect spit-take featuring grape juice. He coughed and sputtered so energetically, Cameron worried about the old guy's respiratory health.

"I've got good data. My sources are tracking astronomical movement of comet-like unidentified bodies and there are increasing signs of elevated thermal levels consistent with alien body heat on the Earth's surface. "

"In other words..." Izzy prompted helpfully.

"In other words," Dogwater said, visibly trying to slow his own excited speech, "alien vessels are being tracked and extra-terrestrial life is starting to show up in greater numbers on the planet—the 'elves' to the 'Santa' aliens, so to speak. Everything Lars Heimdal said would happen is happening. This is the year."

"The year for...?" Cameron asked.

"The first, full-fledged, indisputable alien contact," Dogwater said, actually thumping the table to emphasize his point. "If our calculations are correct, the aliens will enter Earth's orbit in the western hemisphere, specifically over North America, on Christmas Eve. 'Santa Claus' might not be comin' to town, but he is coming to the planet."

Santa's eyes widened. *Oh, dear.*

"And you want to see them?" Cameron said.

Dogwater was stunned. How could anyone ask that? Contact with life from another planet, galaxy, or, hell, another universe—that didn't involve testicle removal -would be the single greatest thing to happen to humankind. How could anyone not want to see that?

"Well, yeah," Dogwater said. "We call them 'the Santas'. Who doesn't want to see Santa?"

Santa's stomach lurched.

"So, what, you perch up on the roof with a telescope, a glass of milk and wave a cookie in the air, hoping Santa sees it? What kind of cookies do alien Kris Kringles like?" Cameron turned to Uncle Milo. "I'm thinking chocolate chip with nuts." Cameron's laugh degenerated to a cough. He took a sip of beer.

Santa, in the guise of Uncle Milo, looking as pale as Dogwater looked flush, nodded weakly.

The color in Dogwater's face intensified. "Please don't laugh at me," he said softly, feeling very embarrassed.

Cameron collected himself and said, "Sorry. And what do you want from me?"

"Well, I need equipment to document the event," Dogwater said, suddenly very self-conscious of how ridiculous this must sound to a nonbeliever. "Cameras, computers, telescope with electronic coordinate adjusters, GPS, lighting equipment, audio recording equipment." Dogwater shrugged.

Izzy, the helpful partner, was temporarily distracted by a solid gold, fully-functional Slinky toy in a hutch that stood on the south wall of Cameron's dining room.

Deep inside Santa's ample gut, his colon seized. He was aware of his breathing becoming shallow. He studied Izzy. Something stirred; a tickle of memory from his naughty/nice archives. He couldn't quite bring it up.

"So, you need money to take a picture of Santa Claus?"

A faint, pained wheeze hissed from Santa's throat.

Dogwater sighed as the color rose in his cheeks. Izzy snickered despite himself.

Cameron crossed his arms. "How much?" he asked.

Dogwater's eyebrows rose. So did Izzy's. Santa's eyes darted from man to man.

Feeling a bit of encouragement, Dogwater cleared his throat and said, "Two-"

"Five," Izzy interrupted.

Dogwater shot a look at Izzy. Izzy just nodded.

"Er, five thousand," Dogwater said, clearing his throat again.

Any rational human being, hearing a half-assed pitch like Dogwater's from a known flake about aliens and such nonsense, would keep his wallet in his pocket and throw the scam artist out.

These days, however, Cameron was not particularly rational, and frequently thought that he himself was, in many ways, an alien. So, he said simply, "Okay. Take a check?"

Dogwater blinked. It didn't sink in. He looked at Izzy, who shrugged. "Uh, yeah, a check is okay." It occurred to Dogwater he didn't have a bank account (the government tracks you through account numbers), but maybe he could go to one of those check cashing places.

Cameron went to get his checkbook. The three remaining men, as men who are strangers often do, took pains not to make eye contact. In this crowd, it was unlikely anyone would mistake eye contact for hostility (except maybe Izzy) and start a fight, but eye contact might lead to a conversation made awkward by unfamiliarity and nobody wanted that.

Santa couldn't resist. "So, uh, Dogwater, is it?"

Dog nodded and smiled politely.

The knot in Santa's lower intestines tightened again as he asked, "Do you really think you can catch, um, Santa Claus?"

"Well…"

"I mean," Santa interrupted, panicking a bit, "if you're awake when he comes, he won't leave you any presents." Santa smiled what he hoped was a smile that put a light-hearted veneer on his panicky tone.

"Yeah, and the Easter Bunny leaves little rabbit shits in your shoes," Izzy said. He and Dog laughed. Santa looked from man to man, not understanding. Santa knew the Easter Bunny and there was no way he'd ever do *that*. Were they kidding? Santa just didn't understand real world humor.

Cameron came back in and handed Dogwater a check. "Here you go, buddy. Go get famous," he said.

"Thank you, Cameron." There were actual tears in Dogwater's eyes. "You'll get every penny back, I swear."

Cameron nodded, internally saying goodbye to his money.

Knowing it's always best to get out while you're ahead, Izzy stood and motioned to Dogwater and then to the door. Dog nodded.

"Well, we should go shopping, I guess," Dogwater said.

"Go forth and multiply or live and prosper a long time or something," Cameron said.

Dogwater looked at his friend. Impulsively, he threw both arms around the man for a mercifully quick hug. An awkward guy moment ensued, then passed just as quickly.

Then the men were gone.

Outside, Izzy snatched the check from Dogwater's hand. "Woo, boy! We got the dough. Gonna snap us some pics of some little green men. Next stop is one of those extremely white guy talk shows on the cable news channel."

"I told you, I'm not doing this to get famous," Dogwater protested. "It's for science."

"Whatever," Izzy shrugged, not buying it.

As Dogwater caught himself picturing the sight of him in a suit and tie, fielding questions from a caller in Wichita on *Larry King Live*, he realized that he didn't entirely buy it either.

Santa laid awake in bed for hours. He stared at the ceiling as he mulled the concept of real world humor. He needed to know if Cameron's friends had been kidding about trying to catch, well, him. They had made other jokes, he guessed judging by the laughter, so maybe they were kidding about that too.

While trying to master the tricky art of the television remote control one day, Santa had come upon a show where a comedian was telling jokes. Santa knew they were jokes because the audience was laughing, but they didn't seem very funny. The comedian talked a lot about sex and cursed a lot. Was that humor? He'd had to change the channel because he suddenly recognized the comedian as one of the former children on his 'naughty' list. Maybe getting a lot of coal and knitted socks for Christmas instead of toys as a child made you curse as an adult. Once again, Santa felt sad about abandoning his believers even after they moved on.

On the other hand, when Holly had visited, she told a joke—Knock Knock. Who's there? Radio. Radio who? Radio not, here I come!—and Cameron had laughed uproariously. Santa didn't get that one either—had no idea it was a very old joke—but it was totally free of profanity and came in the pure, sweet package of childhood innocence.

But then he thought about the comic strip with that crazy duck and chuckled. Today's installment had the duck bumping into things because he had put on a mask and a cape to become "Super Duck" but he put the mask on backwards. The humor in some things was just obvious.

Santa was in self-imposed exile, was jeopardizing Christmas, and couldn't understand even basic real-worlder communication. And now, it seemed, humans were hunting him.

Knock knock
  Who's there?
Santa.
  Santa who?
Santa's in big trouble.

# DECEMBER 17

The morning after Cameron gave Dogwater the five-thousand dollar loan-that-no-one-would-ever-believe-was-really-a-loan for his alien hunting expedition, Santa awoke to a realization.

Izzy Carmichel used to be an altar boy.

No, that wasn't quite right, but as a child, Izzy sang in his family's church choir. Among other things, Santa had been troubled by Izzy, the man, during their meeting the day before and he spent the night subconsciously teasing out this fact about the man's childhood. Izzy was unsettling. With his sarcastic mouth and slothful demeanor, coupled with dark, cold eyes, Izzy was—to use the lingo Santa hoped was still hip—*bad news.*

But there was more. The sweet, little choir boy who went to Baptist church with his family faithfully, was respectful to his elders and even ate all his vegetables, was terribly unhappy. And Santa knew why. Izzy's father was a drunk and an abuser—of Izzy's mother and sister, not Izzy himself. That was something, he supposed. But still, it was a horrible thing and a horrible way to grow up.

Santa always took extra care to bring the best presents during Izzy's "Santa years." There wasn't much he could do directly. He couldn't really knock on the door and tell whoever answers, "Hi, I'm Santa Claus. May I speak to Mr. Carmichel about his parenting?"

Besides, Santa realized, if he started down that path, he'd be intervening on behalf of thousands, maybe millions, trying to stop abuse, poverty, even war, if he took it on. It was too much. Simply too much. Santa had a few magical elven gifts, but he was still just a man.

No, he wasn't. He'd ceased to be a "man" centuries ago. He was now a myth, a legend, a giant among children. A creature of the season, who could do anything for about four weeks, only to be forgotten the rest of the year. Who wouldn't doubt their own existence if that was your reality? Still, who else had such universal, timeless appeal—at least among pre-schoolers? Why, only God himself.

Santa rebuked himself. It was wrong, of course, to even hint that he, a mere mortal (well, *probably* mortal—he had never really figured that out) could be a rival to God even in the limited context of holiday giving. He may be "Saint Nicholas" or "Father Christmas" to some, but he was still a gift-giver, not a life-giver.

Santa chuckled a very un-merry laugh as it occurred to him that at this moment, he wasn't much of a gift-giver either. He lacked the desire to build a toy, decorate a tree. He missed Mrs. Claus, of course. And feeding the reindeer. He always liked that. Blitzen would nuzzle him and look at him with melt-your-heart-eyes.

But what he really wanted right now was to go to the movies. And a waffle. Maybe with chocolate chips and whipped cream. Santa eagerly hopped out of bed to see if Cameron had any.

At nine-thirteen that morning, Cameron sat at his computer not thinking about the manuscript on the monitor in front of him. This was good because in the past hour, all he had written was a single word, four times per line—neatly tabbed—twenty-six lines per page. The word was "jingle." Then, at the very end of the page, by way of conclusion of this thought, he had written in all capitals and in bold print, "BELLS!" That last typed in the font "Baskerville Old Face" which looked, to Cameron, very Christmas-y.

This was not whimsy or some sort of writing exercise. He had no idea he had written this and that was good. On previous occasions when Cameron had read over his draft and seen these types of verbal interludes interspersed with the prose, it upset him. More than that, it unnerved him. He tried, for a while, to brush them aside as fatigue, but that was getting harder all the time, especially since Webster Stanhope made his appearance at Ron's Discount Cow Emporium.

Today, however, so far, Cameron was blissfully unaware of anything amiss. As he scrolled to a new page, his mind slipped seamlessly into coherent sentences. To wit:

"Dexter Morgan knew the jig was up. Conrad Brewster had him cornered. But at least his girlfriend Mandy had huge boobs."

Coherence is a tricky concept sometimes.

Still, Cameron thought, it was not bad, especially in comparison to the continuity glitch that resulted in his protagonist Conrad having been transformed into a dog in chapter twelve, but now in chapter thirteen, being fully restored to human-hood with no explanation whatsoever.

Mercifully, the phone rang.

When he answered, Cameron was greeted by a cheerful, "Well, yes, Cameron, how are you?" It was Everett Franken.

"Fine," Cameron said cautiously.

"Good, good," Everett Franken said. "I was just getting ready for my morning treadmill when I got a call from Wally Bass." Everett Franken's relentlessly upbeat tone dipped ever-so-slightly at the mention of Susan's attorney.

Cameron shoved aside the disturbing image of lanky, pale Everett Franken marching on a treadmill in shorts and black socks that had suddenly crowded his brain.

"What did he want?" Cameron asked.

"He said Susan wants to let you have an extra visit with Holly."

"An extra visit?"

"Yes. Mr. Bass wanted to know if Susan could call you to discuss it."

"An extra visit?" Cameron repeated.

"Yes, she'll call sometime today to make arrangements if that's okay."

"Uh, sure," Cameron said. "Everett, what does this mean?"

Everett Franken verbally shrugged. "I don't know. Mr. Bass didn't explain why. But it certainly doesn't hurt your case."

*No, only I can do that,* Cameron thought.

"You do want the visit, don't you?" Everett Franken was asking.

A beat passed, bordering on being awkwardly long, but still in the safe zone.

"Yes, of course. Uh, thanks."

"Well, then," Everett Franken continued. "I'll let you go. Have a lovely weekend."

"Yeah, you too," Cameron said, adding, "This Saturday morning phone call is costing me a bundle, isn't it?"

"Oh, yes," Everett Franken deadpanned, then hung up.

Cameron held the cordless phone for five seconds before pressing the button to turn it off. It was another full minute before he replaced the phone on its cradle.

*What the hell is going on?* he thought.

At Christmastime, downtown Santa Claus, Indiana is a winter wonderland. Crisp winter air flows over majestic holiday landscapes, infusing the Midwest with yuletide spirit. Images of Abraham Lincoln—a famous Spencer County boy—and Santa abound, filling the air with joy.

That's a lie. Sometimes there's snow. But mostly, like most of the Midwest, December features lots of cold and ice.

Around mid-morning, Santa sat on the deck overlooking the tree-filled lot behind Cameron's house. It was cold, but for a man of the North Pole, a thirty degree day was nothing to get uptight about. He did miss the red wool suit a little though.

The North Pole was beautiful. The air was clear and crisp. The twinkling stars at night came through so sharply, it stopped you cold. But Santa was finding something just as stimulating in the Midwest of America. There was an earthy hue. The trees were plentiful and varied, not all pine as they were at home. He took deep breaths of Indiana air.

Cameron came out on the deck, jingling car keys.

"Hey, Milo, you want to get out of here for a bit?" Cameron asked.

Kris Kringle was intrigued. Another movie? "Where are we going?" he asked hopefully.

"Well, don't you think we should go check out your house? See how bad the damage is? Maybe grab some of your stuff. It's probably sitting there in a puddle of water and soot."

In truth, Cameron had come up with this justification for an outing after deciding that he could not stand to look at Conrad Brewster, the schmuck, screwing up his manuscript any longer. Plus, sitting there waiting for the phone to ring for Susan's call might kill him.

Cameron made sure his phone calls would be forwarded to his cell phone on the theory that if there was a good chance the wait was going to kill him anyway, he might as well not miss the call. Then they climbed into the SUV and set out. Santa still experienced a touch of vertigo as the motorized carriage sprang to life. For a man who flew around in an exceedingly unsafe open sleigh pulled by reindeer, motorized vehicles had quite an unsettling effect on him. Even ones featuring DVD players in the dashboard.

During the short drive to Milo Vestibule's house, Cameron brooded over Holly and his ailing manuscript, now titled *Piss On It*. Kris Kringle filled the silence with commentary:

"Look at those adorable children!"

"That's a beautiful home!"

"Oh my, will you look at that?!" in reference to a string of four semi-trucks. He very nearly had to stifle a ho-ho-ho.

After each outburst, Cameron merely nodded, or, at best, offered a "Yeah…"

They passed a large statue of Santa Claus atop a sign reading: "Dedicated to the Children of the World in Memory of an Undying Love." The two men were struck by that message for very different reasons: Santa because it was like looking at, well, himself, staring down disapprovingly, beating him over the head with his Christmas mission; Cameron because he wondered where he could get a little of that undying love.

The men shoved those thoughts aside and kept driving. Silence cocooned the car, save for the crunch of sand and rock salt under the tires.

Cameron grunted, shattering the funk.

"What is it?" Santa asked, tearing his attention from the squirrels prancing by the side of the road—squirrel were rare at the North Pole.

"Santa's got his own village," Cameron said. "People love the guy in this town."

Santa shifted uncomfortably.

"What's he done for me lately?" Cameron was smiling, but it was a cold, off-putting smile.

Santa opened his mouth as he tried to come up with something that he, in fact, had done for Cameron lately.

Cameron took him off the spot with, "Screw it. Maybe I'll write a tell-all. *How Santa Let Me Down*. Gotta be better than that dog pile I've got on the computer at home."

Cameron actually laughed and Santa decided to take that as a positive sign. Plus, the light—one of two on Santa Claus, Indiana—changed.

Santa's sight-seeing was disrupted by the previously overlooked, but very real, possibility that at some point Cameron might ask for directions to his— meaning Uncle Milo's—house. What would he do? He couldn't really say, "Turn left at the blue house where I left the model train last year. It's right next to the house that always puts out buttermilk for me." Santa started to panic a little.

But Cameron seemed to find his own way. They rounded a corner and approached Milo Vestibule's small bungalow, nestled in a quaintly tree-lined, if modest, neighborhood. When they parked, Santa could finally breathe again. Sharing his rather large frame with Uncle Milo's fairly narrow one was already constricting. Add a little tension, and poor Santa nearly suffocated.

The first thing Cameron and Santa noticed as they parked in the driveway and got out of the SUV was that the picture in the newspaper made the damage look a lot worse than it did in three dimensions. There were some markings that could have been scorch marks around the windows on the south side, and one of the windows on the lower level was cracked, but that was about all that was apparent on the outside.

"I got the sense it was a lot worse than this," Cameron said.

"So did I," Santa replied, a little worried that Flifle's magic was wearing off.

They went up on the porch and stood in front of the door. After a few seconds, Cameron finally said, "Um, Milo, do you have a key?"

"Oh, yes," Santa said, embarrassed. "How silly of me." He started fishing through pockets, not at all sure that he did in fact have a key.

As Cameron patiently watched this production, a squealing child's voice called from the end of the driveway.

"Milo's home!" the voice cried. Both men turned to see a child of eight or nine wearing a snowsuit—despite the lack of any appreciable snow—and a heavy wool cap. He was waving enthusiastically and sprinted as fast as he could up the driveway attacking Santa's legs without the slightest reservation.

"Well, ho-ho...how are you, uh, little boy?" Santa said.

"Fine," the boy with the wool cap with the fringe of red-hair sticking out said. "Where did you go?" he asked.

"Well, I've been staying with my, uh, nephew," Santa said, nodding at Cameron, not really sure if that was the right designation.

Cameron smiled at the boy who eyed him suspiciously before seeming to decide he was okay and smiled back. "What's your name?" the red-haired boy asked.

"Cameron," Cameron said.

"That's a funny name," the boy said in that tone children have that lets them pass off an insult as matter-of-fact conversation. "My name's Wesley."

Cameron considered pointing out "Wesley" was a pretty funny name too, but thought better of it.

"I almost got my birdhouse painted," Wesley said, turning back to Santa, in a tone that suggested this was significant. "But I can't decide whether to use green or purple." This was clearly a very difficult choice. "The top isn't on right, but Mommy says I have to wait until I go see my daddy again to fix it."

Santa nodded along, uncomprehendingly.

Cameron frowned, trying to retrieve a memory. "Milo, you still doing that kids' woodcraft class? Bringing in the underprivileged kids, teaching them a little about woodshop? Birdhouses, and model cars and all that?"

Santa beamed. This was something he knew about. "Yes," he said eagerly. It sounded like a wonderful project. Good for Uncle Milo.

"Are we gonna have class after Christmas?" Wesley asked.

"Well, I hope so," Santa said, realizing he didn't know what would happen—to Milo or himself—after Christmas.

"Me too," Wesley said. "Well, bye!" With that, he bounced off the porch and was gone.

"Nice kid," Cameron said.

"Yes," Santa agreed, watching Wesley run down the sidewalk, presumably toward his own house.

"Should we go in?" Cameron asked.

"Er, oh, yes," Santa said and resumed the key search.

Cameron casually turned the front door knob and discovered the door was open. "Never mind," he said to Santa, who, in desperation, had started checking his shoes for signs of a key.

They entered Milo's small living room. On first viewing, the room did appear to have been recently engulfed in flames. Everything was black with soot and appeared burned. Looking closer, though, nothing was broken, there was no water damage. The smell of smoke was perfunctory, like some sort of canned scent you might use if you—for some reason—were having a fire-themed party. It looked like the room needed a good scrubbing, but not major structural repair. You couldn't really tell where the fire had started. It was as if someone had splashed some Inferno in a Bucket on the walls to disguise them. Santa realized this idea was possibly not far off the mark.

"Doesn't look that bad, does it?" Cameron half-mumbled, still thinking about Wesley's adoration of the old man and wondering if he'd ever be so beloved by a child—his or any other. More likely he'd be the crazy old bastard down on the corner with whom the neighbor kids dared each other to cross paths. He'd have to decide between now and then if he would be one of those crazy old guys who throws rocks or just yells a lot. He'd probably have to get a bunch of cats. Or maybe a mangy dog with a flatulence problem that repulsed most people but would not bother crazy old bastard Cameron in the least.

Santa wiped the soot off a framed photo on the wall opposite the front door with a colorful clown's pocket-type handkerchief, which he then stuffed back in his pocket, despite the filth. The photo showed a group of men in military uniforms. One of them with jet black hair, piercing eyes and a strong chin was clearly Milo. The photo was dated June 9, 1952. Santa shook his head. This must have been during one of the real-worlders' wars. Terrible. The men looked proud and strong though.

"I think the TV might be a loss," Cameron was saying as he drew a path through an inch of grime covering the screen with a finger, then wiped it on his jeans. "You have insurance, right?"

Santa nodded absently. He was now looking at a crudely made wooden plaque lying on an end table which read:

TO MR. MILO VESTIBULE
FROM ALL OF US AT
WOOD CAMP NUMBER 7
WE LOVE YOU

Below the messages, the names of a dozen people, including Wesley, the boy they had just met, were similarly engraved in smaller type.

"Guess you're pretty popular with the pre-teen crowd," Cameron said over Santa's shoulder.

"Yes," Santa said, somehow moved by a dedication to a man he'd never heard of until recently. "I suppose I am." The words were strained a bit through his voice box before coming out.

Cameron paused to wipe some soot off an old picture on a table near the door way to the rest of the house. This photo showed a smiling child giggling at some secret joy. The child was little more than an infant; cute, but at the stage of development where it was difficult to tell its gender. Susan maybe? It was possible. This child had the Wentworth smile and Susan's glowing eyes. The child's look of utter, unreserved joy disturbed Cameron deeply for reasons only Dr. Whipple—if she ever got off the slopes—could explain.

There was not much else to look at in Milo Vestibule's living room, but what was there told the story of a heroic, generous, and loved man. All the things Cameron was not, according to himself anyway. He eagerly moved to the next room.

An examination of the rest of the house revealed no damage at all. There was less and less of the smeary soot the farther they went. The faint obligatory smoke smell was there, biting, but not acrid. Cameron took mental note of the sizeable waste bin full of beer cans in the kitchen and the lack of food in the refrigerator—which was still running. For a house that recently was "gutted" by fire, it seemed remarkably free of signs of intervention by the fire department. The electricity and gas were functional. Nothing was broken. There was not even any sign of water damage. It was all very weird, though Cameron acknowledged that there was little in his life these days that wasn't weird.

To Santa, touring the home of this man whose body he shared, was like walking through a dream. Everything was familiar, but not quite recognizable. The place was unlike any he had ever lived in—certainly a world apart from the North Pole Complex, and obviously far different than his home as a boy in the early centuries. This man, Milo, lived simply, loved, and was loved by children. He was even a woodcarver, a gift-giver of sorts. Santa could, in another reality, be this man, except for the beer. Santa thought again of the bad two sips he had tried that first night at Cameron's house and winced.

Santa had never thought he could have another life and had never wanted one. Or maybe, he realized now, he had never wanted another life because he didn't think he could have one. The realization was profound and heretical somehow at the same time. But maybe this life would suit him just fine.

At Cameron's suggestion, Santa packed a few items—some underwear, a couple changes of clothes, books, some toiletries. Santa spent a long time studying the water pick in the bathroom– what the heck was it?—before settling on the low-tech toothbrush. Now that he had mastered Milo's bridge, he could resume his diligent dental practices.

Cameron hadn't asked if Milo wanted to continue staying with him. There really didn't seem to be much reason to; Milo's house looked pretty fine. They both just seemed to assume—going off some unspoken understanding— Milo would be staying on at Cameron's. That was the right thing. It just was. It was nice.

As they left, locking the door behind them with the key Cameron had found in a work boot that was sitting on the windowsill—only a writer would think, "Hey that must be where the key is"—Santa winced. It was a small twinge. Cameron didn't even notice. The wince was the opening act for a stabbing pain in his head; no, not simply *in* his head, but *within his mind*. It was a thought-headache for lack of a better term. Since he'd had no alcohol recently, Santa started wondering if taking over a real-worlder's body came with side effects.

Back at the house, Cameron's blood pressure spiked. Or maybe it just seemed like that. Whatever it was, his heartbeat took on a big band swing as they pulled into the driveway. There was no real reason for the mood swing—not that his emotions needed much prompting to take his psyche for a spin. Maybe it was because he was now confronted with thinking about Susan's impending call again. Or maybe it was the six cups of coffee he'd had so far today.

As the men entered the house, Cameron glanced at the Christmas tree as he stomped through the living room, noting only that he'd forgotten to unplug the lights before they'd left.

Cameron walked to the kitchen for another cup of coffee. Why not? He'd barely remembered what he did with the sugar bowl before he was seized by an intense hatred of that tree. How dare it make them forget to turn the lights off before they left? His own house could have burned like Milo's. Fucking tree.

He went back to the living room and kicked the holy merry mother of-I'll-be-home-for-Christmas-but-I'll-be-pissed-silent-fucking-night-no-more out of the Christmas tree.

In all his time in the North Pole Complex, Santa had never seen such violence. Teevo, the highly unstable elf inventor, notwithstanding, no one ever raised their voice, much less committed acts of violence.

So even as the eighth, or possibly it was the ninth, candy cane spiraled past his head, only to shatter against the door frame behind him, Santa did not move. What could he do anyway? Tackle Cameron? Get him in a headlock? These were very un-Santa-like behaviors.

Random curses flowed forth from Cameron like an overturned bowl of spiked eggnog. "Falalalala my ass!" "Bite me, Rudolph!" "O, Little Hell-Hole of Bethlehem! Take that!"

"Cameron..." Santa tried, when the cursing subsided. There was no response.

The light strings challenged Cameron's automatic pilot. Cameron had to pull the wire branches out of the faux wooden tree trunk to get the string loose which killed some of his anger's momentum. The jerking motion needed to free the string propelled Cameron's body into a spin. The string wrapped around his legs and he stumbled to the floor.

Cameron sat there, panting and mouthing words that no longer came out fully formed until finally he grabbed a spectacular crystal ornament shaped like a Santa's Castle and said, "It's all wrong! It's not fair!" He threw the ornament and Santa, calling upon the small reserve of Santa-magic he carried to the real world, discretely redirected the path of the ornament through the air with a flick of his hand, rerouting the ball to himself rather than letting it fly into the glass-covered bookcase. He caught it gently in his palm. Cameron didn't notice.

Santa looked at the crystal ornament now in his hand. In front of the castle in this North Pole scene was a small child who—it was clear now—was Holly. The figure looked so much like her. How had he missed it

"Bah fucking humbug," Cameron said, and fell back spread-eagle on the floor.

Santa went over to the man, now in his thirties, but indistinguishable from the sad little boy he used to be.

"Cameron," Santa said, sitting down on the floor with relative ease thanks to elderly Milo's surprisingly limber body. "Christmas is not a time to despair. It's a wonderful time, but there's so much more to life; friends, family, doing good works. This is a great season, but it's not a ...movie with double-buttered popcorn." Santa's mind had gone to thing he'd most recently decided was perfection.

Cameron smiled. "Merry Christmas, Milo."

"Merry Christmas, Cameron."

The blizzard was over.

Later, Santa would contemplate the seismic shift that his words represented for himself. Christmas wasn't everything. Rather than diminish his love of the holiday, this realization somehow increased it. This, in turn, made him feel even more lost.

The phone, which in Cameron's world was always waiting in the wings for its cue, rang.

Both men looked in the direction of the phone. Cameron was trying to orient himself again to rationality and not really fit to answer, but Santa was still a little intimidated by the communication device.

Still, all that ringing after the dramatic tension that had just played out was brutal. Santa would have to be brave. He tip-toed to the kitchen as if he didn't want to disturb the angry noise-maker, then gingerly picked up the receiver. He paused, then said, "Greetings!"

"Santa!" a small, gleeful voice said.

"Hello, Holly," Santa said in a grandfatherly baritone, forgetting to do the Milo voice.

"Did you get my letter?"

"Yes," Santa said, dropping his guard completely. Even if he hadn't seen the letter, he would know what was in it when the time came...if the time came.

"That's good," Holly said. "Can I talk to my daddy?"

Santa looked worriedly at the lump on the living room floor with his legs up on the sofa. He thought about this...then he smiled.

"Yes, my dear. You can."

He took the cordless phone over to Cameron who looked up at him through half-closed eyes.

"Your daughter would like to speak with you," Santa said.

One eye opened, while the other closed. Then he reversed it. Finally, he opened both eyes. When they were more or less in focus, he reached up and took the phone.

"Hi, Holly."

"Daddy, Mommy's taking me shopping tomorrow."

"That sounds cool," Cameron said.

"I rode a horse!" Holly exclaimed, a model of childhood non-sequitur.

"You did?" Cameron enthused, the good dad, even when oblivious to what his child talking about.

"Yeah. I rode...What?" Holly was apparently interrupted and was talking to someone else in the room with her. Then she said, "Mommy wants to talk to you."

"Okay."

Susan got on the phone after muffled sounds of, "You silly goose." Then, clearer, to Cameron she said, "Hi, Cam," in that voice that had allowed her to be the only person to call him "Cam" without verbally driving tent spikes into his head. "I guess you knew I'd be calling?"

"Yeah," Cameron said. "Horses?"

"We went to the open house out at the stables near Rockport. Holly loved it."

"Cool," Cameron said in a mellow tone, still lying on the floor. "So, what's up?" Something about lying on the floor puts one in a casual mood.

"Well, I know there have been problems with, um, the visits in the past," she said, going to the point.

"Yes," Cameron said evenly.

"I was just thinking maybe if the three of us got together for dinner or something, we could talk."

"Dinner?"

"Yes."

"The three of us?"

"Yes."

"Okay," Cameron said without realizing it, stunned beyond the ability to question what he was hearing.

"Great. My house tomorrow night. Are hot dogs and crinkle taters okay?

I promised Holly."

"Yeah. I'll bring desert." It sounded lame, but it was all that came out.

"Cool. I'm looking forward to it. Bye, Cameron."

"Yeah, bye."

*Great,* Cameron thought, *now I have to bake.*

Later, Cameron said he was going to take a nap, though he doubted after Susan's phone call he would sleep. *Dinner with his wife—er ex-wife—and his daughter! Like an almost-kinda-sorta real, functional family.* It would be kind of like "The Brady Bunch" only with less kids and where Mike Brady is insane and hears Tiger the dog talking to him.

After Cameron went upstairs, Santa busied himself cleaning up the winter wonderland of frustration that blanketed the living room. He was a little nervous about having more or less revealed his identity to Holly and needed something to occupy himself. Maybe it wouldn't be so bad, he thought. It wasn't like he *said* he was Santa. He just played along when the child asked if he'd gotten her Santa Claus letter. If anyone asked, he could say he was joking. Ho ho ho. Sure it was a lie and Santa never lies, but in the real world, they do it all the time.

Santa did most of the gathering and repacking of the disgraced ornaments with traditional elbow action, but turned to a little elf magic to makeover the tree. The multi-colored traditional light strings were replaced by glowing, cordless, streams of color and light. The broken decorations were replaced with crystal sculptures, and ornaments with figures—toy trains, Santas, toy soldiers—that moved under their own power, avoiding the suicidal mad dash to the holiday-clogged drug store just for batteries.

Santa sat back to admire his handiwork. For all the beauty he saw in the real world on his holiday travels—and the incomparable beauty found at the North Pole Complex—for Santa Claus, nothing would ever quite compare to a Christmas tree. Not just because it was a Christmas tree, but for what it represented. Love, joy, good will, peace on Earth; all the stuff real-worlds scoffed at.

It wasn't always like that. When he started out his gift-giving life, it was a local affair. He lived among the people he gave gifts to. He saw their grateful faces—young and old—when he brought food to poor people, or candy to children.

Not anymore. Sure, he always saw you when you're sleeping, knew when you were awake and if you'd been bad or good, but Santa didn't feel that he ever really "saw" anyone anymore. His imaginary North Pole world was so remote, so isolated from the real world that he went years sometimes without seeing a real-worlder. Even on his Christmas Eve run he took pains—for obvious reasons—to avoid making contact with them. Not that he would have minded once in a while maybe chatting by the fire with someone for a few moments, but the real-worlders were so gosh darn diligent about being asleep before Santa came, that he never got the chance.

Still, children did love him, even if he could no longer live in the same village or shop in the same marketplaces. But that love rarely lasted past age nine. And the kids who did believe made huge demands. There was a time when kids would ask for their dads to find jobs, their grandmothers to get better. Children still wanted that stuff, but mostly now they wanted CDs (he still wasn't sure what those were), fancy clothes, electronic gadgets. Christmas was a commercial activity for these real-worlders. And losing sight of what Christmas, in all its forms, is really about, Santa thought, led to things like, well, like destroyed Christmas trees.

Santa loved these real-worlders he had met; Cameron, Holly, even Dogwater; though Dogwater's friend Izzy made him uncomfortable. But they were all so sad.

Here was a chance to help people in his own, old village, of sorts, again. A chance to experience up-close, one-on-one giving the joy of Christmas to someone who needed it. It would be just like the old days, when he was a young, optimistic, energetic man. He knew what he had to do.

Benefiting from Uncle Milo's relatively light frame, Santa sprinted up the stairs to his room. He paused to consider whether what he was doing was really the right thing, then nodded affirmatively to himself. He pulled the candy-cane-striped radio from under his bed and set it up on the dresser. Feeling around the back of it, he quickly found a small panel, opened it, and removed a golden metal coil, about the length of a ballpoint pen. It was attached to the radio by a length of wire until Santa freed it with a snap. He went to the window, opened it and flung the item out if it. It fell to the ground, bounced once and laid in the semi-frozen mud of Cameron's backyard.

Santa sighed and smiled to himself. The recall device that was Santa's link to the North Pole was gone. He was free. He would not be going home. At least not right now. For now, he would not even turn the radio on, lest Flifle try to cajole him into coming back. He couldn't. He had a new mission: He was going to be the man who saved Christmas for these real- worlders.

And the first thing he was going to do was find out why real-worlders thought phrases like "the man—or dog or snowman—who saved Christmas" was so funny.

Around the world, at the exact moment the recall device hit the ground, holiday lights flickered and dimmed. The blooms on countless poinsettia plants wilted. Noel shuddered and coughed, signaling a nasty virus coming on.

# DECEMBER 18

It may not surprise anyone to learn the smells of holiday cheer waft through the halls of the North Pole Complex. The scent of baked goods—bread, fresh-baked sugar cookies, gingerbread—along with eggnog with nutmeg, cinnamon, and the like.

What may actually be surprising is to learn that each individual room in the North Pole Complex has a different holiday scent to it. Odder still is the extraordinary fact that those odors do not run together at all. You could be standing in one room enjoying the sweet smell of pine, walk through a doorway, still smelling pine, and emerge on the other side of the door inhaling the mouth-watering aroma of baked ham without the slightest corruption of either smell.

This olfactory beneficence was not an elf creation; at least not an intentional one. The elves have long speculated that it may be a side-effect of the magic that brought the North Pole Complex to life, but no one—at least to common memory—set out specifically to make this nasal nirvana happen.

On this particular night, the elves gathered in a gingerbread-scented room; perhaps a dozen, maybe a few more. Mysteriously, the scent was a little off this night. The gingerbread smelled *burnt*.

Many of the elves looked annoyed at having been called away from the nightly elven-jamboree. Some elves looked anxious, unsure what was going to happen, as being called to these councils was very unusual. And a few of the younger elves simply looked bewildered.

After a period of idle chatter, Doozil strolled into the room from the back with an unconcerned air. He paused to survey his people before they realized he was there. Breathing deeply and brimming with confidence overflowing from an inflated chest, he marched to the front of the room.

At this point, all elfish eyes were upon him, though not with admiration. The elves, generally, are fairly tolerant beings, with no real disputes among themselves of any consequence; not since the olden days of yore. That said, Doozil was not particularly popular and had never done much during his time at the North Pole to remedy that situation.

Santa, however, was determined to overlook Doozil's eccentricities and give him a place in the Workshop. Doozil had, in the minds of most elves, repaid that generosity by being what the real-worlders might have called a royal pain in the ass. He was a slow toymaker, when he deigned to make toys rather than spending his time telling the other elves how to do their jobs. He held little regard for his fellow elves. Perhaps worst of all, he openly criticized the way Santa ran the Complex.

To all elven minds, Doozil was possessed with all the worst characteristics that an elf can have; namely vanity and a lack of altruism. So, it was not surprising that Doozil's arrival in the room was met with not a few groans. The elves had been assembled here without knowing precisely who it was doing the assembly. Finding that it was Doozil made missing out on the elven jamboree all the more excruciating, especially since the sprightly young elf Shivla was going to make her debut performance on the elven harp; a complex device constructed with at least one-hundred strings and no fewer than a dozen levers and pedals.

Doozil moved to the front of the room and stood before the assembled throng wearing an expression on his face that was either great delight or great horror or some combination of both. It was oddly difficult to tell, played out on Doozil's creamy, babyish face. Doozil had rehearsed the face at length and thought it conveyed solemnity.

"My friends," Doozil began, with no apparent sense of irony, "Santa Claus is dead!"

Not surprisingly, there were gasps and exclamations at this. Most of the protests were along the lines of "You're out of your *nebb*" (an elvish word for "head")

Finally, one voice, Blog, a lesser-eld, rose above the others and said, "Foolish boy, you cannot possibly know that."

Doozil motioned for the room to quiet down and said, "No, no, you're right. I don't know that he is dead. But surely you can feel it. There's a stillness in the air, where once it was vibrant with the thrum of the season."

The crowd murmured. There did seem to be an unusual aura these days. The winds wafting in from the real world were not as crisp and magical as they usually were by this time of year. The burnt baked-goods smell in the room suddenly found its way to many elf nostrils and announced itself.

"But that doesn't mean...mean Santa is...dead," an elf protested, barely croaking the last word.

Doozil's head snapped around. "Have *you* seen him lately?" His eyes moved to other elves. "Have you seen St. Nicholas walking our halls? Making our Christmas preparations?"

No one responded. A few shook their heads. It really was very strange.

"I didn't think so," Doozil oozed. "And when I myself went to see our great leader, to ask him why he did not move among his loyal servants, I was brushed aside by his minion Flifle."

Several of the elves looked around the room, noting for the first time that Flifle was conspicuously absent.

"We're now barely six days before C-E time," Doozil said, drawing out "C-E"—short for "Christmas Eve"—as *Ceeeeeee Eeeeeeee* for effect. "Where is Santa? Every year, Santa inspects the reindeer, greases the skids on the sleigh, finishes his holiday bulking up, but not this year." These last words he emphasized with a small fist pounding on the table in front of him.

"Perhaps most disappointing," Doozil continued, not really looking all that disappointed, "he has not been working side-by-side with his elfish comrades to make those model railroads, games, dolls, and books that the children of the world want. During this whole toy-making season, he did not so much as pick up a mallet or saw a piece of wood."

More grumbling. It was true.

"And now," Doozil said, then paused dramatically. "And now, the sleigh is not ready. The reindeer are restless and un-rehearsed. The toy inventory is in a shambles."

"Especially the doll houses," one of the crotchety old elves called out, the words out of his mouth before he realized that he was joining in the heresy and stifled himself.

"And he's not eating his holiday gross of cookies and cakes," another brave voice added.

"And what about the sleigh? It's still got a busted runner," said another.

The elves began chattering in their sing-songy way excitedly.

"You see?" Doozil snarled loudly. "Christmas...is a mess!"

There was no overwhelming round of support, but—significantly—no protest either.

"Every year, when the time got tight, and the pressure was on, Santa has been there for us," Doozil said softly, in what for elves was an impossibly baritone voice. "But this year, where is he?"

A small voice in the back, Shivla, soft at first, but growing stronger, said, "Maybe we could ask Mrs. Claus?"

"I have," Doozil said, all attitude. "She claims all is well. But I think we know better. I fear Santa is in great danger." A pause. "Perhaps *mortal* danger."

"Santa can't die," another elf, a short fat one with a scraggly beard, said. "Can he?" Again, the immortality thing was an unresolved issue.

"Who knows?" Doozil said, with a theatrical shrug. "But we have to face the possibility, however much that may scare us."

"Are you saying...?" one of the few elves in the Complex with short hair and a long nose began, unable to complete the thought.

"Do I think someone wants to harm Santa Claus?" Doozil asks. "I don't know. But I do know this: Flifle and Mrs. Claus are hiding our beloved St. Nicholas from us, for good or for ill."

"So what do we do?" asked a middle-aged female elf with long flowing auburn locks—another rarity among elves.

"We keep our ears open," Doozil said.

There was a grudging laugh at this—elves being quite proud of their large, sensitive, pointy ears.

"And when the time is right, we take action. Whatever that may mean."

Another dramatic pause.

It was a baldly vague call to unity, but it had the desired effect. The looks he was getting now were pleas for leadership, not pleas to go away.

"Go now, my fellow elves," Doozil said, still in that baritone few elves can achieve. "Laugh, play, make toys to stand for the ages. And pray to all that is holy that all will be well."

The elves found themselves filing out of the room at this command.

When the room was empty, Doozil took a deep breath, hugged himself, and giggled a very non-elf-like giggle.

"They're eggs, not your balls," Roberta Hunt told Cameron. Dogwater's sister was helping Cameron bake a strawberry-rhubarb pie with homemade crust, thanks to some canned fruit and veggies Roberta was looking to unload since **her** eviction from the double-wide. There was some disagreement over Cameron's crack-the-egg-on-the-side-of-the-bowl method of opening versus Roberta's whack-the-egg-on-the-counter method, which she thought lessened the risk of eggshell shards in your dessert.

"Why don't you just go to the store and buy something?" Roberta protested, not for the first time this afternoon.

"No," Cameron said. "I promised to bring dessert to Susan's. I can do this. In *The Dead Man's New Hat*, I had a chef character. I spent two days doing research following around the chefs who work with Emeril. I'm ready."

"Okay, *Emeril*, first, get your dish scrubber out of the pie filling.

Cameron moved the offending cleaning utensil.

*Men*, Roberta thought. *You can't bake with 'em. You can't bake without 'em.*

Susan Wentworth's Victorian home sat about as close to the edge of Santa Claus, Indiana as you could get without being country folk. A winding, gravel drive led from the road to the house. The small, detached garage was currently filled with furniture Susan was refinishing to sell, so Susan's jeep sat to the side of the garage. As Cameron pulled into the driveway and parked next to the jeep he wondered what Susan was going to do with the furniture now that she was preparing to move to London.

Cameron climbed out of the car about the time a mid-sized chocolate lab bounded around the side of the house, illuminated by the yard light that shone down the drive area from atop its high perch in the center of the yard.

"Hi, Dave," Cameron said as the dog greeted him, tail wagging, hot breath frosting in the air. Cameron scratched the dog's ears, but Dave was more interested in the pie box in the man's other hand.

The man, the dog, and the pie went up to the front door. A perfunctory knock and Cameron walked in. Susan met him in the foyer as he closed the door.

Cameron was struck by a fleeting pang of ...something. Susan, in a simple sweatshirt and jeans, was stunning. Cameron had always preferred that look to even the sexiest dresses she wore during the marriage when they went to various publishing industry affairs.

He realized he was staring about the same time Susan said, "What's wrong? I don't still have paste on my shirt, do I? Holly and I were making construction paper chains to put on our tree. We had a little mishap."

"Uh, no," Cameron said. Then, in the tradition of clumsy transitions, "I brought pie." He handed her the box.

"Thanks," she said, opening the box. "Ooh. French silk!"

"Yeah, it was supposed to be strawberry-rhubarb, but, well, it's a long story. I don't think Roberta Evans is talking to me anymore."

"It looks delicious. Thank you, Cameron."

A long moment, by pastry gratitude standards, passed.

"Come on in," Susan finally said, motioning to the interior of the house.

Cameron left his coat on the staircase railing to his left and followed.

The living room smelled stridently of pine. Susan had been generous with the pine scent for her artificial tree—that environmentalist thing again. It was decorated in the classic popcorn string, handmade ornament style. There was, though, one of those strings of store-bought twinkle lights with the different speed and light pattern settings—a nod to the cool factor of Christmas.

"Grab a seat. You want a glass of wine?" Susan asked, walking toward the swinging doors to the kitchen.

"Yeah, sure." Even though it positioned him farther from the coffee table where he would set his drink, he sat on the end of the couch nearest the bookcase. On Susan's shelf, Stephen King competed for space with Elmo, Tolstoy, Winnie the Pooh, and Nick Hornby. Books drew the man like a geek to a new computer programming language. The flames in the fireplace were reflected in the glass front of the bookcase.

Susan emerged a minute later with two glasses of merlot. As the kitchen doors swung to and fro, the scent of crispy, fried potatoes—the crispy taters favored by discriminating five-year-olds everywhere—mingled with the pine. It actually wasn't unpleasant.

"So what are you gonna do with that stuff in the garage when, uh, you move?" Cameron asked.

Susan sat on the other end of the couch; near, but not too close to Cameron and said, "Well, I've sold a few more pieces. Mom and Dad are going to take a couple for the house in Florida. I've got an armoire in there that would be great for your house. Hint, hint." She smiled full wattage.

Cameron smiled back crookedly. "So, when do you actually leave?"

"Oh, after the first of the year. I don't have a definite time table yet," Susan said.

"Well, enjoy the fish and chips," Cameron said for lack of anything else to say on the subject.

Susan's smile lost a bit of wattage.

"Listen, about the court case..." Cameron began.

Susan shook her head. "Nah, another time. Let's just hang out."

Cameron shrugged. *Cool.*

While taking a moment to enjoy a sip, this peaceful holiday setting was disrupted by the unholiest bellowing of "Santa Claus is Comin' to Town" perhaps on record.

With a final, shouted "Santa Claus is cominnnnn' to townnnnn!" Holly hopped on one foot into the living room, wearing an oversize Santa hat.

"Bravo!" Susan clapped.

Holly giggled. "Hi, Daddy," she said and scampered over to the troubled writer. She sort of patted his knee and moved away, realizing that she was a little closer than perhaps she wanted to be.

It was enough for Cameron. Forget the book. Forget the exile from the literary community. Forget failing celebrity, hallucinations and psychiatric professionals too busy skiing to fix you. His daughter didn't think he was a freak. Well, she probably did, but not too big a freak to have some physical contact. That was enough.

"Hey there, little elf," Cameron said, improvising. "What do you want Santa to bring you for Christmas?"

Holly thought about it, or, rather, pretended to think about it as she'd deliberated on this many times before and the matter was well established. "A pony," she said finally; a kid classic.

"Where would you put a pony, silly goose?" her mother asked.

Holly was shrewd, for a five-year-old. "A doggie then?" She shrugged in a calculated bit of adorable-ness.

"We'll see," Susan said, motherly. "After the move," she added with half a glance at Cameron.

Cameron looked away.

A moment passed.

"We're moving to a new house," Holly said, now bouncing on one foot.

"I know," Cameron said, nodding in an exaggerated fashion that adults think demonstrate to children active listening.

"It's in another country," she added.

"Called...?" Susan prompted.

Holly frowned. "London, England," she said, keeping the frown.

"Good job," Susan said.

"I know," Cameron said again. He smiled a little. "Sounds like fun."

Holly shrugged.

"Hey, you two," Susan said in a change of subject. "How about dinner? I think your dad can microwave a pretty tasty hot dog."

"I'm the champ," Cameron said.

Holly just studied him.

The hot dogs were hot and juicy; the buns toasted just right. Pickles, mustard, catsup all fresh. The crispy taters were truth in advertising. Holly even enjoyed the fruit cup without protest. The French silk pie, of course, went over big.

Cameron even managed to make the little girl snort milk with the following exchange:

Cameron: "Knock, knock."

Holly: "Who's there?"

Cameron: "Interrupting cow."

Holly: "Interru-"

Cameron: "MOOOOOO!"

Holly: *Snort!*

Cameron Jones does a damn-fine cow impersonation.

When it got to be Holly's bedtime, Cameron was invited to observe the nightly read-aloud session. Tonight's featured text was a book called *Grumpy Goldfish* and the irony was not lost on Cameron. He even got to read a little bit to Holly, starting with the part where the grumpy little goldfish's mother sends him to bed without any fish flakes.

Holly formally introduced her dad to all of her dolls and stuffed animals. He dutifully made small talk with each one. He noted to himself that it almost seemed a little too easy to converse with these toys. He was sort of drawn to them; could feel their little plastic eyes on him. He decided to add that to his next email therapy session with Dr. Whipple.

And, when the procrastination ran its course and it was time to go to sleep, Cameron, not Susan, got the first goodnight kiss.

Cameron Jones: Super Dad.

Well, not yet. Someday. Maybe.

Later, Cameron sat on the couch—near the bookcase, of course, basking in his triumphant father-ness.

After offering Cameron another glass of wine, which he declined, Susan sat on the opposite end of the couch.

"She seems like a happy kid," Cameron said. "You done good, Mom."

"Yes, she's pretty contented," Susan said. "But you're not."

Cameron shrugged.

"Is it your book?" Susan said. Susan was always Cameron's closest advisor—first in line in front of agents, editors, reviewers, with insight into what his manuscripts needed, or what he needed to get them done.

"Partially."

"What else then?" Susan asked, without really needing to ask.

"Why do you have to go all the way to London?" Cameron said, high-tailing it directly to the heart of the matter.

Susan raised her hands in protest. "I really think we should leave that stuff to the lawyers. Wally says-"

"Oh, *Wally says*," Cameron interrupted. "The great legal thinker Wally Bass, who spends so much time thinking up great legal strategy, he can't go shopping for a decent suit. Or a personality. Well, if Wally says we shouldn't talk about it then, we-"

"Cameron, you're being an ass." It was a fairly pretentious insult, but Susan pulled it off.

"I think I'm entitled," Cameron said. "I mean, in a week or so, we get the double-shot celebration of Christmas and—oh, yeah—the anniversary of you walking out on me and—oh, yeah—the anniversary of signing our divorce papers. Well, I guess that's a triple shot. Even *better*. And now, maybe we can add another: the anniversary of you taking my daughter away."

Cameron's voice was high and fast, the evening having moved on from genial family time to contentious family court.

"You know damn well why I left," Susan said, moving to anger just as quickly as Cameron.

Cameron shrugged again.

"Are you still hearing the voices?" Susan asked with a definite sarcastic tone that she didn't honestly feel.

Cameron almost said defiantly, "Yeah, what the fuck about it?" but thought better of it. As much as he hated the idea of litigating his relationship with his daughter, he realized that openly admitting to the child's mother that he was crazy could be very, very bad for his case. In the distance, you could hear Everett Franken tossing and turning in his slumber. Probably still wearing those damn black knee socks.

"Look, Cameron, we've been over this many times. If you'd just get some help..."

"Help? Help for what? I'm *fine*. I had a rough bit, but I'm over it. The book is, well, the book is coming. I'm better than I was. Maybe if I got to see my kid now and then, I'd be better still."

"That's your own doing, Cameron," Susan said, frosting the already chilled conversation.

Cameron shrugged again. What could he say?

"The night I left, you had spent the whole day laying out random crap on the Scrabble board and typing the most bizarre shit." She said "shit" with an inflection that suggested this was not a word she used very much. "It really freaked me out. Not to mention my parents."

Cameron gaped. "That was four years ago. And in that time, I've hardly gotten to see my child. You don't know anything about what I'm like now."

This time Susan shrugged. "Wally thinks..."

"Oh, screw him," Cameron said, raising his voice a bit more than intended. Then he softened a bit. "Look, I'm not mad, okay. You know that. It's just that I love her more than anything."

"I know." Susan said, also climbing down from her high horse.

An excruciating pause.

"Well, this was fun," Cameron said with a half smile.

"Yeah," Susan said. "We should do this every night. Good workout. Tones the abs."

They both smiled weakly.

"Guess that's my cue to leave," Cameron said.

Susan said, "Yeah. Guess so."

"See you Christmas Eve?" Cameron asked.

"Of course," Susan said in a tone crossing annoyance with forced enthusiasm, and achieving neither.

Cameron was pretty sure Susan would be on the phone first thing the next morning telling Wally Bass about his latest goon-binge. But he didn't care. He just wanted to leave. He hastily retrieved his coat, scratched Dave behind the right ear—Dave was a bit more accommodating since the man had no pie this time—and waved a quick sarcastic goodbye to Susan before rushing out into the yard. There was no goodbye return.

Before he climbed into the car, Cameron stopped to whisper a final goodnight and a merry Christmas to Holly's bedroom window. Corny? Sure. Pathetic? Definitely. But he threw in one for Susan too. It couldn't hurt, could it?

As he started the ignition, he said in the general direction of north, "I don't really pray, but being the holiday season, I've got a plea, of sorts: Santa Claus, I've always tried—if not always succeeded—to be nice and I've frequently been naughty. But there's only one thing I want for Christmas this year. Please help me."

By the time Cameron arrived home from Susan's, slamming a succession of doors from the car to the garage to the lower level of the house to the bathroom to his bedroom, Santa was already in bed. He was starting to master the remote control and had tried watching television—he found the talking box fascinating—but had stumbled on one of the premium cable channels that, at nine-fifteen in the evening, was showing naked women with a lot of spirit, but it was definitely not yuletide spirit. Santa, who was alone, got so mortified with embarrassment, he had decided to turn it off and go to bed.

Santa's dream that night began very normally for a Santa dream...

He was leisurely strolling through the Christmas-ville section of the North Pole Complex. The snow was crisp and white below his feet; a glorious North Pole night with lights perpetually a-twinkle. A group of elves played leapfrog. Another group was having a snowball fight—and nobody makes a better snowball than an elf.

Pretty typical Santa Claus stuff. Usually what happens next in these dreams is the reindeer frolic or he eats a cookie with lots of chocolate chips or a group of happy, smiling children run up and hug him. And, in fact, Santa realized that, in this particular dream, he was holding a cookie. A moist, warm, chewy one.

He saw the reindeer. Prancer was, well, doing what he does. Blitzen ran circles around the others in a classic reindeer game.

Santa walked on. The snow crunched under foot in the tradition of every Christmas carol ever. After several more paces, Santa stopped near the elven candlestick maker's shop. He decided something was not quite right. The tenor of the elven songs coming from the castle was off, becoming increasingly discordant.

An explosion shook the ground. Santa's substantial girth tumbled. He looked around, stunned. Elves started streaming out of the castle, screaming, climbing over each other. Santa was horrified to see that two of them were on fire. They ran off into the pine forest before he could call after them.

Then Santa saw him; Teevo, his old workshop leader whose inventions caused the death of Santa's elves. The elf was framed with black lightening, but it was definitely him. With his maniacal grin framed in white beard, Teevo ran up to St. Nicholas. The elf's eyes were aglow with the flames now poking out of the open door of the castle.

"You did this," Teevo sneered. "You—*St. Nicholas*—always trying to do more, visit more real-worlder children. Make more toys. You did this."

"But, but," Santa protested. "I love all the children. I want to make them happy."

"Bah!" Teevo grunted. He followed the flaming elves into the North Pole wastelands.

As Santa sat with a thud in the snow, stunned, he heard a voice from behind him. He whirled, expecting to go another round with Teevo.

Instead, he saw a thin, gruff looking old man. The man was wrinkled and withered, but not diminished as his narrow, glaring eyes attested. He was neither elf nor whatever Santa is. He was a real-worlder.

"Who are you?" Santa asked.

"I'm the rotten SOB who's gonna kick your ass, son," said Milo Vestibule. "Give me my body back."

# DECEMBER 19

Hank Nebble, long-time Christmas tree farmer, awoke early in the morning, put on a pair of sweats and walked out to his backyard, joints stiff with the cold. He looked out over an acreage of Christmas trees, sipped a cup of coffee and waited for his first cut-your-own tree customer. As he gazed out over the land, a steady line of coffee dribbled down his chin onto his work shirt as his mouth hung slack. He was stunned into a stupor for, as he watched, the needles on his fine rows of pines first browned and then dropped from the branches to the ground. It was near instantaneous, like flipping some sort of tree-killing switch. All that was missing was Charlie Brown and the other "Peanuts" characters to laugh at him for being a blockhead who picked stupid trees.

"Rats," Nebble said, only he didn't really say "rats."

The light snow of the previous night had covered Cameron's yard with an incomplete, but not altogether unpleasant, light sheet of snow. Dogwater Hunt gave it not a single moment's gaze as he marched through it.

This was a man on a mission. He absently looked over his shoulder periodically as he walked to see if he was leaving footprints. Alien abductees often worry about leaving signs that the alien tormenters can use to track them. For the most part, though, Dog was focused on the job at hand.

Dogwater Hunt had been deputized by Cameron to decorate the outside of his house in a suitably festive fashion for the season. In truth, Dog lobbied hard for the job as an opportunity to engage in more "therapy." He really thought his exposure to the twinkling holiday lights, so similar to the lights he remembered from the labs or spaceships or wherever the hell the aliens took him, was helping de-sensitize him to those experiences. Roberta was just happy he was getting some exercise.

He scratched thoughtfully at the straggly whiskers on his chin, now chilled and brittle from the cold. Alien anxiety or not, he was determined to do well by Cameron's Christmas. He knew Cameron was counting on the place beginning to look a lot like Christmas for his little girl. He would make sure Cameron had a kick-ass holiday. It was the least he could for the man who had, more or less, single-handedly funded his extra-terrestrial expedition and made his own alien Christmas possible. Repaying such generosity was what the great alien hunter of old, Lars Heimdal, would do.

Standing in the back of the house with a spiral notebook and a pencil, Dogwater sketched a drawing of the house free-hand, but pretty much to scale—all the windows, doors, gutters, and eves in the proper positions. He would later do precise measurements of the front and back of the house, as well as of the light strings he intended to use. Then, he would map out how many lights he could put in a square foot of house to achieve the optimal holiday effect. It was a crude effort, by his standards, but his alien-hunting was taking up a lot of time.

As he stood there scribbling ideas in his notebook, Dog's right eye caught the glint of sunlight reflecting off something on the ground. He looked closer and his stomach seized. It was something golden, perhaps metallic. It looked like an electrode of some kind. Electrodes were very bad things to alien abductees. He looked around reflexively, expecting to see a hoard of slimy (or not), short (or possibly tall), bug-eyed (or perhaps no-eyed) aliens waiting to probe some unnatural orifice with that item.

Seeing nothing, he cautiously bent down to look at the item on the ground. It didn't attack him, which was promising. He poked at it lightly with the pencil. There was no reaction. It occurred to him that perhaps the pencil's rubber eraser had shielded him from some sort of alien death shock, but still, he decided to take a risk. He picked the item up. Nothing happened. It was indeed a zigzag shaped metal item with a dangling wire.

Dog looked around again, looking up this time, still fully expecting his "ride" to be there to pick him up. He sighed and looked at his watch, waiting as one waits for the subway.

But nothing happened. Dogwater frowned at his new-found mystery item.

"What are you?" he said, fully prepared for the possibility that it might talk back, even if it was in an alien language. Inanimate alien objects talking was not unprecedented. The *Dark Matters* website had run a four-part series a couple years earlier about a race of shape-shifting, chatty, aliens living out their lives as kitchen furniture in Pennsylvania Dutch country.

When nothing happened, Dogwater shrugged and put the mystery item in his coat pocket. He was pretty sure this was some sort of elaborate effort by the aliens to trap him. The thing had to be some sort of beacon. It didn't really worry him though. After a dozen or more abductions, his body was so riddled with bits of extraterrestrial metal and probes and tracking beacons and god knew what else, another one wouldn't matter. It was worth the risk if he could get his geeks—friends—in the various labs around the country to study this thing. Besides, he was already marked for... well, whatever they wanted.

He would do a write up on *Dark Matters* about the item. One of his subscribers surely would have some insight. For now, though, he was focused on a bigger issue. Where the hell was he going to find, one week before Christmas, ten lords-a-leaping made from old tractor parts? He desperately needed them to complete his vision for Cameron's front yard. If he didn't get them, his twelve drummers drumming fashioned from old vacuum cleaners were going to look really silly.

"Well, now, I think perhaps you could have handled that differently," Everett Franken said in an even tone, only about an octave higher than the usual, which was perhaps the closest he ever got to anger.

Upon learning of the awkward end to Cameron's visit with Holly by virtue of a short fax from Wally Bass which was written in a slanty font that was subtle, but still conveyed a mirthful jeer, Everett Franken had called Cameron. Cameron was a little put out by the call, having been still right in the middle of editing chapter twelve of the manuscript; a pivotal chapter where, well, not much happens.

"I got a little upset with Susan," Cameron protested. "It's no big deal." Cameron shook the cordless phone in frustration and put it back against his ear.

"Well, if you have trouble getting along with your ex-wife, it could make it difficult to coordinate visitation. That doesn't help your claim for MORE visits."

Cameron sighed. "It was a little spat. We both got our shots in. It cleared the air. Really, it's fine."

"I hope so," Everett Franken said, not convinced. "Have you lined up those witnesses for your hearing I asked you for?"

Cameron sighed again. "I guess Dogwater will come. My brother was going to come for the holiday and stay over, but Maureen is due to have her kid like *now*, so he can't leave her alone to fly out here."

Everett Franken verbally bristled. "Cameron, I told you, we need witnesses who can say how great you are with Holly. Isn't Mr. Hunt the gentlemen with the website?"

"Yeah, *Dark Matters*. He's a good guy."

"Yes." Pause. "Well, we do have the affidavits from your editor friend. And I think the, uh, statement from Holly's former daycare provider will be helpful. Of course, she can really only say how you were when you picked up or dropped off your daughter." From Everett Franken's end of the line there was the sound of rustling papers. "The Winters are supportive."

"That's good."

"But they also are complimentary to Ms. Wentworth." Everett Franken said. "Cameron, the key is you. You have to show the judge what a devoted father you are; how Holly thrives when she's with you. That you can provide a safe, secure, nurturing place for her."

*And a place where Daddy doesn't talk to his imaginary friends,* Cameron thought.

"I'll be ready," Cameron said.

"Good. Well, I need to be going to court. I'll talk to you later. Take care," Everett Franken said. Even the way Everett Franken hung up the phone was cheerful.

Cameron hated that.

The reindeer were out of sorts. Mrs. Claus could sense this as she stood among them in the reindeer stable of the North Pole Complex. A couple stood, a few sat on their haunches, dog-like. A couple more lay with four legs folded under them or splayed out from their bodies, seeming to reach for the heat and light of the wood stove in the center of the room. Several at various times rolled on their sides in apparent boredom.

It was now just five days before the biggest flight of the year—the Christmas Eve toy delivery. Usually by this point, the reindeer were well-rehearsed, loose, flexible, and fighting the urge to get in the air. It was not unusual for more than one to be so prime to fly, that they slept in a hover above the ground.

That was not these reindeer, however. These reindeer arrayed before Mrs. Claus were *lethargic*.

More than that, they were depressed. Reindeer games were at a dead stop. There was no tag. No flight drills. No chase games. The reindeer just sat. Now and then one might execute a half-hearted loop-de-loop, but that was it.

Mrs. Claus stroked the coarse fur on Prancer's neck and felt the huge animal sigh beneath her fingers. The reindeer really didn't talk, but they were great communicators of feeling. Mrs. Claus was sure that Santa could actually communicate with them, but he'd never really explained how; maybe couldn't explain how. She was left, however, to simply read their expressions.

This was not difficult today. Every one of the eight reindeer faces on Santa's elite Team One registered one thing: hopelessness.

"Don't worry, beautiful ones," Mrs. Claus said to them. "Santa will be back in plenty of time for your flight. All you need to do is make sure you're ready." She punctuated this with a gesture simulating taking flight. A couple of the reindeer looked lazily at her, then turned back to chewing hay.

This was very, very bad. Time was running out. Mrs. Claus could see that. When she had sent Mr. Claus off on his—what?—journey of self-discovery, mid-life crisis, whatever it was, she had always intended to allow him as much time as he wanted to work out whatever needed working out. Then he would contact Flifle and Santa would come back home. It should have worked fine. But now things were critical. Christmas was near the breaking point. She would have to talk to Flifle soon about recalling Kris Kringle whether he was ready or not.

Surely, he must be ready to come home, must have "found himself" as the real-worlders called it. Millions of children were depending on him. With only five days to go until Christmas, this was no time to fall apart. Christmas had to happen and it had to happen in five days.

Mrs. Claus became aware that her stroking of Prancer's fur had become more aggressive. Prancer chuffed disconsolately.

"Sorry, dear," she said and patted the reindeer's head.

Prancer grunted agreeably enough, shaking his shaggy head, lightly clipping Mrs. Claus's shoulder with an antler.

Mrs. Claus sat silently watching her elite reindeer sleigh team sink deeper into a funk. After a few moments, Flifle came quietly into the stable, tossing an off-hand wave to Vixen who nodded back. Growing up, Flifle had been one of the elven children on Vixen's personal care team. The two were very close.

Mrs. Claus spoke without even turning around. "I think it's time to bring Mr. Claus home," she said.

Had Mrs. Claus been looking, she would have seen a pale elf, even by elf standards, sweating and shaky. He looked ill, except for the fact that elves almost never get ill.

When she didn't hear an immediate response to what she said, Mrs. Claus said, "I know this...changes things, but I think-"

"Ma'am, there's a problem-" Flifle blurted, then stopped short as he looked around uneasily at the reindeer. Vixen, in particular, watched him carefully. Flifle put on an unconvincing smile and added, for the reindeers' benefit, "- a problem with the selection of tonight's dinner wine. Nothing to worry about."

"What is it?" Mrs. Claus asked.

"Chef wants ancient elven, Santa wants contemporary," Flifle said, easing into the whole lying thing. "Would you come with me to sort it out?"

Mrs. Claus followed wordlessly. Most of the reindeer barely registered the departure, except for Vixen whose eyes never left the elf.

Out on the icy trail back to the castle, Mrs. Claus insisted on knowing what Flifle had been trying to say. It couldn't really have been about wine; the Clauses didn't drink wine.

"Something's happened to the recall device," Flifle said. "It was wired into the radio. It's what we were going to use to transmit the spell that will recall Santa to the North Pole. As long as it's attached to the radio, it sends out a signal. But now..." Flifle shook his head.

"What do you mean something happened to it?"

"I lost the signal. It's broken or-" Flifle stifled the thought.

Mrs. Claus stopped walking. "Or he turned it off."

Flifle nodded.

Mrs. Claus looked out at the frigid twilight of the North Pole. The stars seemed to be waiting for something, for a decision of some sort. A declaration maybe.

"He's coming back," Mrs. Claus said.

Flifle gulped. "He *was* rather upset..."

"I don't care. This is his home. This is his life."

Flifle said nothing.

"He's Santa Claus." Mrs. Claus laughed. It was an uneasy, doubtful laugh. "He's on a little vacation. After sixteen-hundred years, I think he's earned a little time off. But he'll be back."

"Ma'am," Flifle began, then stopped short when he saw that the look on her face competed with the surrounding environment in chill factor. "I'll think of something," he concluded.

They walked the rest of the way to the castle in silence; Mrs. Claus thinking *Kris, come home to me.*

Flifle was thinking *I'll go down in history as the elf who killed Christmas.*

Behind the elf and Mrs. Claus, in a clump of dense pine, the antlers of a reindeer slowly crept through the branches until finally the regal head, broad snout and dark eyes of Vixen were revealed. He shook his head and chuffed uneasily.

And far away, in an intently pink bedroom in the real-world inhabited by a slumbering five-year-old girl being watched over by a floppy-eared stuffed bunny, a small plastic Santa skating in a music box scene pirouetted once, paused, and fell over.

# DECEMBER 20

A dinner theater production of "A Christmas Carol" in Hartford, Connecticut, ground to a halt when the actor playing Tiny Tim forgot the line, "God bless us. Every one." Bob Cratchit ran off stage in tears.

It took a lot of convincing for Holly to get kindly old neighbor Gretchen Morley, who was providing daycare this day, to driver her over to Cameron's house.

Mrs. Morley knew about the pending visitation litigation and didn't want to do anything bad for the child or that would upset Susan. Susan was a delightful young woman of whom Mrs. Morley was very fond.

Still, Holly could be very persuasive. She'd offered *everything*. She would brush the cat. She would sweep the snow off the porch. She even offered to forego her original lunch request—fish sticks and barbecue potato chips—in favor of tuna salad and fruit cup.

And really, what was the harm? Cameron Jones was a little off, but a very nice man and clearly very fond of his daughter. What harm could there be in letting them spend a little more time together? Besides, the child so wanted to deliver a gift to her daddy.

So, ultimately, Mrs. Morley relented. They piled into the sturdy, large sedan left to Mrs. Morley by her husband Hank and drove to Cameron's home. On the drive, Holly sang along with the Mickey Mouse Christmas tape in the player. Mrs. Morley possessed extraordinary reserves of patience as Holly had played this tape ALL DAY LONG. Holly, however, could not stay still. She sang along with several of the tracks (Chip 'n' Dale could really belt out a tune). She danced in the seat. She noted everything of even minor interest they passed on the road with a flurry of exclamation points. All the time, though, she clutched a small square package wrapped in pink, with a red bow. It looked more like a traditional Valentine's present than Christmas wrapping. Holly was very fond of all things pink.

Mrs. Morley interpreted Holly's exuberance to be eagerness to see her father. It was so moving. Young people today, with their divorce and their living together, just didn't cling to family the way her generation had. But here was a family straining to be together instead of giving in to falling apart.

In reality, though, visiting her father was only a secondary consideration for Holly. Mrs. Morley knew about the present, of course, but had no idea of Holly's true mission and wouldn't have understood if she did know.

The sedan struggled to get into Cameron's driveway. The accumulation of plowed snow at the end of the driveway was an afterthought for Cameron's SUV, but a significant consideration for the decidedly-not four-wheel-drive sedan. Eventually, though, she made it in.

The car was barely turned off before Holly had negotiated the seat belt and was out of her seat. She galloped to the front porch with her package and was already straining for the doorbell when Mrs. Morley had just mounted the porch steps.

When the doorbell actually rang, Santa Claus was studying the wall calendar in the kitchen. December featured, oddly enough, the Pacific Ocean looking as crystalline and blue as a picture in any tourist guide. Santa was fascinated by the ocean. Most of the naturally occurring water came in the form of ice at the North Pole. He rarely saw it in liquid form, outside of a bathtub or goblet. It was beautiful. He'd seen the ocean, of course, on his Christmas Eve flight, and perhaps the briefest glimpse on his travels to the North Pole in his early days, but never up close. He'd never listened to the waves. Felt the surf and dipped a toe in. He'd never even stood on a beach. He made a note to himself to do those things before he went "home" again.

When the doorbell rang, panic swooped in. Cameron was gone. Santa realized he would have to greet whoever was at the door himself. This was bothersome. He still wasn't comfortable with these real-worlders.

The doorbell rang again and Santa knew he should do something. It didn't occur to him that he could just stay quiet and let whoever it was think no one was home. That would be a lie. Lying was not something St. Nicholas did. Well, except for that whole stealing a real-worlder's body and pretending to be someone else thing.

Santa went to the door, took a deep breath and opened it. A nervous, uncertain look immediately gave way to a broad smile when he saw the little girl.

"Well, hello there, Holly Jones," he boomed, Santa-like, despite himself. "How are you?"

"Fine," Holly answered.

Santa then noticed the decidedly older woman standing with Holly. In his head, he was startled to hear, "Hello, Mama." He recovered quickly and said, "Good day, madam. I don't believe we've been introduced. I'm St.-" He caught himself and finished, "*Sir* Milo Vestibule."

Mrs. Morley blushed a tad as Mr. Vestibule was a striking older gentleman. His partial bridge was in today and it was stunning. Mrs. Morley introduced herself as well.

"My dear, I'm not used to meeting royalty," she said, picking up on the "Sir." Then, "I'm terribly sorry to drop in without calling first, Sir Vestibule. But the darling child was so excited to see her dad."

Uncle Milo's face turned downward into a frown. "I'm very sorry. Cameron is not home at present."

"Oh, that's a shame," Mrs. Morley said. "We've come all this way for nothing."

Holly interrupted, "But I brought this for Daddy." She handed the package to Santa. "Maybe we could wait...?"

Santa took the gift and smiled. He got a charge from holding presents again. He looked at the child, then at Mrs. Morley. He panicked again. It was bad enough to greet an unknown visitor in his present form. Now he was going to have to entertain. Still, he supposed, part of being a real-worlder was being a good host.

"Of course. By all means," Santa said. He stepped aside, bowed, and ushered his guests—his first non-elf guests in fifteen-hundred years—into Cameron's living room.

Mrs. Morley vowed that they would try not to take up too much of Mr. Vestibule's valuable time. She inquired as to when Cameron would be back.

"Well, I believe he was going to the marketplace to buy..." He paused, trying to sort out what Cameron had said—something about a Computertech 1984B ink cartridge. The only word that made any sense to Santa was "ink" so he said it now. "Ink. He said he was going to purchase ink." Santa nodded for emphasis. "And then he was going to spend the day in Rockport doing research on one of his literary projects."

"Shoot," Mrs. Morley said. "Well, perhaps we could get acquainted for a few minutes." Her eyes fluttered—yes, fluttered—coyly in a manner that totally went over Santa's head.

"Lovely," Santa said, slightly unnerved by Mrs. Morley's gaze, and stepping over quickly to put Holly's gift under the tree. He couldn't deny it felt kind of good to do that.

"Susan told me about the fire," Mrs. Morley said. "I hope there wasn't much damage."

"Not as much as you might expect," Santa understated.

As this exchange continued, Holly's face screwed up in deep concentration. Finally, it brightened and she said, "Mrs. Morley will you go upstairs to my room and get my 'Baby Princess' socks. I left them when I was here last time."

Mrs. Morley looked at Santa. "Do you think it would be all right?"

Santa thought about it. He couldn't think of a reason why Cameron wouldn't want Mrs. Morley upstairs, and said so.

Mrs. Morley excused herself, eyeing Milo Vestibule as she left the room.

As soon as she was out of the room, Holly turned to Santa and said, simply enough, "Hi, Santa."

Santa chuckled nervously, shaking his head. "Now, now, I—I don't even have a beard." A feeble "ha, ha".

Holly assessed Milo Vestibule's lack of facial hair, but appeared unconvinced. "You are too Santa," she said confidently.

"Dearest, that's silly," Santa said. "I think someone has visions of sugarplums dancing in her head." He punctuated it with Uncle Milo's barking laugh.

"But, Santa, I need help," Holly said, turning on full-wattage child charm.

Santa looked at the little girl sitting next to him on the couch and was quite understandably defenseless. How could Santa Claus, of all people, say "no" to a child? Holly was asking for help and Santa had committed himself to helping Cameron's family, hadn't he? It would be ridiculous for him to refuse, not to mention a waste of the North Pole resources that it took to send him here.

Christmas or no, he'd committed to staying here when he snapped the recall unit. That memory was both frightening and exhilarating. This was his life now. Make the most of it.

So Santa lowered his borrowed head to Holly's face and said solemnly, "Holly, dear, look into my right eye."

Without even blinking, Holly did just that. An image formed there and Holly gasped when she saw a perfectly clear, picture-book quality Santa face, complete with bushy white beard and red tassel cap. A mittened hand rose up from below the face and waved at her. Holly waved back. Then the image was gone.

Holly looked at Milo Vestibule, eyes wide. "Is that you?"

Santa nodded.

"Why are you in there?" Holly asked, pointing at Milo's chest.

"It's a long story, little one," Santa began to explain. "I think we should save that for another time. Mrs. Morley will be back soon. Why don't you just tell me what sort of help you need."

"Okay," Holly said agreeably.

"Well, go ahead," Santa encouraged.

She paused as she thought how to say what she needed. "Well, I know you got my letter."

"Of course I did. It was lovely."

His answer was completely honest. He didn't need to see every letter. One of the virtues of being Santa Claus—aside from unfettered access to pastry—is that you just *know* what kids want for Christmas. Just like you know when they've been naughty or nice. This latter set of statistics, of course, he did keep obsessive track of, however on *THE LIST*.

"Let's see," Santa said. "I believe you wanted a pony." Santa galloped and whinnied in his seat.

Holly giggled.

"And, I think you also said something about your mommy and daddy."

"Yeah," Holly said.

"Are you sad because they don't live together anymore?"

Holly shrugged. "I don't know." Then she added softly, "Daddy's kind of weird." She didn't sound upset or frightened. It's just the way it was.

Santa nodded. He didn't know enough about real-worlders yet to know who was weird and who wasn't, but he thought he understood what Holly was saying.

"But I don't want to go away," Holly said, continuing her thought.

"Go away?" Santa asked.

"With Mommy. We're moving to Lun-dun." She added with the pride of self-accomplishment, "That's in England. On the other side of the ocean."

"When are you going?"

Holly sighed. "Right after Christmas."

"I see." Santa was starting to understand why Cameron was spending so much time on his meetings with the tribunal of law-givers. He was trying to keep Susan from leaving with Holly.

"Can you help me, Santa?"

"I'm sure going to try," Santa said, eyes twinkling merrily.

Holly beamed. "Thanks."

"Well, that's what I'm here for."

Holly couldn't resist. "So, what about the pony...?"

Santa laughed. "We'll talk about that later."

Gretchen Morley's voice started in the hallway. "I just don't understand why young men today are so mule-headed about taking a scrub brush to a bathroom."

Mrs. Morley shuffled into the living room. "I'm sorry, dear. I couldn't find the socks."

"Oh, that's okay," Holly said, in a fair bit of acting that conveyed both acceptance and dashed childhood hopes.

"I'm sorry we missed Mr. Jones," Mrs. Morley said.

"Missed me for what?" Cameron said from the hallway.

"Well, bless my soul," Santa said, genuinely surprised.

"Daddy!" Holly said and bounded over to the man for a genuine, unabashed hug. "Guess what?"

"What, kiddo?"

"I just saw Santa Claus."

Santa tensed.

Cameron laughed. "Really? Me too? This is where he hangs out when he's not making toys for good little boys and girls." He tickled the child until she giggled. The irony passed unnoticed, for which Santa was grateful.

"Well, Holly, should we get going?" Mrs. Morley interrupted reluctantly. "We still have to go to the market and get you home before your mom gets there."

"Okay," Holly said.

"But you just got here," Cameron protested.

"Well, her mother will be home soon. She'll wonder where we are," Mrs. Morley explained.

"Well, all right then..." Cameron trailed off.

"Thank you for your time, Sir Vestibule," Mrs. Morley said.

"Er—Milo, please, madam."

"Well, then goodbye, Milo. It was nice to see you again, Mr. Jones." Mrs. Morley's eyes lingered a little as she turned toward the door.

"Always a pleasure," Santa said, trying not to meet her gaze. "Yowza," his inner voice said.

"Bye, San-, Milo," Holly said and waved correcting herself deftly.

"Take care," Santa said.

With that, Santa's first two solo real world house guests were gone. Santa exhaled for what seemed like the first time since the Renaissance. Then he glanced at the still grinning Cameron watching Holly and Mrs. Morley pull out of the driveway.

Santa's mission was clear: He would reunite Holly with her family.

But how?

"Sir Vestibule?" Cameron asked.

Gretchen Morley rued the decision to cash in the two-for-one coupon on economy-size WHAMMO! Detergent today as she lugged the heavy bottles into the trunk while Holy did doughnuts in the slushy supermarket parking lot with the shopping cart.

"Holly, honey," Mrs. Morley grunted. "Come on, now. Get in the car. It's almost time for lunch." She paused to stretch her aching back.

"May I give you a hand?" a deep, smooth voice said from the other side of the open trunk lid.

A head appeared around the underside of the lid. Ben Steene's high-voltage smile was prominently on display, save for one chipped tooth that actually seemed to add character rather than detract from it.

"Well, thank you, dear," Mrs. Morley said and gladly relinquished the detergent bottle she'd been trying to hoist.

Ben Steene made quick work of the bottles.

"Nice to know the world still has a few good Samaritans," Gretchen Morley said.

"I got a boy scout merit badge in soap lifting."

"Well, you're a good boy."

"Well, now that that's taken care of," Ben Steene said, slamming the trunk lid down, "May I buy you and Holly lunch...?"

John Jacob Jingle-Heimer Schmidt Elementary in eastern Pennsylvania, like many schools, has a yearly holiday pageant. The climax of the event features a third-grader dressed as an angel riding in from the darkened background toward center stage on a motorized cart decorated like clouds. This year, the cart made its entrance, carrying eight-year-old Brittany Berger, who waved majestically to the applauding audience. At least, she did until the cart became airborne.

In fairness, the cart didn't go more than five or six feet in the air and no one got hurt. Not seriously, anyway. The litigation, however, is still pending.

In the early days of Santa Claus's legendary run, when the North Pole Complex was, well, just the plain old North Pole, not all the elves were jolly with the thought of rallying around the fat, former real-worlder. Most of the elves of that time had never even seen a human, much less went to work for one.

Many of the elves recognized that Santa Claus was a good and generous human; that it was somehow *right* to dedicate themselves to helping him make and deliver toys, goodwill, and peace on Earth to all the world's children. But, still, there was suspicion.

Almost immediately after the first meeting between the elves and Kris Kringle, work began on a shelter for Mr. Claus, as well as to establish a workshop where the elves could do their work. At first, it was difficult to find volunteers to do the construction.

Now, some sixteen-hundred years later, there was little that the elves wouldn't do for this man. Many of them would never admit that before Father Christmas came along, most elves were quite content to play games and cause mischief. They really just liked to have a good time. The idea of productive work, at one time, was a very foreign concept.

The elves are to be given points for the fact that this particular work they were called upon to do was novel, unprecedented, and really, really hard. For example, wood and other shelter-making materials were extremely difficult to find at the Pole at that time. The elves produced enough for their small huts, but the amount they would need for the massive new castle and workshop—as decreed by the elf elders—was enormous. Finally, the elves were able to cobble together the right combination of ingenuity and magic they needed to fashion their supplies. Still, there were plenty of long days chopping, hammering and sawing to be had; not to mention planning. Elves hate planning. Elves are very much wing-it type beings.

Eventually, the relatively minor grumblings about aches, pains, blisters, and planning gave way to more strident complaints about this real-worlder coming in to their world and bossing them around. The reality was that Santa Claus was beyond extremely grateful for the elves' help and never ordered anyone to do anything. Really, can you picture St. Nick barking at you, "All right, dirt bag, tote that barge, lift that bale!..Ho, ho, ho."? But that didn't change how the elves perceived him at first. Over time, these complaints became louder and were voiced by more and more elves.

One day, when the outer walls of the castle were nearly complete, work stopped completely. The elves, as if of one collective mind, simply put down their hammers all at once, set aside their ropes, stilled their saws. They just stopped working. They'd had enough.

"Elves were not meant for this sort of manual labor," was a common complaint. "We're supposed to make fun, not act as slaves for real-worlders."

A few elves suggested that the true purpose of elves was to make war against dwarves, as they had in centuries past, but by this point in elven history, the warrior-like ways had largely been abandoned. But making toys for *children* was a dwarf pursuit, so the reasoning went. Or worse yet, a *human* occupation. Toy making was a hobby, not a vocation, they thought contemptuously.

"After all," some of the elves complained darkly, "Kris Kringle isn't going to make toys for me." The petulance of the complaint outweighed the absurd logic of it.

The senior elf council allowed the work stoppage to go on for a few days. The elves simply needed to *kerpluck*; essentially elfish for "blow off some steam." No one was really very concerned.

As the days passed, however, the elves didn't go back to work. They were quite happy, in fact, resuming their previous lives; playing games, writing and singing songs. The castle sat unfinished and Santa Claus, today even more beloved than the Easter Bunny and Tooth Fairy combined, continued to spend his nights shivering in a cave.

Santa didn't complain, of course. He knew that his destiny would be fulfilled, pretentious as that sounded. He bided his time making plans for the global gift-giving enterprise he was about to undergo with or without the elves' help.

As the elf strike continued, however, the council of elder elves, which was very fond of this jolly real-worlder who had graced their presence, became concerned that Santa might decide to pack it in and leave. This concern was underscored by the tacit, but not verbalized, concern that Santa might leave them and go to the *dwarves* for help in his quest.

Although the elves and the dwarves had, more or less, stopped making war on each other by this point, that didn't mean they liked each other any better. The pride and bragging rights stemming from having something the dwarves didn't—St. Nicholas—was an unmistakable and enticing reality.

And so it was that the elder elf council by unanimous vote, chose to prevail upon the most preeminent of all living elves for assistance: Trevil of the Northern Realm.

Trevil was, by this time, nearly two –hundred-years-old, elderly even by elf standards. He was an elven war hero many times over (he single-handedly fought back a dwarf invasion in the pre-colony wars a hundred years earlier, armed only with a sling-shot.) He was a statesman and former council leader. He also played a pretty good elven harp. If anyone could convince the real-worlder to stay, it would be Trevil. Except...

Trevil was also a recluse. He had been for years. He lived alone in a non-descript cave deep in the Northern Realm—a chilled, formidable place even by North Pole standards. The elders weren't even sure how they would get him to come down from there. Trevil of the Northern Realm didn't really concern himself with elf matters anymore. No one had seen him in years. He might be dead, though the elves were pretty sure they could sense if that were the case.

As the council sat pondering this by the fire's warmth, a long shadow filled the opening of the council chamber. The elders were a little surprised, but not much.

The shadow entered the room. The owner of the shadow was tall—by elf or human standards—and cloaked in grey. The council of elders stood at once. They knew who it was.

Trevil pulled the hood away from his face. He was striking with a billow of long, white hair and sharply defined features. He peered at the council wordlessly for several seconds then said, "I understand you've been talking of me," in elfish.

The council leader, Shishak, nodded. "It's-"

"It's about the real-worlder," Trevil finished. "He's thinking of leaving."

The elders didn't bother asking how Trevil could know this.

"Will you go to him?" Shishak asked.

"His quest is great," Trevil said, speaking as someone who knew a good quest when he saw one. "The real-worlders, such as they are, need him. I will go."

With no further deliberation or preparations, and certainly no chit-chat, Trevil was off without so much as a "See ya, later."

The elders looked at each other after Trevil left and nodded, gravely satisfied. It would be done. Dremar, the eldest of them all, wept silently.

Trevil hiked straight to Santa's campsite. He never asked directions, didn't need them. Didn't need maps either. He just *knew*.

Santa was ensconced at his writing table next to the fire, compiling the beginnings of what would eventually become his "naughty or nice" list. The elves had begun to train him in their magical arts and he was starting to sense certain things about the real-worlders. He knew when they were sleeping. He knew when they were awake. He knew if they'd been bad or good. Of course, he was also sensing when they belched, when they urinated, and when they, uh, other things he didn't want to know about. He was hoping he'd learn to modulate the frequency he was receiving on—though he didn't call it that—to screen those other things out.

When Trevil entered the firelight of the chamber unannounced and soundless, Santa was not surprised. He had sensed that too.

Santa stood. "Greetings," he said in elfish as he had become quite adept in the language of his new friends.

Trevil nodded. "I am Trevil of the Northern Realm."

"An honor, sir," Santa said.

Then Trevil did something very out of character. He got down on one knee and said, "The honor is mine."

Santa was quite embarrassed by Trevil's display of fealty. Once the awkward exchange had passed, Trevil said, "I come on behalf of the elves. They fear that you intend to leave."

"All of them?" Santa asked skeptically.

Trevil shook his head. "No," he said. "Many of the elves distrust you as a real-worlder, an outsider."

Santa sighed. "I know they do. I just don't know how to dispel their fears."

Trevil studied the human and said, "What is it that you intend to do here?"

Santa shrugged. "Continue on with my work."

"You wish to give gifts to humans in the real world."

Santa sighed again. "I've spent many years wandering from place to place in the real world. I've seen disease, poverty, fear and war. I discovered long ago that I had a gift at making things and acquiring funds to pay for things I couldn't make. I could have used that gift to increase my own wealth; to become a landholder and to rule over others as I have so often seen others do. But I didn't want to. I chose to use my skills to help others. I wish to continue doing so, Trevil. You elves are amazing beings. I have only begun to see the depth of your talents. We could do much good for the children of the world by working together."

Trevil nodded. "I believe that you are truthful. Your motives are pure. But you need to convince the elves of that."

"But how?"

Trevil didn't say anything for a long time, then finally, "You'll think of something. You will stay. The elves will follow." There was no trace of uncertainty in his voice.

"I hope you're right," Santa said.

Not one for long goodbyes, Trevil nodded, turned, and left without further word.

The next morning, the elves were gathered in the main clearing of the elven village making large pots of a breakfast gruel popular with the elves. Santa had not yet taken to it, but he was learning. It was bitterly cold out here in the open, but the elves didn't bother with torches for warmth. They just went about the business of breakfast quickly with no disruptions, as with all things in their lives.

When Santa arrived at the clearing carrying a large bundle, the elves were already busily slurping the contents of the gruel bowls. Santa stood in the center of the clearing for a full minute before someone looked up from her bowl. She only paused a moment before diving back into her meal.

Santa decided he would have to be more aggressive. "Hi, hi, hi!" he shouted, still trying to get the greeting he'd been working on just right.

This drew the attention of two or three more elves, but that was it.

Santa tried the only other thing he could think of. He hoisted his bundle high over his head—an impressive height as Santa is a very tall man. With all the force of his bulk, he slammed the bag down on the icy ground with a WUUUUMP and the sound of crunching snow and ice.

This got the elves' attention. They didn't know what was in that bag, but it made a lot of noise. Many more elves looked at the real-worlder.

"Good then, now that I have your attention," Santa said, "my dear elves, I have something to say."

There was no particular reaction to this announcement so Santa pressed on. "I'm..." he paused. A couple more elves looked. "NOT leaving."

By now, all elf eyes were on him. Many of the most caustic of the elves had been certain that he would leave by now. To hear him say he wasn't, well, that was more consuming than even gruel.

With that, Santa opened his pack and started removing his personal belongings: bundles of clothing, a few odd bits of real-worlder food—cheese and dried meats—a dagger (for defense only), netting he used to catch fish on his travels, and some carvings, including a mallard and an unidentifiable item that wasn't quite finished.

Santa handed the mallard carving to a pretty young elf on his left. He gave the dagger to a slightly older elf on his right. It looked more like a sword for the diminutive elf. The crowd started to murmur.

After handing out a few more items, as the murmurs became rumbles, Santa said, "What is that? Have you something to say?"

Shishak of the elders spoke up at this point and said, "My friend, what is it that you are doing?"

Santa shrugged. "Sir, I'm giving away everything I own."

"Why would you do this?"

"I've heard the elves speak of me. I've heard their suspicions that my desire to work hard only to then give everything away to real-worlders must be a falsity; that I must have some other motivation—wealth or power. I've heard some of the elves think they shouldn't have to work with me for free; getting no money, no land, no possessions in return. So I offer a deal: If the elves will work with me, devote their lives to making the world's children happy, I'll give them everything I own. Admittedly, it's not much, but it's from the heart."

Shishak nodded gravely. "Your words touch me. I am sure they touch *many of the elves as well.*" He squinted pointedly at the assembly of elves.

No elf was willing to return the gaze.

By this point, Santa's bag was empty. He shook it theatrically and glanced around the group. Some of the elves were passing around his possessions curiously, not sure what to make of them.

"I'm going back to work on building the toy workshop," Santa said. "If anyone wishes to join me, you know where I'll be."

Santa dropped the empty bag and it flapped a bit on the ground, the draw string fluttering in the icy breeze.

Santa turned and walked away, the crowd of elves parting to let him pass.

Within fifteen minutes of Santa resuming construction on the workshop by himself, the muffled *whuump whummp whummp* of dozens of heavy boots on snow signaled the return of the elves to Santa's aid. Ten minutes after that, with no speeches, apology or explanation necessary, every single elf was back to work. There was never another word of dissent spoken. Ever. No elf ever questioned the Christmas mission; never criticized or questioned Santa's authority.

Until today.

Doozil once again stood before the elves in the gathering place deep within the catacombs of the North Pole Complex. Vixen was with them, towering over them, his girth even more impressive in the confines of the chamber.

"And that's when I knew that these are dark days for the North Pole, indeed," Doozil was concluding, having already told the elves what Vixen had heard between Flifle and Mrs. Claus. "We must take action."

"Is that really true, Vixen?" one of the elves shouted from the back.

Vixen nodded his regal head vigorously.

The crowd grumbled. They would readily dismiss Doozil as a trouble maker, but Vixen was another matter. The Team One reindeer were the elite, above reproach. It must be true. Santa was really gone.

"So what do we do?" another elf called.

"We must confront them," Doozil said. "Mrs. Claus and our Chief of Staff Flifle. We must end the lies. We will force them to bring our Kris Kringle home. Or..." He paused.

"Or what?" asked a middle-aged elf, arms crossed.

Doozil's grin was devilish. "Or we'll take back our castle, built with the blood of our ancestors."

"And if they resist?"

"We have no choice," Doozil said. "We will do what needs to be done." The words hung thick and angry.

The crowd rumbled something that seemed to start as uncertainty, but gradually found its footing and became determination to act.

Raising his voice above the din, Doozil shouted, "In all these centuries our good and fair Santa Claus has loved and protected us. We will not let these...these criminals ruin the Christmas holiday. Let's go!"

The crowd of elves sprang to their feet with their characteristic agility and flowed out of the room. Doozil smiled and followed, invigorated by the thrill of not being the most hated resident of the Complex.

In the main chamber of the castle, Mrs. Claus sat listening to a CD. It was wired into a sound system that one of the techie elves had set up. She didn't know how it worked. Music just came on every so often, played awhile and then went off. This time, it was a real-worlder called Perry Como who was singing a silly song about a reindeer with a red nose. Honestly, those real-worlders...

The serenity of the winter night—a balm to her trouble mind, stressed over her wandering husband and the precarious state of the season—was shunted aside when Flifle stormed into the room. It was almost comical, as Flifle was clearly not an elf accustomed to running anywhere.

"Mrs. Claus, Mrs. Claus," Flifle said breathlessly. He paused to regain some composure and Mrs. Claus sat up from her formerly reclined position. "Trouble, ma'am. Big trouble," he said.

"What kind of trouble?"

"The elves. They're..."

"They're here," Doozil finished as he entered the room. He stepped aside and let the assembled crowd of North Pole elves file into the main chamber.

Mrs. Claus, eyes wide, looked from Doozil to Flifle—who simply threw up his hands—to Doozil again. She smiled thinly. "Good evening, Doozil."

"Good evening ma'am," Doozil said, all charm.

"What are you all doing this evening?"

"We're spreading a holiday message," Doozil said. Some other elves nodded, a few grunted their assents.

"What's that?" Mrs. Claus asked.

Doozil smiled. "Christmas is cancelled."

# DECEMBER 21

Shortly after the elf coup at the North Pole, all of the radio stations that could be tuned in from Spencer County, Indiana experienced dead air for several minutes during their holiday music blocks. One minute Elvis is singing about how he's going to have a blue Christmas without you, the next minute nothing. The dogs were almost done barking "Jingle Bells" when broadcasting resumed.

Over in England, dozens of cats were electrocuted in freak climbing-the-tree-to-chew-on-the-lights accidents.

In Mexico, revelers in the throes of *Las Posadas*, nine days of candlelight processions and parties preceding the Christmas holiday, stopped dancing and looked at each other. "Eh?" they shrugged, then went home.

And around the town of Santa Claus, Indiana, boughs of holly withered on the eves and lampposts. Every Santa Claus likeness around town appeared to be sticking out its tongue, instead of smiling brightly as they previously had.

At the Cameron Jones residence, the lights on Santa's souped-up Christmas tree went pop-pop-pop! Some of the bulbs literally burst. In others, the glowing incandescence of the holiday simply winked out of existence.

Cameron was cleaning up the mysterious shattered-light mess in the living room when the phone rang. He smiled a grim grin to himself as he bitterly enjoyed how that bastard manuscript—now dubbed *Die, Bitch, Die!*—had allowed a phone call to slip through when he *wasn't writing*. That wouldn't be hard, though. He hadn't touched the computer in days. He was working on convincing himself he was on Christmas vacation.

Cameron picked up the phone and greeted the caller, "Ho, ho, ho. Let you jingle my bells for a quarter," he said.

"Well, hello, Cameron. How are you?" Everett Franken said, unfazed.

"Groovin' on yuletide dreams," Cameron said.

"Good. Good," Everett Franken said, as if he hadn't heard a word of that. "Listen, I won't take much of your time..."

"Because I'm paying double since this is a Sunday," Cameron finished.

Everett Franken laughed politely. "Cameron, we have a problem."

Cameron's amazing—suspicious really—good mood was yanked off the center stage with an angry candy cane. "What now?" he asked.

"I got a letter from Wally Bass by fax today."

Cameron groaned.

Everett Franken continued. "He wants me to meet him in judge's chambers tomorrow. I think....well, I think he's going to ask that the Christmas Eve visitation be cancelled."

"What?!"

Everett Franken's voice retained its calm lilt. "Well, now, he says that Holly and Mrs. Morley paid you an impromptu visit the other day and now Holly has been telling people that you're living with Santa Claus."

"Who?"

"Some reporter. Ben Steene apparently."

Cameron cursed. "Son of a bitch. I told that guy to leave me alone."

"Cameron, I warned you about this."

"Yeah, yeah. So what do we do?"

"Well, Cameron, did you tell Holly that Santa-?"

Cameron cut him off impatiently. "I'm living temporarily with Susan's Uncle Milo. You know that. She's just fooling around."

"The child insists she saw Santa Claus at your house. He talked to her."

"She's five! Kids make up things. You've seen Uncle Milo. He doesn't look anything like Santa Claus. Claus could bench press two of him." Cameron was panicking now.

"According to Wally Bass, you told Holly that Santa lived with you."

Cameron frowned. He tried to remember the conversation, brief as it was. Yes, he had actually said that. "I was *kidding*. Joking around with my daughter."

"Evidently, she believed you."

"This is ridiculous."

"Ordinarily, perhaps. But given your...well-publicized instability, this might not look good."

"What's this Bass guy doing? Every time he gets another court order with my name in it, does it fetch a good price on the Internet?"

"Cameron..."

"Don't tell me to calm down. This is my daughter." Cameron was shouting now.

Everett Franken's tone didn't change. "Meet me at the courthouse tomorrow at one. We can talk briefly before I go in to see the judge."

"Will Susan be there?" He spat the name, suddenly filled with hatred for the woman and her betrayal. "Her and that bottom feeder she got for a lawyer, trying to make a name for himself, taking down the hot-shot writer."

"I don't know if she will or not."

"I'll be there," Cameron said. He depressed the off button on the cordless phone and threw it as hard as one can in a blind rage through the doorway toward the other room.

"Whoa, nice fast ball," Dogwater called, entering the kitchen from the living room, holding the phone Cameron had discarded. He put it on its cradle.

"Maybe Purdue needs a pitcher," his sister Roberta offered, following him.

"Not now," Cameron said, and sat at the table.

"What's up?" Dogwater asked.

"Susan's trying to take away my Christmas visit. Gotta go to court tomorrow," Cameron mumbled.

"No!" Roberta said.

"Yeah," Cameron confirmed.

"Why?" Dogwater asked.

Cameron laid his head on the table. "Don't want to talk about it."

"That's cool," Dogwater said and shrugged. A guy will never probe another guy's feelings uninvited.

A moment passed. Roberta busied herself finishing the clean up of the Christmas tree lights Cameron had started. Dogwater was left, awkwardly, on his own.

"Um, Cameron?" Dogwater ventured.

"Yeah," Cameron answered, head still on the table.

"Uh, could you maybe help with the ladder? Outside? I'm trying to hang the lights out front." It didn't really occur to Dogwater that Cameron may not be interested in having his house decorated now that Holly maybe wasn't coming. The man had a job to finish.

Cameron did nothing at first. Then said, "Yeah, okay." He rose and shuffled toward his parka hanging over the kitchen chair across from him.

"There ya go," Dogwater offered, clapping Cameron on the back as they headed outside.

In the kitchen, Roberta emptied the dustpan into the wastebasket. She crouched to replace the pan under the sink and when she stood up again a starburst played across her field of vision. She stumbled, clutching her temples.

When she'd regained her footing, Roberta ran to the front door and yanked it open. "Dog!" she shouted.

Dogwater had started up the ladder and missed the third rung when Roberta shouted. "What!" he called back.

"Come in here," Roberta shouted back.

"Why?" Dog responded.

"Just get in here."

Dogwater left the ladder propped against the house and stomped back to the porch. Cameron followed, for lack of any particular direction in his immediate life. When they arrived back on the porch, Dogwater said, "What's the deal?"

Roberta winced as a few more sparks shot across her eyes. She said, "I'm *sensing* something."

Dogwater just looked at her blankly.

"Really. I can feel something in the house."

"What are talking about?" Cameron said, surfacing briefly from his fog.

"I'm sensing a presence. No, two presences."

"Well, yeah. *You're* here. *I'm* here. *Cameron's* here...well, sort of," Dogwater grunted impatiently. Cameron just stared ahead blankly.

"That's not what I mean," Roberta snapped. She explained for Cameron's benefit, "I'm a little bit psychic."

Cameron shrugged as if to say, "Okay, so's everybody."

"I'm sensing life forces in the house, other than us," Roberta said. "Two distinct personalities. Or maybe one...but it's split somehow? I don't understand."

"Neither do I," Dogwater said.

Roberta gaped at him. For someone like Dogwater Hunt, so ready to believe anything—aliens, government conspiracies, ghosts and the afterlife, that Elvis was still alive, for God's sake—he was so closed minded when it came to psychic powers or heightened mental abilities. She sometimes reasoned that his aversion to higher mental powers was because he was, well, stupid. But that was probably just sisterly antagonism.

"Somebody's in trouble," Roberta said.

Cameron shrugged again in his so-what-else-is-new mode.

"One of these life forces is being smothered. Cameron, is there anyone else in the house? We have to help them."

"As far as I know, "Cameron said, "the only other person in the house is Milo and he's probably taking a nap. I saw him a little while ago and he was perfectly fine."

Roberta frowned. She started to say something else, but, instead, she went wobbly in the knees, reaching out for the door frame to steady herself.

"You all right?" Dogwater said, in something approximating concern. He was used to his sister's theatrics.

"I'm fine, "Roberta said. "This happens sometimes during my episodes. It'll pass."

"Maybe I should take you home," Dogwater said. "Cameron's got enough to worry about without all your psychic-babble."

"I'm fine," Roberta said, just before her eyes began to flutter.

"Come on," Dogwater said, leading her to the van. "Cameron, I'll finish the lights later, okay?"

Cameron shrugged again. "Whatever." Now that Christmas was a smoldering pile of shipwrecked Noel, twinkly lights seemed pretty superfluous.

Dogwater and Roberta drove away and Cameron walked back into the house. He slammed the door and the strings of lights that adorned the porch overhang fell, one after another, from the house.

"Now where did I put that little fucker Ben Steene's business card...?"

Mrs. Claus would never have guessed how hard it was to install the little buttons onto the video game console controllers until she tried to fit four buttons on a million controllers. By herself.

Now she really, *really* wanted a cigarette.

Granted, the elves had techniques of mass production unparalleled in any other realm, including the real world, but many of the elves would not deign to use them. Still, a couple million buttons is a lot.

But what was Mrs. Claus to do? The elves wouldn't make the toys, so there was no one to help use all those magical techniques and equipment. The lack of elves in the workshop was unprecedented. It was almost heresy. Santa was still, well, absent. It was up to her to make Christmas happen. If necessary, she would drive the sleigh herself. This would not sit well with the reindeer, who were understandably accustomed to the jolly old elf and did not like change at all. The year that the elves had successfully lobbied for colorful Christmas Eve costumes for the reindeer had been an unpleasant one indeed.

Mrs. Claus was taking a breather before again tackling the toy bin. After that it would be on to the production of several thousand pairs of designer sneakers (who would ever prosecute her for trademark infringement—even if she did know what that was?) When she was up to her kick-boxing toned hips in shoe strings, she really would miss Santa then. At one point in his existence, he had been an excellent cobbler.

Flifle ran into the workshop, door slamming with a hollow echo unimpeded by the sounds of busy elves hard at work making toys which ordinarily would have absorbed the noise, because there weren't any.

"Mrs. Claus," Flifle called.

"Over here," she called back from behind a stack of crates, some filled with completed game units, others with the guts of future game controls. Flifle found Mrs. Claus sitting cross-legged on the floor with piles of wires and controller buttons covering the lacy expanse of her apron. "Pull up a crate and grab a controller...or a thousand."

"Ma'am," Flifle said, not really paying attention. "I think I've found a way to get Mr. Claus back."

"What do you mean? You said we lost contact with the recall unit."

"I know," Flifle answered, face pulsing red, probably from exertion. The poor elf had been running again. "But I...I found a spell. It's old and I don't know if it's ever been used, but..."

"*Where* did you find a spell?" Mrs. Claus asked, standing and letting the buttons sprinkle to the ground like red dye number five raindrops.

Flifle's flush deepened. "I pulled out some of...Teevo's old spell books."

"What?"

"I'm sorry, ma'am. I know it's forbidden, but these are unusual circumstances."

"Are you actually suggesting we use some of that maniac's magic on Santa Claus?"

Flifle could have pointed out that they had already done so, which is how they got into this mess, but he thought better of it. Instead, he said, "Ma'am, we need to get him back. Time is running out."

"Don't you think I know that? But scattering his molecules all over the atmosphere with Teevo's magic is ridiculous." Mrs. Claus felt a chill.

"Most of Teevo's inventions work pretty well," Flifle offered. "Except for that one..." He left unspoken the mass production machine Teevo had created that killed those elves and led to Teevo's undoing.

Mrs. Claus glared. "I should banish you from the Complex for even mentioning his name."

"I know," Flifle said, struggling to convey patience. But he didn't look away. "But, ma'am, we're in trouble. *Christmas* is in trouble. Santa Claus would not want the holiday to end like this."

Mrs. Claus nodded, though at the moment she wasn't so confident about Santa's frame of mind. No, that wasn't fair. Mrs. Claus had essentially pushed Kris Kringle to go on this little journey. Maybe she should have seen this coming. Maybe she should have seen how really lost her husband was. Still, what was done was done, as Santa was wont to say.

"All right," Mrs. Claus sighed. "What do we do?"

Flifle shifted from one foot to the other, looking decidedly uncomfortable. "Well, the spell itself looks pretty simple," he said. "Basically, it removes the Santa life force from the body it's inhabiting."

"Will the real-worlder be okay?" Mrs. Claus asked, suddenly ashamed that only now was she really considering what might happen to the real-worlder they invaded.

"I believe so," Flifle said. "But..."

"Yes?"

"Like I said, the spell looks pretty simple, but it's designed specifically for Teevo."

"You mean you can't do it?" Mrs. Claus slumped.

"I couldn't do it anyway. I'm not a magic elf. I'm a production elf."

"So, it's hopeless," Mrs. Claus said.

"Well, maybe not," Flifle said. "A lot of elf magic is tied into the specific elf the spell is made for. That elf's life force gives the spell its power. Elves of the same house have similar blood, so they have similar life forces. I think as long as it's someone in Teevo's family line who performs the spell, it will work."

Mrs. Claus brightened a little. "Do we know any relatives of Teevo?"

"Well, most of them left the Complex after, well, after Teevo's problems, but there is one here." He gulped nervously, hesitating to say it.

Mrs. Claus suddenly understood. "Doozil," she said. "Second cousin to Teevo, twice removed."

Flifle nodded.

Like most of the elves, Doozil resided in a dormitory-like wing of the castle filled with elf-size bunks. When Mrs. Claus and Flifle found Doozil there, they were not surprised to see that he was alone. Except when they were in their bunks sleeping, or when the work of the North Pole required it, the elves kept their distance from Doozil. Doozil was a royal pain in the *schnafu*.

Doozil reclined on his bunk, writing with a quill pen in a tablet balanced on his knee. Flifle thought to himself darkly that he was probably writing compliments to himself; "Doozil is the greatest." "Doozil is the smartest of all the elves." "Doozil's ears stay naturally pointy."

Several seconds passed before Doozil looked up from his writing and only then it was in response to Mrs. Claus saying, "Doozil, you will look at me."

"Will I?" Doozil said, eyes with creepily flowing lashes lazily moving toward the First Lady of the North Pole.

"If I was the elf who shut down Christmas," I don't know if I'd be so impertinent," Flifle said stiffly.

"Can't be any worse than being the North Pole Complex Chief of Staff who banished Santa Claus."

Flifle clenched his teeth. "So, where are your friends?" he asked sarcastically.

Doozil didn't take the bait. "Probably out doing run-of-the-mill elf things; somersaults, pranks, coveting pots of gold."

"That's leprechauns," Flifle sneered.

"Oh, yes," Doozil said airily.

"Enough," Mrs. Claus said. "Doozil, we need your help."

Doozil's one eyebrow rose, dipped, and rose again. "Really? Well, I'm not making any toys, if that's what you want."

"You want Santa Claus back, don't you?" Flifle asked.

Doozil hesitated. "Of course..." It was only moderately convincing.

"*Don't you?*" Flifle repeated.

"You need me for something?" Doozil asked.

"Yes," Flifle said evenly.

"We've found a way to retrieve St. Nicholas," Mrs. Claus said.

Doozil's eyes narrowed. "Truly? That's contrary to your plan, isn't it?"

Flifle threw up his hands. "For the last time, we were trying to help Santa, not overthrow him."

"Yes, so you said."

"Doozil," Mrs. Claus interrupted. "We need your help."

Doozil studied Mrs. Claus as he considered this. "You found one of my counsin's spells, didn't you, Flifle?" Doozil peered intently at the chief of staff.

"Yes," Flifle answered.

"I had assumed those were burned after Teevo's...departure."

"No," Flifle said simply, not feeling inclined to offer any further explanation.

"Which one do you have?" Doozil asked, becoming more interested.

Flifle reached into his vest pocket and pulled out a brittle piece of parchment, yellowed with age and covered with elfish markings.

Doozil took the paper gently and, of all things, sniffed it. "This is a powerful spell," he said. "Definitely too dangerous for the likes of a production elf like you."

Flifle smacked Doozil in the side of the head clumsily, but effectively. As Doozil rebounded from the surprise, about to retaliate, Mrs. Claus executed a gentle, but persuasive, kick-boxing hold to dissuade him.

"Enough," she said. "There's no time for this." Then looking at her two North Pole elf colleagues. "Ever."

Instantly regaining his composure, Doozil closed his eyes and seemed to inhale the ink on the page. Flifle guessed he was picking up a residual essence of his lost relative. Elves had a heightened perception for their own kin. Smell is one of the senses most able to stimulate vivid memories. Of course, in this case the dear-departed was, by all accounts, insane, making the value of the effort, Flifle thought, questionable.

"Will you help us?" Mrs. Claus asked.

After another long moment, Doozil opened his eyes and glanced at the writing on the parchment. The words, written in stark, almost frantic, elven script, entranced him and he read the whole page quickly. He muttered a "hmm" or "oh!" now and then.

"Well," Flifle asked sharply.

"The spell is difficult, but not impossible—for a member of Teevo's family line."

"Like you," Flifle said, barely able to contain the sneer.

"Yes," Doozil said, without a trace of embarrassment.

"So, you'll do it?" Mrs. Claus asked.

Doozil shrugged. "I don't know."

"You don't know?" Flifle asked.

"Well, it's not without risks," he said. "I certainly don't want to go down in history as the elf who killed Santa Claus." He laughed. Mrs. Claus and Flifle did not.

"You just said you could do it," Flifle said.

"I can," Doozil assured absently, suddenly quite distracted by his quill pen.

"Christmas needs its Kris Kringle," Mrs. Claus pleaded. Then she simply blurted, "And I need my husband."

Doozil, already extremely pale by genetics, blanched even further for a moment, then resumed his normal color. "Yes, I understand..." He paused, then affirmed, "Very well, I will help you," he said magnanimously.

"Thank you Doozil," Mrs. Claus said diplomatically.

Flifle said nothing.

"What do you need from us to get this done?" Mrs. Claus asked.

"Well," Doozil said thoughtfully, "In order to make the spell work, it requires a Teevo family conduit—that's me." He did not say, "That's me since Teevo was killed here," but the tone was there. "And also a collective of elves to feed their life energy to the spell." He paused, tapping the quill lightly on his tablet. "I need an assembly of North Pole elves—three or four dozen, no more—to meet in the main dining hall of the castle tonight, in three hours. Can you handle all that?"

"They'll be there," Flifle said stiffly.

"Good," Doozil said.

"Anything else?" Mrs. Claus asked in the sweet, grandmotherly tone that made her a household name—despite rock-hard abs and a butt you could bounce a quarter off.

Doozil sighed. "Only to be left alone with my thoughts; to prepare myself to ascend to my glory."

"Just don't forget who we're doing this for," Flifle cautioned.

"Oh. Of course."

"We'll leave you alone then," Mrs. Claus said, as she and Flifle started to turn away.

Doozil suddenly sat up straight. "Oh! There is one other thing I need," Doozil called after them.

Mrs. Claus's sweetness never faltered. Flifle just shook his head.

"What is it, Doozil?" Mrs. Claus asked.

"A cookie. Sugar, frosted. Some of those little blue sparkly things on it," Doozil said. "Make that two cookies." He flopped back on the bunk, with a dismissive wave.

Within a short time, as Doozil instructed, Flifle had gathered elves in the main dining chamber of the castle, approximately seventy-five of them. Flifle knew if he only brought four dozen elves—despite what Doozil had said—that somehow Doozil would find fault with Flifle's failure to bring more elves. Well, he'd show that little elf-twerp.

Many of the elves were rather put out, being torn away from their new lives of play, play, a few hijinks, and more play. But they came because, well, it was Santa they were thinking of after all. It cost Flifle a promise of maple syrup in the morning gruel every day for a week—and he had no idea how he was going to get it when the nearest maple tree was, literally, a world away—but they were there.

A good half hour after the designated meeting time Doozil had insisted on, he finally arrived in the chamber. He was dressed all in white, a stark contrast to the colorful outfits elves usually wore. The standard pointy hat with jingle bells was gone. Doozil's ordinarily thick, slicked back hair (notably an unusual style for elves who preferred long and free flowing), was now in a tangled heap on top of his head.

Doozil walked wordlessly to the center of the room, elves parting to let him through. A few elves in the back snickered that perhaps this was finally execution day. Doozil stood, eyes closed and hands clasped in front of his face, saying nothing for several more seconds. The elves started wondering if they should wake him up.

Finally, Doozil said, "My fellow elves, we are gathered here tonight because one of us—the greatest of us—our dear Santa Claus is in trouble. His soul is lost in the real world and he cannot find his way home. I call upon you to help me convey the words of one of our most resourceful, most loved elves in all of our history, Teevo, across the expanse from our realm to the real world to retrieve our lost comrade—nay! Our lost leader."

A couple elves choked on the assertion that Teevo was "loved" by anyone. One elf, in fact, did a classic comedy spit take with ale upon hearing this. Doozil didn't notice.

"As I recite these words—Teevo's words—I need you to give me your energy, the life force that makes elves the great race that they are. Will you do this?"

Nobody said anything.

"I say, will you do this?"

Still nothing but a few uncomfortable seat shifts.

Flifle spoke up and said, "Just get on with it."

Doozil was unflappable. "The words I speak now are words of the ancient elven tongue. Many of these words are not even used today; lost to the ages. But although the phrasing and meaning of the words may be unknown to many today—outside of Teevo's line—their power is not diminished. I, and I alone, as the last surviving relative of Teevo's family, possess the ability to use these words, and I shall do so now."

Flifle huffed impatiently, wanting Doozil to pick it up. The Christmas season was ticking away.

Doozil closed his eyes again, swooped his arms above his head, turned clockwise three times, lowered his arms, and launched into a string of old-Elvish words, a chant, lasting four minutes. He barely paused for breath. How a little elf like Doozil could have such a lung capacity was unknowable, but he did it nonetheless. By the time he finished, he was drenched in sweat.

The assembled elves were, despite themselves, impressed by the spectacle. True, many didn't understand the words Doozil said, but as they were the old versions of words they used in the modern age, they could pick out a few phrases here and there, like an English speaker reading a text in Old English.

When he was finished, Doozil opened his eyes and said nothing. He was clearly fatigued.

"Is that it?" Flifle said.

"No, I have now to give the command that will summon the soul of St. Nicholas, freeing the real-worlder with whom he has joined, and bringing Santa home to us." He rattled off twelve more words. Frowned, repeated them, and then uttered a strangled gargle. He shouted the words now in a gravelly mess, the sweat beading on his forehead again.

"The chasm between here and the real world is wide and treacherous," Doozil said hoarsely. "Still Teevo's words are powerful. I do not understand how this could be..."

"How what could be?" Flifle asked.

Doozil looked stunned. "I cannot reach him." There was something very akin to fear in his eyes.

"No!" Mrs. Claus shouted, having, until now sat in uneasy silence near Flifle.

Doozil stammered, "I have failed," he said, then collapsed.

The crowd gasped and all chattered anxiously.

Flifle sprinted through the crowd to the front of the room and hauled Doozil to his feet. Shaking him by the folds of white cloth around his shoulders, he said, "You told us you could do Teevo's spell. What by the oaths of Gandish happened?"

"Santa's levila is fused tightly with the real-worlder," Doozil said softly. "This spell will not separate them. He is lost to me."

A groan rose up from the middle of the crowd.

"Well," Flifle sighed. "I guess then he's lost to us too. Christmas really is over."

As Doozil spooled out the retrieval spell in that elven hall, Santa was in Cameron's living room surveying the light strings on the tree that, oddly, had no functioning light bulbs anymore. Not a single one. A stabbing pain filled his vision with lightning bolts. He groaned, and stumbled to the couch.

Cameron and Dogwater, hearing the groan, rushed in from the back door through the kitchen. "Milo! What is it?" Cameron asked.

Milo looked at Cameron, but it wasn't Milo at all. In place of his eyes were images of terrified Santa Clauses. Milo's face twisted in silent agony. The Santa images grew and left Milo's eyes. Santa's agonized face floated about the room. Milo's stared expressionless from atop the writhing old man's body on the couch.

The Milo head turned and looked at the Santa head, horrified. "What the hell are you?" Milo shrieked. Then it turned to Cameron and Dogwater. "Help meeeeeee," he screamed. The Santa head simply looked bewildered and disoriented.

The Santa head spun around Milo then circled the room. It flew between Cameron and Dogwater. Dog dove for cover behind the tree, protecting his privates and waiting for the mother ship to pick him up. Cameron couldn't move. Every circuit in his mind that governed coherence and reason shorted out. He was certain that Webster Stanhope—"Suck my tail fin, ya bastard!"—would pop out of Milo's ass next.

The silent, shimmering spectacle lasted for two full minutes before the Santa head collided with the Milo head. They shattered in mid-air in a shower of ephemeral sparks and were gone. Milo, whole again, collapsed on the couch, sleeping.

"Fuck me," Dogwater said, peering cautiously around the tree, amazed he was still here and not off being probed, and equally amazed that he hadn't pissed his pants.

"Fuck me too," Cameron said absently. He turned without further word and went upstairs calmly.

"Cameron?" Dogwater whispered, but the auxiliary battery operating Cameron's vital functions in crisis mode didn't allow him to respond.

Dogwater hesitated. Check on Milo? Check on Cameron? Get the hell out? He went with option "C," slamming the door behind him and not looking back. Milo never moved.

Dogwater was so eager to speed away from this place that he didn't even notice the out-of-towner in the expensive shoes scampering across Cameron's front yard toward the rental car, pen working furiously over a reporter's notebook.

# DECEMBER 22

Santa Claus awoke the next morning feeling as rested as he ever had waking up in the feather bed in his cozy room at the North Pole. He yawned and stretched contentedly as he rose to meet the day. He had a vague sense that something had gone on the night before, but he couldn't recall.

Kris Kringle pushed aside the covers, sat up, felt around on the floor with his feet for his slippers and when he found them, he stood up in them. His stomach rumbled and he decided to head downstairs for breakfast.

As St. Nick shuffled past the dresser, he caught a glimpse of Uncle Milo in the mirror and thought not much of it, having gotten used to the vessel that carried him by this point. Quickly his groggy early morning gears shifted, however, and his subconscious became very alarmed. So he looked again.

What he saw was Uncle Milo's skinny body and Uncle Milo's face, but on that face was a silvery white, bushy, flowing *Santa Claus beard*. He knew it was a trademark Santa whisker festival because, well, the man had been wearing it around for nearly a couple millennia. How could he mistake it? And there it was on Milo's face. Milo Vestibule was a clean-shaven man by habit and Santa had dutifully continued the habit for him, though it had been ugly going the first few days. When he had roused himself from the couch and gone to bed the night before, he had just one day's growth of whiskers; this, however, was several years, nay centuries, worth of beard.

Kris Kringle tugged, pulled, yanked. It wouldn't move. He had another vague inkling of some significant event the night before, but the realization tantalized his conscious memory while withholding satisfaction.

Santa forgot breakfast for the moment. Instead, he went straight to the bathroom to try and get rid of this tell-tale sign of Santa-ness. He knew that having a white beard by itself wouldn't make people guess he was Santa

Claus, but he also knew people around him like Cameron and especially his suspicious friend Dogwater, would think it very odd that it grew overnight. He would rather not have to explain this.

He found, however, that getting rid of the evidence of his Santa-ness was going to be impossible. The first two razor blades snagged and became useless in the flowing white curls; the two after that snapped apart. He gave up on shaving it off. Seeing no options, Santa decided to just go with it. If anyone asked, he'd claim to have been diagnosed with some glandular thing that made his facial hair grow really fast. Surely people would buy that. Everyone believed Santa, even if they didn't know he was Santa. Right?

Santa showered and dressed, being very conscious not to wear anything "Santa-like" in red or green, lest he call attention to his whiskers. He stuck with old blue jeans and a plaid work shirt. He was somewhat dismayed to see by the end of the grooming process that his standard grey Uncle Milo eyebrows had become bushy white Santa brows. This was very bad. Pretty soon he'd have rosy cheeks and a cursed cherry nose and it would all be over.

Santa noted with relief that Cameron's second floor bedroom door was closed. He was apparently still sleeping. This would give Santa more time to come up with an explanation for his hairiness.

He ate pancakes with chocolate chips and whipped cream this day. He was getting to be a good cook, though the microwave was off-putting and Cameron's "Home Java-nator" coffee maker was eons beyond his comprehension. He tried reading the paper, but the real-worlder news made him sad. He watched some television—he was starting to like television—but was afraid to progress after he got to the channel with the women exercising in form-fitting leotards. He was afraid what they might be doing on the next channel. So he went back to "Price is Right" instead, though the currency part of it was a little confusing.

But still, Santa couldn't shake the feeling that something bad was going on in this house. Even looking out the windows was unsettling. Instead of bountiful rays of morning glory, this morning was lifeless and dark, the sky streaked with gray, much like the inside of a naughty child's coal-filled stocking.

Well, Santa would deal with that anxiety, but first his more immediate problem was the outside of his head, not the inside.

As the morning wore on, Cameron still did not come downstairs. Santa started to think there was something wrong. He was supposed to meet his lawyer at two and it was almost noon.

Finally, at one-fifteen, Santa decided to go check on him. The bedroom door was still closed. He rapped lightly at the oak and heard nothing. He knocked again and still no response. He gingerly opened the door and said, "Cameron, I don't mean to disturb you, but I believe you have an appointment with the, um, barrister."

The room was dark, the shades pulled. He could hear Cameron breathing softly, but after he spoke, he heard the ruffling of covers and a muffled yelp.

Santa peered around the door, hiding as best he could, the lower half of his face. "Cameron, are you all right?"

Cameron was lying in a fetal position, staring with eyes the seemed to glow cat-like in the dark room. He glared at Uncle Milo.

"You don't want to keep Mr. Franken waiting," Santa said.

"Stay away from me," Cameron said hoarsely, with a mixture of fear and, well, more fear.

"What is it?" Santa asked. The alarm-signaling tingle was back.

"I don't know who you are, or what you are, or how you got in my head, but you have to get out. I don't see you. I don't believe in you."

Santa was stunned. Cameron, of course, was speaking to what he perceived to be a hallucination based on what he'd seen the night before—a bifurcation of Susan's Uncle Milo and Santa Claus and a spectacle of floating heads– but Santa was struck because he'd heard "I don't believe in you" so many times before from his beloved children as they entered adolescence, losing their faith in their former hero. Santa was speechless.

Unconsciously, Santa stepped into the room, revealing his bushy beard. Cameron freaked. "Oh, shit," he said. "I knew it."

Santa started to say, "Cameron," then stopped short when he realized what he'd done. He tried ineffectually to cover his beard with his hands and stepped toward Cameron, frantically shouting "It's glandular!"

"Get away from me!" Cameron shouted and sprinted out of the bedroom. He was fully clothed and rumpled in his outfit from the night before. He soared down the stairs and was out the front the door before the considerably older Uncle Milo/Santa Claus could catch up.

"Cameron, wait. Please," Santa called, but the front door slammed shut and Cameron was in the car and gone before Santa got to the porch.

Traditionally, the week of Christmas is a slow time at courthouses. Lawyers are disinclined to try a lot of cases that week. Nobody wants to work during the holidays, plus going for the judicial jugular so close to the day of goodwill and peace might be bad for public relations. It would be awkward to get a big judgment against somebody or send somebody's dad to jail right before Christmas dinner.

A few things do still go on, such as family law cases involving celebrities, even fading ones. Still, the parking lot was pretty empty when Cameron squealed in, which was fortunate for Cameron's insurance rates. He stopped the car over portions of about three spots in the end of the lot farthest from the courthouse.

Cameron fumbled with the seatbelt before realizing he hadn't been wearing it. He jumped out of the vehicle and sprinted toward the courthouse. A sheriff's deputy walking through the parking lot watched him curiously to see if there might be trouble—no one ever ran to meet a court date—and also because he vaguely recognized the man, maybe from the cover of one of those books his wife read.

Cameron was halfway to the courthouse when Everett Franken intercepted him, having just parked his own car. He'd missed the dramatic entrance and his own arrival had been characterized by very precise, slow turns, culminating in a master's approach to the parking spot and perfect alignment of the vehicle between the lines. It was Everett Franken's nature.

"Well, season's greetings, Cameron, how are you today?" Everett Franken called, smiling a confident, friendly, lawyer smile. When Cameron turned and Everett Franken took in the unshaved, unkempt appearance and wrinkled clothes, he had the answer to his question. The smile faltered a bit, but remained in place. Poker faces weren't just for card players.

"I'm crazy, Ev," Cameron said, his voice high and reedy. "How you doin'?"

Everett Franken glanced around, but didn't see Wally Bass anywhere. His old, rusty Buick with the missing muffler wasn't there yet. "Cameron,

I think we should go inside and talk."

"I don't want to talk," Cameron protested. "When I talk, weird shit comes out. Plus, now I'm living with Santa Claus. I guess I could talk to him; maybe tell him what I want for Christmas. Wonder if he'll let me sit on his lap. No, never mind."

"Cameron, really," Everett Franken protested, trying to lead him toward the courthouse door.

"No, Everett. Please, just tell Susan she wins. Holly was right. My brilliant little girl called it—Father Christmas is sleeping in my guest room, using up all the hot water, and hogging the Fig Newtons."

"Cameron," Everett Franken tried again. "Let's just go sit down and talk-"

Cameron cut him off. "I'll give up my Christmas visit. I can't subject Holly to...to her freak of a father, anyway. Not like this, not after last year. The guy is Santa Claus to me, but maybe to her he'd be, I don't know, a seven-headed alien that shoots fire out his butt."

Cameron was making little sense. Everett Franken knew Cameron didn't really want to give up his visitation, but he also knew there was no way he was putting Cameron in front of the judge like this.

"Well, be that as it-"

"Just cancel all of it," Cameron blundered on. "Christmas. The modification application. Let Holly and Susan get as far away from me as possible." He smiled darkly. "It'll be my present to them."

"Cameron, I think you should take a few moments to..."

"You take a few moments!" Cameron shouted, attracting the deputy's attention again. The retort made no sense, but he was frantic.

Everett Franken read his client's face. He saw there an expression of deep conviction that this was the right thing to do, warring with the deeper belief that it was not, in any sense, the right thing to do. Everett Franken had seen that look many times on many clients' faces.

"Well, Cameron, here's what we could do," Everett Franken said. "I could go up and explain to Wally Bass that we understand Ms. Wentworth is concerned about what Holly has said about Santa Claus living with you in the guise of Milo Vestibule."

Cameron flinched.

"And that, of course, calls into question the ability of Mr. Vestibule to serve as a third-party go between for visitation purposes," Everett Franken continued. "So, in light of the difficulty finding another neutral third party so close to Christmas, we propose canceling the Christmas visit—to be made up later, perhaps over New Year's."

"And the modification?"

Everett Franken sighed. "You're upset. Now is not the time to make a decision on that. Let's talk about that later."

Cameron considered this and the portion of his sanity that wasn't overloaded and was at least somewhat functional, realized maybe chucking the whole thing was irrational. Maybe he could pull out of this. Maybe *I'm not crazy, just...ill*. Of course, that is *exactly* what a crazy person would think. He was too confused right now to argue.

"Fine, Everett, do whatever. I just can't handle this today."

Everett Franken nodded. "I understand," he said, though he didn't really. He realized he would have to give some thoughts to a continuance of the modification trial to allow time for a psychological work up. Then there would be the battle to keep those records away from the press. Everett Franken was not used to the additional strains of representing a national celebrity—there were few in Santa Claus, Indiana—and he didn't like it much. But he did like Cameron very much.

Everett Franken sighed. He patted Cameron's shoulder and could feel the man shivering faintly beneath a sweaty shirt despite the brisk Midwest winter breeze. It just now occurred to him that despite the high twenties temperature, Cameron wasn't wearing a coat.

"I gotta go," Cameron said abruptly.

"Well, Cameron, I think we need to plan for-"

"Save it," Cameron snapped, then softened. "Later, okay? You don't need me for this, do you?"

"No," Everett Franken said, knowing his client needed to go more than Everett needed him to stay.

"Thanks," Cameron said. "I'll talk to you later." His voice sounded almost even again.

"Goodbye, Cameron."

Cameron smiled weakly and turned toward his car just as Susan Wentworth pulled her jeep into a space about ten feet away. She tried to smile cordially as she got out of the vehicle and gave a short, awkward little wave.

"Bite me," Cameron responded, and not quietly—the sheriff's deputy was very curious now. "You won. Merry fucking Christmas."

With that, Cameron marched back to his vehicle, wrapping himself in his own arms as best he could for some measure of warmth against the steady chilled wind and also for the small amount of security the gesture provided.

At an intersection featuring a Santa cutout on all four corners, Cameron fumed even as other drivers honked when he failed to take his turn to proceed through the intersection. He was finally about to step on the gas when he heard a familiar voice.

"Merry Christmas, Cameron."

Cameron glared through the passenger side window. Ben Steene toasted him with a tall plastic-topped cup of coffee. "Have you told Santa what you want yet?"

"Yeah," Cameron grunted through gritted teeth. "You on the business end of a long stick."

"Pardon?"

Cameron shrieked and jumped out of the vehicle, engine still running. A few passers-by paused to watch the show. In an instant, Cameron was in Ben Steene's face, which didn't seem to faze him in the least.

Sipping his coffee, Ben Steene said, "That coffee place on the corner has amazing muffins. I ate like three of 'em."

"Stop it," Cameron said.

"Yeah, I know. All that cholesterol."

"Stay away from me."

"The doc says I should switch to decaf too."

"And my family."

"I mean, I already gave up smoking. If it's not one thing, it's another, am I right?"

"I'm serious, Steene," Cameron grunted. "Write what you want about me, but stay away from them."

"That include your Uncle Milo Claus?" Ben Steene asked. "Quite a little fireworks display at your house yesterday."

Cameron gulped. "Um...what?"

Ben Steene just smiled. "Gonna be quite a story. Could be a Pulitzer in it. Too bad I didn't have a camera though. Maybe you and your buddy St. Nick could stop by for milk and cookies."

Even at such close range, Cameron landed a very effective left to Ben Steene's nose. Blood and expensive coffee house coffee went everywhere.

"There," Cameron said. "Go get yourself some decaf." He dug a five dollar bill from his pocket and tossed it at Ben Steene. "On me."

When Cameron returned home, after swinging through a drive-thru to get two large cheeseburgers and two fries—really, what's the point of promoting heart health and living a long life if you've lost your family?—he went into the house, tossed his keys onto the table by the door, and ignored the mail sitting there.

Had he looked at the small stack of bills, letters, and magazines, he would have seen a postcard featuring a stunning Swiss mountain scene sent to him by Dr. Marjorie Whipple, or rather someone in her employ. The card was addressed to *Ms.* Cameron Jones. The scene, devoid of the cozy informality of personal vacation snapshots, was as predictable and coldly formulaic as his life was not.

Cameron went to the kitchen, tossed the bag of food on the table and went looking for a beer. It was only about two in the afternoon, but what the hell.

As he emerged from the refrigerator, he heard Uncle Milo step lightly into the kitchen. *Great, now he wants to sneak up and kill me*, Cameron thought. *I should put jingle bells on the guy.* He slammed the refrigerator door.

Cameron turned and when he saw Uncle Milo, he said, Oh, Christ..."

"No, Santa Claus," Milo said, taken aback. He still had the bushy Santa beard, but had added a Santa hat and red coat with white fringe—not the original, but a close second found in Cameron's basement—that was much too large for Milo's wiry frame.

"That's not funny," Cameron said darkly and pushed past him to the kitchen table. He started to unwrap a burger as Santa gaped awkwardly.

"Cameron, it's time I told you the truth," Santa said. "I am Santa Claus.

Or Kris Kringle if you prefer."

"Or St. Nicholas?" Cameron said through a mouthful of beef.

"If you like."

"How about Father Christmas?"

"I have many names, Cameron," Santa said patiently. "I want to tell you..."

"Forget it. You're not really here, so you're just wasting your breath. Why don't you go back to the South Pole and tell Webster Stanhope I'm ready for him? Little fucker's probably frozen in an ice cube." He held up his cola—it had come free with the value meal. "When I'm finished with this, I'll fill it with tap water. Webster can swim his fake fishy ass off."

"It's the North Pole I'm from, actually," Santa said, helpfully. "And I don't believe I know Mr. Stanhope. Is he a friend of yours?"

Cameron barked. "Something like that." Cameron shoved several fries into his mouth.

Santa sat uncomfortably across from him until finally he couldn't stand it any longer. "Cameron, I really am Santa Claus."

"Fine. Whatever," Cameron said.

"What must I do to convince you?" Santa pleaded.

Cameron thought a moment. "What did I want for Christmas when I was five?" he asked, eyes narrow.

Santa considered, his Santa hat slightly cocked to one side, and finally said, "A puppy."

Cameron nodded. "And what happened?"

"I brought you one. A little brown and white one. Adorable-" then Santa stopped short. His face darkened. "Cameron, I'm sorry." This was the puppy that died.

Cameron smirked, then chewed and swallowed another fry. "And what did I want for Christmas when I was eight?"

Santa thought again. "You wanted an air rifle," Santa said.

"Did I *get* one?" Cameron asked, sounding very much a like a prosecutor grilling a reluctant witness.

"No," Santa said cautiously. "But that was because your mother clearly didn't want you to have one. I can't give gifts that parents object to."

Cameron's eyes rolled. "And what, may I ask, did I want for Christmas when I was eighteen?"

Santa's eyes widened. He nodded sadly. "You wanted your father to get better."

Cameron tossed a hamburger wrapper toward the sink as he stood, knocking his chair backward on the floor. "You're a pretty good guesser, Milo or St. Nick, or whatever you're calling yourself."

Cameron got another beer from the 'fridge. "And did he live?" he asked as he turned back to the table.

"No, he died when you were just nineteen," Santa said softly. "I'm sorry."

"Save it...Christmas Boy," Cameron shouted, fumbling for an insult. "Tell you what. As long as I'm crazy anyway, let's see some Christmas magic. You know a little Santa-action. Climb down a chimney. Or, I know, whip up a magic snowman from some of that slush under the car. I don't have any coal for eyes, but the dog crap would make great buttons."

"Cameron, I really only go down chimneys on Christmas Eve. I don't think it would be appropriate..."

"No," Cameron nodded, exaggeratedly, "We wouldn't want Mr. Christmas to be *inappropriate*."

Santa's thick white eyebrows knitted together as he thought hard what he could do to convince his friend—and he did consider Cameron a friend—that he was really telling the truth. This was hard because, being Santa Claus, he couldn't conceive of anyone thinking he was lying. Santa doesn't lie; well, except for the thing about pretending to be Uncle Milo.

He had to do something. He thought, then he smiled, eyes all a-twinkle, as the perfect idea came to him. Santa said, "Cameron, I think I can show you something that will prove I am telling you the truth. Will you join me in the living room?"

Cameron looked at Uncle Milo, grabbed a couple more fries and chewed thoughtfully. "What the hell?" he said, then wiped his hands on his jeans and stood. He followed Santa into the living room.

The tree there looked again how it had when Santa had redone it. Santa had earlier in the day repaired the lights again, mostly to have something to do. He stood in the center of the room and motioned to Cameron to sit on the couch. Cameron flopped down and looked lazily at Santa, waiting for the show to start.

Santa was nervous. At the North Pole, the only audience for his magic consisted of the elves and Mrs. Claus. The few and infrequent times he did magic in the real world, it was for children; making the characters in a snow globe dance, displaying a glimpse—but only a glimpse—of the magical beauty of the North Pole. They were a much more accepting lot than cynical adults. But now if a display of magic was what Cameron, an adult, needed to resurrect his faith in the spirit of the holiday, he would do it.

Santa took a deep breath, said a few magic words to himself, and waved his hand.

The re-decorated Christmas tree in Cameron's living room began to shimmer, even though the lights were not plugged in. The colors—reds, golds, greens, and silvers—blurred and melded, almost creating a brand new, never-before-seen color of amazing brilliance. Eventually, the tree ceased to be a tree at all, just a blob of color. And then it reformed. It was a tree again, but not the same one it had been. This tree was more *traditionally* decorated—popcorn and construction paper chains.

Next, presents sprung up from the floor underneath the tree, like so many festive flowers. And then, there was the distinct sound of a baby crying. At this, Cameron became more alert, despite himself. A baby slowly came into focus, wearing a red and green jumper, lying happily on the floor near the tree, enjoying a ribbon of gold dangling from a low branch, giggling at it. This was a very happy child.

Next to the child, nearer the tree, a slightly younger version of Cameron— complete with the scraggly beard he tried for a while—appeared, as if with a snap of the fingers, cross-legged on the floor.

Cameron's—the Cameron watching all this—mouth dropped. Magic Cameron was staring intently at the gurgling child. "Ho, ho, ho, little Holly," Magic Cameron said. "Welcome to your first Christmas. I hope you like your presents. Mommy picked out most of them, but I'll take credit for the ones you like the most." Magic Cameron lowered his head closer to the child, glanced around and whispered in a stage whisper, "Just remember when you're older that I wanted to get you a hockey stick, but Mommy said you weren't old enough."

Cameron's heart thudded.

"But you will be someday, won't you?" Magic Cameron added. "Will you remember this day? Probably not. But I will."

With that last statement, Magic Cameron, the baby, and the tree and presents all disappeared, slowly fading into an eternal new year that is always on the horizon, but never quite arriving. The old tree—that is to say, the new tree—stood in its original place as if it had not been disturbed.

A single tear hovered without falling from Cameron's right eye. "How did you...?" he started.

Santa waved his arms. "Christmas magic." Little gold sparks floated lazily from his finger tips and fell harmlessly to the floor where they faded away.

Internally, Cameron debated. Either he was getting crazier and his hallucinations were having hallucinations, or this guy really was Santa Claus. He supposed a third possibility was this guy was a really good magician/con artist, but he couldn't guess what the angle would be. Revenge for *Quality, Not Quantity*, perhaps?

Santa sat next to Cameron on the couch, "Well?" he asked.

Cameron turned his head slowly to the bearded, but still skinny, curiosity sitting next to him. "Just stay away from my stockings, okay? I know we've been bunking together, but, dude, I hardly know you."

"Ho, ho, ho," Santa chuckled good-naturedly. He didn't get the joke.

But Cameron didn't care.

Out on the lawn, there nearly arose such a clatter as the ladder that had been leaning against the house nearly toppled. Dogwater Hunt—who had returned to put finishing touches on the house decorations—had near nearly knocked the ladder over when he stepped back from the living room window absently; the window where he had just seen vindication of his faith in Lars Heimdal. He had found his Christmas alien.

Dogwater sprinted back to the van. Ben Steene, cigar between his teeth and sporting a bandaged nose, was waiting for him.

"In a hurry, Mr. Hunt?" Ben Steene asked through a mouthful of hand-rolled Panatela

"Yeah, could you move buddy?"

"Sure, if you give me a ride downtown," Ben Steene said, turning and climbing into the passenger seat of the van before Dogwater could formulate a protest.

"Hey," Dogwater started then glanced at Cameron's house. He needed to go get his equipment and get back here to record whatever that thing in Cameron's house was. The clock was ticking. He ran around and jumped into the driver's seat.

As they drove, Ben Steene held up a business card so Dogwater could see what it was and laid it on the dash. "I'm with *Perils of Prose-Masters.com*, Mr. Hunt," Ben Steene said. "Name's Steene."

"Cameron's a friend," Dogwater said. "I don't talk to reporters about him."

"Of course." Ben Steene nodded. "But what about that thing we just saw?"

Dogwater nearly swerved off the road.

Be careful what you wish for.

The real-worlders say that a lot. And for them, it's a reasonable caution. The real-worlders live in a finite world bound by the limitations of availability, the ability to pay, and mortality.

For elves, however, all things are available—think of a thing and it can be created or you can get it or you can travel to another world to find it. "Paying" for something is virtually unheard of; all the elves share whatever they have. Mortality is not, at least not yet, an issue for the North Pole elves; not since the elf-dwarf wars subsided. Thus, for elves, the notion of "wishes" is simply that, a notion. And yet...

Even an elf as intelligent—he might say brilliant—as Doozil is not immune to the seduction of wishes. His wish: to get back at that vile carpet-bagging, real-world interloper to the North Pole: Santa Claus. Santa was, after all, the man who led his dear cousin Teevo to his death. Santa clearly didn't recognize Teevo's genius. Doozil could relate. And Teevo was killed by Santa.

So, Doozil had had no qualms about stoking the flames of elf rebellion. He'd planned to do it anyway, but the timing of Santa's departure from the Complex was an advantageous coincidence. It did his little elf-heart proud to see Mrs. Claus and Flifle strain and struggle; to have the elves listening to him, doing as he said. The luster of his tarnished family line was going to be restored.

But still...Doozil was rocked by his failure to retrieve Santa with Teevo's spell. The irony of this was not lost on him. Doozil had come to the Complex, put up with the scorn of his fellow elves, for the sole purpose of undermining Kris Kringle to make him go away. And now, when the man was gone, he was actually shaken by the absence.

Doozil shuddered. Could it be, he actually missed the man? Sitting in the darkened south tower of the Complex, a sanctuary of worship for the elves surrounded by stained-glass and filled with the aroma of fresh-baked bread, he sought the answer to that question. He realized that he did, in fact, miss the man; missed him very much indeed.

But Teevo was dead at Santa's hands. Doozil could not forget that.

*No, not at Santa's hands,* Doozil thought. *Santa loved Teevo, as he did all the elves. Teevo was passionate and—sometimes—a little reckless.* That thought stung, but Doozil faced it. *Santa loved everyone. He was generous and good.*

Still, Teevo deserved better. He was mocked, and Doozil was mocked. And now Teevo lay dead. Long dead.

Why did Doozil feel so sad instead of angry?

What was he to do?

"So, Cameron sprouted, like, a magic beard and talked to an invisible baby?" Izzy Carmichel asked, rubbing his eyes. He'd been up most of the previous night playing the new sniper game he rented for Dogwater's video game console— that he'd borrowed six months earlier—and smoking lots of pot.

"No, man, listen," Dogwater said, launching again into his story for the third time, almost literally, as he teetered on the edge of the ominously stained couch in Izzy's trailer.

"No, no, I got it, man," Izzy said. "So when you gonna call that reporter dude?"

"I'm not," Dogwater said.

"Say that again?" Izzy said, struggling to an upright position. "Are you nuts? This is your ticket to the big time, man."

"He wants to write about Cameron. It'll embarrass him."

"That reporter dude could put your little space bug on the map. You said he saw it too right?"

"Yeah."

"Well," Izzy began, inching closer to Dogwater. "You don't do something and he's gonna claim that little discovery for himself."

"I never thought of that..." Dogwater said, trailing off. He could see his name fading from the science books and off the plaque on his Nobel Prize and being replaced by Ben Steene's. Life was so much easier when no one shared his weird little passions.

"So the thing was gone when you got back?"

"Yeah, I dropped off Steene-"

"Without telling him shit," Dogwater added.

"Right. I went back to the house and everything was quiet. Cameron didn't even answer the door."

"So you didn't get no photos," Izzy said. "You got anything else?"

Dogwater dug into his parka pocket and pulled out the strange, gold, zigzag shaped object he had found in Cameron's yard days earlier. "Well, you ever see anything like this before?" he asked as he tossed it onto the coffee table where it clinked dully against an empty peanut jar.

Izzy reached for the object, dropping it again almost immediately, his hand snapping back to his chest. "Shit, man. It's hot."

"What?" Dogwater asked, touching the thing tentatively. It had indeed gotten warm. It was also vibrating gently. What was this thing?

"Get it out of here, man," Izzy said. "I'm screwed if you burn the place down. No insurance."

"You're still gonna help me Christmas Eve, right?"

"What else I got to do?" One eye remained on the softly humming object.

"Well, I'm gonna need a camera. No, a camcorder. A good one. Or two. With tripods. Some actual, up close video of Santa Claus will really put *Dark Matters* on the map. Can your boy at Electronic Junction get me any?"

Izzy shrugged. "I guess, if you still got some of that writer's money left. But is that all you're after? Some cool pics for your website?"

Now Dogwater shrugged. "Yeah. I want the truth to see the light of day finally." It didn't sound at all cliché sautéed in Dogwater's simple passion.

"That's my boy," Izzy said. "Now get out of here. I got to get some sleep. I hear the "Sniper Killer 3" calling me out on another mission tonight."

"You thought about looking for a job?" Dogwater asked.

"Yeah," Izzy said simply with no follow up.

Dog shook his head and headed for the door, after he picked up the mystery wire. It was cooler now. "Later," he said as he went out.

"Don't forget," Izzy said. "Not a word to that reporter. Our future depends on it."

The door slammed behind Dogwater without further word.

Izzy stared at the ceiling above his couch for a few minutes. *Dark Matters.* He snorted. If it wasn't porn, it was just wasting Internet space.

But then he quickly sat up as a thought occurred to him: what if Dogwater wasn't being loony this time? What if conspiracy boy really had stumbled on something? A video of Santa would be worth some cash.

Sure it was ridiculous, but Izzy was along for the ride—what else did he have to do? It felt right, somehow, that Santa Claus would be coming here. His brain was too tired to realize that this may be because the town was called "Santa Claus," but he would realize it later, while high again, and would laugh until the tears flowed.

So, yeah, maybe he should help Dogwater get St. Nick live on videotape. But wait, video can break. It could come out fuzzy. It could be doctored. It could be stolen by the likes of, well, by the likes of himself. If a video of St. Nick would make money. What could they get for the man himself? All two tons of Kringle ass worth. *Millions.*

Izzy went to the small bedroom at one end of the trailer and pulled a shoebox from under a pile of laundry next to the futon. He opened the box, revealing a SIG-Sauer P-232 pistol.

What was the going rate for a jolly old elf, bound and gagged, dancing on a stage in Vegas? Izzy was going to find out. Dead or alive. True, dead would make it harder to do the dancing part.

Oh, well.

# DECEMBER 23

Two days before Christmas, KidTown Toys, Inc. was sticking firm to its decision to only ship a dozen units of this year's hottest toys on the theory that, "Well, no one has killed anyone over it yet."

Santa sat quietly in his room. As Christmas approached, the reality of the choice he had made to walk away from his old life was sinking in. It was time to join his new life. And the beginning of that, he thought, was at Milo's house—*his* house now. He felt a sudden urge to go there; to immerse himself in his new life.

But how would he get there?

Cameron was all but comatose so that was out. Maybe he could get there himself. Santa Claus, Indiana was not that big. It was pretty cold though, at least for Milo's body.

*I could drive*, Santa thought.

No, he couldn't. He'd never driven a car in his life. That's ridiculous.

*Milo knows how to drive.*

True. And Santa knew Milo was inside him somewhere. Maybe it was time to convert the take over of Milo's body into a partnership.

But how?

"Um," Santa cleared his throat. "Excuse me, sir? Uh, Mr. Vestibule?" He said all this softly, tentatively.

Nothing.

"Er, Milo, this is Santa Claus speaking. I know we got off to something of a rocky start, but I think-"

"Well, I want a drink first." The voice was unfamiliar and echoed. Santa looked around, eyes wide, before he realized the voice was inside his head.

"Milo?" Santa asked.

"Yeah, it's kinda dark in here, you know. How about turning on some lights?"

"Sir," Santa's eyes—Milo's eyes, actually—welled. "It's so good to know you're all right. You are aren't you?"

"Still breathin'"

Santa noted the steady rise and fall of his chest and nodded agreement. "Sir, I'm sorry I had to borrow your body."

There was a pause.

"Oh, that's okay, I wasn't too busy."

Santa breathed a relieved sigh. "Thank you, sir."

"So what's up?" Milo asked.

"Well, do you know how to drive a, uh, SUV-mobile?"

"You mean a car? Yeah. I drove a tank in Korea, so I think I can handle an SUV. Why?"

"We need to go for a ride," Santa said.

It took a full five minutes to get down the stairs from the second to the first floor. Now that Milo had been revived, both men were trying to operate one body. Walking was a stuttery, jerky affair. Santa thought it felt like trying to will your leg or arm to move after it has fallen asleep, only without the prickly needles feeling. There was some disagreement between Milo and Santa whether to use the right or left hand to pick up Cameron's keys from the kitchen table.

Getting behind the wheel of Cameron's SUV, after Santa tried to start the vehicle by inserting Cameron's house key in the CD player, Milo spoke up again. "Maybe you should let me take over for a bit."

"Oh thank you, sir," Santa gushed. He closed his eyes wearily. They reopened a moment later and all the jerkiness was gone.

Now fully in control, Milo confidently started up the SUV and sped out of Cameron's driveway.

Santa enjoyed the brief respite. He was a little uneasy when Milo caused their arm to make an obscene gesture at another driver that cut them off, but, still, it was nice to have a break.

They pulled into Milo's driveway. "We're here," he said.

"There you are," a young woman's voice called.

Milo/Santa turned to see Cindy Lew Woo, college student and pharmacy delivery-woman extraordinaire.

"I was worried about you," Cindy Lew Woo said. "You didn't answer the door." She rattled a pharmacy bag. "Your delivery."

"That's so nice of you, honey," Milo said. "Come on, give us a hug."

Cindy Lew Woo waggled a finger at Milo, then relented for a big bear hug.

"Oh, my," Santa whispered inside Milo's mind, struck by the fit, curvaceous young woman.

Milo was more direct. "Yowza," he grunted.

Cindy Lew Woo laughed and gave Milo the bag. "I like the beard," she said.

Milo grinned wolfishly. "It's all for you, my dear."

"Flatterer. Now remember, I'll be back in two weeks. Don't stand me up again." She grinned.

"Yes, ma'am," Milo saluted.

"Bye-bye."

"Au revoir," Milo said.

Cindy Lew Woo bounded to her car and drove off with a wave.

"Goodness," Santa sighed.

"Well, I'm spent," Milo said. "And I'm tired."

Santa heard the echoing yawn in his mind. It actually tickled. He could feel Milo's soul retreat back into the interior folds of his brain.

Santa stepped nimbly, but cautiously, testing his control of his regained legs. He didn't fall. That was good.

He walked up to the porch. From the recesses of his mind, he heard a faint, weary whisper, "There's a key behind the windmill blade." Then another yawn.

Puzzled, Santa looked around. He noticed, perhaps for the first time, a small wooden windmill perched on the edge of the porch, more decorative than functional. He examined it, felt around the slightly rough edges of the blades, and finally hit upon a small metal box duct-taped to the back. Santa found it was not necessary to remove the sticky tape in order to slide the box open and therein found the key.

"Good job," Milo said, sleepily.

"Thank you, sir," Santa replied, getting used to the idea of talking to a voice inside his head. He was starting to wonder why Cameron fussed so much about voices in his head.

Santa worked the key in the lock and went into the house, where he stopped cold.

"Holy balls," Uncle Milo exclaimed through the mouth he now shared with Father Christmas.

"You said it," Santa agreed, without really recognizing what he had agreed to.

The men looked around the room with one set of eyes and saw perfection. It was Milo's living room again. Not a trace of soot or water could be seen. Even the faintly acrid smell of smoke was gone; replaced by...lilacs?

The place was cleaner than it had been before the takeover of Milo's body. Santa started to say, "How did the elves get here?" but caught himself. He didn't know how much Milo understood about what was happening and didn't know how to explain it.

Apparently having rallied a bit, Milo tugged their joint body toward the television. Santa quickly saw why. Someone had left a note. He picked it up and read: "Dear Uncle Milo, I know you don't like people making a fuss, but I came over and cleaned up the house for you. I was surprised [the author inserted a smiley face here] by how little damage there is. Yay! Anyway, enjoy your clean house. There's frozen lasagna in the fridge. Also, I got rid of your empty beer cans (you really should cut back, you know!). Take care. Holly says hi. Love you, Susan."

"Well, that's very nice," Santa said.

"Yeah, I guess," Milo said simply, but Santa could feel a warmth coming from him.

Santa strolled around the room. He looked at the furniture, the carpet, the pictures on the wall. He had seen all this before, of course, but now he *really* looked at it, through eyes that really understood and cherished what he was seeing.

"You're not gonna steal anything, are you?" Milo asked nervously, despite the absurdity of Santa using his own body to steal his stuff.

"No, no," Santa said, "I was just-"

"'Cause it ain't the Plaza, but it's all I got," Milo said.

"You have a lovely home," Santa said, trying to ignore the lack of color, music, elves or woodland creatures.

A thought occurred to him. "Say! Are we near the ocean by any chance? I would so enjoy visiting. I couldn't see it from Cameron's, but surely here..."

Milo chuckled. "Sure, only about a thousand miles that way." He took control of their right arm to point to their left. "If you start walking now, you might make it by next Christmas."

Santa frowned at this. Geographic distance was a much bigger deal in the real world.

"Say, I think we're getting hungry," Milo said. Sure enough, their shared stomach started to growl.

"Where is your dining hall?" Santa asked. "Who is in charge of the cooking?"

Milo chuckled again. "Well, I usually eat in front of the TV by myself. And I do all the cooking. If you can call microwave dinners cooking."

Santa shuddered at the thought of the appliance spawned of black magic.

The doorbell rang. It rang again. There followed a rapid succession of rings.

"So answer it already," Milo said.

Santa was a little uneasy. He still found greeting guests a stressful chore, but he was a real-worlder now. When in the real world, do as the real-worlders do. He opened the door.

Wesley, the little boy from Milo's birdhouse building class stood on the porch wearing that same silly stocking cap as in the previous encounter.

*Wesley*, Milo said inside Santa's head, sounding pleased.

"Hi, Milo," the boy beamed. Then, getting a better look, his eyes got large, "Santa!" he shrieked, throwing his arms around the man.

""Ho, ho-" Milo stopped Santa's laugh short, seeming to whack a neuron with another neuron to get his attention.

"I thought maybe Milo came back," Wesley said. "But this is really cool!" The boy actually quivered with delight.

It did Santa's formerly Noel-boosting heart good. He knelt down to the boy. "And it's good to see you too."

Wesley looked at Santa's beard. Then, in a complete absence of adult-style reticence, he tugged at it; really digging his tiny kid fingers into the hairs and pulling.

As the Northern Lights that Santa knew so well from home played across his field of vision, he heard Wesley say, "See? Only Santa has a beard like that."

*That's gotta hurt*, Uncle Milo muttered.

"Wesley, my dear boy," Santa managed to say as he blinked a couple small tears from his eyes, "If I was Santa, what would I be doing here?"

"I dunno."

"And look at me, I'm too skinny." Santa patted Milo's flat stomach.

Milo grumbled from his corner of Santa's mind.

"You're Santa," Wesley shrugged confidently. "My little sister still believes in you. I don't really, but she does. I *used* to believe, but Benny at school says Santa's not real. I didn't believe him when I didn't like him, but now he's got the really cool new Power-Game video game console and so he's okay. If he says there's no Santa, I guess there's not." The dissonance between insisting Milo was Santa while at the same time insisting there is no Santa Claus was lost on Wesley.

Wesley looked a little sad at this. "I kinda wish Santa was real though. Did you ever believe in Santa?"

"Once, yes," Santa said simply.

Wesley turned as if to walk out the door, then turned back, looking slightly embarrassed. "I kinda miss him," he said. "Don't tell my little sister though, okay?"

Santa nodded, then heard himself saying, "I kind of miss him too."

*Me too*, Milo said.

As Cameron so often did in times of turmoil, he sought refuge from the stressful—to the power of ten—experience of talking to a man you thought was an elderly relative of your ex-wife, but who you now find out is Santa Claus. He didn't even consider calling Dr. Whipple again. Even she wouldn't believe this.

He sought refuge at his computer. For a good portion of the day, he'd been staring at the monitor, though only in the last few minutes did he turn it on. Before this, he'd tried watching television, but this close to the holiday all that was on was one old, lame Christmas movie after another and the occasional weather report about the blizzard predicted to follow Santa into the Midwest on Christmas Eve. Little did the meteorologists know, Santa had traveled on ahead. Ho, ho, ho.

He tried reading a book, but the quiet room just set the stage for the endless loop of "Jingle Bells" running through his head. He didn't know if this was a symptom of the season, a symptom of living with jolly old St. Nick, an auditory hallucination, or all of the above. Whatever it was, it made concentrating impossible.

So, he decided to write. Focusing on the act of typing might help center him. The fact that he had not written *anything* yet, despite six hours in front of the computer, was a minor detail.

Cameron shook his head, settled his mind—more or less—and started a new chapter in the manuscript now going by the title *Knee Deep in Insanity*. He actually thought the book was going pretty well at the moment. His hero, Conrad Brewster, had just solved a major piece of the plot's puzzle. Cameron found that Conrad Brewster was having a much easier time of things since he'd stopped being a dog and embraced his inner guinea pig. That really opened up the plot possibilities.

Cameron typed: "Conrad Brewster knew that it was only a matter of time before Mira realized that he was on to her. This didn't concern him. He'd nibble her heels and leave little poops in her shoes. Conrad Brewster knew that once she did find out the secret, he would be ready. If she came for him, he'd simply call in back up. No question, Kris Kringle—who is alive and well—would knock her into last Christmas."

Cameron stopped typing. What was that last part? He re-read the words on the screen, cursed, and deleted the offending portion.

*This is nuts*, Cameron thought. *Even nuttier than me.* It really was impossible for a seventy-seven-year-old man to wake up one day and be Santa Claus. Wasn't it?

"Shit," he said, out loud. "Maybe Milo is crazier than me. Or senile."

It occurred to him that maybe the fire at Milo's house had rattled the old man more than it seemed. This got him thinking about the fire. The fact that he had really seen very little structural damage, beneath the layer of black soot, hadn't really impressed him all that much at time, but it was odd. No standing water from the fire hoses or broken windows either. It really just looked like the special effects department sprayed some fire-damage-in-a-can around the house, but why? It did seem a little weird even to his foggy mind.

Make that very weird.

And what about that magic show; the image of himself and Holly under the tree on Holly's first Christmas? True, he didn't trust his eyes much lately, but it really did seem real. Real real. Really, really real.

And there was that startling, even spectacular, beard growth Uncle Milo had experienced overnight. Surely the man could figure out how to tie that into a nice career in shaving product commercials.

Or, just maybe it was all true...

Cameron grinned a little. This all sounded like half-assed plot points for a novel, maybe call it *My Ex-Uncle's a Kringle* or maybe just *Nick!*

Cameron barked a hoarse laugh, slightly taken aback; it was not a sound he heard from himself much lately.

No, it was ridiculous. The man was *not* Santa Claus. Cameron knew he'd have to go and talk to Milo, make sure he was okay, and that he understood he wasn't really Santa Claus. The idea of one crazy person trying to convince another crazy person he's sane amused him.

"You sure about that, buddy?" a gravelly voice said. The thick, snarky voice could only belong to one person...er, fish—Webster Stanhope, floating goldfish. "What if he's telling the truth, then?" the goldfish said, voice burbling through an accumulation of hallucinated water floating in empty space around him. "You'd be a royal bastard not to believe him, wouldn't ye? I'd sooner ravage a pig than cross the word of Santa Claus."

Cameron turned to face the fake fish. "You're a big Santa Claus believer?"

"Aye, that I am," Webster said. "Good man. Can't hold his liquor worth shit, but a good man nonetheless."

"So you've met him?"

Webster Stanhope slapped the water with his tail fin. "No one gets to meet Santa Claus. He just is. Knowing he's there is enough."

"How can you be so sure?" Cameron asked, leaning close enough to the floating water puddle to almost wet his nose.

"Everybody believes in Santa," Webster said, almost managing to shrug his fins. "Or should."

"But why?"

"Gods, man! How can you be so dense?"

"Sorry," Cameron said.

Webster Stanhope sighed a little air bubble. "Everybody knows that Santa Claus is the single greatest being ever, after the almighty himself."

"But, again, why?"

Webster Stanhope sighed, sending little air bubbles to the surface of his suspended puddle. "Because he brings joy to millions every year and asks nothing in return. Who wouldn't get behind that?" Webster Stanhope explained. Then, pointing an accusatory fin, "You, you scribble some shit on a page, slap a cover around it and sell it for $24.95. When was the last time you gave up anything?"

"So the guy gives stuff away? Big deal. What's he ever done for me?"

Webster Stanhope managed to curl his fish mouth into a smirk. "So, that's it. You don't believe in Santa Claus because ya had a crappy childhood. The elves chopped down your tree and shit all over the holiday, huh?"

"Basically," Cameron said.

"Well, you can't blame Santa for your problems."

"I'm not blaming him," Cameron said. "I stopped believing in Santa Claus back when I'd only had a few crappy Christmases. I've had a lot of sucky yuletide goodness since then that has nothing to do with him."

"All the more reason to believe in Santa Claus," Webster Stanhope insisted. "Kids grow up and stop believing. Then they bitch and moan about how crappy the real world is. Well, crap on yew!" He swirled around with an impudent flip of his tail, and did, indeed, make a fish deposit. Fish crap floated for a moment, twirling in the hallucinated water. It sank to the lower end of the pool and actually broke through. The fish crap picked up a little speed as it headed toward the floor, but faded from existence before it hit the carpet.

"Bad tuna for lunch," Webster Stanhope said. "Sorry...not!"

Webster Stanhope swam to edge of his water puddle. Cameron leaned in again, this time his nose did cross the water border. But it didn't get wet. Hmmm. Cameron noticed he couldn't smell the same faint aquarium smell that had been there before either.

"Ya got to believe in Santa Claus because ya got to believe in somethin' in life," Webster Stanhope said.

"What bumper sticker did you get that off?" Cameron asked.

"That's all there is to it." Another fish shrug.

"What about God?" Cameron asked.

Webster Stanhope flopped his fins in a most aggravated fashion. "Don't get me started," he groaned. "God wants you to pray, and be devout and follow all the little Commandments. Santa Claus, though, doesn't ask for anything, except that you be *nice*. In fact, he asks yew what you want. Then he goes out and gets it for ya. You don't like that. Well, fuck you , you English bastard."

"Uh, actually, I'm American."

"Whatever, asshole."

Cameron looked at the grumpy fish, and waved his hand through the puddle. It was dry, both the hand and, oddly, the water. Webster Stanhope just glared with his unblinking, fishy eyes. Cameron thought about the sorry state of his life that led to talking to a fish. "Well, Webster, it occurs to me that with Santa around, I have plenty of imaginary friends. You've been taking up too much of my imaginary time."

"So get rid of me," Webster said. "No sweat off my sack." Never mind that fish, strictly speaking, don't have sacks.

"Great. See ya." In one slow-motion chain, Cameron tossed a glass of actual water that had been sitting on the desk at Webster. Webster and his puddle melded into the droplets of water—Cameron actually thought he could see hundreds of little Websters in the individual drops as they splattered onto the glass fronts of the bookcase. Then he was gone.

"Wonder if Dr. Whipple is in from the slopes," Cameron mused.

Izzy sat on the old lime green couch in his dumpy trailer watching Dogwater fiddle with a handheld global positioning satellite unit; one of the many electronic devices Izzy's former employer, Electronic Junction, had unwittingly provided.

"Do you know what you're doin', man?" Izzy asked.

"Of course," Dog answered. "I've used these lots of times." He pushed a button and the GPS beeped back angrily. The thing was not yet convinced that Dogwater was where he actually was.

"No, man, I mean with this Christmas alien stuff."

Dogwater sighed. "Do I have to tell you about Cameron's living room again?

"I heard you the first time," Izzy said. "I just don't know why you think you're gonna catch an alien tomorrow night."

"Three dimensional holographs. Not even holographs. Fully physical forms that came out of nowhere and moved and talked. Cameron and a baby. That's alien technology," Dogwater said. "I don't know if that Milo dude's an alien or being controlled by an alien or what."

"Or Cameron maybe," Izzy offered.

"Maybe," Dogwater said thoughtfully. "Maybe. Anyway, I think Cameron's property is the epicenter for alien activity in this region. So that's where I'll be Christmas Eve."

"Got your alien rat trap all ready? Put some moldy cheese or somethin' in there. What do aliens like, anyway? Swiss? Maybe if they got wings and stuff, you could just put out a big sheet of flypaper." Izzy chuckled at the thought of a Martian wiggling around on a big yellow sticky note.

"I didn't say I was going to *catch* one," Dogwater said. "I just want to see it. Document it. That's why I wanted all these cameras and stuff. So I could record it. You know this."

"Well, if you're going to all that trouble, why not just catch one?"

Dogwater laughed. "What, you think the aliens will just land and walk up to us and shake hands?"

"If they have hands," Izzy replied. "Could be flippers."

Dogwater smirked. "Look, I know a little bit more about alien... interactions than you do."

"Oh, yeah," Izzy nodded. "All those probes up your ass."

Dogwater offhandedly held up his middle finger than let it fall. "It's not going to work like that. Lars Heimdal was very clear that every year an unidentified object follows the same path across the sky and it's always in the sky over our area between one and two a.m.. I just want to track that flight and get an image of the object on film."

"I'll make you a deal," Izzy said.

"What kind of deal?" Dogwater asked suspiciously.

"You let me take one of those cameras," he gestured to the assorted cameras and camcorders, "and if I can get my own picture, I can sell it to whoever I want."

"I don't know, Izzy..."

"You don't know? I got you all that stuff. Ain't asked nothing in return. I agreed to sit my freezing ass up on the writer's roof with you Christmas Eve. I deserve something for my trouble."

Izzy had a point. He wasn't getting paid and the man was out of work.

"I'll think about," Dogwater said.

Izzy crossed his arms and thought for a few more moments. "And, if I can catch me an alien, I'll do it."

Dogwater's head snapped up sharply. "You're going to do what?"

"A picture won't cut it when you can have one living and breathing and hopefully only bleeding a little," Izzy explained.

"I thought you didn't even believe in any of this," Dogwater said.

"I don't. I don't," Izzy said. "But it don't hurt to be open-minded. Reporters be crawling all over my ass to get a look at my space bug. Probably want to do some sort of reality show; call it 'So Your Momma's Dating an Alien'. I'll clean up." He peered at Dogwater. "Unless all this *Lars Heimdal* stuff is just shit."

"You're delusional."

"Yeah? Well, I'll bet that Ben Steene joker'd love to get a piece of this action. You tell him your theory?"

"Of course not. He just wanted to know who the guy with Cameron was. I don't think he was a believer."

"Too bad," Izzy said, shaking his head. "He'll be eatin' his heart out when all the other rags buy up our story."

"Look, Izzy, I really don't..."

"That's the deal, man. I get me an alien and you get to use all this stuff. I'll even help you set it up. Otherwise it all goes back to the store. Before you say 'no', don't forget: if I catch one, you'll be famous too. Money and girls be crawling all over your ass too." Izzy appraised Dogwater and reconsidered. "Well, you'll get money anyway."

Dogwater deliberated internally. It was unlikely the aliens would actually land, or if they did, that they would land in Santa Claus, Indiana. Even if they did land, an alien life form that had the capability to travel to Earth surely could outwit an unemployed stoner like Izzy. It probably wouldn't hurt to agree to Izzy's proposal. And he really did need Izzy's help—his corroboration of what they would see, if nothing else.

He also supposed, a tiny part of him did warm to the idea of catching an alien; exacting a little revenge. He didn't want to hurt one, just show them that humans weren't all weak lab rats. And, it was true, the money was enticing. He fingered Ben Steene's business card in his shirt pocket. He was sure the reporter couldn't resist a scoop like this, no matter how cool he acted in the car after witnessing whatever was going on in Cameron's house.

Dogwater finally said, "All right. Deal."

"Cool," Izzy replied, digging through his pockets for a celebratory joint.

Dogwater's blood began to run very cold.

Up at the North Pole, it was cold too; inside the Complex, as well as outside. Mrs. Claus stood in her husband's study, stoically looking out at the frozen landscape, frayed nerves teetering on the brink of despairing hysteria. It was now barely twenty-four hours until the fabled Christmas flight would ordinarily take place.

But this year, no Santa Claus would be on that flight. There was no way to contact him. He hadn't found his way back on his own, if he'd even tried. Since the failure of Doozil's effort to retrieve Santa with Teevo's spell, the elves had seen no reason to go back to work. Piles upon mounds of toys remained unfinished; trucks without wheels, dolls without clothes, and computer games without solutions.

Christmas was over.

Not in the strict sense, of course. Christmas would still occur, but it would be without the Christmas magic that only Santa embodies. Many children would find their Christmas wishes unfulfilled. Their parents would rightly tell them that there was more to Christmas than presents, but presents—and more importantly the love and goodwill that come with them—were every bit as important as the other aspects of the holiday.

Even if you don't receive a single gift from Santa Claus, it seemed to Mrs. Claus, his absence from the season would leave you cold, without the warmth of the holiday. Mrs. Claus knew that well. She was feeling it now; that and the lost warmth of a companion, a husband.

The world was already feeling the loss too, probably without realizing it. Holiday events were failing. People were moodier. There was less peace in the world. Mrs. Claus could feel all this. She was afraid what things would be like by Christmas morning. Much of the world didn't celebrate Christmas, but all of the world craved fellowship and harmony. The absence of Christmas would leave a void that would ripple through all communities. Was it an exaggeration to fear the end of civilization? Unfortunately, she didn't think so.

And even if Santa did return eventually, on the twenty-sixth or whenever, what then? The Christmas spell was broken. Would the Clauses be banned? What does one do as an ex-Mr. or Mrs. Claus?

As far as the elves were concerned, they would go back to doing what they used to do best: recreation and fun. After all, where do imaginary characters go when their imaginary world doesn't want them anymore? It's not like they can go enroll in medical school or get jobs at the local fast food joints.

For Mrs. Claus, the question marks hanging over her future would have to wait as a small voice from the other side of the large oak desk that dominated the center of the room said, "Um, excuse me, ma'am?"

Mrs. Claus turned slowly and saw no one. Most people would think that meant they were just hearing things, but this was the North Pole. Mrs. Claus just lowered her eyes to peer over the desk. She saw there the blue and silver locks of the sprightly young elf girl, Shivla. She was tugging on the sleeve of a clearly reluctant Doozil who looked ready to bolt.

"Hello, dear," Mrs. Claus said sadly. "Doozil."

"Hello," Shivla said nervously. "Um, Flifle said to tell you the lights on the outer gates of the Complex are fading. All the trees in the Christmas garden have sunk back into the ground. Also, the eastern wing of the castle has gotten really, really cold."

Mrs. Claus nodded faintly. "I know," she said. "Christmas—as we know it—is dying."

Shivla nodded, perhaps even more sadly. "I miss Santa," she said. She gestured encouragingly to Doozil who shook his head.

"Me too," Mrs. Claus replied simply, eyes flashing quickly but coldly toward Doozil.

The three experienced a silent night for the next few moments.

"Um, ma'am?" Shivla queried.

"Yes."

Shivla shifted nervously from one foot to the other. "I think Doozil knows how to bring him home."

Shivla was nearly airborne as she dangled by a wrist from Mrs. Claus's hand while they swept into the workshop. Doozil struggled to keep up. Flifle was already there, caked in sweat and grease, putting the finishing touches on his one-hundred-fiftieth wagon of the day. He was pretty sure none of the children on Santa's list had asked for wagons, but it was all he knew how to build and he had to build *something*.

"What is it, ma'am?" Flifle asked, putting aside his mallet reluctantly, eyes burning into Doozil. Doozil noted that Flifle's hand hesitated ever so slightly on the mallet's handle.

By way of an answer, Mrs. Claus turned to Shivla and said, "Tell him what you told me."

Shivla looked at Doozil, who said nothing. She shifted uneasily. "Um, we know how to bring Santa Claus back," she said.

Flifle's eyes widened. "You do?"

Shivla looked again at Doozil, who was still silent. Then, in a great departure from character, she whacked him in the back of the head.

Doozil stammered. "Well...well, the type of transponder recall unit that you used has a back up, a failsafe switch."

Flifle smacked his forehead with a grease smeared hand, leaving a black smudge above his eyes. Why hadn't that possibility occurred to him? He was the chief of staff after all.

Shivla continued. "I think if you press that green button on the master unit, it should activate the back up transponder and recall Santa from the real world to ours immediately."

Flifle, stunned, just shook his head and grinned. "That's it. We can get him back." Then a thought occurred to him, "Why didn't you tell us that before?"

More uneasy shifting. "Um, I'm sorry." Tears welled in the corners of Shivla's eyes, softening Flifle's mounting rage.

"I told her not to," Doozil said. "It seemed...well, Teevo...I don't know...I was wrong."

Rising to his full elf-height, Flifle stepped toward him.

Mrs. Claus stepped between. "Well, it was good of you to tell the truth now," Mrs. Claus said, living up to her motherly image.

Flifle grunted.

With a definite tone, Mrs. Claus said, "We will speak of this...unpleasantness no more."

"Of course," Flifle said with effort.

Mrs. Claus smiled. "Good, then. Well, Flifle, shall we bring my husband home?"

"Yes, ma'am," Flifle grinned, and sprinted from the workshop. Mrs. Claus and Shivla followed close behind. Doozil hesitated, wanted to flee back to his bunk to cocoon himself in the covers, but instead found himself running to be with the others.

On the way, Flifle asked, "But what if he's broken it?"

"It doesn't matter. The failsafe is self-contained on the recall unit. It would interpret a break as an emergency," Doozil explained.

"You better not be lying this time," Flifle warned.

"No," Doozil mumbled. "No more."

Flifle's small office that adjoined Santa's much larger one was dominated by the large desk. Flifle went straight there now and pulled a heavy black cloth from the object parked in the center of it. The object was a radio; the twin of the one they sent with Santa Claus so long ago—weeks, months?—right down to the candy cane antenna.

On the side of the radio was the transponder-recall unit in gold, identical to the one on Santa's radio. Below it under a small panel was, just as Shivla said, a green button; the failsafe mechanism.

Flifle was terrified. Once again, they were relying on Doozil. What if he was wrong? What if he was only jeopardizing Kris Kringle to serve his own twisted ends? He considered voicing this real possibility, but the suddenly recharged look on Mrs. Claus's face—so different than the pained, frustrated one of these last days—made him unable to say anything. They had to try.

Flifle looked at Mrs. Claus, who nodded eagerly. Then he pushed the button.

The gold wire coil of the transponder vibrated softly and emitted a hum. Somewhere across the great expanse between the imaginary world and the real world, the identical transponder unit was doing the same.

Lightning crashed through the center of the office, shattering a bust of an elf elder. The three elves and Mrs. Claus took cover behind the sturdy pine desk.

The castle shook. Windows cracked or blew out completely in several rooms on all floors. The fact that the elves had to a great extent abandoned the castle actually turned out to be fortuitous when the shards flew.

An image began to swirl like a localized typhoon through the echoing corridors of the castle like a bull in the proverbial china shop, only this bull had a relentless, gaping maw that consumed everything in its path, chewed it, and spewed splintered wood, plaster and glass out in return. The cyclone arrived in Flifle's office without knocking, unless you count ripping his door off the hinges. It was a blur at first, but quickly gelled into the outline of a human.

Mrs. Claus held her breath. Flifle clenched and unclenched his fists. Shivla wept nervous tears. Doozil—much to his surprise—found himself tearing up a little too.

The being, the legend that all of the North Pole and millions of real world children were devoted to, and the man that Mrs. Claus loved, was coming home. Christmas was saved.

It was mere seconds before the murky human outline became a solid, living, breathing human form. Flifle started to erupt in an elven cheer—in defiance of his usual reserved demeanor—but the cheer sputtered and died in his throat.

Mrs. Claus gasped.

Shivla outright fainted.

Doozil just shook his head.

Standing in the middle of the office of the elf chief of staff at Santa's castle at the heart of this vibrant, imaginary Christmas world, looking very confused, and protectively covering his ass with his hands was the man who would soon resuscitate Christmas:

Dogwater Hunt.

# DECEMBER 24
## CHRISTMAS EVE

The elves around the North Pole Complex knew Santa Claus was home. They heard the racket—felt the racket—the night before. It could only be the bumpy return of someone from the real world that could make such a boisterous entrance. Granted, very few had physically made the trip across the void from imaginary world to the real world other than Santa on his Christmas flight, but they knew anyway. St. Nicholas was among them again. In the end, where else was there but home for the holidays?

In the elf commons, there was much rejoicing with dancing, singing, food and drink. No ordinary gruel today. Today's cauldron had dates in it—a rare and exotic delicacy at the North Pole. Sure, the elves enjoyed their furlough, their break from the grind of the workshop, but they missed the toy making too. Over the centuries, it had become part of their souls. Plus, the castle was battered and devastated. They didn't know why and didn't really care. There would be plenty of repair work to occupy them after the holidays. They loved that.

This joy, ironically, presented a problem. Mrs. Claus and Flifle had, of course, worked hard to make the elves excited about their leader and about Christmas again, but now that they were, all they wanted was to see the leader. Mrs. Claus could hardly show them the stranger they had drawn into the Complex from the real world last night.

The human had not been particularly talkative. When the recall was complete, he had squeezed his eyes shut, yelled something like, "Screw you, you bastards. You won't get any cooperation from me again this time either." And then he simply sat on the floor saying nothing. Neither Flifle,

Doozil, nor Shivla understood many of the words, but the tone made them nervous. Mrs. Claus was uneasy too. No real-worlder from the outside had ever set foot in the Complex. What would he do? What would the elves do to him?

Flifle immediately summoned the one self-defense spell he knew and put Dogwater to sleep. Dog had remained unconscious all night, sleeping peacefully in a spare room of the residence wing. If there had been anything funny about this situation, it would have been an amusing sight to see the three small elves, Flifle, Doozil and Shivla, and Mrs. Claus (though admittedly buff from all the kick boxing) lugging the stout real-worlder from the workshop to the residence draped in a spare Santa Claus coat in case they were spotted.

Now this morning, Mrs. Claus and Flifle sat in uneasy silence in the Clauses' sitting room, busying themselves with drinking some sort of beverage kind of like elf coffee.

"What if the real-worlder," Mrs. Claus began, breaking the silence, but then pausing before uttering a word that was all but banished in the North Pole, "killed him?" The word was disturbing on many levels; fear for her husband, and memories of her own life as a real-worlder in a land where killing was all too common.

"Well, I don't believe he'd do that," Flifle said quickly. It was more positive thinking than cogent assessment. He'd never met a real-worlder before.

As if on cue, from the next room, Dogwater's high, panicky voice rang out, "Get off me you sons of bitches, or I'll cut your hoo-has off and feed 'em to you...if you have any!"

Flifle and Mrs. Claus exchanged frightened glances and scurried into the bedroom.

Dogwater, tangled in red satin sheets, was backed up in the corner of the bed against the wall, evidently preparing to go toe to toe with an elderly elf and Shivla who had brought Dog his clothes, freshly washed and pressed, as well as a Santa-style breakfast of eggs and toast, cinnamon rolls and a dozen cookies. Wasn't that what all real worlders ate?

The elves were staring at Dog with wide eyes as his head pivoted from one to the other. "Come and get me! Just try it!" he shouted.

"Sir, please be calm. There is no need to fear. The elves will not harm you," Mrs. Claus said soothingly, sounding almost grandmotherly, even as she calculated the series of body blows she could inflict if necessary to subdue the real-worlder with the least damage.

Dogwater's narrowed, suspicious eyes locked on Mrs. Claus. She looked like someone familiar, kind of like his Aunt Miriam. "Did they take you too?" he asked in a stage whisper.

"Take...?" Mrs. Claus asked, confused. "Oh, no, I live here. I'm Mrs. Claus. Welcome to the North Pole, my new friend." Mrs. Claus curtsied; the elves bowed.

Dogwater laughed. "I'll give you credit," he said. "This beats the hell out of the stainless steel lab and the strobe lights." He looked around. "All right, let's get the probes over with." He sighed and started to loosen his pants when Flifle stepped forward.

"Sir," Flifle said, screwing up his courage for his first alien contact. "We are elves. You are in Santa Claus's castle."

"Oh, I get it," Dogwater said. "This is some sort of hallucination. A trick so I don't know what sort of tests you're doing. What is it this time? Teeth drilling? Eyeball peels? Swapping the fingernails with the toenails?"

Mrs. Claus walked over to the bed slowly as an image filled her mind, borrowing from Santa's bag of tricks. No, not an image so much as a word, a name:

"Percy," Mrs. Claus said.

At the sound of his birth name, one he had quit using not long after acquiring speech, Dog's head snapped to her, their eyes locking. "What did you say?"

Another word floated into Mrs. Claus's consciousness. "Dogwater, I mean. It's all right." Such an odd name, but it worked.

Dog slumped on the bed. "You know my name?" The aliens never called him by name. They never called him anything; never said anything.

"Yes," Mrs. Claus answered, then frowned. "And I know you've spent an awful lot of time on Santa's naughty list." She shook her head. "Shame on you for looking at those dirty computer pictures."

Dog gaped.

Mrs. Claus beamed. "But I suppose everyone deserves a break. You were mostly a good kid. Well, except for that thing with the neighbor girl, when..."

"Okay!" Dog interrupted. "I'm convinced."

He studied the pointy-eared elves before him. "Are you guys hobbits?" The elves just blinked.

"Oh, right. No fuzzy feet. Sorry." He looked around. "Where am I again?" Dogwater asked.

Concerned maybe his defense spell had injured the human, Flifle said in a more patient, soothing voice, "The residential wing of Santa's castle at the center of the North Pole Complex. I'm sorry we had to disable you."

Dogwater nodded, unfazed. "Okay. Why?" He climbed cautiously down from the bed. Surely, the hobbits—er, elves—wouldn't jump him, would they?

Now it was Shivla and the old elf's turn to back away nervously.

Mrs. Claus, however, stood her ground. "We thought you were, well, we thought you were Santa Claus," she said, as if this made total sense.

Dogwater patted his flat stomach and smirked. "Well, I can see why you'd be confused."

"Have you seen him?" Mrs. Claus asked earnestly.

Dogwater hesitated, his heart clutching in his chest. But then he realized when you're standing in a roomful of elves and someone claiming to be Mrs. Claus, for you to say, "Well, yes Santa Claus is hanging out at my friend's house," probably wouldn't sound too crazy.

"Yeah. I mean, I think so. He made a three-dimensional hologram of my friend appear in his living room. I mean, the guy said he was Cameron's Uncle Milo or something, but that beard was something else..." Dogwater blushed and retreated into his common awkward silence, certain that, as usual, he sounded ridiculous.

Shivla gasped. Flifle and Mrs. Claus exchanged looks. Dogwater assumed they were shocked by his ridiculous words, forgetting again that these were *elves*.

"Doozil's transference spell may have started to take effect. Maybe the effect is progressive. First a beard, then..." Flifle said, trailing off, not having any idea if that was even plausible.

"But my husband is still gone," Mrs. Claus moaned.

"True," Flifle said

"You're trying to get him *back*?" Dogwater asked. "Shouldn't he be here by now? It's Christmas Eve. Isn't it?"

Mrs. Claus shrugged. "It's complicated."

"Santa was...visiting your world for a time. We activated our recall unit, thinking it would transport Santa back here, but we got you instead," Flifle explained.

"Recall unit?" Dogwater asked. "You mean this?" He fumbled with his jacket that Shivla had left on a chair next to the bed the night before and pulled the gold transponder from the right-hand pocket. "I knew this was not of our world."

"Yes, that's it," Flifle said. "The question is: how did *you* pass through the barrier from the real world to the imaginary one? It's long been known that no real-worlder—save our sainted Claus—can make that trip."

Dogwater just shrugged. "I've traveled through a lot of strange places. Guess I'm used to bumpy rides."

Flifle looked at Dogwater thoughtfully. The beady elf eyes peering over the long nose and beard made Dogwater nervous in a way that shiny black alien eyes never could.

"Ma'am," Flifle began, still staring at Dogwater. "I have an idea how we can get Santa home in time for Christmas, assuming Percy- er, Dogwater will help us."

Dogwater gulped and—for a horrified second—thought he made water. By Christmas miracles, he did not.

It would not be the first miracle of the day.

Cameron Jones was not really a sappy man. Until today.

He sat on the floor of the living room with a beer bottle and the remote, eyes fixed on a young woman on television singing "I'll Be Home For Christmas." It was, frankly, not a particularly good rendition, but the words dragged Cameron's psyche out to the alley for a thorough beating.

Failed father, failed writer, pathetic loser who can't even enjoy a Christmas visit with his daughter because either his live-in visitation supervisor was a lunatic who thinks he's Santa Claus, or Cameron himself was a lunatic who thought his live-in visitation supervisor was Santa Claus. Hell, maybe both.

Cameron turned to his right. "This song really grinds your guts, you know?" he said to Santa Claus, who sat next to him on the floor in a close approximation of cross legged; not bad for a body in its seventies and a soul in its, well, hundreds. His beard was still brilliant, but tangled and matted. He had skipped the beer, but a large bag of cheese puffs leaned against his thin Uncle Milo torso, his undershirt streaked with unnaturally orange "cheese" dust.

"It's over," Santa said softly. "Noel no more. I've killed Christmas." He could not believe he'd let his own inner demons destroy something so magical, so special as the yuletide spirit.

"Me too," Cameron agreed, waving his beer bottle and taking a swig. Cameron laughed a dark laugh; Santa laughed not at all.

A pounding on the door. Cameron glanced blithely in that direction. Santa's eyes didn't move from the spot of Christmas tree twinkle light that played across the floor of the gloomy room, reflecting off the windows. The blinds on one of the several windows in the living room remained open, but the sun was losing a battle with the gloomy, gray day outside. Snow was coming.

The pounding continued. This time, Izzy Carmichel's voice joined it. "Hey, writer man, you in there?"

Cameron sighed, grunted and stood. He shuffled to the door and opened it on a wide-smiling Izzy, loaded down with two boxes and two paper bags with handles. All had various bits of electrical cable or tools sticking out; one also held a sub sandwich.

"What's going on, Izzy?" Cameron asked, though he didn't really care.

"You seen Dog, man?" Izzy asked. "He's supposed to help me set up all this stuff on your roof. Gonna bag us an alien tonight." Pause. "Or maybe ol' St. Nick himself."

Santa's head snapped toward Izzy, who hadn't noticed him. A prickly cold flowed through Father Christmas's veins. The announcement, however, was not enough to motivate him away from his position leaning against the couch. He wasn't Santa anymore. What was there to worry about?

"Whatever," Cameron shrugged and closed the door.

"Thanks, man," Izzy called through the closed door. The next sounds were the clanging and banging of a ladder against the front of the house and Izzy climbing around, whistling "We Wish You a Merry Christmas."

Cameron slumped back down on the floor, lying spread-eagled as if he was about to make a snow angel in the living room. "I want my life back," he moaned.

"Me too," said Santa, softly. Then he crunched a cheese puff disconsolately and held it in his mouth for a long time before barely finding the energy to chew.

"You want what?" Dogwater asked. He was sitting on a bale of hay in the reindeer stable. The reindeer were in a ring around him, eyeing him suspiciously, except for Comet, who chewed some hay, clearly unimpressed with the real-worlder.

Shivla giggled. "You have to show the reindeer they're special. You have to be affectionate toward them. They're really just big babies." She patted Dancer between the ears. Dancer huffed appreciatively. "Go over to one of the reindeer and give him a rosy-nosy. You know, rub noses," she said.

"That's dumb," Dogwater protested.

"It works," Shivla shrugged.

Dogwater sighed. "Which one?"

Shivla thought, then said, "Donder. Definitely. He's the leader of the group. He guides the team on the Christmas Eve flight. If you can win him over, you're in." She pointed at the largest of the eight reindeer.

Donder was more interested in something he could see through the cracks between the boards in the south stable wall.

Dogwater gulped and longed wistfully for the days when alien abductions meant only torture. He walked cautiously over to Donder who lazily lolled his large head to the side, so he could see the approaching real-worlder.

"Hey, buddy, how you doin'?" Dogwater asked, by way of introduction.

Donder just blinked at him.

Dogwater looked at Shivla who nodded encouragingly.

"Well, here goes," Dogwater said. He leaned in toward the reindeer's impressive head, mindful of the massive antler rack extending out on either side of him. Donder was built more like Seabiscuit than Bambi.

Dogwater shook his head a few times, nowhere near the reindeer's snout.

"Get closer," Shivla hissed.

Dogwater gulped again and moved in, touching noses with Donder ever so briefly. Donder sneezed and shook his own head. There was a pause;

during which Dogwater was sure Donder would convert to carnivore-ism and rip out his throat.

Instead, Donder raised one hoof and waved it in Dogwater's direction, then set it back down.

"You did it," Shivla praised, effusively.

"That's it?" Dogwater said.

"They're reindeer, Percy, not puppies," Shivla said. "That's all you need. Donder has accepted you."

"Cool," Dogwater said.

Mrs. Claus had watched all this from the doorway of the stable. "How's it going in here?" she asked.

"Fine," Shivla said. "Percy, I mean Dogwater, is a natural with reindeer." She blushed slightly.

"Good," Mrs. Claus said.

Dogwater frowned. "Mrs. Claus, I don't think I can do what you're asking. I mean, do you *really* expect me to pilot a flying sleigh pulled by flying reindeer through the sky and land it on Cameron's house in the middle of North America...in the real world?" The real world—imaginary world distinction was still making Dogwater's head hurt.

Mrs. Claus shrugged. "Yes. That's exactly what I expect you to do."

"But I've never even been on a plane. Air transportation is not really my thing."

Mrs. Claus just blinked. She had never been on a plane either. She'd left the real world long before airplanes were even a notion of a possibility. "You'll be fine," she insisted. "The reindeer really do the driving. Mr. Claus just sort of guides them; encourages them. You can certainly do that. Just look how Donder has taken to you."

Dogwater looked at the reindeer which appeared to be falling asleep. He gulped again anxiously.

"Besides, time is running out," Mrs. Claus said. "That recall spell was the only chance we had, we thought. It didn't work." There was pain in Mrs. Claus's eyes. "And it looks like sending the sleigh is the only option." The pain took on a tinge of hope and just a dash of a twinkle.

"Ma'am, why didn't you just do that before?" Dogwater said.

"The sleigh is, well, obviously magical. Santa magic," Mrs. Claus explained. "Its magic is based on Santa's aura, in part, but also his presence—his...

dimensions. Santa is a very tall, human, real-worlder. Quite frankly, none of the elves have the same soul, not to mention the fact they aren't tall enough to fit the structure of the sleigh. I'm a real-worlder, but it just doesn't work for me. I'm not...male." She bridled for just a moment, then relaxed. "It's just the way the magic works. You're not as...round as Santa, but Flifle thinks that your dimensions and the fact that you also have real-worlder origins—like Santa—might be enough to trigger the magic and power the sleigh."

Mrs. Claus paused and gazed at Dogwater; gazed into him, in fact. "If, that is, you truly believe in Christmas. You do, don't you?"

Dogwater thought about this. Did he? He believed in a lot of things: aliens of course; shadow governments certainly. He didn't know if he believed in Santa Claus. Still, something (perhaps messages from one of the implants) told him this was where he had to be and what he had to do. He supposed if this all worked out, he definitely would have to look at becoming a believer. So, for now, color him a believer in the possibility of holiday magic.

"Yeah, I guess I do," he said to Mrs. Claus. "I'm getting there anyway."

Mrs. Claus beamed. "I knew it. Well, should we go?"

"What? Now?" Dogwater said, suddenly afraid.

"Yes, why not? Shivla and the stable elves will get the sleigh and the team ready. I'll take you back up to the castle to get dressed for the flight."

Without time for protest, Mrs. Claus led Dogwater by the arm away. Donder looked after them, a little sad that his new friend was going away.

Within minutes, the reindeer were hitched to the sleigh and positioned in the center of the Complex, the traditional starting point for the Christmas Eve flight. Donder had, in the silent reindeer way, reassured the other nervous reindeer that taking the early flight was okay.

This was not the "real" Christmas Eve flight, but in many ways it was even more important. The Complex elves, decked out in their finest outfits, per tradition when the reindeer made a flight, were assembled in a loose oval around the sleigh. The south end had only a few elves who were prepared to scatter when the sleigh came through on its take-off run.

One end of the oval broke to allow Mrs. Claus, followed by Flifle, to approach the sleigh. Flifle was nervously testing the wind with a damp index finger. They, in turn, were followed by Dogwater and Shivla. The elves erupted in cheers at the sight of the man who would save Christmas.

Dogwater was decked out in a borrowed blue elf hat, heavy wool pants, thick boots, and Santa's trademark red coat. When asked why he was going to be wearing that last item, Mrs. Claus said simply that it helped the magic to work. Plus, "It will have special significance for him, I hope. It will make him want to come home." Dogwater was just grateful for the warmth. It was sure to be a cold flight.

The assembled crowd continued to applaud and Dog was sufficiently embarrassed, and not just because of his silly hat. Shivla tugged gently at his sleeve. He turned. She beamed coyly and handled Dogwater an oversized candy cane with red and green stripes.

"In case you get hun-hungry on the trip," she stammered and blushed aggressively.

"Uh, thanks," Dogwater said, taking the thing. He awkwardly shoved it into a cavernous pocket of the Santa coat. Then, feeling dozens of beady elf eyes on him, he waved awkwardly at the crowd. This prompted more cheers and whistles. A few of the elves did cartwheels.

"Should I give a speech or something?" Dogwater asked Flifle.

Flifle shook his head. "No. Most of them don't speak human anyway. They wouldn't understand you. Santa usually speaks elfish."

"Thank God," Dogwater said. Then, "Sorry."

Flifle just looked at him.

"Ready to go?" Mrs. Claus asked.

"I guess."

"Remember," Shivla said. "*Leningul* means to go left; *reningul* means to go right."

Dogwater reflected that the elf commands made no more sense than human horse-riding commands—*gee* and *haw*. Why couldn't people just say what they mean? No wonder the world was messed up. Did his planet really deserve to have Christmas back?

Flifle pulled Dogwater around toward him. "Now, Dogwater, remember, the flight goes very fast."

"Well, the man does cover the whole world in one night," Dogwater agreed.

"Yes, well, this is a level of speed you're probably unfamiliar with. But it's not just that. Time and space are different in the sleigh's vortex. They distort."

"So that Santa can hit the whole world in one night," Dogwater said.

"Right," Flifle said, as he brusquely guided Dogwater to the sleigh. "Just remember the instructions Shivla gave you, and you'll be fine."

As he climbed into the sleigh, Dogwater glanced at Shivla who wore an expression of great anxiety that Dogwater didn't find particularly inspiring.

Dogwater awkwardly picked up the reins. The reindeer instinctively snapped to attention. Donder, in the lead, chuffed eagerly. Dog looked at Mrs. Claus whose own expression was something like joy dipped in a crunchy fear coating.

"Bring our St. Nicholas back to us," she said simply. "Don't let Christmas die."

"I will...er, won't," Dogwater promised. "You know what I mean."

Mrs. Claus nodded, a trace of a smile cracking tight lips.

Flifle, in turn, nodded to Shivla. Shivla hustled over to the reindeer and said loudly. "Now, Dasher. Now, Dancer. Now, Prancer and Vixen. On, Comet. On Cupid. On Donder and Blitzen!"

One by one the reindeer stood. Dogwater just had time to say, "Hey! Isn't that from *'Twas the Night Before Christmas* before the sleigh took off across the complex courtyard, still low to the ground, the oval of elves opening up and cheering the sleigh on.

"Oh, shiiiiiiit!" Dogwater screamed, dropping the reins and clutching the leather sleigh seat. Shivla's reindeer guidance instructions—*leningul* and *reningul*—flew out of his head along with a tiny bit of vomit.

The elves cheered as the reindeer ran faster and faster. Their cheers rose with the sleigh as it became airborne. It went up, up, up and away (Dogwater actually did picture Superman in his mind and even he was screaming too.)

The tears on Mrs. Claus's face glistened in the glow of the courtyard torches.

In the unearthly still of Christmas Eve night, unmatched even by the calm after a fierce thunderstorm, not a creature was stirring at the Cameron Jones residence. Well, not unless you count the tall man banging a hammer into a plywood platform on the roof. Izzy was busily constructing a sort of crows nest and cursing Dogwater for not showing up for the alien hunt. Izzy felt like an idiot up her by himself, even if he was about to become a very rich alien-bagger. The peppermint schnapps was helping his mood, though, if not his carpentry. It was also providing good insulation against the bitter cold wind that was picking up.

Inside the house, Cameron was in bed in a position approximating, but not achieving, nestled and snug. He stared at the ceiling, glowering at every thud and crash on the roof. Dogwater's and Izzy's alien quest was depriving him of the only joy he had now: sleep. Christmas? Bah humbug.

Down the hall, Santa was opening the blinds on his bedroom window for about the twelfth time. A light, but steady, snow was beginning to fall, covering the frozen dead grass with a slowly thickening coat of white. It was, he had to admit, shaping up to be a perfectly glistening, lustrous, Christmas snow. He opened the window and stuck his head out to feel the cold calm of Christmas Eve night on his rosy cheeks one more time.

So this was it. Christmas Eve was here. He fleetingly thought perhaps one of the elves had filled in for him, or maybe Mrs. Claus, but he knew that wasn't true. Christmas—Santa Christmas—was over.

It was for the best. He was old, out of step with a world of children who didn't believe in him anyway. And there were plenty of psychologically-scarred adults that had been left in the wake of his post-believer abandonment of them; Izzy Carmichel, Cameron—and elves like Teevo too.

He heaved a sigh and scratched his still thick beard. He supposed he would have that little souvenir of his past life forever. He absently patted his stomach and was alarmed to feel that it was rounder than it had been. Too many cheese puffs and chocolate chip waffles. Maybe Uncle Milo was packing on the pounds. Santa realized that as a real-worlder again, maybe he should lay off the deserts. He had to take care of himself now, maybe start working out. If Mrs. Claus could see him now. That thought stung, so to cover it, he chuckled a low, "ho, ho, ho," then realized he would have to do something about that laugh too in his new life as Uncle Milo: Personal Claus to the Jones Family.

Santa looked out at the night sky and found the Christmas star. It was shining brightly as always; brighter, maybe, than even the day before. This pleased him. The constellations were the same in this sky as they were at the North Pole, even if not as bright. He admired them all, scanning each one, counting. His count, however, came out uneven. There was an extra star. And it was *moving*.

Not just moving; it was streaking across the Northern Hemisphere. Fast. And getting closer.

"Shit," Santa muttered, then clamped a hand over his mouth like a kid caught cursing at the church social.

Santa's eyes widened. He'd never seen what he was now seeing from this perspective on the ground, but he knew what it was. A miniature sleigh and eight tiny reindeer, illuminated with a crisp, magical light. But who was the little old driver?

Up on the roof, Izzy dozed drunkenly by a small heater precariously perched on the custom-built platform. With the schnapps bottle in one hand and digital camera in the other, Izzy was ready for fame to glide in, if he woke up.

The sleigh swooped down through the atmosphere, drawing closer to the house. Dogwater crouched on the floor of the sleigh, clutching the bench seat and facing away from the reindeer, petrified. The reins flapped around freely, whipping him occasionally. The reindeer, however, knew the way and flew on unconcerned.

"Oh, god, oh god, oh god!" Dogwater screamed. He turned, resting his hands on the floor of the sleigh, eyes firmly shut. "I'm gonna die. Or puke. Or die puking," he said loudly. "Fuck! Land already. Give me ground!" This was immediately followed by an image of a fiery sleigh wreck and he wished he could take the words back.

Santa wrinkled the curtains on his bedroom window in sweating, flexing hands, mesmerized by the beautiful spectacle. He could almost reach out and touch a reindeer hoof.

As Santa drew in his head and was turning around, the sleigh approached the house, passing over the near comatose Izzy, and gracefully slid to a perfect landing on the roof. The flakes of snow churned up by the landing prickled at Izzy's face. He grunted and rolled over in the lounge chair he had hauled up to the roof.

"Damn you, Dasher," Dogwater groaned. "Dammit Dancer. You too Prancer, Vixen, Comet, and Cupid. Donder—blow me!" Dogwater hissed, eyes still firmly shut. "And BLITZEN, I'm gonna punch *you* in the nose next chance I get." Blitzen was in the rear position, closest to the sleigh and had, well, perhaps one bucket too many oats before the flight. In response to Dogwater's threat, Blitzen made a noise something like a raspberry.

Dogwater slowly began to realize the sleigh wasn't moving anymore. He opened one eye, felt dizzy, and the other eye opened automatically as he toppled from the sleigh, a victim of vertigo. He slid part of the way down the back side of the rapidly icing roof. "Oh, shit," he said with uncharacteristic calm as he managed to catch hold of the gutter. Momentum carried his body forward and he swung out into the air and down.

Down in his bedroom, Santa heard the thud on the roof, the prancing and pawing of hooves mingled with the slamming of a body and the scraping of said body sliding down the roof. He had a fleeting image of the embodied spirit of the season coming to find him and give him a wedgie.

To Santa Claus's great surprise, he saw his own boots dangling outside as Dogwater swung out over the roof and collided with Santa's window, cracking it. Santa regrouped with amazing speed and fumbled with the window lock before awkwardly pushing it open.

"Don't let me fall! Don't let me fall!" Dogwater called continuously, even after he had awkwardly clambered inside.

This new "Santa" was stout and not particularly tall, Santa thought, and twitchy. Santa laughed in spite of himself. The young, scared man in the oversized red coat reminded him much of himself from centuries earlier.

Dogwater rubbed all his extremities. Everything was cold, but nothing was broken. "You okay?" he asked the man in the room, adding, "Santa." It sounded funny saying that name like you would "Fred" or "Ignatius." But it felt good. It resonated pleasingly.

Santa nodded. "I was about to say the same to you, *Santa.*"

The bedroom door flew open and Cameron stomped in, red-eyed and hair askew. "What the hell is going on here tonight?"

Santa nodded at Dogwater. "Cameron," he said, "I'd like you to meet Santa Claus. The new one apparently."

"Ho, ho, ho," Dogwater warbled, knees still wobbly from the flight.

"Oh, Christ," Cameron groaned.

Down in Cameron Jones's kitchen, over steaming mugs of coffee—for which Dogwater and his tingly extremities were extremely grateful—Dog described his magical, terrifying flight from the North Pole back to the real world. In the interest of dignity, he left out the part where he threw up over Greenland. And Iceland. And New Brunswick. Especially New Brunswick.

Cameron stared intently at his friend, trying to decide if he was a hallucination. At one point, he even poked the man in the forearm with a fork, eliciting a non-hallucinatory response of "Ow! Son of a bitch!"

"Santa, they need you back at the North Pole," Dogwater said, still rubbing his arm. "Everyone misses you."

"Do they?" Santa asked.

"Yeah, of course. They're just sitting around, not doing anything," Dogwater said. "The elves aren't making toys. Mrs. Claus is pulling her hair out. That little elf, the nervous one with the rod up his butt, Fivel? Fili?

"Flifle," Santa assisted.

"Yeah. I think he's gonna have a heart attack. They all want you back. It's Christmas. " He looked his watch. "Pretty soon it will be anyway. The night is moving fast. Some parts of the world are already starting to look at Christmas morning. Right here in Indiana, we're only about two hours from midnight. That's a lot of make up toy-flinging."

"I just don't know," Santa sighed, laying his head on the table.

"Santa, look, when I flew over here"—it still sounded insane—"I saw no Christmas lights. Not a one. This town is usually lit up like, well, like a town called 'Santa Claus'. But tonight, nothing. Christmas is dying. Can you really let that happen?"

"I'm tired," Santa moaned, the sound muffled by the table.

Dogwater slammed the table with a ferocity that surprised even him, making Santa jerk his head back, wincing. "It's not about you," Dog said. "It's about the children. They need their Santa Claus."

"But," Santa paused. "But I'm not that person anymore. That life is over. I'm sharing Milo's life now."

"Fuck that. Don't you see how ridiculous that is?" Dogwater said, voice cracking slightly.

Inside his head, Santa heard Milo's voice. *It is a little weird, buddy.*

"Dog, I'm pretty sure dropping the F-bomb with Kris Kringle is a guaranteed ticket to cat poo in your stocking."

"I don't care," Dogwater said, jerking one arm and spilling his coffee. He paid it no notice. Dogwater stood up with ferocity, not blushing, stammering, awkwardness. He commanded Santa to do the same.

Santa looked bewildered, but stood and Cameron wondered fleetingly whether Dog was going to punch Kringle in the face. That would put a nice little night cap on what had shaped up to be a record-setting shitty holiday.

Instead, Dogwater moved behind the troubled old elf, removing the Santa coat he still wore and draping it over its original owner's shoulders.

Dogwater turned the man toward him, grabbed the lapels, and said, "You are St. Nicholas. You're not..." Then he blanked. He was on such a great roll, he'd forgotten the man's name.

"Milo," Cameron offered, head in hands.

"Milo. Thank you," Dogwater continued. "You are Father Christmas. Santa Claus. St. Nicholas. And a bunch of names in other languages I can't pronounce. "

"But the non-believers...," Santa protested.

"Right now," Dogwater continued, ignoring him, speaking in measured tones, "All over the world, there are millions of children trying hard to fool you into thinking they're not naughty and trying to figure out what the hell a sugar plum is so they can have visions of it dancing in their heads. All so you'll show up and bring them something special. So you can either go do you job, or sit here on your ass and feel sorry for yourself." He clutched a little on "ass," as it seemed awkward using such language with such a wholesome a creature as Santa Claus.

"They don't believe," Santa said. "Maybe once. But no more."

"Bullshit. What about those thousands of letters you get? Millions maybe. What about your picture being on every goddamn thing at Christmas except pictures of Jesus? What about countless cliché movies, annoying songs, and lame books about you? And don't get me started on those stupid commercials for razors, radial tires, and incontinence undergarments."

"I see what you mean, but..." Santa strode stiffly to the sink, watching a thin drip from the faucet.

"What about Holly?" Cameron muttered.

Dogwater's head jerked toward Cameron. Santa's eyes widened, his distress deepening.

"Holly?" Santa asked.

"Yeah, Santa," Cameron said, shifting awkwardly. "She's asleep at her house right now expecting to wake up tomorrow and find all sorts of great stuff that *you* left for her. I'm not there for her. I've failed. You can't. How do you think she'll feel when there's nothing?"

"Well, I don't want to hurt her. She's such a dear..." He turned toward the kitchen, studying the variety of pizza delivery place magnets.

Dogwater sighed. "Either be there for the children, or be there for yourself. You pick," Dogwater concluded.

Something in that sentiment resonated for Cameron, offering a tiny glimmer, even in the blackness of his mood.

When Santa turned back around, he was weeping. Seeing this caused Cameron, for the first time throughout this entire exchange, to feel something more than vague annoyance. You try looking at an innocent little puppy crying and not feel moved.

The tears glistened on Santa's increasingly ruddy cheeks and cherry nose. He stroked the white fringe on his lapels and looked at Cameron. "What do you think, Cameron?" he asked.

Cameron looked back and nodded, for the first time, not at the face of the gentle, old ex-relative, ex-visitation supervisor, Uncle Milo, but rather into the face of Santa Claus himself. It was a pretty far journey to come to this place, at his kitchen table. He was face to face with a man who, until this month, had been no more real than Webster Stanhope.

Given all his rotten holidays, Cameron was tempted to say, "You know what, Santa? Screw you!" But...but...wasn't Christmas about faith? About hope? About good will toward others? No, really, wasn't it? Cameron thought he'd heard that somewhere, but wasn't sure.

No, Christmas was about Holly. Beginning, middle, and end.

If there was anything Cameron was sure of these days, anything at all, it was this: having a chance to be there for a child, let alone millions of children, is what it's all about. You get your shit together and you do it.

"Go," Cameron said, finally. "Go now. You're needed. And wanted. Go be Santa Claus."

Santa smiled. Cameron was right. Dogwater was right. Mrs. Claus had been right. He *was* Santa Claus. He could doubt his own identity, his own existence, but he still had a job to do.

"If I go, will you be all right?" he asked Cameron earnestly.

Cameron, who didn't really realize the extent to which Santa had invested himself in him, shrugged. "Yeah, I'll be fine. Well, fine as usual," he said. "With all my other problems, being the guy who stands in the way of Christmas would probably not play well in family court."

Santa turned to Dogwater. "All right," he said. "What will happen to him? Milo, I mean. We're still joined and I destroyed the recall device."

Dog smiled and reached over to fumble with Santa's left coat pocket. He pulled out a pipe, perfect for clenching in one's teeth—until Santa recently quit—and set it aside. He reached into the pocket again, dug out a pair of spectacles, a set of chattering teeth—from when Santa had a sense of humor—and the oversized candy cane Shivla gave him. He nodded awkwardly at the others as he shoved that last item into the inside pocket of his own long coat he'd been wearing under Santa's. Dog switched to the right-hand pocket and found what he was looking for: a small wire device similar to the recall unit that Santa had snapped off the radio.

He handed the device to Santa and said, "Flifle told me to give this to you. Just press the green button, and you and Milo will instantly separate. Milo will be just fine. And you too. Well, in theory anyway."

"You'll take care of him?" Santa asked Dogwater, gesturing to Cameron.

"Uh, sure," Dogwater said.

"And, you'll take care of each other?" Santa said, looking at the two men.

Dog and Cameron exchanged awkward guy looks. "Yeah," they mumbled. "Of course."

"All right, then, let's do it," Santa said.

"Great," Dogwater said. He handed Santa the recall unit and stepped across the room, well out of range of whatever was about to happen. Cameron followed, wondering if his homeowners' insurance was paid up.

Santa stepped to the center of the room. "Should something...*unplanned* happen, I love you both," he said.

"Ho, ho, ho," Cameron said.

Santa nodded gravely. "Yes, indeed." He pressed the green button.

An ear-piercing squeal filled the room, but was quickly replaced by the crisp peals of silver bells. The room was bathed in green and red light. Milo's body twirled, not in pain, more like dancing. The light obscured the spectacle, though Cameron could make out two arms and two legs, flailing eerily.

Up on the roof, Izzy was jolted sluggishly to consciousness. He spun around in his seat trying to figure out what the hell was going on as the red and green beams of light shot out through the windows.

Back in the kitchen, both Cameron and Dogwater tried to follow the progress of Santa's two arms and two legs, as they were the only parts they could make out. But then, gradually, they realized there were four arms and *four* legs. Then two heads; one with the bushy Santa beard, the other clean-shaven. Milo and Santa separated, their shapes peeling away from each other and revealing themselves like the layers of a folded piece of construction paper transformed into a paper snowflake.

Within moments, the bells and lights were gone. Two distinct humans stood in Cameron's kitchen: Santa Claus, jolly and plump, complete with Santa suit; and the other, a rail-thin bewildered, old man in sensible slacks and cotton work shirt.

Dogwater was, well, giddy. This was going to make an *excellent* piece on *Dark Matters*.

I don't care if Dr. Whipple is setting a world Alpine ski record while having mind-blowing sex, when I call. I'm gonna have to talk to her about this, Cameron thought. Or drink a lot.

"HO HO HO," Santa roared, successfully rattling the window panes. The yuletide rallying cry had been repressed, cramped inside Milo's wiry frame for nearly a month waiting to burst.

Up on the roof, Izzy flopped out of the lounge chair and crouched, listening intently.

Milo Vestibule looked around the room, eyes lingering on Santa, and said, "That's it, no more creamed chipped beef before bed," and immediately fell into a deep sleep standing straight up. Cameron and Dogwater gently led the man to the couch and laid him down, unsure what else to do with him.

When everyone was reasonably confident that Milo was okay, Santa said, "To the sleigh," in a hands-on-hips pose that was amazingly devoid of cheesiness.

"I'll get the ladder," Dogwater said, sprinting to the porch.

"Come, Cameron, feel the holiday spirit," Santa said in a booming Santa voice.

Cameron started to shrug reflexively, then grinned a little. "Don't mind if I do."

Outside Cameron's front door, fluffy white snowflakes were riding streams of accelerating wind. With the snow crystals illuminated by Dogwater's holiday lighting strung around Cameron's porch and windows, Cameron couldn't help but experience a greeting card moment. It was like walking into one of those cheesy holiday specials from the '70's. For the briefest moment, he was sure he saw Andy Williams in a festive holiday sweater stroll into the driveway crooning "Winter Wonderland."

Dogwater sprinted toward the ladder that Izzy had left in place leaning against the front of the house. Santa was not far behind.

Santa Claus is a man well over six feet tall and easily three-hundred pounds. And yet, Cameron was impressed with how lightly and gracefully the man moved. In that red suit, it was like watching a really, really fat, sunburned flamingo. Without a moment's hesitation, Santa ascended the ladder, which strained surprisingly little under the great weight. Nevertheless, Cameron took up the ladder-bracing position. The death of Santa Claus on his property would be difficult to explain to the insurance company. Dogwater immediately followed Santa up the ladder.

At the top, Santa reached one hand over the gutter to begin to hoist his girth up onto the roof, now nearly snow-covered. He had just started the maneuver when a large object that Dogwater would later learn, to his dismay, was a camcorder, flew past St. Nicholas's head. It neatly knocked off his Santa cap, which Dogwater below caught with one hand.

"Santa, you okay? Just wait..." Dogwater protested, yelling a little to be heard over the wind. At this moment, Dogwater remembered Izzy and his TV tabloid dream of catching the Santa Claus aliens. This was going to be bad.

Not really comprehending what had just happened, Santa retrieved his hat from Dogwater and climbed onto the roof. When he spied his beloved sleigh team, he cried "Hello, my beauties. How I've missed you." The reindeer stamped their feet and shook their heads. Curiously, they all shook their heads in the same direction; toward the back of the sleigh. Even as Santa patted and cooed at each of his reindeer, they rolled their eyes, trying in vain to signal Santa.

Dogwater climbed onto the roof just in time to see Izzy spring up from behind the sleigh, Sig Sauer pistol in hand, point it at Father Christmas and fire. "Got you, you space-son-of-a-bitch," he said as the bullet left the chamber and cracked the holy night.

Santa wobbled as the bullet passed harmlessly through the white tassel ball on his hat. He looked in the direction of the shot and could make out a man standing there, the Christmas lights and Cameron's yard light providing some illumination.

"It's Izzy, isn't it?" he asked, as if he was greeting an old friend. "What do you intend to do with that?" Santa pointed at the gun. "Someone might get hurt," he added, with no sense of alarm.

Aiming for another shot, Izzy growled, "Only you, motherfu-,"

"Izzy, no!" Dogwater shouted. Almost on reflex, he grabbed the oversized candy cane—the one Shivla had given him—in his coat pocket, as if he was a great yuletide warrior, unsheathing a sword. With the curved end, he struck out and jerked Izzy's gun arm just as he fired. A second bullet left the gun, this one crashing through Cameron's roof and—amazingly—through the bedroom window over Cameron's head.

"What the hell is going on up there?" Cameron yelled. He got no response, perhaps because it was obvious.

Izzy, still a little drunk, dropped the gun and Dogwater swooped down to scoop it up before it slid off the roof. He tossed the gun to Santa as he tackled Izzy. Santa caught the gun, but fell backward on the icy roof and slid down its slanted front, even as Izzy and Dogwater wrestled each other down the backside—Dogwater relentlessly pounding Izzy with a giant stuffed reindeer from the back of Santa's sleigh as they went. Santa's legs dangled over the edge of the roof, his coat riding up, and he very nearly was mooning the Christmas star.

Without thinking, down on the ground, Cameron moved over to Santa's position, a good ten feet from the ladder and stood as if he would—what?—catch the man?

Still struggling with Izzy, Dog yelled, "Cameron, get your ass up here."

Cameron hesitated, thinking he'd go with the catching-the-fat-man plan instead, then thought better of it. He scaled the ladder. By the time he got to the roof, Dog appeared to be getting the better of Izzy. Bits of toy reindeer stuffing filled the air.

Cameron, on all fours in deference to the now slick roof, crawled over to Santa and grabbed his two green-mittened hands. He tried to hoist the man up, but it was a tough go. "Dog, a little help," he called.

Dogwater looked back toward Cameron and then with one action-movie-quality right cross, he sent Izzy sprawling back on the roof, momentarily stunned, if not unconscious. Reasonably certain the punch sprained one, if not two, fingers, he rushed over to Cameron and each man took one of Santa's arms and hauled him to safety. Several shingles took the brunt of the effort.

Santa hugged both men gratefully. "Ho, ho, ho," he chuckled. "Thank you. What brave gentlemen you are."

"Yeah, yeah," the guys muttered.

"I think there will be something special in your stockings tomorrow," Santa said, eyes twinkling.

Out of the corner of one eye, Dogwater spied Izzy crawling beneath the sleigh, sliding on his stomach toward the ladder.

"Cameron!" Dog shouted, pointing. Cameron whirled and nearly lost his balance on the slanted, icy roof. Izzy slid the rest of the way toward the ladder and grabbed it. His weight pushed the ladder forward. Man and ladder tipped forward, away from the house, but instead of falling to the ground, the ladder bumped the oak tree in the middle of Cameron's front yard. Izzy quickly scampered down it and ran away.

"Dammit, he got away," Dogwater said.

"Never mind that," Santa said, sounding more like his normal, baritone self. "He will get what is coming to him in time."

"But," Dog started to protest.

Santa just shook his head, laying a finger aside of his nose. On first glance, it looked like he was some sort of Mafioso giving the sign that someone was going to be rubbed out.

It took a moment for Dogwater to realize Santa didn't mean what he thought he meant. He looked at his watch, "Santa, time's wasting. You've got to fly."

Looking out at the Christmas star and then at the horizon, Santa agreed. "Yes. It is time I go home. If I hurry, it may not yet be too late for Christmas to come. You two have shown me the way. Thank you."

More guy awkwardness.

The jolly old elf sprang to his sleigh and whistled the reindeer to action. He rattled off each reindeer's name and—hand to God—Cameron could swear the reindeer smiled as their names were called.

"Cameron, Dogwater, come. I will give you a lift down."

"Uh." Dogwater hesitated, then remembered he'd already lost most everything he'd ever eaten somewhere over Canada and climbed in the sleigh. Cameron hesitated too, certain he was achieving a whole new level of insanity.

The sleigh, heedless of the weather or the laws of physics, launched effortlessly into the air. It floated effortlessly down to the ground where the runners were quickly buried in the accumulating snow.

Cameron and Dogwater shook hands with St. Nicholas and climbed out of the sleigh. Impulsively, Santa sprang from his sleigh and embraced Dogwater in a massive bear hug. "Thank you," he said simply.

"Uh, sure," Dogwater responded in a tone muffled by red-dyed wool.

Santa was on Cameron giving him the same treatment before the man could react. Santa loved these real-worlders. They were good men and now maybe once again believers in the spirit of Christmas, the power of good will toward all. This was the validation of his existence he'd sought. It was real and it was true.

"Well, it looks like I'm ready," Santa said.

"It's been...interesting," Cameron said, originally planning to say "fun," but he'd decided that wasn't totally accurate. "Seriously, though, thanks for...for everything." The writer was at a loss for the words to describe his own feelings.

"Ho, ho, ho," Santa said, then frowned. "I'm just sorry I won't get to visit the ocean. Your calendar made it look so beautiful."

Cameron didn't really know what that meant, but said, "Well, you could always visit."

"Perhaps I will," Santa said, though he knew he likely would not.

"You could sleep on my futon. I don't really have any extra pillows, but I guess I could get some..." Dogwater offered with total earnestness.

"Thank you, Dogwater," Santa said. Then, stepping back into the sleigh, he stood straight and tall and said, "Farewell, gentlemen."

Cameron and Dogwater waved awkwardly.

The sleigh and reindeer flew out of sight, trailing a comet of glittering magic dust behind. Santa pumped a fist in the air triumphantly.

And they heard him exclaim, as he drove out of sight, "Yahoo!" which wasn't very literary, but there it was.

After several moments of silent observation, Cameron said, "Well, that's that." He shrugged, partly to end the affair—which he was not yet entirely convinced was real—and partly to try and shake off Andy Williams, who was still hanging around at the end of his driveway, or possibly just in his head, droning on and on in his dopey red and green sweater, not clearly identifying himself as hallucination or simple flight of imagination. Bastard better remember to turn out the lights before he leaves, Cameron thought..

Dogwater stood quietly, holding the candy cane in one hand and Izzy's Sig Sauer in the other, the decapitated toy reindeer at his feet. He was cocooned in the swirling snowfall that was falling with no inhibition now. Putting the candy cane back in his pocket first, he took off his blue elf hat and looked at the white snow crystallizing on it. The little pellets of snow, upon closer inspection, were perfectly formed, extra large, snowflakes of all different shapes as if they'd been manufactured in a factory, not just blobs of frozen water. He smiled a little and realized two things. One was that Roberta's prediction had come true, complete with candy cane, gun, reindeer head, and snowfall. There was no way she'd ever let him forget that.

The second thing Dogwater realized was that Christmas really was a magical time where anything could happen.

Dogwater sighed. In Roberta's honor, he danced a little joy-to-the-world, peace-on-Earth, goodwill-toward-men (more or less) holiday jig. Suddenly, pausing mid-jig, he realized a third thing.

"Shit!"

In the night's excitement, he'd forgotten to get even one picture, video, or audio recording of his prized Santa Claus alien. In the afterlife, Lars Heimdal would surely be waiting to kick his ass for being such a punk.

"Ho, ho, hosed again."

# DECEMBER 25

There are few things that combine magic and the world's natural splendor in quite the same way as the Christmas morning sunrise.

Now picture that, overlaid by a little red sleigh, aloft in flight, with eight majestic reindeer in the lead, muscular legs pumping through the reddish, early morning light.

And, at the helm of that sleigh, a delightful, bearded old man, white hair flowing in the wind, laughing joyfully over the sound of empty toy bags in the back of the sleigh flapping in the wind.

That Christmas morning, as Santa made the same landing approach at the North Pole Complex he'd made so many times before, the run complete, the toys delivered, and the man weary from the night's work, he wept devastatingly happy tears.

It had been—what—less than a day earlier when he'd been set to abandon this place forever; had been set never to wear the Santa hat again or play with the elves, or feel the power of the jet stream on his magical run.

It felt good to be home. No, it felt *really* good. The Complex had never looked more inviting to him. This was where he was supposed to be; doing what he was supposed to do. All over the world, many children—and not a few adults—were waking up early in anticipation of his having been there. The would be enjoying special family time, making lifetime memories, thanks in no small part to him. How could he have ever walked away from that?

Santa knew, as he watched that sunrise, that he would be just fine. Any lingering doubts about this melted as he landed in the courtyard of the North Pole Complex and saw assembled there hundreds of elves—men, women, children; young and old. When the runners touched earth, the crowd erupted in elfish cheers.

Santa climbed from the sleigh, patted all the reindeer between the antlers, per custom, and turned to wave at the crowd. The cheers increased.

Then the crowd parted and Mrs. Claus stepped forward, unable to contain herself, and executed a round-house kick of joy, before sprinting forward to hug her husband.

"Ho, ho, ho," Santa said.

Then he hugged Flifle. And Shivla. And a bunch of other elves. The man's a hugger. The sound of an elfish flute could be heard in the back of the crowd, playing a traditional holiday tune.

A small hand tugged at the large man's coat. Santa turned and looked down into the pale, creamy face of Doozil, who looked back sheepishly. The crowd immediately became quiet. "Welcome home, Mr. Claus," he said.

"Thank you, Doozil."

And for Doozil, the biggest hug of all.

Cameron and Dogwater took Milo home shortly after Santa departed. Milo was sleepy, but seemed otherwise unharmed by this whole ordeal. Then the two men saw in the early hours of the Christmas morn drinking and coming to grips with the night's events. They brought in the electronic equipment from the roof, but left the observation platform there. It could come in handy, Dogwater had argued, and Cameron had been too tired to protest. They considered boarding up the broken window that Dogwater had cracked and where the bullet went through, but decided they didn't feel like it. They also opted not to call the police about Izzy. What would they report? An assault on St. Nick? Being out in the country, no one probably heard or paid attention to the shots Izzy fired anyway.

A few hours after Dogwater had finally left and Cameron had gotten a little sleep, he was awakened by a muffled sound, familiar but distant. It was faint, but echoed in the empty house. He shuffled on his bathrobe and stumble-stepped downstairs to the living room, still a little buzzed from the night before. The noise grew louder, took on more definition; a plaintive whine. He continued following the noise to the kitchen, where he spied on the table the long, carved pipe Dogwater had pulled from Santa's coat the night before. So much for passing all this off as a dream. Still, he touched it just to make sure. It was real.

There was a yelp and Cameron pinpointed it to the cupboard nearest the refrigerator. The door was slightly ajar.

Wondering if perhaps Webster Stanhope had taken to whining, Cameron cautiously swung the cupboard door open. On the top shelf was something Cameron first thought was a clear jar of cookies. Then he realized they weren't cookies—not human ones, anyway—but rather dog biscuits. What the hell?

Then he saw it.

On the bottom shelf, curled in a tight, fuzzy ball, was a puppy. A chocolate Labrador retriever, perhaps a couple months old, looked up at Cameron with moist eyes, and let out a sharp little yip/whine.

Cameron rocked back on his heels. "How did you...?" he asked as he reached in and gently picked the shivering thing up. He might have left the cupboard open last night, but that didn't answer what was really the bigger question: How did the dog get there? Looking for dog biscuits presumably. But how did the biscuits get there?

The puppy's heart pounded furiously against Cameron's chest. Cameron now saw that the dog's green collar had a red bow and a card attached. Holding the flopping puppy in one arm while trying to hold the card with the opposite hand was awkward, but he managed to read the sweeping calligraphy that spelled out, "A dog won't bring your daughter back, but maybe the two of you can give each other a happy home. Love, S.C."

Cameron thought about this, about all that had happened this month. This puppy, by far, could be the most realistic hallucination yet. On the other hand, something this warm and fuzzy—happiness is a warm puppy, after all—how could it not be real?

"Come on, you. I'll show ya around the place. Then we'll work on a name."

That seemed okay with the puppy and they walked into the living room.

As he passed by the tree, Cameron spied something underneath he hadn't noticed before: a small package wrapped in pink paper. He smiled. Could Santa have left another special surprise?

Cameron set the puppy down, knelt under the tree and, with no concern for the bow, the wrapping, or the tape, ripped the package open. Puppy pawed at the wrapping and made short work of the ribbon, batting and gnawing it. What Cameron now held made him laugh out loud. It was a framed, crayon drawing of a stick figure man, with straggly dark hair, holding an oversized pencil, and a smaller stick figure person wearing a dress. Below the figures was a caption: "I love Daddy. From Holly." And a bunch of hearts and flowers.

It was all he ever wanted.

When Milo Vestibule awoke in his recliner—in the pristine, soot free living room of his home—he felt more refreshed than he had after any night's sleep in his life. Sally, his faithful old cat, sat on his chest, delicately licking a paw and keeping one suspicious eye on her master. Milo had a vague, dream-like memory of riding in a car in the dark with a weird little guy in a blue hat, but it was a tenuous thought and faded away quickly. Sally, too, had some vague impressions of having traveled far, but her memory had faded just as quickly as Milo's. She hopped down from the recliner and went in search of food.

Milo stood and stretched. On the mantle, oddly, was a plate with two sugar cookies. Milo didn't bake and should have been suspicious, but he ate one anyway. It was mighty good.

Below the plate was a note written in a bold hand. It said:

> *Milo:*
>
> You wouldn't understand the events that led me to write this note and you have no memory of why I thank you, but I do thank you, nonetheless. Thank you for helping me to see the magic of Christmas again. And, more than that, thank you for being you, for you know the true joy of giving of your time and talents for children. In your garage, you will find a little something to help you in your own quest. Live well and long.
>
> -Santa Claus

Milo ate the other cookie and considered this skeptically. Later, when he finally decided the curiosity was too much to bear and went out to his garage, he would find an array of serious woodworking tools including lathes, drills, electric saws, and enough lumber to build a house—for people, not birds. He didn't know who his benefactor was, but the children in his class would be building the finest birdhouses ever for months to come.

When Dogwater woke up Christmas morning—in the closet, naturally— he, per habit, turned on the computer to check his email. Instead of the usual desktop icons, numbers started scrolling across the black screen, along with various letters "N", "NE," "SW," etc.

"What the hell?" Dog cursed, but then the numbers were interspersed with the encouragement, "Look here!!! Look here!!!" The little alien alert bell started ringing. Dogwater realized, excitedly, "They're coordinates!" and turned on the printer.

"Thank you, Santa!"

As the flurry of wrapping paper at Susan and Holly's house died down and Susan's parents, Earl and Myrna, were starting to think about a mid-day nap before Christmas dinner, Susan was enjoying a cappuccino and staring absently at the Christmas tree. Behind her, she could hear Holly showing her grandmother—again—the large, apparently simple, wooden crate that held a very realistic holographic image of a horse that Santa had brought her. She had gotten her pony.

Susan's eyes wandered lazily to the tree and she noticed an envelope stuck in the branches. Her brow knitted. What was that doing there? She looked around as people do when something odd shows up as if the answer would appear magically behind them, then walked over to the tree and pulled out the envelope. Her name and address were on the front.

"Mom, what's this?" she asked Myrna.

"Oh, I forgot. Mrs. Morley brought that over last night. She said the mailman had delivered it to her by mistake. It had your employer's name on it, so I thought maybe it was a bonus check or something." This explained why she'd hung it on the tree.

Susan shrugged and opened the envelope, which bore a red rubber stamped

"HAPPY HOLIDAYS" on the front. Inside was a piece of paper bearing the letterhead of her employer, Currier & Ives. The letter was short and to the point and ended with the signature of the company vice-president to whom she reported. She didn't notice, but may have been interested to note, the initials at the bottom of the page where the typist's would usually go: "SC."

Despite the shock of the letter's contents, a small smile cracked the corner of Susan's mouth. She sighed and put the letter in her back pocket.

"Well, what is it?" her mother asked.

"Oh, just a company Christmas bonus," Susan said vaguely. She looked at her daughter, directing the holographic horse to leap holographic bales of hay—a gift that surely must have come from Cameron who loved his daughter enough to find such an extravagant gift.

Izzy made it back to his trailer in the early morning hours, bitter and cold, certain the cops would haul him in. He'd taken the long way home, on foot. Relieved to finally be there—maybe have time to light up and take the edge off before the police got there—he went inside.

A large box sat on the coffee table. It was white with a big red bow.

"Who's here?" Izzy shouted, looking around. No one answered. "Don't fuck with me." Still no answer.

Izzy shrugged and took the lid off the box. Anything he might have guessed about the contents of the box, what was actually in there was not even close. It was a skateboard. Not just any skateboard; a vintage Sundancer eight-wheeler, the one he'd desperately wanted—thought he'd die without—as a kid. It was the same board his father had opted not to give him, offering, instead, a ringside seat to a Christmas morning beating of his mother.

A note attached to the skateboard said simply. "Sorry this is about twenty years late. It can't make up for all you've seen in your young life; for all that has happened to you. Just remember: whether you're 'naughty or nice' depends more on who you are than what you've done or where you come from. Love, Santa."

Izzy cried long repressed tears—also about twenty years too late.

Ben Steene poured another mug of eggnog and turned down all the lights in his apartment, save for the aluminum pre-lit Christmas tree he'd picked up at the drug store on the way home. He settled back to enjoy his traditional holiday by logging onto Ho Ho Hos.com

Ben Steene's bells were preparing to jingle when he heard on his terrace the click-click-click of hooves. Or possibly a burglar.

"Fuck," Ben Steene muttered and went for his gun in the desk drawer. He heard someone fiddling with the French doors that led to the terrace. He leveled the Glock toward the doors and shouted. "Don't do it, asshole."

The doors shimmered and melted into a large fireplace, through which Santa stepped, bending and straightening with ease. The fireplace changed back into the doors.

"Hold it right there," Ben Steene said, leveling the gun with one hand and fumbling with his cell phone in the other.

Santa sighed. "More guns? Really, I don't understand you real-worlders."

"Dammit," Ben Steene cursed, discovering he couldn't get a signal on his phone.

"Merry Christmas, Ben," Santa said.

"Get out of here, old man," Ben Steene sneered. "I'll shoot."

"Put that thing away," Santa ordered.

"Don't push me."

"You owe me, Ben."

"What?"

"When you were a kid, I gave you that pellet gun even though your mother was sure you'd shoot your eye out."

"Pellet gun?" Ben Steene said, his gun hand dipping a little.

"Does this look familiar?" Santa waved a mittened hand and an image of a shiny metallic gun hovered in front of him.

Ben Steene's eyes widened, partly for the gun, partly for the visitor. "Santa?" he said. He distractedly set the gun on the desk.

Santa bowed. "Or Kris Kringle, if you prefer." That felt good.

"So it was you I saw through Jones's window the other day. Not just a trick."

Santa nodded.

"So why are you here?"

"It's Christmas, Ben," Santa said.

Ben Steene glanced at the bare space under his tree.

"Presents later, Ben," Santa said. "First, we need to talk."

"About what?"

"You cannot publish an article claiming Cameron Jones is unstable. The authorities will keep his daughter from him."

"How did you...?"

By way of answer, Santa held up a scroll bearing the heading "NAUGHTY/NICE." He shook his head. "You've been quite naughty, haven't you?"

"I just report the news."

"But you know I exist"—it felt good saying that—"Cameron wasn't wrong to believe in me."

"He's bonkers," Ben Steene scoffed. "Washed up. The readers love a has-been. Sorry, Santa. The First Amendment clearly..."

"Oh, pish," Santa grunted. "Cameron's daughter needs him."

"That's not my problem, Santa." Ben Steene shrugged. "I have a job to do."

Santa's brow furrowed, his eyes were still baby blue, but now they were an angry, tantrum-throwing baby blue. He stalked stiffly over to the reporter. Ben Steene was a tall guy, but not compared to Santa. When the men were nose to nose, Santa said, "You will not write that article." There was no malice there, just a simple expression of fact.

Ben Steene returned the icy stare, but he gulped just a little. "Or what?"

Impulsively, Kris Kringle stepped forward, fists clenched. Santa looked at the man for several long moments. Then he swiftly reached into his coat pocket. Ben Steene flinched at what may be coming.

"Or you won't get this," Santa said. He held up a solid gold, hand-held TV/stereo/GPS/glucose tester/video game/Internet hook up/electronic organizer. It was a thing of beauty. It would take a month just to figure out how to turn it on.

"Deal," Ben Steene quickly said.

Gifts for guys are so easy, Santa chuckled to himself.

Around the world that Christmas morning, church bells rang as they always did, but the sound was a little crisper than it had ever been. Christmas morning cinnamon rolls were tastier. Families hugged a little tighter. No one realized why these things should be—probably didn't even consciously realize anything was different. No one knew how close they had come to losing the spirit of Christmas, but for the efforts of a few true believers—belated believers, perhaps, but still believers—in Santa Claus, Indiana and some determined elves in an imaginary world only a few special humans would ever see. All those people knew was that no matter what else was happening in their personal worlds the rest of the year, on this day, their hearts swelled with unmistakable peace and joy.

Ho-ho-ho!

# DECEMBER 26

"Are you sure about this?" Everett Franken asked, standing with Cameron outside the courtroom.

"Yeah," Cameron said softly, a man at peace. "I don't want to fight the visitation thing anymore. If this new job in London makes Susan happy, then I'm happy for her and she should go."

"Look, Cameron, if this is about the mental health allegations-"

Cameron shook his head, "No, I know I'm not crazy." He paused. "But I'm not well either. I think, though, that even if I can't replace the part of the deck I'm missing, I at least need time to re-shuffle the cards I have."

"All right," Everett Franken sighed, sounding a little disappointed. "I'll let Susan's lawyer know we're dismissing our petition to modify the visitation."

"Thanks, Everett, really," Cameron said. "Happy Chanukah, by the way.

"Thank you. You're a little late."

"Sorry. Sue me."

Everett Franken laughed and shook his head. He turned to walk away when Susan scurried in.

"There you are," Susan said.

"Is your lawyer with you?" Everett Franken asked.

"No, not yet. He's not always real punctual."

"I just told Everett I'm dropping the case. I'm not going to fight you anymore," Cameron said.

"Oh," Susan said, abruptly. "Well, thanks, but I was just coming to tell you that I'm not moving."

"What?" Cameron asked.

"I got a letter from Currier & Ives. The merger didn't happen. There's no London job." She pulled the letter she'd opened on Christmas Day from her purse and waved it for emphasis.

"They didn't fire you," Cameron said, genuinely concerned.

"No, no. It's kind of cool, actually. I'll be telecommuting. Work from home." With emphasis, she added, "Here."

"Wow," Cameron said, completely at a loss for anything better. "So what will we do about the visits?"

Susan frowned. "Cameron, you need help."

Cameron nodded.

"But Holly needs her father," Susan continued. "Now, since she is convinced my Uncle Milo is Santa Claus..."

A faint smile tweaked Cameron's lips.

"I don't think we can use him as a visitation supervisor anymore," Susan concluded.

"Then who?" Cameron asked, stiffening a little.

The corners of Susan's mouth twitched slightly upward. "I'm not really even sure, I mean I don't know. We'll figure it out, okay?" This statement melded into a question delivered half at Cameron and half at Cameron's lawyer.

Everett, very lawyerly, said nothing. Cameron, however, shook his head vigorously.

"I know I need help," Cameron said. "I'll call Whipple. No, forget that, I'll get a doctor more interested in Jung than yodeling." Cameron borrowed that line from *The Deadman's New Hat*. He was pretty proud of it.

Now Susan nodded vigorously. "Good."

"So could we increase the visitation maybe?" Cameron broached, sidling up to his ex-wife.

"Let's just go one step at a time," Susan said. "If you can string together a few visits without jolly old St. Nick, we'll see."

"Fair enough," Cameron said, not entirely confident he was done with his new yuletide buddy, but now was not the time to think about that.

"Merry Christmas, Cameron," Susan said, beaming.

Yes, Cameron reflected. In the end, it really kind of was.

"Please, sir. Won't you reconsider?" Flifle pleaded nervously.

Flifle was standing in the Clauses' living quarters watching them stuff clothes into ancient, but little used, suitcases. Santa and Mrs. Claus wore matching Hawaiian shirts and straw hats and looked appropriately ridiculous.

"Too late," Santa said. "The bags are packed. I've got my..."—reaching for the right world—"...shades, and my flip-flops."

"And the sunscreen," Mrs. Claus added, trying to coax the lid of her suitcase down over a pair of sandals.

"After a millennium and a half, we've earned a vacation," Mrs. Claus said. "We're going." She nodded toward Mr. Claus, who nodded back. The two hoisted their suitcases and headed for the door.

"But, sir," Flifle protested. "At least tell me where you're going."

"To a magical, beautiful place full of peace and joy."

Flifle was puzzled. "Where is that, sir?"

Santa turned, lowered his shades from his eyes—his eyes, how they twinkled!—and said, "The Real World, of course. It has the most beautiful oceans. And the waffles aren't bad either."

For more of William Pepper's writings, and a
few podcasts, check out:

## www.carnivalofglee.com

Email Bill at **carnivalofglee@mchsi.com**

Printed in the United States
127752LV00002B/97-141/P